'Shades of Brian Moore's *Lies of Silence* abound in this no-... an Irish republican paramilitary who becomes first ... then hunted.. ... resists clichés and stretches the tension out to a bitterly abrupt end in which there are no winners.'   *Guardian*

'A fresh perspective on the Troubles.'   *Observer*

'This confident debut alternates between two characters and invites us to speculate on the connection between them (the truth of which is tantalisingly deferred). The scenes dealing with young Aoife are beautifully handled. Though her story is harrowing, there are moments of humour and warmth that would seem to confirm her plaintive dictum: "It's not always cruelty that shows through."'   *Financial Times*

'Very impressive.'   BBC Radio Ulster

'No word is wasted, no imagery subdued in this powerful book... An emotional rollercoaster with a very thought-provoking ending where the true value of life is considered.'
                                                                          We Love This Book

'A deftly written, confident debut.'
                                                  Jess Richards, author of *Snake Ropes*

'Combines a gripping narrative drive with a deep sensitivity to the language, thoughts and emotions of its characters.'
                                                                  Times Higher Education

'A mature exploration of a controversial and difficult subject... wisely choosing to place the human – not the political or paramilitary – story at the centre of the novel.'
                                                                          Gutter magazine

'By turns lyrical and brutal, Liam Murray Bell's novel is a gripping and unforgettable literary debut. Interweaving an acutely observed coming-of-age story with a chilling account of one woman's involvement in Republican paramilitary activity, *So It Is* unflinchingly examines the devastating impact of violence on individual lives. This is a first novel of astonishing maturity from a talent to watch.'   Paul Vlitos

'Bell uses our present peacetime context to examine the impact of all that has gone before. The interwoven narrative of a contemporary character who seeks to bring some retribution to bear upon those figures that live amongst us still in Northern Ireland – those with plenty of secrets and lies in their closets – interestingly seems to offer some catharsis to our villains in their attempts to deal with their own past.'

Culture Northern Ireland

'Had me close to tears… If you like your books gritty with more than a hint of truth… then you will enjoy this one.'

newbooks magazine

'Vividly and sympathetically written.'   Whichbook

'*So It Is* explores the physical and psychological devastation of the Northern Irish conflict on many levels with sensitivity and compassion… intelligent [and] carefully constructed.'

Pamreader

'[Bell] knows how to tell a tale… It's an ending with no winners. Women, Bell would have us believe, are here no different from men… A challenging political thriller cum coming-of-age story.'

bookoxygen

To read an extract from So It Is,
turn to p.281

The BUSKER

LIAM MURRAY BELL

Myriad Editions

Published in 2014 by

Myriad Editions
59 Lansdowne Place
Brighton BN3 1FL

www.myriadeditions.com

1 3 5 7 9 10 8 6 4 2

A CIP catalogue record for this book is available
from the British Library.

ISBN: 978-1-908434-37-1

Printed on FSC-accredited paper by
CPI Group (UK) Ltd, Croydon, CR0 4YY

For Orla

BRIGHTON

'Fuck it,' I say. 'It got us a bed for the night and a hot meal.'
'And a bottle of wine.'

'Château Shite.'

Neither of us mentions the benzos. We sit underneath the overhang of the promenade on Madeira Drive, eating the greasy kebab scraps we fought the seagulls for. One of the fat bastards we defeated watches us from the stones of the beach, his head twitching from side to side and his throat raising a note that is both question and protest.

'Here.' I fling him the curved yellow chilli pepper. 'That'll teach you, you beady-eyed wee gobshite.'

'You didn't need to do it, though, Rab; we could have managed,' Sage murmurs.

'Let it go. We needed the money, simple as that.'

'Still, not like that.'

I shrug and look out to the pier. All the rides have closed for the night and the neon is starting to fade to ghostly twists and turns out at sea. Shouts and shrieked laughter drift from the beachfront bars, further along the seafront. At the tideline, a group of teenagers is trying to build a fire. They've only got damp, rotten wood.

'I'd been thinking of doing it for a while,' I say.

'We could've got you a gig instead. There's a friend of mine up in Kemptown who said…'

He sniffs, then snorts the lie back up before it's fully out.

1

'There were other things we could have done, at least.'

'Like what – sell our bodies?' I do a little dance for him, shaking my shoulders. It lets the draught in underneath my blanket. Sage watches dispassionately. He has wrapped his own blanket, stiff with stains and salt air, over his shoulders as a shawl. The dress shirt he wears beneath it bulges open at the bottom and a fold of white stomach, with a scrawled dark signature of hair across it, shows through. He doesn't seem to feel the chill.

'I used to teach a class on social theory – ' he begins.

'Let it go,' I repeat.

'Your guitar,' he continues, 'was your livelihood, your means of production. Give a man a fish and he'll eat for a day, but give a man a fishing rod – '

'Is it not "but teach a man to fish…"?'

'Let me finish.' He gives me his stare. 'Give a man a fishing rod and he'll sell it and buy a fish.'

'Ha.' It's mirthless, a word rather than laughter. 'It seems so, mate, it seems so.'

It wasn't meant to be this way. When I came down from Glasgow I had big plans. There would have been no chance of me pawning the acoustic guitar Maddie gave me for my eighteenth for the sake of a bed, bath, bite, bottle and benzo. Maybe I'd auction it off after the second album, to fund the coke habit or to crinkle handfuls of cash on to casino cloths – for charity, even – but I'd never have pawned it. Not for fifty quid. Not that guitar, the one from Maddie.

'It's not even the gigs,' Sage says. 'It's the busking.'

Since we arrived in Brighton, I've spent my days sitting outside the shops on Church Road or at the underpass on Trafalgar Street, leading from the train station down to North Laine, picking out folk songs and covers but avoiding my own material. It's a chore, scraping seventy-two pence in loose change from a Springsteen song or a pound coin for some Dougie MacLean. I don't tell Sage that, though. I don't want to admit to him that I'm sick of it.

2

He's taken a deep wheeze of a breath. It's his windbag way of launching into a lecture or supplication: get it all out in one go so that no one can interrupt him.

'Busking is your way of participating in consumer culture, your only marketable skill in this capitalist system, the only thing that you can trade off.' He takes a breath. 'That guitar was a symbol as much as anything, Rab – of your willingness to participate in the sham and shame of it all.'

The seagull has haughtily hobbled away from the chilli pepper. I feel a flicker of frustration about that, because I'd harboured this vague notion that he might swallow the whole thing, pause to blink at us in alarm, and then explode into a fluttering of feathers. No such luck, though. He lives to fight another day.

'I'm proud of you,' Sage concludes. 'In a way.'

'Left with only the blanket on my back and the song in my heart.' And the single benzo I kept back from last night. Sage doesn't know about it. I tucked it into the top of my sock as soon as I realised that the pawn money wouldn't stretch to more than one night of the high life.

'The kids down there have a guitar.' Sage points at the shadows on the shore. The fire beside them wisps out smoke, but there are no flames to speak of. They're all probably educated to Oxbridge-entry level, with Duke of Ed. awards and internships and gap years abroad stitched into their CVs like Scout badges, but not one of them can build a fire.

'What are you saying – steal it off them?' I ask.

'I would never say that.' Sage picks at his lip underneath the fringe of his grey-streaked beard. Dry skin, maybe even the beginning of a cold sore, comes loose and is flicked to the side. 'But you could ask them for a go, maybe, to keep your hand in.'

The boy who is plucking away at the guitar is making a sound that the chilli-canny seagull would be proud of, and someone is running their mouth up and down a harmonica

3

by way of accompaniment. If I did go over there, if they were to hand me their instruments, I could give them a song that might earn me a swig from their cheap chest-pain cider, or a toke from the broken bone of their joint. Equally, though, I could earn myself a kicking. Sage should know that as well as anyone; he's suffered more beat-downs than me in his time. He's been woken with spit and piss. Or by being dragged down the street in his sleeping bag. You can't rely on strangers to leave you in peace, never mind show you kindness.

'I've no interest,' I say, 'not really. Tell me a story instead, Sage. I'll close my eyes and you can tell me a story and I'll see if I can sleep.'

I know this suggestion will please him. He used to be an associate lecturer at a university up in London. There were half-filled halls of students listening to him once upon a time. If he closes his own eyes, if he recalls his research word for word, then he can be back in academia for a moment or two.

'Have I told you about the factory owner in China?' he asks.

I shake my head, keeping my eyes closed. It doesn't sound like 'once upon a time', but it might be perfect for sending me to sleep.

'Well, just outside this city in China...' He clears his throat. 'Just outside is this factory where they make electronic components for these high-end American smartphones...'

His voice changes, shifts to a lower register. It's a radio voice; it reminds me of the books on tape I used to listen to as a child. There's a rough rasp to it that mixes melodiously with the shushing of the sea. If I listen imperfectly, if I mingle and meld the two together, then it reminds me of the whispers Maddie used in the moments before sleep.

'A robotic arm could do the work, but labour is cheap and injuries are ignored so they use men, women and children instead. Children especially. They only need to say they're of age. The manager is too fond of their nimble fingers to ask for documentation...'

4

My mind drifts to a memory of my last cup of coffee: holding it between the heels of my hands, curling my fingers in towards the scalding polystyrene.

'The American company eventually gives the smartphone a limited release in the city: only a hundred will be sold. And the factory owner finds out about this and decides to take advantage – he wants to buy up the phones and sell them on at three times the price. So, when the launch day arrives, he has a long queue of these factory workers waiting, each of them with a white armband on so the minders can identify them...'

Maybe it's the caffeine that's keeping me awake. I don't even like coffee, not really. But it keeps you warm and it keeps you walking that bit longer. Until, eventually, you find somewhere to slump and sleep.

'Those in the queue without an armband – businessmen and trendy types – catch wind of this and start protesting, and it builds to a riot. The store doesn't open and the phone isn't sold, and there's outrage all round. Everyone turns on the workers: the minders beat them for giving away the scheme, thinking of the loss of the bonus the factory owner promised them; and the businessmen and trendy types shout, "What were you queuing for when you don't *want* the phones, don't *need* them the way we do".'

It doesn't lull me to sleep as Maddie's voice used to. It's an emotionless story, without soul, that's delivered in that flat, factual way Sage has. He's expecting me to join the dots; he's led me to the water but he's damned if he's going to tell me how to drink.

Opening my eyes, I glance across at my older companion. His own eyes are tightly closed; he's probably imagining standing silently in front of a seminar group and waiting for the sharpest of the students to pass comment. I reach down into my sock for the last benzo. It has a stray thread caught in its markings, so I pick that off and slide the pill under my tongue. Then I look across at Sage again. He has one eye open, watching me. There is accusation in his stare.

'What's your point?' I ask, peevishly. 'That the factory owner was a prick? That both the minders and the workers were underpaid?'

He shakes his head. 'No, you've missed the point, as usual.'

'What was the point?'

'You just took a pill, I saw you.'

I shrug. 'It was the last one.'

'You could have shared it, though.'

'Let me sleep,' I say, and curl myself in against the concrete curve of the wall. The change of position ruptures the cocoon of my blanket, but my thoughts begin to slip and slide towards sleep in spite of the numbness of my fingers and toes. The shifting sea advances up the stones of the beach and washes over me, but the tide is warm and it carries me off in the undercurrent –

I am along the shore at the nightclub beyond the car park, standing on the stage and watching the crowd beneath me, as they lap up against the footlights. Their murmurings are a constant background noise, occasionally interrupted by a screeched call or cry. Then I strike the first chord and all becomes calm. They part, right down the middle; they fold away to either side to create a path for Maddie, who stands at the back of the room, distinctive with her cropped blonde hair and that olive-green summer dress that falls from her shoulders and has to be hitched back up.

I don't play beyond the first chord because I realise that I'm holding the guitar Maddie gave me, with the untrimmed strings spraying out from the tuning pegs. My fingers fall from the fret and I step forward to the microphone.

'I have a story to tell,' I say. 'About this guitar.'

The crowd draws a breath. Maddie takes a step forward, then stands, waiting, in the centre of the parted sea of people. Her widened brown eyes are on me, those eyes that make me feel as if I'm on the cusp of saying something profound, that the next thing to come out of my mouth will change everything utterly. For better or worse.

'Maddie,' I say, 'I had to pawn the guitar, this guitar.'

There are a couple of hisses and catcalls from the crowd on either side of her.

'I had to pawn it, because I needed a bed and some pills.'

'And food, don't forget!' someone shouts.

'And food,' I concede, with a smile. 'But I got it back, Maddie. I must have.' I wave it in the air in front of me. 'It was only a matter of time until I got it back.'

Maddie is still looking up at me, but she's not smiling. Instead there's this look of intense concentration on her face, with the wrinkle of a frown on her forehead. I've only ever seen her look that way once before. I need to continue before the crowd, who are losing interest, burst their banks and she is carried away on their current.

'So I went back to the pawn shop,' I say, 'and there was this seagull on the counter. And he told me that – '

'Seagulls can't talk!' someone objects.

'Fine,' I say into the microphone. 'He let it be known that I could have it back in exchange for a yellow chilli pepper. Just a single yellow chilli pepper.'

Her frown has deepened. She glances away, off towards the back of the room as if looking for someone else.

'And so I went searching around Brighton for a chilli pepper,' I say. 'It's not that I didn't value your gift, or that I think it's only worth the chilli pepper, but the seagull – '

'Are these meant to be lyrics?' someone shouts, from the crowd.

The booing starts towards the back of the room, but it builds as it reaches the front and it breaks as it reaches the edge of the stage. Hands stretch out to clutch at my trainers, dragging my feet out from under me. 'That was meaningless!' they chant. 'Mean-ing-less! Mean-ing-less!'

The guitar has fallen to the side and is being driven, again and again, against the microphone stand until the wood

7

splinters and breaks. Lying on my back, I twist my body and reach out a hand towards the wreckage of it, but the crowd have lifted me and are pulling me down from the stage, pulling me under, the weight of them on me as the air is squeezed from my lungs. I gasp and grasp and –

I wake with a crick in my neck that can't be stretched away and a sense of rising panic that doesn't fully leave me even after I've rubbed at my eyes and spied the yellow chilli pepper lying discarded on the concrete, with the seagull nowhere in sight.

There's no way of telling the time, but there's the soft orange glow of sunrise out at sea and the first yawning groans of traffic from up on the main road.

Sitting upright, I look across at Sage, who has slumped forward on to his knees and is snoring softly and trailing a line of saliva down the leg of his well-worn corduroy trousers. He is middle-aged, although I have never asked for specifics. His brown-grey hair is greasy and lank and settles into slicks at his sideburns so that it seems to melt like plastic into the untidy tangles of his beard. The skin that shows around his nose and eyes has been browned by the sun and wind, weathered rather than wrinkled. His eyes, when they are open, have enough by way of sharpness to hint at his intelligence, but the way he spills out from the top and sides of his charity-shop clothes means that he will never again be called handsome. Even after a wash and a shave, even with a suit and a dousing of aftershave, he'd still carry himself with that awkward loping gait that shows the weight he's been lugging around all these years.

'How does a homeless man get to be so fat?' I mutter to myself, half-expecting a chorus of boos for my unkindness, for my lack of charity. There is no reaction, though. The crowd has gone. Maddie too.

I'm back to grey. To a day of walking until my feet pulse with pain, then resting until the cold gnaws. Of seeking something of substance to dull the nerves, numb my skin and draw myself inwards. Enough warmth to see me through until I can find a kipping point – beneath a child's slide in a playground, in a doorway with a covering of cardboard turning to mulch, or a shelter down by the seafront – where I know I'll wake with a policeman kicking at the soles of my shoes, telling me to move on.

Rising to my feet, I wrap the blanket tightly around my shoulders and begin to shuffle towards the stones of the beach. There is a tap beside the oyster stall and the ice-cold water from it will remove the fur that seems to have grown, like mould, across the surface of my teeth during the night. Collecting the water in my cupped hands, I drink. The water tastes faintly of last night's kebab. I belch deeply and roll the flavour around on my tongue.

The fire down on the shore is out, and there's a spattering of rain starting to hiss out any remaining embers, but I decide to make my way down anyway, to see if the youngsters have left anything worth salvaging. They might have set down a sloshing of cider, or a cast-off roach that has enough clinging to it for an early morning smoke.

I lift the plastic cider bottles, but they've drowned their half-smoked joints in the alcohol so that both are useless. Swinging my arm, I lob a bottle up and out towards the sea, watching as the liquid inside spills out in an arc. A seagull, startled by the movement, lets out a scolding cry and swoops off to another part of the beach.

In among the charred wood and blackened stone of the fire, something glints. Like a magpie, I'm drawn to it. I wipe ash away from it until I can see its markings. It's the harmonica. A nice one: twelve-hole, chromatic, with a wood inlay. It is warm to the touch as I lift it.

Holding it an inch or so from my mouth, I blow up and down the length of it. Fractured notes, incomplete scales, sound out. I take a corner of my blanket and polish at the metal until the scorched scars from the fire fade. I raise it to my lips and blow a chord. Just one chord. And then, in the early morning, with no way of telling the time precisely, I begin to sing with all the breath in my lungs. The words are caught by the wind and swept along the length of deserted Brighton beach.

LONDON

'Morning, Rob.'

I hear a voice and know, without looking, that it belongs to Pierce Price. It is a slow voice, a voice that carries a nasal note and adds a throat-clearing as punctuation at the end of every sentence.

'What are you doing here?' I ask, into the pillow.

'Checking on my investment, buddy.'

Turning slowly, so that I don't irritate the hangover, I peer up at him. He pushes his glasses up his nose with his index finger. I'd love to reach up and slap him right across the cheek, to see if it dislodges the bright grin. In the state I'm in, though, it would probably hurt me more than it would him. There is a shard of glass behind my eyes. Squinting into the early morning sunshine causes it to reflect blindingly, and movement causes it to shift and stab anew.

A bit of coke would sort me right out, no doubt. A zip-line to wakefulness, to a clear head. And Prick Price will have some. He always has a baggy – takes it with him like a packed lunch so he can swap the tastiest morsels. I'll have to wheedle for it, though; I'll have to pick his pocket or start with a 'please sir', because he's a right fucking Dickensian villain about the stuff. 'Bud*dyyy*,' he'll say. 'What kind of manager would I be if I let my prize asset do that before he was even out of bed.'

I go through the motions anyhow. It'll be excruciating for a minute or two, but it'll make the rest of his visit bearable.

Question asked, I close my eyes and drown out his reply with the dub-step thumping in my head.

'Go on,' I say. There's a routine to it. What you ask for three times will come true; he's a simple man, is Pierce Price.

'Really, Rob, it would be better if you did the work first, maybe, and then relaxed later.'

Rab, I think, it's fucking *Rab*, you bell-end. 'Be a mate for a minute, Pierce,' I say. 'Be a mate, not a manager.'

'I'll make you a deal,' he says. 'I'll give you a line now if you promise to bring a new song to the studio tomorrow.'

'Absolutely, mate, absolutely.' I'd sign my soul away for the line he carefully trails out on to the bedside table, for the credit card he uses to chop it into shape and for the rolled-up fiver he hands over so I can snort it up.

Pierce is constantly nagging at me about studio time. It's recording, not rehearsal, he says. As if the creative process can be scheduled: ten-thirty, write generation-defining anthem; eleven, cup of tea and a custard cream; eleven-thirty, record track in one take plus another for safety; then an early lunch before a fucking rinse and repeat in the afternoon.

'It looks like you got cashback on my idea, anyway,' Price says, as I collapse back on to the bed.

'Cashback?' I think he's talking about the fiver that I've crumpled protectively into my fist – and the way the coke is fizzing about inside, dissolving that stubborn shard behind my eyes and tweaking energy into my muscles, means that I'm ready to fight him to the death for it. 'What the fuck does that mean?'

'I ran into her on the way up,' Pierce says.

'Who?'

'I don't know her name, do I?' He smirks. 'And I won't judge you if you don't either. But I told you that my plan was a good 'un. The Price is right, my friend – the Price is always right.'

I try to remember back to the night before. It was Pierce who'd suggested I make the trip to the camp at St Paul's. The

Occupy movement, he said, very trendy. Give you something to write about, give you some protest lyrics.

Felicity. I remember her name. Flick, for short. A performance poet, being filmed beside the neoclassical pillars by a French camera crew. Like them, I hadn't understood a word that came out of her mouth. Except for that line about the government throwing out the baby and keeping the bathwater – I'd liked that. For the most part, though, I'd not been listening. I'd been inspecting the way her curled black hair was piled like knotted wool on the top of her head, and admiring the way that strands of it straggled down her cheeks as though a cat had clawed them loose.

She made a pleasant change from the earnest chappie with slicked-back hair and glasses who'd taken me to the side and spoken, at length, about the similarities between the Mafia and capitalism: banks as casinos, laundering money from toxic mortgages; lobbying as loan-sharking, with political funding holding an expectation of being repaid many times over; and companies running the equivalent of a protection racket, threatening to leave the country and rough up the economy if they don't get their way over tax.

Until I'd found Flick, I'd been thinking of calling it a day. The camp is good for a wander, granted, but there's a lot of standing around waiting for something to happen, and I'd struggled to strike up conversation with the clutches of folk sitting around.

'Nice-looking girl,' Pierce says. 'You could write a song about her, maybe.'

'No,' I say.

'OK, OK.' A pause. 'Did you learn anything, then, buddy?'

I shake my head, but it causes the hangover to rattle the edges of my cocaine high. So I drag a hand up from the warmth of the bedclothes and rub at my eyes until they tingle, then burn.

'Anything about Occupy London, or about the riots?' Pierce pauses to shift his glasses again, mentally sorting through the hashtags in his mind. 'Student fees, youth unemployment, anything like that?'

'We spoke about Palestine,' I say.

That scares him. He's liable to drop a settlement-worth of bricks out of his arse at the mention of it. 'Not *Palestine*,' he hisses. 'You can't sing about *Palestine*.'

Flick had placed a hand on my fretboard halfway through my work-in-progress song, just after the lyric about the St Paul's camp being a settlement in a foreign land, turning into a fortress for those willing to take a stand. No, she said, with a soft smile that stirred both irritation and lust. That's not quite right, she said. That makes us the aggressors, and we were here first. The city of London – small c – was here before the City of London – big C. They're the Israelis; we're the Palestinians.

'It's all in hand, Pierce,' I say.

'By the end of the week we really need to clock up some proper studio time.'

'Definitely. I'll have a new song for you tomorrow.'

It's not the songs, though. I could turn up with Lennon and McCartney tomorrow and the session musicians we've got in would make it sound as if Sergeant Pepper had taken the Lonely Hearts Club Band hostage. Half the studio time is wasted on the producer editing out the torture – cleaning blood from the tracks.

Once Pierce has left and both cocaine and hangover have dulled to a numbness, I take my guitar to the window of the hotel room and look across London to St Paul's. I can't see the tents, only the dome of the cathedral itself, but I set to thinking about Flick anyway. Maybe I can write about giving her a night in a budget hotel room, away from the fabric catacomb – shit – or moving her from ground-mat to top-floor flat – shitter – tents to vol-au-vents – doesn't even fucking rhyme.

Maybe I could write about the way that she clutched and clawed at my back, as if trying to break through the skin, and

14

how I struggled to get into a rhythm because she was always stopping and taking up a new position. Then, finally, when I got into my stride, when I was grunting, gasping, gulping towards my goal, she pushed me out of her so that I spilt up into her belly-button. And I knew that I should be grateful for the cheat's contraception, but I throbbed and felt deflated. Because she'd not been lost in the moment; there'd been no pace or intensity to it for her. She'd been lying there judging, measuring the moment at which I should be withdrawn.

Afterwards, she explored the room and tentatively fingered a miniature brandy bottle from the mini-bar. I smiled and said yes, that's OK, it's all paid for. Over the past six or seven weeks money has been draining from the account like sand through fingers, but I'm still confident there'll be enough for a castle. Eventually. Once I've finished recording and we can move on to the release and begin thinking about touring.

'How does it work?' she asked, then.

'What?'

'Your record deal. Do they just give you free rein and you go off and write an album?'

'Not quite. They give me an advance.'

'An advance on what?'

'On future royalties.'

'Like credit?'

I shrug, then nod. She cracks open the bottle of brandy and tips her head back to drain it. Her naked body, stretched away from me, has no tan or trimming. There is a bruise, like a birthmark, down near her left hipbone, and her dark brown pubic hair is matted with what we've just done.

'And who writes the songs?'

'I do,' I say, fascinated by the way she scratches at an itch just beneath her right breast without caring that I'm watching. 'Well,' I continue, 'they have final say, of course.'

'Of course?' She stops scratching.

'Yes. They're the producers, they're the label, they're the ones with the experience. They know what sells.'

15

'They're your songs, though.'

I nod. 'And?'

'So surely you know what you're trying to say, and surely that's more important than what's going to sell?'

'Of course.'

'Sooooo…' She drags the word out, and lifts the bedsheet up and over herself, suddenly coy. 'What are they about?'

'My songs?'

She nods. She has wrapped the sheet into a toga, covering all but her face, one shoulder and her arms.

'I played you one,' I say. 'Earlier.'

'Yes, but what was it about?'

'It was about Occupy, about the movement – '

'What was the message, though?'

I shrug and reach off to the bedside table for the menu. It is late and I've smoked skunk at the camp, shared two bottles of red at the pub and blown my load into this near-stranger's belly-button, all without pausing for food. I have no patience for sitting on the sheets sifting through the sentiments behind my songs. I am hungry. Bloody ravenous.

'Room service?' I ask, waving the menu at her.

'Do they have lobster?'

I'm not sure if she's asking ironically, so I answer anyway. 'I think this place is more cheese toastie than lobster thermidor.'

'I love the way you say that – the*rrr*midor,' she says, rolling it more like a pirate than a Scotsman, and crawling up the bed towards me on her hands and knees. 'The*rrr*midor. Is the food on credit as well?' she asks.

'Of course it is,' I say, smiling. 'Free ride, baby.'

GLASGOW

We always meet in the woods behind Hyndland station on a Friday evening to get drunk, even if it's pissing down. It's tradition and, Glaswegian weather or not, we stick to it like religion. A close-knit cult of five: three boys, two girls. No ceremony or idolatry to it, but a fair amount of confession and quite a bit of – unintentional – prostrating. There's only one rule: drink until you can't see the woods, can't see the trees.

It's on a mild night at the end of January, a few weeks into 2011, that Ewan brings Maddie along to even out the gender balance. Six of us now: three boys, three girls. He's always had a roving eye for the ladies, Ewan, and it's roved further afield since he left school last summer to get himself a full-time job at a shoe shop. This is the first time he's brought someone along to be inducted into our weekly meet at the woods, though; the first time any of us has brought someone along. These aren't fairytale woods, and if you're looking for a fairytale romance then you're better off going to the cinema in town, the café up at Broomhill Cross, or the pub down on Dumbarton Road that doesn't ask for ID.

'Nice to meet you all,' Maddie says softly, bringing a hand up to give a wee wave.

'Did you wear heels up that path?' Teagan says. 'That's honestly absolutely mental. You're lucky you didn't break your leg.'

'Ewan gave me a piggy-back.'

17

Ewan gives the rest of us a wink.

To get to the woods you have to walk up a stony path, on a steep incline, to the side of a hut with 'Night & Day Security' on a sign above it. The shop, nestled underneath the railway bridge, used to sell alarm systems, but it was broken into so many times that the owner tired of the irony and closed down. The path itself is neglected and overgrown: roots show through to trip you, thorny bushes pluck at your clothes, and the ground cracks and oozes moisture. At the top of the hill the path disappears into bogland, which sucks your trainers from your feet and sends splatters like stitching up the inside legs of your jeans. Only the wooden planks, thrown down in the worst of the wet weather, will lead you safely across to the fallen tree-trunk where everyone sits to drink.

'Look what I brought.' Ewan unfolds his jacket to reveal a litre bottle of vodka. 'It's going to be some night, guys.'

'Where the fuck did you get that from?' I ask.

'This one – ' Ewan nods over at Maddie, who's crinkling her nose as Gemma spreads a ripped plastic bag out across the damp bark and indicates for her to take a seat with all the flourish of a *maître d'* at a high-end restaurant ' – can pass for eighteen at the corner shop down beyond the university.'

'You serious?' Cammy looks over at Maddie in admiration. 'Fuck me, that's good. No more need to beg students to jump in for us or steal an inch from our parents' bottles, then?'

Ewan nods. 'I think the Paki in there might have a thing for her, to be honest.'

'Ewan!' Maddie's voice is sharp but, as I sit myself down on the opposite end of the fallen tree, I'm not sure which part of Ewan's comment she's censuring. Whatever the race of the shopkeeper, I can certainly see why he might have a crush on Maddie. Oval-faced, with blonde hair cropped close and brown eyes that linger for a moment rather than flitting off as most people's do, she's pretty, certainly, but thoughtful-looking with it. The kind of girl you'd notice in a bookshop rather than in a nightclub.

It's Teagan who begins the interrogation, once the cap has been twisted and the bottle begins to be passed from hand to hand.

'What school do you go to, Maddie?'

'Cleveden Secondary.'

'What age are you?'

'Sixteen.'

'You doing your Highers?'

'Yes. Maths, English, biology, modern studies and drama.'

'Five.'

A pause. Teagan only did four, and she's resitting one of those this year. Gemma takes up the baton.

'How did you meet Ewan?'

'At a concert,' she says. 'Though I had to drop my ticket three times before he finally noticed and picked it up for me. You need to give these lads plenty of opportunities to prove themselves gentlemen, you know.'

'You like him, then?' Gemma asks, smiling.

'Sure.'

'How much?'

A shrug.

Ewan doesn't try to shield her from it, or even seem too bothered about her answers. He's more interested in the vodka than the vodka-buyer. Soon enough the bottle is going between me and Ewan only, with the girls moving on to a bottle of white wine that Gemma pinched from a family party and Cammy complaining loudly about the *crème de menthe* he's siphoned off from his gran's supply but sipping away at it nonetheless.

'You know Ewan's a bum, right?' Teagan asks.

'How d'you mean?' Maddie replies.

'Well, he's left school and he smokes dope more or less constantly and – '

'I have a full-time wage,' Ewan interrupts. 'Which is more than any of you have.'

'And he's my manager,' I back him up.

'*And* I'm his manager,' Ewan agrees, taking the bottle from me.

'Manager for what?' Maddie asks.

'I'm a singer,' I say, with a shy smile that the vodka stretches into a smirk. 'Singer-songwriter. I have a couple of songs up online, if you search Rab Dillon. D-I-L-L – '

'Are they any good?'

'They're mostly covers.'

I could tell her that I've changed the simple strum of the Nick Drake song to what my Uncle Brendan calls 'pinch and tickle' fingerpicking to make it my own, or how I changed the melody on the chorus of the Tom Waits song. Instead, I settle for a slight shrug that I hope will mark me out as a modest musical genius.

'Here, Dildo.' Ewan pushes the vodka bottle against my chest. 'Let's have a competition: who can down the most.'

'Right.' I accept the bottle, and the challenge, without question.

'Stupid fucking alpha males,' Teagan mutters.

'Stupid fucking – '

I don't hear the end of Ewan's reply because I've raised the bottle to my lips and I'm grimacing down as much of the vodka as I can. Cammy doesn't help matters by thumping me on the back, supposedly in encouragement, so that the backwash bubbles up into the bottle. Stopping, I hold it out to Ewan, who repeats the process, except he uses a flailing arm to stop Cammy from helping him out. Three or four passes later, the bottle is empty. I win, by volume, in that I drank from the bottom of the red label down to the dregs, but it's Ewan who finishes it off, throws the empty bottle into the weeds at the side and holds his hand out for Maddie. They rise, then, to go off and find somewhere quiet. There are catcalls and wolf-whistles from us all but, while Ewan turns around to give us a wink, Maddie pays us no heed and just keeps walking.

As soon as they've been swallowed by the bushes, the debrief begins.

'Bit up herself, don't you think?' Teagan says.

'She's quiet, is all.' Gemma replies.

'I'd fuck her.'

'Cammy!'

'What? You saw the eyes on her – blowjob eyes, those.'

'You'd fuck that tree if it had a hole small enough for your cock,' I say.

'What the hell are blowjob eyes, Cammy?' Teagan asks.

'Big wide eyes that stare up at me, all innocent, even when she's got my cock – which is a perfectly respectable size, by the way – in her mouth.'

'You watch too much porn, Cammy – far too much.'

'Even still,' he says. 'I'd give her a face like a painter's radio.'

'What do you think, Rab?' Gemma asks, cutting off Teagan's disgusted squeal.

'She's not bad. Seems nice enough.'

'He's gay for Ewan, though,' Teagan says. 'So he's not worth asking.'

'What I'd not give for a go on those tits, anyway.' Cammy concludes. 'As Tea says, I watch a *lot* of porn, and those are the nicest tits I've ever seen.'

Within the hour, I'm in a position to confirm Cammy's observation. I don't intend to catch sight of Maddie's right breast, ladies and gentlemen of the jury, but when I go stumbling off into the undergrowth for a piss there's this rustling to my left and, as I start my stream, I squint over towards the movement and noise and see skin through the leaves. A perfect curve, pert and pale, with goose-pimples that are being smoothed by Ewan's clutching, dirt-streaked hand. Turning mid-stream, I take a step to the side and peer to make out the pink dimple of the nipple. Then, cock in hand, I find my eyes travelling up to meet Maddie's gaze. Over Ewan's shoulder, she stares steadily across at me. A second passes; two, three. We watch one another, each in a compromised position, before I start to scrabble with my fly and belt buckle, covering myself and turning away. Maddie, for her part, makes no effort to hide her exposed breast or to alert Ewan to the fact that his best mate is peeping at them through the trees with his dick in his hand. Instead, with her eyes still fixed on me, she lets out a moaning gasp that carries across to me on the breeze.

It's about half an hour later that she emerges from the bushes and comes to sit next to me on the fallen log. Teagan and Gemma have gone off to the chip shop to get themselves a fritter roll and flirt with the young Italian who works the fish fryer, and Cammy is trying drunkenly to climb a tree, swaying and snapping branches as he goes, but I have found myself unable to move. Either the vodka or the woodland sex-show, or both, have left me solitary, silent, and rooted to the uprooted tree-trunk.

'Where's Ewan?' I ask.

'He went off to pee or find someone or something.' Maddie waves vaguely in the direction of the trees. Her hair is matted and mussed from lying on the ground and she has a smudge of dirt beneath her right eye but, to my eyes, she looks as if she's been carefully made-up, modelled for a calendar shoot – cavewoman, maybe – with her white woollen jumper off one shoulder and the denim of her jeans camouflaged with a thin layer of dirt, twigs and leaves. 'He's very drunk,' she concludes.

'Who is?'

'Ewan.'

'Right.' I nod, meet her gaze, then remember the last time we locked eyes and look away. There's silence for a spell, until Maddie reaches into her pocket and brings out a packet of cigarettes.

'You smoke?'

I nod and take one. Then I root in my jacket for a lighter and lean across to light hers. She cups my hand until it

22

catches, her breath shallow, and, as her eyes come up to meet mine, all I can think about is Cammy's earlier comment – blowjob eyes.

'We didn't do anything, you know,' she says, after a drag.

'What do I care?'

'Just… we didn't do anything. Other than a fumble in the jungle.' She lets out a giggle at that, only a trickle of laughter. 'Fumble in the jungle sounds dirtier than I meant.'

'You like him?' I ask.

A shrug, again.

I look about myself, at the few stray strands of grass sprouting through the mud, at the plastic bottle that held Cammy's *crème de menthe*, the empty white wine bottle that has rolled over to rest against a bent and broken sapling and the torn plastic bag, curled by the breeze, which Maddie sat on earlier. To the side of this litter, trampled by a careless foot, is a single snowdrop with its white bloom bowed towards the ground. I rise and lurch across to it, leaning over to pluck it free. 'For you,' I say, clumsily presenting it to Maddie.

'Thank you,' she says, wasting no time in pinching the bloom free from the stem and placing the white flower in behind her ear, tucked into a fold of blonde hair. 'They were my granny's favourite flowers.'

'Is that right?'

Smoke rises from our fingers as the cigarettes slowly smoke themselves.

'What do you sing about?' Maddie asks.

'This and that,' I reply. 'It's mostly covers, like I say.'

'What do you write about, though, when you do write?'

'Whatever comes to mind.'

She nods. 'Are you any good?'

'My Uncle Brendan taught me to play.'

'Right. And are you any good?'

Brendan, my uncle on my mother's side, wanted to be a folk singer in the mould of Ewan MacColl or Dougie MacLean. So in his teenage years he taught himself to play guitar and patiently waited for the pitching squeal of his voice to settle. It never did. He bided his time again, until myself and my cousin Gerard were old enough. Gerard never showed an interest, but I liked some of the American stuff he passed on to us. And the invented names for the techniques – like 'pick and jab' for hammer-on. Over the years I've learnt enough to leave me, at the very least, campfire-ready.

'I play an acoustic set on a Saturday night at a coffee shop up along Great Western Road,' I say eventually, rather than answering directly.

'Oh.' She takes a drag. 'I'll need to come and see you.'

'That would be good, aye.'

'Ewan can take me.'

I look down at my cigarette, half-smoked, and then grind it out against the rough bark. Throwing the butt down to join the discarded snowdrop stem in the mud, I stand and stretch. 'Where is Ewan anyway?' I ask.

'You already asked that.'

'I know, but I wonder what's keeping him.'

'You worried he's neglecting me?'

'Will I go and find him?'

She shrugs. Again.

'I should go and find him,' I say, and set off into the scrub. Using my leading arm as a blunt machete, with branches whipping back at me, I clear a path through the trees. I follow the same route as I did half an hour ago, making for the spot I'd last seen Ewan. With Maddie.

She intrigues me. There's a self-possession about her, a quiet assurance that seems entirely at odds with the bitchy narcissism of Teagan or the eager-to-please friendliness of Gemma. Maddie seems to know her mind, seems unashamed at being seen half-naked by a near-stranger and unabashed by the fact that he was holding his cock at the time. She's unfazed by being brought by Ewan to meet us all, and unconcerned whether we like or loathe her. She's un – she's anti – she's – *fuck* –

24

At first, when my foot hits something solid among the foliage I feel a lurch in my stomach. When I crouch over and see that it's a denim-clad leg, I briefly have a panic that I've stumbled across a body in the woods. Maybe it's a homeless guy who's wandered off in search of some shelter, or a murder victim dumped out in the wilderness. Reaching out a hand, expecting the corpse to be cold and stiff, I find that it's warm and that it stirs to my touch. With a groan, it rolls over on to its back and shows its face.

It's Ewan, there's no doubt. I recognise his clothes, his trainers and the majority of his features. It's hard to make out his face, though, because in his drunken state he's chosen to lie, face-down, on a bed of nettles. His cheeks and forehead are reddened and swelling, the skin beginning to blister.

'Ewan, mate.' I shake him. 'You OK?'

'Eee-fff-kkk.'

'Your face, mate – that must hurt to buggery.'

'Fff-kkk.'

'You're blootered, aren't you?'

'Mmm – '

'You want me to just leave you be?'

A contortion of the head – might be a nod – is enough to send me on my way, back to the fallen tree and Maddie. Before I leave, though, I take Ewan by the feet and drag him clear of the nettles so that he can twist and turn in his sleep without it doing him any harm. I do think about going searching for some dock leaves, to maybe make Ewan a pillow of sorts, but I decide I've done enough. After all, I've had just as much to drink as Ewan; I've just had the good sense not to let it get me off my face. The swelling will go down of its own accord after a day or two. It'll hurt like hell in the meantime, without a doubt, but it'll do no long-term damage.

'Did you find him?' Maddie asks, as I fight my way through the enchanted forest back to my fair maiden (fuck, vodka taking hold) – through the bushes to the fallen tree.

'I think he must've gone out the back way,' I sniff. 'Maybe went off home to sleep it off.'

'Did you see him? Did he tell you that?' It's the first time Maddie's self-assurance seems to crack – the first time she seems genuinely worried. Her forehead creases and she bites at her bottom lip.

'He's wrecked, Maddie, that's all it is.'

She nods. Clearing her throat, she stands, failing to notice that the movement causes the snowdrop to be dislodged from her hair and fall to the ground.

'You fancy going to the off-licence and getting some beers?' she asks. 'I'm not nearly drunk enough yet.'

'A woman af-after my own heart,' I reply, grinning.

She holds out her arm for me and I take it, the vodka-glow smoothing out any guilt I might otherwise have felt. I should be worried about Cammy, up in his tree, watching proceedings, or about meeting the girls on their way back from the chip shop and having to explain why I'm arm in arm with Maddie. I certainly should be sparing a thought for Ewan, lying on the pine-needle mattress of the woods with his face bubbling and distorting. As it is, though, all I can think, all I can focus on, is the likelihood that, when we get to the wooden boards laid out across the bogland, Maddie will ask me for a piggy-back.

BRIGHTON

We set up early in the morning outside the Royal Pavilion. Sage digs deep in his tattered rucksack and finds his Mozart tie, shell-coloured with black musical notations and a silhouetted Wolfgang Amadeus on it. Puffing his chest out beneath it, he strides back and forth across the path, waving his arms like a conductor. I stand on the fringes of the grass and play my harmonica. I wear fingerless gloves, and my breath comes out of the other side of the metal grille as sighs of steam.

'The magnificent Rab,' Sage cries. 'Hear him play, hear him sing!'

There are groups of tourists milling around, mostly schoolchildren. They look up at the ice-cream-scoop domes of the Pavilion only for an instant before looking back to their phones. They listen to their headphones rather than to me. They ignore Sage completely.

I'm not too worried about their indifference. I have no interest in the youth market, nor in breaking through to the Americans who've sauntered up from the seafront. With my eyes closed, I'm just content to breathe runs and licks out into the cold September air.

'Excuse me, mate.'

I open an eye; my melody trails off. 'Yes?'

There's a guy in a checked shirt, chinos and a black body-warmer standing in front of me. He wears his hair up in a shark's fin and, when he smiles, he shows a flash of white teeth beneath his thin moustache. These details give him the look of a predator.

'This is my spot,' he says, motioning with his guitar case.

'Really?' I say. 'I'm sorry, I didn't realise…'

'No worries. I've played here every day this week, though.'

I nod. Instinctively, I tuck the harmonica into my jacket pocket and shuffle backwards on to the grass. My thinking is that if he takes a swing, if he starts a fight, then all my valuables will be hidden and I'll have a soft landing for when I take a fall.

'What's happening?' Sage is over to us now.

'This is my spot,' the newcomer explains. 'Don't worry, you had no way of knowing.'

'No,' Sage replies. 'This is public ground.'

'Listen, mate –' the newcomer lays a hand on Sage's sleeve ' – this right here is prime location. This is where the tourists come. No offence to your friend, but you can't be taking up prime location with harmonica-playing and begging.'

I stay quiet, flushed with embarrassment.

'He sings as well,' Sage says, ignoring the last word.

'How do you sing and play the harmonica? You'd need to leave off one to do the other.'

I nod. 'That's how I do it.'

'We were here first,' Sage points out. 'That's the end of it.'

'How about a compromise?' the newcomer says.

'No,' Sage says.

'What kind of compromise?' I ask.

'Well, what kind of stuff do you play? We could busk together, maybe, and split the profits down the middle.'

'Sounds good,' I say.

'Absolutely not,' says Sage.

The newcomer introduces himself as Luke and I step to one side to let him stand on the grass next to me. Sage stands in front of us to protest, windmilling his arms as if to block

28

us from the view of the gathered tourists. Ignoring him, Luke takes out his guitar, tunes up, and then begins to play The Beatles. Old classics: bird seed for the tourists. It's easy for me to harmonise with him, with both voice and instrument.

'We were here first!' Sage shouts over us, a discordant backing singer. 'He didn't even ask – not really!'

Those placing money in the guitar case don't pay him much attention, they do their best to ignore him, and I'm doing the same. Luke is a decent guitarist and vocalist, and between the two of us we pull in a small crowd consisting of Spanish students, two stag-dos, a hen-do and what looks like a Women's Institute outing.

I'm used to people staring off to the side or just beyond me. As if I'm on the other side of one-way glass and they can't quite see me, though they've an idea I'm there. So it's nice to have folk doing a shoulder-dance or a head-bob or sharing a smile. Usually busking is about gathering as many pity-clinks as possible before the police or the cold moves us on. Not today, though. Today I'm enjoying myself.

It's only half an hour later, when Luke takes a couple of coins from the case and goes off to get us cups of tea, that Sage can make his objections fully known. In the meantime he's taken a sulk and a seat on a bench over towards the museum. As soon as Luke strides off, though, he's over to me and grasping me by the shoulders as if to shake me to my senses.

'This was our spot,' he hisses.

'What does it matter?' I reply. 'I'm enjoying playing with someone. Besides, is it not you who's always going on about collectivisation, pooling resources and all that shite?'

He sighs deeply. 'He dictated to you, though.'

'He offered a compromise.'

'On his terms.'

There's a pause. Sage stares at me through it. Then, with his hands still on my shoulders, he turns me and pushes me over towards an empty bench. We sit and he leans back.

'Rab,' he says. 'Let me tell you the difference.'

'Between what?'

'There is a story…' Sage begins.

I have a hollow hunger in my stomach, and I concentrate on that more than on Sage's story. Which is about a man who uses force and threats to get a job over another candidate, then offers his rival a role as his assistant. I'm almost certain that Sage has made it up on the spot; it's not one of his best. I offer no comment and the story trails off as Luke returns with the teas. He's brought three of them. In spite of all Sage's griping and heckling, he's brought back a tea for the man in the Mozart tie.

As he makes his way over to us, I lean over to Sage. 'You see that? He's brought you a tea.'

Sage just shakes his head. 'You don't get it, do you?' he says. 'He thinks he's better than you.'

'You're criticising him, but he let me sing with him.'

'It was a hostile takeover, Rab. From first to last, a hostile takeover.'

There's precious little conversation over our tea at first, so I ask Luke where he's from and how long he's been playing. He's from Worthing, further along the coast, and he's been busking since he was sixteen, for nearly five years now. He goes to Sussex University, studying dentistry, and he'd rather busk to bring in money than work as a waiter or a barman.

'In my experience,' Sage says, smoothing his tie, 'students are the worst. They think they'll change the world, think they'll change the system, but they end up reaffirming it instead. Especially *dentists*.'

'Why dentistry?' I ask, choosing to ignore Sage, since his own teeth look as if they've been used as a firing range by miniature soldiers – cratered, chipped, cracked, scorched with brown and black.

Luke shrugs. 'Good wage, good benefits, chance to work for myself.'

Sage snorts derisively. It kills the conversation for a moment.

'What about yourself, Rab?' Luke asks.

'I got a record contract straight out of school, just over a year ago,' I say. 'Came down to London to record the album and ended up in debt to the record company and without – '

'Capitalism sucked his soul,' Sage interrupts. 'It bled him dry and left him eviscerated in the gutter. Sorry, I should explain: to eviscerate is to disembowel or to remove an essential component.'

Luke blows on the surface of his tea, creating ripples. Not yet a storm in a teacup, but not far off. It's in situations like these that Sage is at his worst. When all that's called for is a *normal* conversation, or a casual chat. Don't get me wrong, I owe him a lot, but I can't be arsed with him when he's like this.

'Did you release the album, then?' Luke asks.

I nod.

'Any good?'

I shrug and look down at the sleeve of my jacket. There is a stray thread. I pull at it until it snaps, then look back up at Luke. 'How do you judge these things?' I say. 'I mean, it sold next to no copies and the label didn't take up the option for the second one, so…'

'Are you proud of it, though?'

I have to think about that. I remember back to the day, a week or two ago, when I was wandering about around North Laine. The tight-knit streets with their market stalls and cafés spilling out on to the pavements were the perfect place to spend the sunny days busking. When I still had my guitar, that is. You'll see all sorts down that way – some in sunglasses that cost no more than a few quid and others in designer ones that cost a few hundred – but no one judges you for having trousers that are too short in the legs or a T-shirt that is tie-dye-discoloured beneath the armpits. It was so muggy-warm that my guitar kept slipping out of tune, and I had to pull my tuning fork from my pocket to strike against my kneecap or the cobbles at my feet.

After busking, I was browsing through the second-hand CDs in a music shop – the kind with cardboard dividers and handwritten price tags – when I came across a copy of my first and only album: *Measures Taken*. It was a little worse for wear: the corner had snapped away and left a split like a fork of lightning down the case and the CD inside had a thin maze of scratches across the surface. Still, I considered paying the three-quid asking price. With my fingers fumbling through the change in my pocket, I thought about buying it. Because I don't have a copy. Out of all those thousands that were pressed, I don't have one.

And what stopped me, above and beyond my hunger, my thirst and my thoughts of a hostel bed that night, beyond my lack of a CD player even, or the vague notion that some scout might stumble across it, buy it, and 'discover' me for the second time... beyond all of that was... what was it?

'I'm not too sure, mate,' I reply to Luke, with an uncertain smile. 'It was a bit of a crazy time, to be honest.'

'Still, quite an achievement to have an album out.' He looks at me, then lays a hand on my arm as if to console me. 'And you're a brilliant singer, mate, I'll tell you that. You've got that gravel tone to your voice like a young Bob – '

'Thank you,' I interrupt, before he can get out the surname.

'Maybe, if I have any gigs going, you could come along and help me out?'

'I'd like that.' My smile broadens. 'Cheers.'

Sage holds out his clenched fist between us. It is a gesture somewhere between a military salute and a child raising their hand in the classroom. He means it as a protest. We both turn to him.

'As your manager, Rab,' he says, 'I would advise against it.'

'What?' Luke frowns. 'Are you for real?'

'This *boy* – ' Sage speaks only to me ' – is clearly a charlatan. He's only looking to exploit your talents. After all, he's training to be a *dentist*.'

Luke stands and looms over Sage. 'What is your problem, buddy?'

Sage tries to maintain his dignity as he squares up to Luke, looking off into the distance as he rises to his feet and straightening his tie before standing nose-to-nose against him. The effect is undermined slightly by the broken zip on the fly to his corduroys which, as it has a tendency to do, flaps open.

I want to step in, but I don't want Luke to withdraw his offer of us gigging together and I'm mindful that Sage is likely to interpret any calming measures as disloyalty, as a betrayal.

'You're only out for what you can get,' Sage says calmly, slipping into his lecturer's voice. 'You muscled your way in on Rab's busking spot and now you're thinking about exploiting his talents to make up for your own shortfalls.'

'And what's your deal, *mate*?' Luke replies. 'Are you a homo, or just a sad old man with nothing to do?'

'What does my sexuality have to do with it?'

'I'll take that as a yes.'

'Take it any way you choose.'

We're beginning to gather a crowd again, but not in the positive way we were before. This time the stag-do guys edge closer in anticipation of a fight, the Spanish schoolchildren look up from their phones and consider recording it all to put on YouTube, and the WI ladies discuss whether it's a matter for the security guards in the Royal Pavilion or the police officers down by the pier.

'Look,' I hiss, 'why are we making a scene, anyway?'

'I've forgotten more than you know.' Sage stabs a finger into Luke's chest. 'I used to teach at university level. I used to give lectures. And not one of them was about bloody *teeth*.'

'*Used* to.' Luke smiles, showing his perfect teeth.

'I'm outside the establishment now, where I want to be.'

'You're a greasy old man who hangs about with Rab here to make yourself feel important.' Luke turns to me. 'No offence, mate.'

33

'None taken,' I murmur.

'You're everything that's wrong with society – ' Sage begins.

'Listen, Luke,' I interrupt, trying to defuse the situation, 'how about we get busking again? There are a lot of folk about, and we could make a killing if we played some more.'

Luke looks across at me and nods. Before stepping away from Sage, he hooks a finger in underneath the Mozart tie and flicks it up so that it hits Sage on his chin. I can see that Sage is bristling with anger, that he's ready to launch into a speech, so I quickly reach into my pocket and lift the harmonica to my mouth. I run off a scale before he can open his mouth and then step over on to the grass to stand beside Luke.

'Ladies and gentlemen, any requests?' Luke calls out.

'Fuck off and die!' Sage calls back.

We ignore him.

'"Sweet Caroline",' one of the stag-do lads shouts. 'Bill here's getting married to Caroline next week.'

Luke looks at me. I shrug, then nod. It's easy enough to come up with a quick lick on the harmonica, an approximate melody, to replace the opening instrumentals and, after Luke's come in with the vocals and guitar, the whole crowd join me for the three notes after the chorus – *duh, duh, dah* – and we've suddenly got ourselves a sing-along that drowns out all but the worst of Sage's shouts.

It all goes really well, and after we've finished that one someone shouts out that we should sing 'Come on Eileen' in honour of another bride. She's called Evelyn rather than Eileen, so we change the words accordingly and continue our impromptu karaoke session on the lawns of the Royal Pavilion.

All the while, though, I'm keeping half an eye on Sage, who goes slouching off towards the flowerbeds but then turns and comes back to sit himself cross-legged on the grass to the side of me. Luke's too busy working out the chord progression to 'Layla' to notice, but I see Sage snaking out an arm, lifting a note from the top of the heaped piles of coins in the guitar case and tucking it into his coat pocket.

I see him, but I say nothing.

LONDON

I decide to walk from the hotel to the trendy bar even though Pierce offers to send a car. I say that I want a breath of fresh air. I actually want a pint, or two, before I show up at this bar called Che and have to play my guitar in front of all the press and hangers-on that the label have invited. Pierce has licked the arse of some radio producers and pluggers to get them to turn up, promised them great things by way of protest and social critique, and he's told me that *Measures Taken* will largely sink or swim on the basis of tonight.

No pressure, then.

With my first pint, in Marylebone, I sit and brood on the name-change. It's been a month since my identity was altered, Price coming into the studio with Bower, from the label, and beckoning me out of the recording booth. Bower is in charge of the Agitate imprint, which my album will be released on, though he looks more like a Kazakh weightlifter than a music executive. While Pierce stood in the background, listening in, Bower placed a hand on my arm and said, 'We need to talk.'

'You breaking up with me?'

I said it with a smile, but then I had this wee clench of panic in my chest because maybe, just maybe, it was going to be *that* conversation. Days before the CD was pressed, with the cover art finalised – the lettering near enough a copy of The Specials and the picture of me holding up my guitar in the style of Woody Guthrie – just months before the release, and they were going to pull me to the side and say, *It's all been a terrible mistake, son.*

'Nothing like that.' Bower tried a grin, but it turned out crooked.

'Well?'

'It's just that the marketing department thought...' Bower cleared his throat '...well, we all thought that your name was Robert Dylan, with a "y". But, on examining the contracts and what-have-you, we've discovered that it's actually with an "i".'

'That was no secret,' I said, breaking into a smile. 'And, like you say, it was on all the contracts; you must have noticed it before now, surely?'

'As you know, a lot of that was handled by our parent company, through the A&R department and the lawyers.'

I shrugged. It wasn't a problem, so far as I was concerned.

'That's what comes of leaving the paperwork to the bloody secretaries, I suppose,' Bower continued. 'Anyway, we feel that one change from Bob Dylan is good marketing, but that two loses the connection, you know?'

'Sorry, I'm not sure I do.'

'Let me explain...' Pierce stepped forward and passed a hand over his forehead, taking away the sheen of sweat. 'They feel that Bob to Rab is good. It gives the impression that you're Scottish. But to have Dylan, with a "y", changing to Dillon, with an "i", as well, makes it difficult to maintain the link.'

'But hang on...' The answer I wanted to give was full of swear-words, so I had to take a moment to filter them out. 'I *am* Scottish. I *don't* have a link to Dylan. My name *is* Rab Dillon, with a *fucking* "i".' One sneaked past the censors.

'And they're sympathetic to that,' Price said. 'But from a marketing point of view – '

'Show him the CD,' Bower said, in this growling voice that made me wonder if he meant to say 'gun' and got the two mixed up.

37

Price half turned, turned back, all the while nodding and flustered. It took him two attempts to wrestle the CD – it was a CD, not a gun – from his suit jacket and there was this tearing sound as he got it free. He handed it over to me. It was familiar, in that the photo was me standing in my Guthrie pose staring off beyond the camera, but there was a massive typo there in The Specials lettering: 'Rab Dylan: *Measures Taken.*

'We've made the decision, son,' Bower said, stretching forward to offer a handshake. 'Because you need any leg-up you can get. In this business, the first album can be released and forgotten about on the same day. At least, this way, people will take notice.'

'Do I have a choice?'

'This is the name the label is behind; this is the name the label wants.'

'D-Y-L-A-N.' I sounded it out.

'It sounds the same, let's face it,' he said. 'It's cosmetic detail.'

I looked at his hand. It was a fleshy hand, with some dry skin over the knuckles. I reached out and shook it.

'Excellent,' Pierce said, trying a chuckle. 'It's almost biblical, isn't it? A "y" for an "i".'

And now, in that pub in Marylebone a month later, I imagine what the reaction to my name-change will be from the folk back up in Glasgow. My mum, my friends… Maddie. They'll think it's a mistake. They'll presume that the CDs will all be taken and melted down, that some typesetter somewhere will lose their job and that new CDs will come out pristine and new and *correct*. But they won't. For the rest of my days, there will be a CD of my music out there that doesn't *quite* bear my name.

Leaving the bottom inch of beer in the glass, I rise from my bar stool, lift my guitar, and make my way out into the streets of London. It's just gone five-thirty and the city-slickers are streaming out from their offices and marching towards the

Tube/train/bus. The streets outside the pubs are scattered with the quick-one-after-work crowd, and the restaurants are waving people inside for the pre-theatre menu. In this mix of natives and tourists I don't want to take out my *A–Z*; I don't want to show myself up and admit that I'm lost. In spite of the well-creased spine, the map feels like a failure. I try the GPS on my phone, but it buffers and then shows me a map of the West End of Glasgow – from the last time I used the bloody thing. So I settle for walking on another couple of streets, ducking into the quietest bar I can find, a wine bar down a side-street, and sitting myself down to plan my route in peace and quiet.

'What can I get you, sir?'

It's bloody table-service. Nothing worse than table-service – you can't see the beer taps to make your selection and you can't drink at your own pace; got to time it to coincide with the to-ing and fro-ing of the bar folk.

'Beer,' I say, looking up at the young waiter with the pencil-thin moustache and glasses.

'Any particular one?'

'Whatever you've got on draught.'

'We only serve bottled beer.'

'Whatever you have in bottles, then.'

'We have Peroni Nastro Azzurro, Sagres, Blue Moon – '

'Peroni is fine, cheers.'

'Very good.'

'Exceedingly good.'

He ignores my final comment and makes his way off to the bar, and I take comfort in the fact that it's harder to surreptitiously spit into a bottle than a pint glass. I sit and leaf my way through the *A–Z*, working out the way from Marylebone down to the Soho bar. I imprint the directions on my brain, wanting to avoid the shame of taking the blue, red and white book out again in the street and having to stand spinning, in the centre of a crowd, like a fucking tourist looking for Trafalgar Square.

I'm still not fully settled in London. Maybe because I've been so busy with recording. It's the kind of city you need a base in, some soil for your roots, but I never seem to be in the same place for more than a few hours at a time. Too fucking expensive to stand still – the hotel seems to charge per cubic centimetre of air breathed, the cafés pass on the cost of flying the coffee beans over from Kenya, and the bars bill you for their alcohol licence if you stay for more than a swift pint.

Pierce is suggesting that I go back to Glasgow for Christmas next month, to save some money. Recharge, he said; maybe stay on for the Celtic Connections festival in the New Year. As a punter rather than a performer. I'm not keen, though. I'd rather spend the time exploring the capital, enjoying my freedom from the recording booth. Because, come springtime, I won't be able to walk these streets for fear of being mobbed.

When the beer comes I swallow it down in a couple of glugs, leaving more than two inches at the bottom in case there is waiter-backwash in there. Then I leave a fiver on the table, thinking first that it might be too much of a tip, and then that it might actually be less than the list price in a place like that. Never mind, it's more than enough for a single bottle of beer. Besides, I'm cutting it fine if I want to get there in time for the sound-check.

Che is a bar that lives up to its name. The iconic print of Guevara is up everywhere, not just with the usual red background but with all manner of reliefs behind, like the Warhol pop art of Marilyn Monroe. It strikes me as odd, to be honest, that this icon of revolution is plastered over the walls in more colours than the Dulux range, but I smile and nod at Price when he says, 'Isn't this the perfect place, *hombre*? The Price is always right.' Above the bar, the word '*Revolución*' is stencilled in blue and white, but the taps are all the regular beers that you would get in any high street pub, and the spirits are the same ones I drank when I was seventeen. When I go to take a leak, the picture above the Gents sign is Che with a cigar and I wonder what the image for the Ladies is, but I decide not to go looking for it in case it's just the same image with blonde Marilyn hair Photoshopped on.

'So,' Pierce says, when I return. The table he sets my beer down on is (or was) a hubcap. Revolution in Soho extends to – maybe ends with – hubcaps being turned into tables. 'We'll start at around half-seven. Just two or three songs. Give them a flavour.'

'A flavour of revolution,' I say, with more than a flavour of sarcasm.

'*Exactly*,' he says. 'Exactly.'

After tuning up the old-fashioned way, with my tuning fork, and going through the sound-check, I sit at my hubcap and drink until I feel detached. Not until I'm drunk, but until the nerves are gone and replaced by this vacant disconnection from my surroundings, from the people that are beginning to cluster around hubcaps in slim-fitting suits and streamlined skirts. Two kisses, one on each cheek, and a smile. I've never understood that; never felt comfortable going from cheek to cheek when the equivalent in Glasgow would be a nod or, at the very most, a handshake. Pierce brings people across to kiss and be kissed, but I say very little and they soon go drifting off to other hubcaps.

Over the past couple of months, while I was recording, I've grown used to spending the days playing my music and the nights slowly and steadily drinking in the corner of pubs where everyone else seems to know one another. Those worlds colliding should be my Big Bang moment, but it feels like an anticlimax, to be honest.

When the time comes, I step up to the stage – not really a stage, more a corner of the floor with a Cuban flag as a backdrop – and make sure I'm tuned up. The venue is small, it should hold no fear for me, but I know that the people around the hubcaps have turned up just to hear me; they are no casual crowd, they're professionals and they can make or break me.

'Ladies and gentlemen,' I say, into the microphone, 'my name is Rab Dylan.'

I resist the urge to spell it out for them and settle for an opening chord instead. The song is called 'Hiatus' and it's about a student taking time off from his degree to go and join the Occupy camp at St Paul's Cathedral. I have no experience of university and only my time with Flick to draw on for the Occupy part, but I'm proud of the song. It talks about 'the trade in ivory towers' and 'letters after your name, so that you can shift the blame'. It is explicit, it is confrontational, it is activism in song form. But, as I stand there, I can't shake the feeling that it's a little… just a touch… *thin*.

I think of that first day visiting the camp. Pierce gave me a notebook to take with me and, as I went from group to group, I should have been scribbling away. There were people talking about corporate tax avoidance, about scrapping the Trident nuclear defence system, about introducing a financial transaction tax on the banks. Why do we need austerity, they said, when we can raise the funds this way instead? And I knew those were the arguments I should have noted; that those were the debates Maddie would have plunged into head-first. But, until I met Flick, I'd struggled to even dip my toe in the water. Standing on the edge of the groups, I felt like a kid on the first day at a new school listening to the other kids gossiping about teachers that I didn't know.

In the end, the only thing I wrote down that day was a detailed plan for a waste disposal system. An older gent in socks and sandals shouted it out to me, along with, 'You've got a pen and paper – write it down, for Christ's-sake.' It had separate columns for compostables, recyclables and reusables – but it didn't help in the least when I sat down to write the song.

It's not just the lyrics, though. My mind flashes back to another day in the studio, a month or so ago, when Pierce came up and tapped on the glass of the isolation booth. He mouthed at me and I shook my head, indicating that I couldn't hear by pointing at the headphones on my ears. The sound engineer pressed a button and the music in the cans stopped.

'What about some brass?' Pierce called.

'Brass?'

'Trumpets, horns, the likes of that.'

I shake my head, speak into the microphone. 'Guitar and harmonica is fine.'

'I don't know…' He pushed his glasses up his nose. 'I've been listening to a lot of Miles Davis.'

'Right. And if you'd been listening to Rolf Harris would we be putting a fucking didgeridoo over the top of it?'

'It's missing something, is all I'm saying… it needs more depth…'

I stepped up to the glass, misting it as I gave him my answer. He couldn't hear because I wasn't speaking into the mic, but he caught the mouthing.

On the stage at Che, though, I think he might just be right – *the Price is always right*. In the silent bar, with only sips and cleared throats for company, the acoustic guitar sounds tinny and faraway. I launch into the harmonica solo at the end, but I've never quite got used to the rack that loops around my neck, so a couple of the notes slide off into approximations of themselves. It's not a disaster, but the applause at the end is polite rather than rapturous. Maybe that's just the crowd, though; maybe that's just the occasion.

I play another – about the London riots – and a final love song that almost didn't make it on to the album. A break-up song. If I'd had another week, another day in the studio it probably wouldn't have been on there, but I was running late as it was and Pierce had given me this soppy smile and called it 'touching' so I'd shrugged my shoulders and given it the nod. It's about Maddie, that one, although it doesn't mention her by name. It's about her decision, in those final days of the relationship. I called it '3.17am' because that's the precise time she called to tell me.

43

After the three songs, as I make my way back to my hubcap, it's the final song that seems to have made an impression. Two girls approach me – they come as a pair. One says, 'I loved the emotion in that last song.' And the other says, 'Was it written for your wife? For your girlfriend?' I smile, and I shake my head and I let them feel the callus on the tip of my guitar-plucking finger as I lean over the bar to buy them a drink. They might have been paid by Pierce to be there – might be part of the service, one of the perks – but, in that moment, I don't care. As long as they don't ask me questions about my lyrics, as Flick would, or prompt me to analyse my performance, like Maddie. It's all simple, straightforward. I get them both a cocktail, I get myself a double whisky, I put the whole lot on my credit card, and then I walk them, one on each arm, over to the hubcap in the corner.

GLASGOW

Maddie comes in and orders a chai tea. At the sink, I hear her voice and fumble as I lift a soapy coffee cup. It falls and chimes out, calling attention to my cheeks, reddened with embarrassment, and my half-apron, browned with coffee stains.

'Hi, Rab,' Maddie calls.

I wave awkwardly, the broken handle of the cup in my hand.

'I thought you were singing tonight?' she asks.

'I do… I am,' I say, avoiding the eye of Cesare, my boss. Cesare lets me play two or three songs at the end of my shift as long as the shop isn't busy and provided the sweeping and mopping has been done to his satisfaction. He's a stickler for details, is Cesare, and I'm worried that the broken cup might see the last-minute cancellation of the evening set.

'I'll see you in a bit, then,' Maddie says, and takes her tea over to the sofas. The shop is small and full of corners, so she is not in my eyeline, but I can picture her slumping down in the sag of the leather sofa and casting a disappointed eye over the paperback books on the shelf, the gramophone in the corner and the film posters from the 1950s and '60s that line the walls. Retro chic. I can hear her sigh in the steam from the coffee machine, and the impatient tapping of her fingers in the water drip-dripping into the sink. I look up at the clock: twenty-five minutes until the end of my shift.

45

'She is your girlfriend, yes?' Cesare says, coming over. He stands uncomfortably close. His breath smells of biscotti, sweet and stale.

'Just a friend.'

'You are trying to impress her, though?'

I nod, then put my hands into the lukewarm water to rummage around for the broken pieces of the cup.

'She is pretty,' Cesare says, not in his usual tone. There is a gentleness to it, almost a wistfulness, so that the word is nearly drowned out by the rasp of the coffee grinder from behind. 'You must not keep the lady waiting,' he says. 'Finish the dishes in the sink and then go and play your guitar.'

'Th-thank you,' I manage.

'And you will pay for the cup from your wages, yes?'

I rush the rest of the washing-up, barely grazing the cups with my sponge before setting them up on the draining board. It takes me only a matter of minutes, then I unknot my apron and lift my guitar. There is a chair set out, in front of an oriental rug that hangs over the rising damp. I do not tune up, or introduce myself. Instead I sit and launch straight into some Leonard Cohen. My fingers, either from sweat or soap, slip and slide from the strings, and my voice creaks and cracks on the high notes.

'Thank you,' I say once I've finished, in response to the polite scattering of applause. I look over to the sofas and Maddie leans forward to flash me a smile and a thumbs-up. Dragging my hands across the knees of my jeans, I take a minute to tune my guitar and settle myself.

She came to see me play, I think. She came and she didn't bring Ewan. At that moment, with the knowledge that I have her full and undivided attention, I desperately want to play her something special, something from the heart. I can think of nothing, though. All the covers speak of other people, and all my own songs have echoes of my friendship with Ewan.

I play a King Creosote cover, then decide to play some Dylan. My nerve fails me, though, when I consider playing

46

'Absolutely Sweet Marie' and changing the name. The lyrics might needle some guilt from her about coming to see me without Ewan. I settle on 'Buckets of Rain' instead. Then, happy with the borrowed sentiment in my set, I leave my guitar propped up against the chair and make my way over to where Maddie sits.

'That was great,' she says, rising. I feel the button on her coat sleeve catching my cheek as I lean in to give her a hug. She smells faintly of sweat. Among the familiar aromas of the shop – the cloying sweetness of vanilla, cinnamon and sugar, and the bitterness of coffee – the sourness of it is not unpleasant.

'What did you think?' I ask, as I take a seat beside her, even though she's already answered that. Then, catching sight of her tea on the table, 'Was there something wrong with your chai?'

'I don't think so.'

'You didn't drink much of it.'

'I don't really do hot drinks.' She shrugs. 'Coffee shops aren't about the drinks anyway. You're just paying for time. Time to sit and chat, or read, or write… or listen to music.'

'Right.' I'm confused for a second, unsure whether to be insulted by her scorn of my workplace or flattered that she's come in in spite of it, to hear me play.

'Are you done?' she asks.

'I am.'

'Will you walk me home?'

'Of course.' I rise to collect my guitar. As I zip up the case, I glance up at the clock and realise that there are still ten minutes of my shift left. I have taken the last fifteen minutes at fast-forward, and now I need to pause and look across to Cesare.

'When is your next shift, Rab?' he calls.

'Tuesday evening.'

'See you then.' He winks and clinks a cup on to the top of the coffee machine. 'Have a nice night, yes?'

As we walk home, Maddie leans towards me and I feel her coat brush up against my jumper. I feel it as keenly as the touch of skin against skin. I am alert and aware of her every movement.

'Ewan's a dick,' is her opening line. 'Simple as.'

I'm not too sure how to respond. Without speaking, I watch Maddie as she takes out a cigarette. Using her teeth, she delicately tears a strip from around the tip before lighting it. The spare paper is rolled into a tight ball and thrown down to settle against the concrete like a single stray hailstone.

'Why did you do that?' I ask.

'What?'

'With the cigarette.'

'Oh, I read somewhere that it makes for a smoother smoke.' She smiles. 'You don't get any paper with the first drag, you see.'

I nod, then look down at the pavement. It's been raining and there is a reflective sheen to the streets and a freshness to the air. It is a Saturday night and the pubs are casting light, laughter and shouted conversation out on to Great Western Road.

'Force of habit, really,' Maddie says.

'Why is he a dick?' I ask.

'He's just a child...' She drags on her cigarette. 'Like, if we're going to the cinema and I ask him what he wants to see, he'll just shrug. But then, once we've seen what I want to see, he'll fucking *complain* about it, you know?'

'Is that not him complaining about the film rather than about you, though?'

'Maybe, aye. But there are other things, more intimate things, and he'll just go silent. And – '

'Are you boyfriend and girlfriend?' I ask, my voice catching.

She shrugs, then goes silent.

'He's a good mate, and a good lad,' I say, aware that I'm trying to convince myself as much as her. I've known Ewan since we were five years old. I can't remember the first time we met, but my mum has a picture of it somewhere: our first day of school. Me in my uniform, grinning, and Ewan in the background, with his bowl cut squint across the fringe, making a pretend camera with his fingers.

'He's a good mate,' I repeat. 'But, if you're not happy with him, then… as in, there's nothing stopping you from…'

'I don't think he'd even be upset,' she says. 'He's one of those guys who doesn't even break stride. Like, there's this cat who hangs around my mum's house, right, and he's only got three legs but he goes off stalking the birds like he's got all four, and with every step he hobbles and half-falls, but then he forgets again and keeps on going towards the birds with this awkward fucking limp.'

'What's the fourth leg in that analogy?'

Maddie looks across at me, then flicks her cigarette down to the concrete. 'If you don't know, Rab, then I'm not telling you,' she says.

I feel as if I haven't drawn breath, not properly, since I asked the boyfriend/girlfriend question. Maddie is giving me clues, but not enough to work out the puzzle. Soon we will be at her house, up beside Westbourne Gardens, so the next question is crucial.

'Are you with him?' I ask.

'Like, do you mean, have I *been* with him?'

I shrug. 'Yes.'

'I've tried,' she says. No more than that.

'Right.' My thoughts are drawn to the evenings spent in my attic bedroom, up at my parents' house, writing lyrics with Ewan – spliffs and songs – and I remember the reaction of my best friend to the porn hidden among the folders on my computer. The single shake of the head, the lack of a laugh as I made the awkward joke about needing, every once in a while, to strum myself rather than my guitar.

Ewan has an odd attitude towards girls. A mixture of confidence and indifference – the exact opposite of me. On

49

a night out it's Ewan who'll chat away – hand on arm, eye-contact – while I stare at the floor. When they show interest in him, though, he tends to go wandering off and leave them with me. He'd make the perfect wingman, really, if I could only get my eyes off the ground.

'I like him,' Maddie says. 'But he's closed-off.'

'Right.'

'Not like you,' she adds, softly.

We are outside her house now, and I wonder what to do next. We have already hugged, so it's the safe option, but I'm thinking of going for the kiss on the cheek, unusual in Glasgow, just to let her know – without saying it – that I'm... well, that if she –

'Thanks for listening, Rab,' she says. 'And congratulations on tonight. It was great, really.'

'Cheers.'

She steps towards me, but her face is bowed down towards the ground. She is a foot shorter than me, so her forehead nestles in at the crook of my neck and I feel her breath on the collar of my jumper. The fabric seems to rise to her lips as she breathes in and fall as she breathes out.

Maddie raises her head; I peer down. Maddie on her toes; me bending my knees. Then we are nose-to-nose, eye-to-eye. She tilts her head and I place a hand on her back to draw her closer.

At first, the kiss is dry and tastes of tobacco. I focus on the twitch of her mouth as she smiles, the flick of her tongue. My hand comes up to the nape of her neck, to the shortest strands of her tomboy haircut, and I move my fingers up towards the crown, savouring not only the feel of it but also the sound, a rustling as soft as stirring in the night-time.

The next day, Ewan and Cammy come over to my house. It's our usual Sunday routine, hanging out in my attic bedroom, listening to music and playing football games on the PS3. All my thoughts are maddeningly, madly Maddie.

When Ewan arrives, I sit and whisper-wish that we will steer clear of the subject, that no mention will be made. Lately he's been bringing over the early Karine Polwart albums, which is an improvement on the Fairport Convention phase he went through. We listen to 'Scribbled in Chalk', then he puts on a Burns Unit album which has Polwart singing alongside King Creosote and others.

After Cammy arrives and we've played four or five matches on the PS3 I begin to grow annoyed by the fact that Ewan is still talking about the collaborative nature of Scottish folk music and asking me whether I think it would be worth listening to Joni Mitchell's back catalogue.

'You and Maddie, then?' I say, after scoring against the run-of-play.

'What about us?' Ewan replies. His tongue is sticking out from the corner of his mouth, as he frowns in concentration and twists his controller this way and that to get his virtual players to run in the right direction. 'What the *fuck* is that? How did you get past him there? It's fucking *cheating*; the game's fucking *decided* I'm going to lose.'

'Are you going steady?'

'Going steady? What is this, '50s America?'

I think of the movie posters Maddie sat beneath last night: the swooning leading ladies and the moustachioed men supporting them around the waist. I try to imagine Maddie filling the first role then, briefly, wonder what I'd look like with a moustache. It wouldn't work, I've tried it before: it came in thin and blond, and when I tried to darken the hairs with shoe polish I was called 'smudge' for a week and then 'Adolf' for months.

'Fine, then,' I say. 'Are you going out with each other?'

'We're having a good time, just,' Ewan replies. 'She's a real live wire, is Maddie, I'm a big fan of her work.'

'Has she given you a blowie yet?' Cammy pipes up.

'Jesus, Cammy, you're obsessed…' I shake my head. 'Has she, though?'

'We've done some stuff,' Ewan says. 'I'll say no more than that.'

Have you like fuck, I think. You've thrown a pebble in the water, mate, and you're trying to convince us it's a tsunami.

'And are you boyfriend and girlfriend?' Cammy asks.

The question, with its echoes of the night before, makes me wince, but Ewan doesn't notice because he's doing some wincing of his own. I've just run through to score my second and Ewan responds by throwing his controller across the room and rising to his feet.

'Let's get stoned,' he says. 'Fuck this game; it's *decided* I'm going to lose anyway.'

Ewan is generally a laid-back guy, but he sometimes shows his temper. Like the time, when we were seven, that he thought I was cheating at Monopoly so he launched a terrorist attack against the high-end hotels of London and tore up the financial system. Or when he got so frustrated with Subbuteo – that game where you flick plastic footballers around a felt pitch – that he kneecapped both his centre-forwards and left his goalkeeper's arm dangling by a thread. We call them his 'limit-breaks', these fits of rage, and try to avoid them, or at least tiptoe past them.

We turn off the console and roll a joint. I feel the acrid smoke scour at the inside of my throat as I inhale. I splutter it back out, thinking of the time my mum climbed the ladder and knocked on the hatch door just seconds after I'd taken a bong. As I opened the hatch, my mum sniffed questioningly at the fug of smoke and asked what it was. 'Erm... um...' I replied, my thoughts slow. 'It's the smell from the computer monitor overheating: the dust burning in the vents.' She accepted it without further comment.

'Did I ever tell you – ' I begin.

'The story about the computer monitor overheating,' Ewan finishes the sentence. 'Yes.'

Cammy laughs. 'It's like your go-to story, Dildo, every fucking time.'

'Right.' I smile, but I'm wary now of saying anything else in case it is just a repetition, in case everything is unoriginal. I'm paranoid I'll get pelters for whatever I come out with. So, instead of speaking, I switch off the music and lift my guitar.

Usually, over a weekend, I'd record at least one track to upload online. Just a cover. At first, it was all the old folk songs that my Uncle Brendan taught me. Scottish airs and American blues. Then, about a year ago, I played Bob Dylan's 'Masters of War' and Ewan edited a video to go along with it that showed still images of the aftermath of drone strikes in Pakistan and Afghanistan. It got close to seventy thousand views.

After that, I did a cover of Ewan MacColl's 'Dirty Old Town', with some pictures of Glasgow that Cammy took, and a version of Woody Guthrie's 'This Land Is Your Land' with a still image of the Saltire flag. Ewan suggested we change the lyrics to Scottish place names and that, but I struggled to rework the later verses about dust and deserts so I kept to the original in the end. It still got a few thousand views.

Today, though, I don't play protest songs. Instead, I start a succession of chords. It sounds good, so I play it again. And again. Again. And then Cammy begins drumming on the floor with a pen and Ewan picks up the old acoustic with the missing B string and plays the only two chords he knows – G and C major – over and over.

'Someone fucking turn on the laptop and record this shit!' Cammy says.

'You do it,' Ewan says.

'I'm keeping the beat. You're the one doing shite-all, you do it.'

'No, I'm – '

'You do it, Ewan, quickly,' I say, feeling as if there's something momentous, some musical epiphany about to occur and that, if we don't capture it, I'll spend the rest of my days picking at my guitar trying to recreate it.

53

Ewan lays down the acoustic – '*Fuck sake!*' – and makes his way over to the computer. The way he slams his fists down on the desk like a toddler having a tantrum causes Cammy to look at me and laugh, and we lose our rhythm for a moment, but we regain it by the time Ewan has everything set up and is ready to hit 'record'.

'Now,' Cammy says, straight-faced, 'you sure you can remember your chords, Ewan?'

'Fuck you,' Ewan says. 'Fuck you. At least I've got an instrument; you're drumming with a fucking *pen*, mate. The only thing you have is a bloody *biro* and you think you're changing the world. Well, you're not, OK? You're fucking not.'

He's started recording before he's finished ranting, so the tail end of his outburst will be over the start of the track, but I decide that it's easier to edit it out later than to get him to begin again. Besides, there's a false start on 'Bob Dylan's 115th Dream', so it might even be worth keeping in. Closing my eyes, I wait for the regular G-C-G-C plod from Ewan to start up again and then start singing. The lyrics come easily.

'I spied you through the undergrowth… and you spied me… but it wasn't for him, no, it wasn't for him to see…' I bite at my lip. 'You came to find me, to hear me sing… and you stayed for tea… but it wasn't for him, no, it wasn't for him to see…'

'It wasn't for him to see,' Cammy repeats, in falsetto. I ignore him.

'I kissed you on the long walk home… and you, you kissed me… but it wasn't for him, no, it wasn't for him to see…'

The drumming has stopped. The G-C-G-C has stopped. I also trail off. I keep my eyes shut, though. I've gone too far. I've basically just confessed, in song, to kissing my best mate's girlfriend. Fucking ridiculous thing to do, like something from a bloody opera, or one of those teen-shite movies set in an American high school.

54

I open one eye. I'm expecting to see an acoustic with a broken string flying towards me, or at least a fist. I'm expecting a limit-break from Ewan. There's no acoustic, though – no fist. Instead, Ewan is spread out across the futon squirming and writhing as if in agony. He's trying to laugh, but it's coming out in gulps and dry heaves. Cammy watches him and alternates between frowning and bursting into these wee chuckles of bemused laughter.

'I thought it sounded good, man,' Cammy says to me. 'Not bad at all.'

'It's not... it's not...' Ewan gasps. 'It's not the song... it was the fucking... the fucking falsetto... from that ballbag...' He points at Cammy and drags in a deep breath. 'What the fuck was that meant to be?'

I grin, then laugh. 'The lyrics were good, though?'

'They were fine.' Ewan is gathering himself, wiping at his eyes. 'They were fine. It was just that biro ballbag over there.'

Cammy opens his mouth, but I speak first.

'We start again, then,' I say. 'With no backing vocals from Cammy and no laughter from Ewan, OK? Try to keep to the rhythm. I really feel like I might be on to something here.'

BRIGHTON

I find him in the doorway of a solicitor's office up on Church Road, his blanket drawn up over his head. He snores like a foghorn, steering the early commuters away from the chipped concrete steps. I nudge him with the toe of my trainer. He splutters but doesn't wake.

'Sage?' I hiss.

He is a notoriously heavy sleeper. I left him once, in the daytime, in Preston Park, and returned to find him sprawled out across a bench with a gaggle of gathered teenagers sticking chewing gum into the bristles of his beard. I stayed back, unconvinced of my ability to chase them off, and waited for them to tire. The only thing that woke Sage was one of the teenagers trying to stuff a wad of gum up his nostril. He rose then, his face decorated with more baubles than a Christmas tree, and flailed his arms until the teenagers scattered.

'Wake up!' I try again.

'Rab?' The voice is thick with catarrh, but he hawks it up and a phlegm-missile flies out from beneath the blanket to land on the solicitor's door and dribble down the paintwork. It is still early so there are no suits. He sits up and peers at me over the top of the blanket. 'Well?' he says.

'Morning,' I say.

'Is that all?' He fixes me with his stare. 'Do I not get the speech? Do I not even get the bloody speech? *I know thee not, old man,* was what I was expecting, *make less thy body hence and more thy grace. Fall to thy fucking prayers*, I was expecting – '

'Sorry about last night,' I say.

'Ah, so there *is* an apology, is there?' He clears his throat again. 'I've not been banished, then? Well, thank fuck for that, Rab. After all, what the fuck would I do without you, eh?'

I'm too hungover to unpick his sentences. Instead, I hold out my peace offering: a bottle of half-full 'blended' wine. This morning I traipsed around the debris of the party, pouring dregs and sediment into one bottle. If I had to guess, I'd say it's four parts red wine, two parts white, one part vodka, and one part expired cough medicine that I found in the bathroom cabinet.

'Sorry,' I repeat. 'I ended up crashing on a sofa afterwards.'

'We were supposed to meet down on Brunswick Terrace.'

'I know, sorry.'

'Instead I had to deal with those Rough Sleeper people for an hour, trying to convince me that they could help, that they had the answers…'

This is bad news. Sage despises the Rough Sleeper folk, a team of well-meaning workers who walk the streets and chat to those who're sleeping rough. They found a family of four in a tent on the beach last year and rehoused them, and they often put up temporary hostel beds for the runaways, but they can offer little more than advice and the occasional meal to the likes of Sage. I get on OK with them – they're pleasant enough. For Sage, though, they're the Jehovah's Witnesses on the doorstep or the sales call when you're making the dinner.

'At least they weren't the Churchies, eh?' I say, trying to lighten the mood.

'I waited, Rab,' he says, twisting the cap from the bottle.

'I know. Like I say, I'm sorry.'

He swallows half of the liquid away in one draught, then grimaces. 'First opportunity you get, Rab, you forget about old Sage. First opportunity.'

'I didn't forget. I just couldn't…'

Last night I had a gig, with Luke, at a bar just off West Street. Quiet venue, with complimentary bottles of beer and folded notes as payment. The walls were decorated with beermats and there was graffiti on the stairs down to the toilet, so it wasn't the kind of place where they'd sneer at the stain on the left shin of the trousers I found in the bins round the back of Churchill Square. The perfect gig to get me started again, to get a feel for it.

Afterwards, Luke invited me back to his mate's student flat up in Elm Grove. I'd been nervous about that, thinking that they'd all be sitting around sipping sherry and discussing Nietzsche. Not a bit of it. It was a glorious hovel: someone had smeared 'Welcome to Hell' on the front window with ketchup, the cooker was so encased with grease that the gas could no longer be lit, and fruit flies were so omnipresent that each and every person there was clapping out a constant flamenco rhythm.

In the midst of it all, her poetry gloriously riffing off the drum and bass that pulsed through the flat, was Flick. I shrank back when I first saw her, thinking that the months since I'd last seen her had not been kind to me, but she raised a hand and smiled and her lyrics trailed off…

'Rab!' she called. 'Fuck me, how are you? You've lost your clean edges.'

'Um, thanks.'

'What brings you here?'

'I had a gig, in town.'

'You look great…' She leant in and hugged me, and my first thought was that the natural end to her sentence would be 'and you smell… well… *ripe*'. Instead, though, she gripped me by the shoulder and looked me in the eye. 'You look great.'

'Thanks, you do too.'

'What are you doing with yourself these days?'

'Well, I've gone… freelance.'

She smiled and reached over to the counter for her beer. 'Tell me all about it.'

That's how I ended up missing the meet-up with Sage. It wasn't malicious, or even forgetful. It was just that I'd not seen Flick since my second visit to the Occupy camp at St Paul's, the disastrous stay a month before the album launch, and it felt good to rebuild bridges. Besides, it had been so long since I'd had the opportunity to sit with a beer and a beautiful girl and feel the hopeful rush of telling (white) lies in anticipation of feeling a more powerful rush later in the evening.

I told her about the split from the label. The outline of the story was right, but I shaded it all a bit differently. Like when a child is given a colouring book and they make the grass pink and the sun purple – still recognisable, but not quite right. Artistic differences, I said, because they tried to change my sound, my look, my *message*. I made it sound as if the grass was pinker on the other side – this side – of the fence.

Sage doesn't care about all that, though. He'll not listen if I tell him how we shared a joint or two and drank our way through the beers in the bag at our feet. There'll be no sympathy from him if I tell him that I got strung out and then I struck out; that Flick departed at five in the morning to get an early train up to London and left me to sleep alone on the sofa for long enough to entice a hangover but not long enough to feel rested.

'Did you get paid?' Sage asks. He sips his marvellous medicine. 'How much?'

I reach into my pocket. It rustles reassuringly. 'Twenty quid.'

'Is that all?'

I nod. The actual amount was thirty-five, but I'd bought myself a chilli-burger after the gig and then chipped in with Luke for some booze and a bit of dope. Still, twenty isn't bad. There was a time when it would have all been spent.

'It's enough, anyway,' Sage says. He is leaning back against the paintwork, his shoulder against the spit from earlier. It will add another shaded stain, another crusted covering, to his blanket. 'It should be just about enough.'

'For what?' I ask.

'I've been thinking…' He leans forward and his fingers pinch the air in front of his mouth, as if shaping his words as they're spoken. 'Last night, when you abandoned me, I got to thinking. The problem is *this*.' He knocks his knuckles against the step. 'The city is made of concrete; it's hard and unyielding. It's unnatural. We need to return to nature, to the very root of things.'

You're havering, I want to say. Complete gibberish. Instead, I nod.

'Ideally,' Sage continues, 'we would have a bit more by way of seed money – no pun intended – but the principle remains the same. It's a simple existence: foraging, cooking roadkill, picking berries and mushrooms, whatever.'

'Sage,' I say, gently, 'you'll need to spell it out for me.'

'We don't *need* the city.' He reaches forward and grasps me by the wrist. 'We're outside it anyway, metaphorically speaking. We don't use the houses, or the shops, or the *banks*. So why not return to nature, eh? Live hand-to-mouth the way we were built for.'

'You mean leave Brighton?'

He nods. 'I mean going out to the South Downs. We use the money to buy a tent – you can get a simple one for fifteen quid – and the rest to buy basic provisions. Then we live off the land.'

'It's nearly the end of September.' I frown at him. 'We'll be frozen.'

He waves away my objection. 'We can build a fire. There's firewood everywhere; there's open land. All we need is the tent for cover when it rains. That's all we *need*.'

'Sage.' I say it softly, sympathetically. 'I don't want to.'

He snorts, then smiles. 'Lad, you've only been conditioned to think that you need all these *things*.' He points out at the empty street, at the shuttered shops and the flats with drawn curtains above them. 'It's only marketing and indoctrination that tell you that you need all this bullshit: a credit card, a car, a commute. All you really need, Rab, is food and shelter – '

'And company,' I cut him off.

He reels backwards, as if I'd taken a swing. 'What's that?'

'It's not the city itself I'd miss,' I say, 'but the people in it.'

'Am I not people?'

'Not plural, no.'

'Am I not the only one you talk to? Properly, I mean. Day-to-day.'

I stay silent.

'Let me tell you a story…' he begins.

I sit myself down on the step next to him and tune him out. I'm thinking of Luke and the gig the night before, with the sound of conversation and clinking glasses coming from the tables in front of us. Then the party, with all those folk sitting around discussing music and politics and not a single one of them clearing their tacky throat to say, 'Let me tell you a story.' And Flick, who sat on the sofa next to me and listened as I told her about the last days of the singer-songwriter dream, her face crumpled with concern as she chewed the polish from her nails with her yellow-edged teeth. Finally, I think of the shower I took this morning in the flat. *No need to ask, we're all mates.* Hot water, shampoo, even lotion for after, to quell that itch I've been getting in my arse-crack.

Sage's story is one I've heard before. It's about the old penguin pool at London Zoo – how they built this concrete Modernist building for them. Functional. It was an experiment that would eventually lead to improved social housing for humans as well – clean lines and open space. But the penguins got sunstroke from the glare off the concrete and their joints ached from walking on the hard surfaces. The point being, as Sage tells it, that the structures of the city are an unnatural habitat: they confine and restrict us. Chaos is our natural state.

'I know you think society's broken, Sage,' I say. 'And it may well be. But that doesn't mean *people* are broken too. Society is only the framework; you can't go turning your back on everyone within it, surely.'

'The idealism of youth,' Sage sighs.

'Besides,' I say, 'where would you get drink out there in the wilds?'

'There'll be *shops*, Rab. I'm not saying we should be going to the Arctic Circle or the surface of the moon. We stay in touch with civilisation, certainly, but without relying on all this shit.' Again he waves a hand at the street. A bus swishes past. 'We get ourselves a space of our own.'

The night before, over the first beer, Luke had leant forward and placed a hand on my arm. 'I'm not being funny,' he said, 'but one morning you'll wake up and that old faggot'll be trying to bugger you. He'll be using his fingers to stuff his floppy prick into your hole, mate, and, with the weight of him on top of you, you'll just have to lie there and take it.' He laughed afterwards, but when I tried to duck away from the party to go and meet up with Sage, he said, 'Away to get buggered by the blubber, are you?'

And it isn't that I'm frightened of Sage, definitely not, but more that he might misinterpret the companionship for something else. Especially given the circumstances in which we first met. All this talk of rural living unsettles me, causes wee ripples of anxiety, because it's when two people are in isolation, when they're detached from the world, that...

'Actually, what I was thinking,' I say, 'is that we could maybe try our hand at squatting. Now that the weather's turning colder.'

Sage squints across. 'You mean breaking and entering?'

'You've been reading the bog-roll again, haven't you?'

There's a running joke, between the two of us, that whenever we find a copy of the *Daily Mail* we set it aside for use as toilet paper. Any other newspaper or magazine is fair game for reading material, or even for supplementary warmth in the night, but the *Mail* is only for the wiping of the arse.

It was Flick who raised the idea of squatting. She's living in an office space in London, along with seven others. Quite a few of the folk from the Occupy movement have taken to communal living. You're golden, she said, as long as there's one person in the squat at all times and providing you display a notice-thingy on the door so that visitors know that you're aware of your rights. They've just changed the law so that it's illegal to squat residential properties, but if you look hard you can still find a commercial property to live in. She was even willing to lend a hand, she said, with sourcing somewhere. And she said it all with this smile that lit a flickering hope that there might be a future for the two of us, at some stage down the line.

'I'm not sure I'd advocate that,' Sage says, trying his best to sound superior in spite of the trail of mucus that bubbles out from his nose. He sniffs it back in and tries again. 'Every time I've been in a squat it's always been rat-shit and used needles. Most of the time it's bleaker than sleeping rough, Rab. At least outside there's fresh air.'

His history of squat-living is news to me. I've heard his stories of horror hostels and brutal B&Bs, but he's never mentioned these squalid squats before. Although, from what Flick said, he's right about the state of most of the buildings. You need to get in before the place has been pissed in, shat in, set alight or opened to the elements. Most of all, you need to get in before the owner's had the chance to sabotage it. There are squats with electrical wires left exposed, broken glass scattered on lino floors, trip wires stretched across doorways, concrete poured in toilet bowls. Friends of hers have had fish guts pushed in the letterbox, tiles stripped from the roof. They've been literally smoked out with cardboard stuffed into the chimneys.

It doesn't have to be like that, though. It can be respectful, mutually beneficial. We can be caretakers.

'It would just be us, though, Sage,' I say.

'Just the two of us?'

I nod. 'In a disused office or shop space or something.'

'In theory,' he says, slowly, clacking his teeth together afterwards, 'I'm not against it.'

'It would only be temporary,' I say. 'We'd be ready to move on as and when.'

I'm enthusiastic about the idea because I'm thinking that, once we're settled, I can maybe invite Flick to switch squats, to re-situate her protest to the seaside. And maybe, if I had somewhere to store it, Luke would lend me the guitar I played on last night – the acoustic – so that I can start songwriting again.

'We could even hold public lectures,' Sage murmurs to himself. 'Marx, Žižek, Chomsky.'

The last two names mean nothing to me, but I nod eagerly.

'Here's the solution,' Sage says. 'We still use some of the money to buy ourselves a tent, but then we find ourselves a suitable squat and pitch the tent inside. That way, we're not using the building so much as the space inside. We're self-sufficient and ready to move on at a moment's notice.'

'Is that not a – ' I stop myself before I say the word 'compromise'. It's true that ninety per cent of what Sage comes out with is contradiction, but the other ten per cent is stubborn refusal to acknowledge it, so it's best just to keep the peace and combine squatting and camping. 'Sounds like a good idea.'

'Excellent,' he says. 'Now, then, do you not think you owe me breakfast after last night?'

'Are we not saving for this tent, though?'

'I think you can stretch to a celebratory bacon sandwich, Rab. Don't be stingy – share the wealth. After all, not all of us had the luxury of sleeping where you slept last night.'

As he rises, the Nirvana cover of Lead Belly's 'Where Did You Sleep Last Night?' starts to repeat in my head. An earworm. For the first time in weeks I could answer the lyrics with 'under a roof', 'on a cushion', 'out of the wind', 'in the warm', rather than the usual 'in the corner of the covered car park' or 'under the arches, on a stack of cardboard'. Yet Sage – fucking Sage – is making me feel guilty for that one spell of sofa-surfing, that one night where the sleeping wasn't so rough.

We begin walking. Sage lets out these sighs and groans as he lumbers along, as if his joints are creaking-cracking hinges that need oiling. Partly to drown him out, partly to draw out the earworm, I start whistling the tune. Then I sing the opening lines softly, under my breath, thinking first of Flick and then, more sharply, of Maddie.

LONDON

'It's the perfect stage,' Pierce says. 'There are already all sorts of musicians, writers, and poets making use of it, y'know? Because there's the iconic building of St Paul's Cathedral, then the tents all around – clustered around. It makes for the perfect photo opportunity.'

'Can I not just turn up, take a few snaps and fuck off again, then?'

'No, no.' He shakes his head. 'We're going for *authenticity*, Rob. This time it has to be more than just a visit. This time you're going to become a native.'

Prick Price let himself into the hotel room early this morning – well before ten am – and started hammering a tin mug against a tin plate right beside the bed: *clank*, *clank*, *clank*. When I opened my eyes, he gave me this smug smile and called out, 'Are you ready to get your camping badge, scout?'

I made a grab for the mug – thinking it might fit rather neatly up his arsehole – but he danced out of reach and gave a girly giggle.

'What in the fuck is all this, Pierce?'

He held up a carrier bag. 'Time to move to new accommodation,' he said.

'What does that mean?'

I felt a jolt of panic, because I'd grown fond of my hotel with its breakfast in bed, laundry left outside the door, room

66

service, minibar. They'd even had a go at cleaning the frayed fabric of my trainers when I'd left them, skewed and whiffy, out in the hallway.

'Great idea, I think,' Price said, hopping from foot to foot like an excited toddler. 'Just for a few nights, to try to drum up some publicity.'

'What *is* the idea, though?' I asked, resisting the urge to add 'you knob'.

'We move you into the tent city for a couple of nights.' He grins. 'Get you settled in, then invite some of the journos down, get some stories running and take some publicity shots for the launch.'

'You've got to be joking – '

'I know, perfect timing, eh? A month until release.'

Of course I put up resistance to the idea. Staying the night is entirely different from making a tourist stop – 'Here is St Paul's Cathedral, note the disaffected youth circa 2012, next stop Madame Tussaud's' – because at night it's not a hop-on, hop-off deal; you're there for the duration. It quickly becomes apparent, though, that it's not Pierce Price himself who's come up with this pitch – it rarely fucking is – but Bower and the label's marketing department. They've this angle they've been working on: 'Actions speak louder *with* words. Rab Dylan, *Measures Taken*'. It's a tag-line that paints me as an activist who uses music to spread my message, they say, and they're anxious that it doesn't come across vice versa. Solution: urban camping trip.

'Besides,' Pierce says, pushing his glasses up his nose, 'and I'm not trying to tell you off here, but there have been concerns about how long your advance will support you… erm… financially.'

He holds out his hands in a gesture of appeasement.

'Not that we don't have faith that you'll make it back – you will – but a more prudent lifestyle, just for a bit, might put less pressure on album sales.'

'Concerns, eh?' I say.

'From higher up,' he says, pointing at the ceiling.
'We're on the top floor.'

An hour later, I'm on the Central Line making my way to St Paul's, with a rucksack on my back and my guitar balanced against my legs. I've dressed the part – grey hooded jumper, khaki three-quarter-length trousers and tattered trainers – but I'm a bit worried about the fact that my tent is entirely scuff-free and my rucksack still has the price label hanging from one of the straps. To grease the wheels – to endear myself to the ninety-nine per cent – I've packed ten pre-release copies of my album, a bottle of blended whisky, and some assorted merchandise that the label sent over for approval. I come bearing gifts.

As the Underground clatters me closer, I start to feel more positive about the whole enterprise. Maybe it wasn't too good to be perched up in that hotel room, with no connection to the public. Perhaps I can play an open-air gig or two to give something back, to thank those in Occupy who inspired the songs on the album. I might even see Flick.

Emerging from the station, I sniff questioningly at the air. I'm expecting there to be a sourness, a fustiness – like clothes that have been folded away while still damp – but instead there's a smell of freshly ground coffee that brings back memories of Cesare and my part-time job up in Glasgow. I listen intently, anticipating a folky campfire medley and the chatter of excited political debate. There is an off-key whistling and the distant sound of traffic. The tents around me look slumped and empty, but there's a group of people gathered in a hollow over by the steps to St Paul's. They sit on fold-away chairs and talk quietly among themselves. Above them a slung banner sags, so that I can only make out 'Capitalism is…' Maybe they're running a caption competition – fill in the blank – with a guest spot on *Newsnight* for the winner.

When I walk over, they all look up but say nothing. 'Hi there,' I say. 'I was wondering whether… if Flick is around at all?'

'Flick?' A girl with blonde hair, an Irish accent and a nose that seems to have been chiselled to a point speaks up. 'Who, or what, is Flick?'

'A performance poet. Spoken word. She lives here.'

'Does she now?'

The group – five of them – look at one another. I count two shrugs and a shake of a head before a guy with dark hair tied back in a ponytail and metal braces on his teeth glints out a smile and reaches into his pocket. For a moment I think he's reaching for a knife – a gun even – but he brings out a battered mobile phone and starts stabbing at the buttons.

'I think I know her.' His accent is northern. Not Manc or Geordie, but definitely northern. He is cocooned in a sleeping bag, against the February chill. 'But she doesn't stay here, mate. She's up at Finsbury Square, I'm pretty sure – '

'I met her here,' I say. 'Before Christmas.'

'I've maybe got her number, hang on...'

As I wait, I look down at the cobbles. There's no conversation from the rest of them and I feel awkward and ill at ease. How the fuck do you make an introduction when there's a group – a clique – and you turn up unannounced and uninvited? There should be a welcoming committee, I'm thinking, for Occupy. There should be someone to greet you and show you around, if they want to make it a truly inclusive movement. Not this wary silence.

'I'll give her a text,' the northern guy says. 'Tell her you're looking for her. What's your name?'

'Rab.' I see it as an opening and I seize it. Maybe my white knight imaginings of turning up and playing a benefit concert were a bit wide of the mark, but I can make an impression on these few folk, surely? 'Do you mind if I wait with you guys?'

'Of course,' the Irish girl says, and for a second I'm uncertain whether she does or she doesn't, but then she points at an empty plastic chair.

The two girls beside me seem to be quietly and methodically carrying out a war of attrition over a blue-checked blanket, with one pulling it slowly one way and the other responding with a tug or grab that reclaims the lost territory. Next to them an acne-scarred teenager lolls back in his deckchair, as though dozing on a beach, although he wears two jackets and a purple patterned bobble-hat to keep out the cold.

I sit down and fumble with the neck of my guitar through the case, as though picking out chords. If I were a different person – a ballsy busker – I'd unzip and actually play them a song or two. I've heard of comedians who stand at the side of the stage and introduce themselves in the third person, but I don't have the brass neck to do that. I need someone with no shame – I need Pierce Price – to say, 'Do you guys not know who the fuck this is? This is Rab Dylan – he's going to be fucking huge.'

Then I remember the merchandise. I have key-rings, badges, stickers, T-shirts even...

'I brought some stuff...' I say, unbuckling my rucksack.

'Oh, yeah?' Bobble-hat leans forward and I see the glazed look in his eyes for the first time. There is a tremor to his fingers as he passes one hand restlessly over the other. 'What you got?'

'T-shirts, badges, key-rings, CDs...' I trail off as I realise that key-rings might be a touch useless for tent-dwellers. And I've not seen a CD player – I'm not sure whether they even have electricity hooked up. Still, they could download the album taster from the label's website, couldn't they? On to their smartphones or whatever. 'And whisky to share,' I finish.

Bobble-hat rocks back into the deckchair, disappointed. The Irish girl, her sharp nose raised in the air, looks across at me. There is suspicion in her gaze that wasn't there before. She folds her arms. 'Most people bring food,' she says. 'Or books for the library.'

'I'm a singer – ' I begin.

'And why are you offering us whisky mid-morning?'

'It'll keep if you'd rather – '

'What are you after?' she asks.

'Nothing,' I say. 'I'm here to help.'

'What's with the bribery, then?'

'It's not bribery, I'm – '

'Are you a plant, is that it – an *agent provocateur*?'

I'm taken aback by her bluntness. I'm even more taken aback by the phrase I don't recognise and the way she spits it at me like the worst of insults.

'No,' I say. 'I don't know what one of those is.'

'So you don't work for the government or the police?'

I shake my head. Jesus, how fucking paranoid are these people? I just wanted to show up and camp with them for a couple of days, maybe play them a song or two, I didn't know I'd need to prove myself. Reaching into my bag, I pull out a T-shirt and hand it to her. She unfolds it and inspects the front – it has the album cover, blown up large, across it.

'I'm a singer,' I say. 'That's all.'

'Right.' She hands the T-shirt back to me.

'You can keep it, if you like.'

She waves it away.

'I could play you a couple of – *shit*!'

A hand lands on my shoulder from behind, causing me to jump up from the seat and send it toppling to the ground. The guitar follows, sounding out like the toll of a bell as it hits the cobbles.

'Bloody hell,' Flick says. 'You're tightly strung.'

I stand for a moment with my fists clenched – more wedding dance than boxer's stance – before relaxing and stepping forward to give her a hug. She's (inexpertly) chopped her curled hair short, to just below her ears, and there's a nose-ring that's new. She's looking good, though – and she's also looking pleased to see me.

'Have you come to join us, then?' she asks.

'Where do I sign up?'

She laughs and places a hand on my shoulder. 'Why don't we go somewhere and catch up?'

I agree eagerly, thinking that she means the pub or a coffee shop, but she leads me over to the cold concrete steps of St Paul's instead. We climb up to a column and sit with our backs against it. Beneath us, to the right, the breeze moves through the tents as a rippling rustle. It carries with it a murmur of conversation and the faint aroma of cooking – cumin and garlic. People mill around, but most of them seem to be looking up at the cathedral – solid, austere, grey – rather than down at the tents – colourful, covered in sloganised ideas, and in danger of being lifted by the wind.

Carefully, delicately, Flick raises a hand to her mouth and begins biting the skin at the sides of her nails. 'So what have you been up to?' she asks.

'This and that,' I say. 'Gigging, mostly.'

Over the festive period, I haunted some of the folk venues in Camden, Islington and Hackney. Trying to get my name out there. I was thinking I'd be the Ghost of Christmas Yet to Come – 'I saw him, yeah, just before he took off' – so I queued with the floor singers for a turn on the open mic. The nights were always billed as 'nu-folk' or 'folk-rock' but ended up feeling more like something organised by my parents. I did them, though, for the sake of my future fans, who'll come to see me in the proper venues – Bush Hall, the Union Chapel, King's Place, Cecil Sharp House – and remember the time I appeared at some grotty little pub in Clerkenwell as a warm-up act for a girl who played Coldplay covers on a ukulele.

'Excellent,' Flick says. 'Anything big?'

I shrug, shake my head.

'And what is it you're doing here?'

'You'll like it, actually,' I say, unscrewing the cap from the whisky bottle and taking the first searing sip. 'It's a publicity drive. The idea is that I spend a few nights here and really tap into – '

'Are you just passing through, then?'

'Like I say, I'm here for a couple of nights.' I smile across at her and offer her the whisky bottle. 'I'm here to help.'

'Rab...' She takes the bottle and lets out this small sigh. 'The people here have been around since October, more or less four months. It's not easy, you know? Most of the time it's a struggle just keeping people motivated, keeping them fed and warm, mediating disputes and, well – '

'I'm not trying to – '

'Let me finish.' She holds out a hand. For some reason her eyes have closed, tightly, and she's speaking tensely and deliberately, measuring each word before slotting it into her sentence. 'I would hate to think that you would exploit that, Rab. I would hate to think that you would use all the hard work, all the struggle, to further your own career.'

'My album,' I say, 'will shine a light on the Occupy movement, Flick – will be a mouthpiece for all these folk.' I sweep an arm out to indicate the tents beneath us. 'It'll let them address their issues from a half-decent platform, rather than over a megaphone as a... because they're only preaching to the choir here, isn't it?'

My sentence unravels slightly at the end, because her accusation has stung me. There is a tone of disappointment and weariness about it that brings back memories of 3.17am and that phone call from Maddie. *You can't possibly understand, Rab*, the tone says. *You might try to, but you won't be able to*. Condescension, that's the word for it. Not sneering, but pitying condescension.

'Occupy London,' Flick whispers.

'What?'

'It's important that you realise that this is Occupy London, not simply Occupy. It's part of a larger movement, certainly, and it's tied to Occupy Wall Street and the violence at Occupy Oakland, and it is inspired by the Arab Spring to an extent, but it's also local. It's local as well as global.'

'Well – ' I take another drink of whisky ' – I'm intending my music to be both local and global as well. We're already in discussions with a label in the States and – '

'What I mean...' Flick places a hand on my arm. 'What

I mean is that Occupy is massive and diverse and full of contradictions. Even Occupy London is, never mind Occupy as a whole. There are activists here who see it as an extension of things like Climate Camp, and those who see it as a direct protest against the banks. What I mean is – '

'That's the power of it,' I say. 'That it draws support from all these different places and ideas, that it speaks to issues that affect us all.'

'Ye-es.' She says this slowly. 'But you can't gloss the differences. And you can't show up and presume to speak for all these different people with all these different agendas, making these grand statements while they struggle against eviction orders. If you haven't been here – '

'If I haven't been here I have no right, is that it?' The whisky ignites my shortest fuse. 'Why the fuck not, Flick? It's all grist to the same mill, isn't it? I release a song about Occupy *London*, folk pay attention to the arguments, we all fucking win.'

'Ah!' Flick raises a palm to her forehead. 'Of *course*! Why didn't we think of that? In fact, why didn't we just put out a tweet: hashtag fix capitalism, smiley-face.'

'At least people will listen to the songs, engage with them.'

'But here's the fucking point, Rab.' She's turned towards me, her eyes wide. 'This is the point – would you be here if it wasn't for the album? Honestly and truly? Would you?'

'It's a contemporary issue, Flick, and I write contemporary music.'

'It's a bandwagon.' She lifts the whisky bottle and I note that her hand shakes as she takes a drink. 'For you, at least, it's just a bandwagon that you can piggy-back on and – '

'Which is it? Bandwagon or piggy-back? There's a mixed metaphor in there, love, and you're supposed to be a poet.'

'You're such a cunt.' She shakes her head. 'That first night I thought you were just naïve, and it was endearing, but you're just a cunt.'

She rises and skip-trips down the steps in her hurry to get away from me. I watch her go, with angry words burning in my throat but refusing to form into something I can shout – something I can scream – after her. Better to let her go. I was hoping that the day would turn out differently, that I'd be able to play a few songs in the sunshine and then enjoy an evening under canvas with Flick, but the sky is overcast and my only groupie has renounced her sexual privileges. I decide that I'll take the professional approach – see one night through and contact Price in the morning to arrange the publicity shots and then get me the fuck out of here.

What do I do in the meantime? How do I spend my day? Pierce told me to interact with people, maybe get myself in a working group or speak up at the General Assembly. *Participate*, he said, get yourself a profile within the movement. But boredom is already itching at my thoughts. Besides, it's bloody *cold*. It's not heated debate I need, just a bit of fucking heat. Using the whisky bottle as a crutch, I push myself upright and scan the tents spread out below. There's bound to be a gap on the fringes where I can squeeze my tent in, later. For now, though, I'm going to go and find a pub that has the shadowed corners and hollow eyes I'm looking for. A quiet bar – a drinkers' bar. If I talk to anyone, it won't be from choice. On a telly in the corner the headlines will scroll, unread, across the bottom of the screen.

I make my way back down to the group at the foot of the steps. The Irish girl and the northern lad have gone, and the two warring girls have fallen asleep with the blue-checked blanket draped between them, covering one knee of each. Bobble-hat is still there, though. He'll ask no questions, but he'll answer if I show him my money and ask him where I can lay my hands on some coke. He's the kind of company I'm looking for.

I sit down in a plastic chair and nudge him with my elbow, waiting for him to stir and fix me with that vacant stare.

GLASGOW

She sits on me, naked, pinning my wrists back against the headboard. She laughs before she kisses me and shifts her weight so that my cock springs out from beneath her and rests against her thigh. Bringing her legs together, she wriggles, and my breathing becomes shallow.

'I could just climb on,' she says.

'What?' I strain to raise my head from the pillow to kiss her.

'Nothing to stop me having my wicked way, is there?'

'I think we should wait,' I repeat.

'It's not every day you'll have a girl sitting buck-naked on you, Rab, you know that?'

I nod, but then shake my head. Two days before, at the supermarket with Gemma and Teagan, I'd looked at the condoms in their plastic security cases and thought about it, maybe… but we'd only kissed three times and I decided that there was no need… surely she wouldn't want to… not yet, at least.

'We could just cheat,' Maddie says, and grins. 'As long as you can control yourself.'

'I just think that… without a condom…'

'We could even just put him in a wee way, to check the fit?'

'We should wait.'

I don't think we should wait – I deeply, desperately, despairingly don't – but we don't have protection and we've only just started seeing each other. And she's still seeing Ewan. This would be my first time – I haven't asked if it would be hers – and I don't want there to be cause for regret afterwards. There doesn't need to be any great hurry, does there? We can be patient, surely.

'It's better to be safe, Maddie,' I say.

She releases my wrists. 'Two friends, both alike in dignity,' she mutters.

'What does that mean?'

There was no indication, earlier in the day, that it would play out this way. When she arrived at my house – still in her white shirt and school skirt – she showed little interest in anything other than the telly in the corner. There's this Aussie soap actress – with blonde hair to her slender shoulders and a sly smile about her lips – who looks a bit like Maddie. Truth be told, you'd have to turn the brightness setting down and squint sideways to concede the resemblance, but an ex-boyfriend had told her it was uncanny and she'd been vicariously embroiled in the small-screen drama ever since. So, while I nuzzled at her neck and plucked distracted kisses from her lips, she watched this troubled twin going through a month of heartbreak in half an hour until a hasty engagement, in the last moments of the episode, that drew a sigh of satisfaction from Maddie. She turned to me, then, and kissed me as if I'd gone missing in a fire and been declared dead but then returned two weeks later to accuse the arsonist and propose to her in front of the ex-fiancé (also the arsonist, obviously) who'd jilted her at the altar.

'Do you have something…' she looked around the living room '… maybe not down here, maybe up in the bedroom…' she leant in for another kiss '… something I could use to tie you up?'

Once we'd made our way to my attic bedroom, Maddie ignored the ties hung over the shirts in the wardrobe, the dressing gown cord hanging over the hook on the back of the door and the belts tucked away in my sock drawer. Instead, she guided me as I rolled off her tights, giggled as I tugged at her skirt until the zip gave way and grinned as my fumbling fingers fiddled with shirt buttons and bra strap.

Stretched out across my single bed, she looked up and said, 'Now you.'

It took me only seconds to shed my clothes. My shirt went flying over to land on the desk in the corner, sending stacked sheets scattering, and my jeans were hook-kicked to drape over the chair beside. Socks and boxer shorts went up into the air like celebratory fireworks. I didn't see where they landed.

'Here,' she whispered, taking my right hand and placing it against the stubbled firmness of her pelvis. We both clenched our breath between our teeth as my fingers went searching, then both let it out as the resistance gave way. I found the melting warmth and began beckoning her on...

It was only once she'd twisted her face away from my kisses, started this vowel-heavy panting noise – *eeee* – *aaaa* – *oooo* – and whispered, urgently, '*Faster...*' only after she'd dragged her nails across the mattress and lifted the bedsheets, in fistfuls, from the neatly tucked corners. Only then did she turn me, by the hips, until I was lying on my back. She straddled me and lifted my hands, by the wrists, until I felt the rough wicker weave of the headboard against my knuckles.

'Now, as I was saying, do you have something I can tie you up with?' she asked.

'Why?'

'I like to be in control.' She grinned. 'Is that not OK with you?'

'Just...' I hesitated. 'I think we should wait.'

Two days later, out walking Maddie's dog Silo in the grounds of Gartnavel Hospital after school, I remember the butchered Shakespeare she used in those moments before she rolled away and got hurriedly dressed – 'two friends, both alike in dignity'.

It's a phone call from Ewan that brings it back to mind.

'Don't tell him I'm here,' Maddie squeals, and darts behind a tree. Silo stays where he is, his lead taut. He's a mongrel, no doubt about that, with a bit of bloodhound in the mix. His saggy jowls and long ears are ragged and trail in the muck. Maddie says he has sad eyes, but I reckon he just looks stoned. He stares up at me as I hold my phone out at the space where his owner used to be.

'Ewan can't *see* you,' I say to the tree. 'It's a phone call.'

'But if *you* can see me,' it replies, 'he might hear it in your voice.'

I shake my head, then answer the phone. There is a moment's anxiety, just a tightening of nerves, because it's possible that someone's seen me out walking with Maddie. Ewan's shouted splurge of words is about something else entirely, though. He's managed to get me into a showcase competition for singer-songwriters, in a city centre club, which has a studio recording session as a prize for the winner. Better than that, even, the judge is a music manager from down in London.

Without telling me, Ewan took the rough cut of that song about Maddie, recorded on my laptop, and entered it. Along with my cover of 'Masters of War'. He jazzed up my CV a bit as well, by putting down my weekly slot at Cesare's café as something close to a residency and listing open-mic nights at the Queen Margaret Union as gigs. Still, that's what a manager's for, I guess.

'Are you not bloody *excited*?' Ewan screeches down the line.

I feel guilt, more than anything. 'Of course I am, mate,' I say. 'But bricking it a bit, you know.'

'Well, you've got a week to get over your nerves. Valium, smack, masturbation – whatever it takes – just make sure you're loosey-goosey by next Thursday, OK?'

'OK.' I pause. 'Listen, Ewan – thanks, mate. That's awesome.'

'No worries. I'll call you later, you fucking superstar.'

I say goodbye and tuck the phone away in my jeans pocket. Then I take it back out again to make sure that the call has disconnected. It has. Maddie steps out from behind the tree, with an eyebrow arched. Silo has been looking up at me expectantly since the phone started ringing. They both seem to be waiting for me to speak.

'He's got me a gig,' I say.

'Thank fuck.' Maddie lets out a wee giggle. 'I was sure that was going to be about me... He didn't mention me at all, then?'

I shake my head. 'It's a really good gig, with industry professionals.'

'When is it?' She hooks her arm around my waist. 'Can I come?'

'Next week,' I say. 'Thursday. But Ewan'll be there.'

She nods, bites at her lower lip. 'I'll have a chat with him before then.'

We start walking again. To our right are the psychiatric wards of the hospital, to our left the train tracks leading to and from Hyndland station. The tarmac path weaves through the space between the two fences, fringed by patchy grass and sprouting weeds.

'The other day,' I say, carefully, 'up at my house, you quoted the opening line to *Romeo and Juliet*. Well, you changed it, but you kind of quoted it at least...'

'Mr McIntosh would be proud, eh?' She grins.

'Who's Mr McIntosh?'

'My drama teacher.'

'Oh, right.' I smile. Silo has gone wandering off. His retractable lead spools out through the silence. 'What did you mean by it?' I say.

'What was it I said again?' She frowns.

'Two friends, both alike in dignity.'

'Right.' She tightens her grip on my waist. Her head nestles in at my shoulder and I have to angle my body to accommodate her. 'It was just a joke, Rab, a throwaway comment.'

'Was it about us not having sex?'

She nods. I feel the tip of her chin against my collarbone.

'Because I wanted to wait,' I say. 'And Ewan…'

She nods again, then looks up at me. 'Yes.'

'You've got to know, Maddie,' I say, looking off to the side towards the psychiatric ward, to where Silo's lead disappears into a thick clump of bushes, 'you've got to know that I really want to. That I will.'

'Really?'

'Like that.' I try to snap my fingers, but they don't really catch.

'Why wouldn't you, then?'

'Because we didn't have a condom.'

Yesterday I went round to the chemist on the corner and thickened my wallet with enough condoms to raise a throat-clearing from the elderly pharmacist behind the counter. The wallet bulges in my pocket now. I would gladly suggest to Maddie that we take advantage of the great outdoors, but the only likely location is the bushes, and I suspect that Silo is making use of them to create a smell worthy of his name.

'That was the only reason, honestly?' she says.

'Yes.' Guilt takes the conviction out of my voice. 'Although, there is Ewan as well.'

'Eunuch Ewan,' Maddie says.

'Can you not…' I begin, drawing away from her. 'He's my best mate.'

'Sorry.' She squeezes back in towards me and raises her face for a kiss. 'I'll talk to him, I promise.'

I kiss her. At first we walk blindly on, but we stumble, slow and stop as the kiss deepens. 'Are your mum and dad still out at work?' she asks.

My dad is a curator down at the Hunterian Museum, and most days he gets so absorbed in his work that he only realises that it's time to go home once the building is empty and echoing. My mum is a different matter – she watches the clock for five pm – but the solicitor's office she works in is at least a fifteen-minute walk from the house.

Maddie takes my phone out of my pocket, purposely grazing her hand against my erection on the way down. She checks the time on the screen. 'Four-fifteen,' she says, handing me the phone.

There is a message from Gemma, probably about the gig. I ignore it. 'We should have an hour or so,' I say, smiling. 'Good enough?'

'Silo!' Maddie shouts. 'Heel, boy!'

BRIGHTON

For the past few weeks we've been using the pitch, but not the putt, of the miniature golf course along at Hove lagoon. Just while we search for a suitable squat. We put our fifteen-quid tent up before it gets dark and take it down before it gets fully light. Sage is scornful of the small clutch of rough sleepers who camp underneath the archways, but I've shared my bottom-shelf vodka or the odd can of Special Brew with this Danish teenager, Freddy, who's taken to repaying me by telling me about growing up in Fristaden Christiania, an autonomous commune in Copenhagen; and I've shared a smoke with this jittery dope-fiend who calls himself Mossy. They're not bad blokes, especially if all you want is a bit of company while you drink.

I need the booze, to be honest, so that I can face the cramped conditions of the tent. Sage lies on his back, dragging deep snorting snores from the air, with his blanket over his legs and a coat across the rise and fall of his stomach. To fit, I have to lie on my shoulder and slide in at the side of his bulk, with my back to him. It's a delicate operation, though, because the single-sheet canvas of the tent collects the condensation and if I rest up against it then I develop damp patches on my clothes that seem to worsen as I shiver myself to sleep.

Over the first couple of days, I followed Sage's example and kept to myself. I would greet Mossy with a nod, of course, or pass my roll-up to Freddy for a drag, but I didn't hang about with them the way I do now. Instead, I spent my time up at the day centre with Sage. It was only on the third day that I started walking with Mossy up to his spot on Church Road where he sells the *Big Issue*. Even then, it took a day or two before I reached into my pocket for the harmonica and started playing. But, ever since, Mossy has sold a ton more copies by hopping from foot to foot in time to my music with this manic ska/cossack crossover dance, all the while shouting, '*Big Issue*, hey! Help the – hey! – homeless!'

I'd rather be standing there with this shrunken, toothless, bouncing bum than sitting through the sessions up at the day centre – which always seem to be about how to fill in the form that can be sent off to get the form that we can then fill out to get an appointment with someone who'll give us a form. Over a cup of tea afterwards, Sage repeats the word 'Kafkaesque' over and over, or shortens it to 'Kafka'. Mossy's mantra is catchier, and gives me the opportunity to run out a backing track of harmonica licks.

After a couple of hours of helping Mossy out, I go searching for Freddy. He's a thin wee bugger, likely to drift off in a gust of wind, but as often as not I find him slumped and still. That boy was born holding a tarnished spoon, cooking up. Most of the time it's easy to ignore, because the heroin just evens him out. It's without it that he's a tweaking, squeaking mess. Like a rat in death-throes. With it, he readily agrees to come skipping with me and we tour the big bins round the back of the shops looking for food, drink, and anything else we can use.

Sage notices my absences, though. He complains about always being alone when the Street Services team come to visit, and he moans that it's usually left to him to get the tent up. Then, about a week into our stay, he launches into a lecture about my new friends. It's dark when I arrive back with a loaf of brown bread a few hours shy of its use-by, and a bag of bruised oranges that have been flown from Valencia to end up in landfill.

'You think you're better than this, don't you?' I say to him, once he's done. I've been waiting, calculating the moment to hit him with this accusation.

'Yes,' he replies. '*Everyone* is better than this, Rab.'

'What?'

'That's the point – no one should be living like this.'

'Even Mossy and Freddy?'

'Of course.'

This surprises me. When he was needling me about spending time with users, I thought he was sneering at them. Fuck, that's how it works, isn't it? You find someone lower than yourself – worse off than yourself – so you feel better by comparison.

'They're not bad people,' Sage continues. 'They're just the last thing you need right now.'

'But they're friendly,' I say, opening the plastic-wrapped loaf and tearing at the bread. 'And it's a way to – '

'They're decent, Rab, but they're also junkies.'

'So?' I chew on the bread. The wind gusts in from the sea, trying to rip our tent up from its roots. Our weight – Sage's weight, mostly – is the only thing keeping us from ending up in traffic along Kingsway.

'This,' Sage says, 'rough sleeping, is humanity brought low. It's those moments after you trip, you know, when you stumble or stagger on for a step or two. And you might regain your balance, or someone might reach out to catch you, but the likelihood is your chin will hit the ground. Hard.'

'Right, OK. But then are Mossy and Freddy not in the same position?'

'Exactly.'

He says no more than that, letting the silence settle. A fresh, sharp smell cuts through the dankness of the tent – he's dug his dirty fingernail into the skin of an orange.

'I don't understand,' I say. 'What is it you're getting at?'

'What's the last thing – who's the last person – you should be grabbing on to if you're falling, Rab?'

'A junkie?'

'Not necessarily, no.'

'Someone else who's falling, then?'

There's a movement in the dark – could be a nod. Anger flares inside me. Because, at the heart of it, Sage isn't judging *them* – Mossy and Freddy – he's doubting *me*. Even though every time I've been offered that stuff, I've answered by holding up a can and repeating three words like a catchphrase: 'Beer not gear, lads, beer not gear.' Pills and alcohol only.

'You both end up flat on the ground,' Sage says. 'And it's fucking difficult to get back up with a habit.'

'We've got our own habits, Sage.'

'True. With *that* habit, then.'

The dry bread is paste in my mouth. I chew and chew, but can't swallow. I grope for an orange and grasp at Sage's foot instead.

'Sorry,' I mumble, and continue to fumble until I find the oranges. 'Listen, though. I've never gone near a needle or… well, I've never – '

I've been close to needles, of course I have. I've sat with Mossy while he's cooking, with Freddy while he searches – his arms, his legs, between his toes – for a usable vein. And I've seen the look on their faces. The spreading smooth-soothe, like drawing a hand across a wrinkled sheet. But, in spite of that, I've never –

'You're on the margins, though,' I say. 'You're cutting yourself off from the folk around you.'

'The margins of the margins, eh?' Sage sniffs. 'You ever think that might be intentional?'

'Why?'

He shrugs. 'Same reason I don't want to go to hostels. The stuff is bacteria. It spreads, no matter how bloody careful the staff are, no matter how closely they work with the users.'

'These are people who understand what you're going through, though.'

'They only understand their habit – it's only that for them. It's their warmth, it's their forgetting, it's their fucking oxygen.'

Mossy is ex-army, ex-convict. His back is bowed, shoulders hunched forward. Freddy is younger – still upright. Nearly all his movements are involuntary, though – tics, tweaks, twitches. The two of them are often together, but I've never seen them speak. Not to each other. They watch each other cooking brown; that's the extent of their friendship. Still, they're decent to me, and I object to Sage dismissing them, defining them by their drug-taking.

'Whatever fucking burdens you're carrying, old man,' I say, 'they're not mine. We share this tent, no more than that. If you want to declare yourself God of the gutter, then that's your call, but I'm going to talk to the rest of them – help them if I can…'

'You've only got an obligation to yourself, Rab.'

'And to you, right? That's what you're saying. Help yourself and – oh, while you're at it – give me a fucking hand too, right?'

'I'm only looking out for you.'

'You've no fucking *obligation* to.'

'No,' he says. 'True.'

'That's settled then. I'll keep whatever company I like, and you keep yourself to your-fucking-self.'

We don't speak after that. I have nothing more to say. Instead, I peel my orange and listen to Sage's deep, wheezing breaths. They soften, then slip down a register to a bass note a tuba player would be proud of. And, in the gaps between the snores, I lie and whisper-curse the idea that I owe Sage so much as a second thought.

The next day, unsure if I'm proving Sage right or wrong, I leave Mossy on Church Road and go up to North Laine in search of a job. I'm still bringing in spare change from my weekend playing with Luke, and Mossy is good about passing me a can from his slim profits, but I need a steady wage if I'm going to get my guitar back. The one Maddie gave me.

It was never meant to sit in the pawn shop this long. The idea was to get some ready cash to see us through, then settle down to earn enough to get it back. Problem is, with only a harmonica to busk with, I've not been as successful with the shun-smile-clink ratio. Same amount of tight, apologetic smiles, probably, but it's only with Luke at the weekends that the coins really start clinking. Now that the colder weather's set in, I'm thinking that an indoor job might be preferable in any case.

I'm looking for 'help wanted' signs in the windows of the cafés, bars, boutiques and antique shops. If I were doing this properly I'd saunter into every place that looked likely and ask if they were hiring, but the aim is to speak to as few people as possible. I've always left that to others – Ewan, Pierce, Sage even. My neck has always lacked that layer of brass – especially back in London when I should have been hustling for gigs – but the rough sleeping has started to eat at my thin skin, too. If I were to walk into that tea room, or that chocolate shop, I'd probably be greeted warmly – sweetly – and they'd tell me if they were looking for someone, happy to ignore the splattered stain across the knee of my jeans and the sour smell that creeps out from my armpits. Nine times out of ten, they'd be polite. But it's the anxiety of that one time, of them turning up their nose or getting out the hose. The possibility that they'll note all the signs of the street – unshaven, unwashed, unkempt, unsteady – and daub 'undesirable' on me with their eyes.

It's on the road up towards the station that I finally find a handwritten sign in a steam-misted window asking for counter staff. It's a coffee shop. If I had a CV – fuck, I should have gone to the day centre and got them to help me with a CV – most of the lines would be taken up with Cesare's café back in Glasgow. Barista, cash-handler, food preparer, dishwasher, guitarist, and occasional painter. The thought of going in and listing all that, though, counting it off on my fingers, leaves me trembling. It would be like a mangy, flea-bitten mongrel limping up to Crufts – it's still a dog, but it shouldn't expect a fucking ribbon.

In my pocket, along with a few other odds and ends, is the last of a packet of painkillers. Two pills. I was keeping them for tonight, but I'm in need of them now. Right *now*. I have no time for swallowing them whole, waiting for them to take effect, so I duck around the corner and crouch in a doorway. Using my fingernail, I try to crush them against the palm of my hand. They don't break apart easily, though, so I put them down on the concrete and grind them to a powder with the butt of my harmonica. Once I've got enough, I put it on my fingertip and snort. Then I gather up the bigger pieces and chew at those too.

Ten minutes later, pleasantly numb, I go into the coffee shop. There's no queue, but I hover by the display case of cakes for a minute anyway, aware that the eyes of the girl behind the counter are on me. She has a pink streak in her blonde hair, which is twisted up in a bun, and red lipstick. She leans her forearms against the till. It's not guaranteed that she'll accept me as a customer, never mind as staff.

'Hi, there,' she says. 'What can I get you?'

'I… erm…' I realise that I should have brought enough for a cup of something. 'Nothing for me, thank you. I was just wondering about the sign in the window?'

'Counter staff?'

I nod. This is the moment. She looks like an extra in a high school film and I'm petrified she's going to act like one – curl of the lip, sneering smile, and then the put-down line: 'Oh, yeah, the sign doesn't say no dregs but – no dregs,' or just the simple: 'You're joking, right?' She's pretty; she doesn't need to be witty.

'Give me a minute,' she says, instead.

'No worries.'

As she steps into the back of the shop, I imagine her holding a hushed conversation with a colleague. *The steam might lift the filth, at least, but he's sure to* steal, *isn't he? Sure to treat the tip jar like a begging bowl.* She comes back quickly, though, with a pad and a pen.

'The manager's not in just now,' she says. 'But if you leave your name and number then he'll give you a call.'

'Name and number,' I repeat slowly, avoiding her eye. I've not owned a phone since my last days in London. I sold it in exchange for a single folded note. I can't remember if it was a tenner or a twenty.

She hands me the pen. I look at it and then at the blank page. How do I deal with this? Do I write my name and 'c/o Hove Lagoon pitch-and-putt'? Do I come clean and hope she suggests coming back later? Do I just turn and bolt?

In the end, flushed with shame, I scribble down eleven digits. The first two are zero and seven, but then I just go for random numbers. Above them, I write down 'Ewan'. Someone, somewhere, will be getting a wrong-number call over the next day or so.

'Thanks... Ewan,' the girl says, looking at the page. 'I'll get him to call you as soon as he gets back in.'

'Cheers,' I murmur, and make for the exit.

That's it – enough for the day. I tried, I failed. The thought of stepping into other shops – bell above the door tinkling – and having to face up, waiting for the crumple and crush of rejection, fills me with dread. I'm not up for round after round of it. Better to throw in the towel now.

I walk back along the seafront. By the pier, the promenade is thick with people. I edge, shuffle, mumble my way through them, and find myself a slipstream where I can walk in a straight line, with my eyes focused on my feet.

When I was sixteen or so, my mum decided to go back to university. Part-time, with day-release from her work because it was a business administration course and they thought it would benefit the company. Two weeks in, she burst into tears at the dinner table, over a chicken salad. I just blinked at her, but Dad put an arm around her shoulder and asked her what was wrong. 'I just feel so *useless*,' she said. 'They're all so capable and confident – but it takes me ten minutes to build up to saying anything and then ten minutes to recover. I'm wrung dry by the end of it.' A fortnight later, she left the course. I've never really understood that moment at the dinner table until now.

In London, I played to rooms filled with people. Well, rarely filled, but I played to decent enough audiences. And that held no fear for me, especially once I'd picked out the first chord. I didn't think about all those out beyond the lights as individuals, just as a crowd. There wasn't this reckoning – this calculation – that every one of them, taken in isolation, has more than I do. At those gigs, in those rooms, the majority of the folk would have been glad to swap places with me. Now, among the throng at the seafront, I'd be lucky to find just one.

Along the promenade at Hove are neat sentry-lines of beach huts. They are all locked up for the winter. As I walk past them, though, I find myself inspecting the rusted padlocks and wood panels that have come away, slightly, from the rest. If I could find my way inside, just for the night, then I could curl up and enjoy the feeling of being surrounded by a solid structure. Not the tent that sways and shrieks in the wind or the cardboard mattress under an overpass or in a doorway, where the best you can hope for is three sheltering walls. It's been so long since I've been able to shut a door against the world.

There's a hut painted lime-green with a door that looks ajar. I step across to it, but there's a chain padlocked across the front. Besides, there are joggers and strollers passing by, sure to see. If I want to get in, to any of them, then it would have to be at night with bolt-cutters and a crowbar. Neither of which I have.

I make my way up to the pitch-and-putt. Our tent is already up and, from the bulge against one side of it, Sage seems to be inside. Unable to face him, I go in search of Freddy instead. He usually has some pills, to manage his comedowns. He's not underneath the archways but Mossy tells me – his words thick and slurred – that he's gone to the public toilets at the seafront.

Sure enough, Freddy is inside the brick-box building. Alone. He stands at the mirror. In his left hand is a filled syringe. I watch as he tips his chin back, stretching his neck, then begins prodding at the skin down near the collarbone with the tip of a finger. He hasn't seen me – too intent on what he's doing. It only takes a moment before he's satisfied, then he raises the needle and slides it into his neck. He pulls the plunger out a touch, before pushing it all the way in. Then his arms fall to his sides, leaving the thin, empty syringe dangling from his pale neck.

I clatter my way outside. My body convulses, as if flinching away from what I've just seen. Sliding down the outside wall, I sit and grip my head in my shaking hands. Closing my eyes brings an image of Freddy pulling the needle out and splatter-spurts of blood spraying out of him – across the mirror, the sink, the tiled floor that he slumps down on to – so I keep my eyes open. I watch the doorway, digging my fingernails into the palms of my hands. How fucking stupid – how fucking desperate – do you need to be to stick yourself in the neck? Hit the wrong vein – hit an artery – and you're in a paralysis-stroke-death lottery. Hit the right fucking vein and you get – what – the same fucking high?

Freddy emerges a minute or so later. He casts his blank gaze around – it passes over me – then he makes for the beach. He's fine. Better than he was five minutes ago, even. But I'm not sure I'll ever be able to look at him without cringing at the memory of that syringe hanging from his neck. I've seen him shoot up before, I've seen others shoot up, but never in that Russian roulette way. What if an abscess forms? Fuck, there's all those stories of junkies losing their leg from infection after injecting into their groin. What if that happens in his bloody neck?

A wave of nausea crashes over me as I get to my feet. I retch – a dry heave – and have to brace myself against the wall. Then, uncertain and unsteady, I turn away from the sea and towards the pitch-and-putt.

Sage lies on his side, facing towards the Kingsway. If he is asleep, then, for the first time since I've known him he's not snoring. I can hear his breaths, though, shallow and regular.

It isn't yet dark outside. There's enough by way of twilight to cast a bluish tint, from the canvas, on to Sage's skin. His arm, in shirtsleeves, lies outside the blanket.

Without a word, I kick off my trainers and lie down behind him. Still shaking, I draw my own blanket up over my shoulders. I hesitate, listening to his breathing. Then, I raise one hand to my neck – protecting it from the memory of what I've just seen – and reach the other arm out to curl around Sage. If he notices the tremble to my hand, he doesn't say. Instead, he edges backwards an inch, into my spooning embrace. And I am grateful.

LONDON

'Five minutes,' the voice calls. 'Five-minute warning, then the tents will be cleared.'

I lie and listen. There is a rustling and a whispering outside, movement and voices. The lit screen of my phone shows that it is just past midnight. I have been asleep for an hour, no more. After thirty-six hours of coke- and caffeine-fuelled wakefulness, I have only been allowed one hour of rest before being roused.

'Bailiffs,' someone says. 'And riot police too.'

'Peaceful, everyone, remember,' someone else says, and the three words are taken up and repeated, echoing like a mantra. 'Peaceful, remember, everyone. Everyone peaceful, remember. Remember, everyone, peaceful.'

'Fuck's sake,' I hiss.

It's not that I care whether or not they clear the camp – for all I care they can set it alight so that the tents crumple like microwaved crisp packets – but they could have the decency to do it in the daytime. Where were they earlier when I was scrounging for cardboard to use as a ground mat? Or when that fanny with the dreadlocks gave me that lecture about how it's the producers who shape the music industry, not the artists? Or when my final snort of coke went missing from the pocket of the jeans I'd left inside the tent? At any of those points I'd have been glad to be evicted, forced out into the welcoming warmth of the pub or back to the hotel.

'You're in violation of a High Court order,' the voice calls. 'Move on.'

I stretch and scratch and stuff my things back into the rucksack. It only takes a moment. Outside, there is a gathering of high-vis-vested men, with policemen behind. The policemen stand impassively, watching, as the bailiffs walk from tent to tent.

'Clear your things,' one of them says, as I emerge.

'Absolutely,' I say. 'No worries, mate, no worries.'

He peers at me, weighing my words for sarcasm. There's none, but he's expecting more than politeness and passivity from me. He's expecting me to react like those off to the right, who're dragging wooden pallets in an attempt to form a barricade, as if they're in revolutionary France. He'll get none of that from me, though – provided I can take my guitar and my rucksack, I'll jettison everything and everyone else.

'Do you not want to take your tent?' he shouts after me, as I saunter off towards the police lines. Most folk are making for the steps up to St Paul's, there are banners unfurling and chants starting up, but I have no interest in prolonging the protest.

'Keep it,' I call back. 'Take your son camping.'

'It'll be thrown away…'

'I honestly couldn't give a fuck.'

The interview with the *Guardian* was yesterday morning, over by the Tent City University, with the photographer positioning me so that he could angle the lens upwards and get the black stencilled words on the white marquee roof into the shot. Emboldened by coke, I gave a lecture of my own, on the importance of music as a means of social commentary. The journalist – what was her name: Jenna? Jemima? Jeeta? – recorded each and every word of it, even when I started gurning 'reason-rhyme-reason-rhyme-reason-rhyme' in an endless loop that I thought bard-worthy at the time.

In any case, with the interview done, it doesn't matter to me whether my tent is thrown into the bin-lorries lined up to the side of the bailiffs, or whether the likes of the Irish girl and Bobble-hat get carted off. And Flick? Fuck Flick, she had her chance.

Beyond the police there's a clutch of press, awaiting developments. I briefly wonder if journalist Jemita is among them, but then remember the single shake of the head she gave when I asked if I could buy her a drink and decide she's not worth the trouble of a search. Instead I go up to a blinking boy with a microphone. He looks like a work-experience kid, with glasses and a rash of dermatitis across his chin, but he's got a camera pointed at him so I figure he must just be one of those presenters who's been prematurely promoted from the kiddie shows to fill the twenty-four-hour news cycle.

'Do you know if there are any pubs still open around here?' I ask him.

'It's a Monday,' he replies, frowning. 'Well, Tuesday morning now…'

I nod. 'But do you know of any pubs I could still get a drink at?'

'Have you just come from the Occupy camp?'

'Yes.'

'Where are you going now, then?'

Jesus, they should have kept this clown on CBeebies. Twice I've asked him for the nearest pub and then he asks me where I'm going. They'll let any simpleton loose with a press pass these days.

'Well,' I say, patiently, 'I'm either going to the pub or back to the hotel.'

'Hotel?' he says. 'Did you not just come from the Occupy camp, though?'

'*Yes*,' I repeat. 'I did.'

'And you'll be staying in a hotel tonight?'

'I will indeed.'

'Can I interview you, maybe?' He points towards the camera.

'I doubt you could even interview fucking Peppa Pig, mate.'

'What?'

'Listen…' I shake my head '… just fuck off, yeah.'

With that, I walk off and leave him staring after me. The last Tube will be leaving soon and I'm anxious to be on it, but I spin as I walk down Ludgate Hill because I'm not sure where the nearest Underground is: Mansion House, maybe, if I double back on myself? Or St Paul's station if I loop round to avoid the police cordon? Then there's City Thameslink, straight ahead, but I'm not certain where the Overground trains from there go or what time they run until. Come to that, where am I going to? Back to the same hotel?

Pulling the phone from my pocket, I dial Pierce. It rings. And rings.

'Hello, Rob?'

I'm expecting his voice to be bleary, irritable after being woken from deep sleep. That's what I want after my own rude awakening. But Price sounds excited to be up past his bedtime; he's torch-under-the-covers, midnight-feast gleeful.

'Why is it so *quiet* with you?' he asks. 'I'm reading a live blog about it, but I can't find a stream of it anywhere yet. Can you see any cameras?'

'Pierce…' My tone is firm. 'Does the booking at the hotel still stand, or should I go somewhere else?'

'What?'

'Should I go to the same hotel or somewhere else? Simple question.'

'Where are you, buddy?'

'Near City Thameslink.' I've actually just caught sight of the station. 'But it's fucking closed. Fuck. Pierce, what's the nearest Tube?'

'Hang on – you've *left*?'

'St Paul's, you mean?'

'Yes.' He sounds panicked now, breathless. 'Did you leave the camp?'

'They moved everyone on, didn't they? That was the point.'

'And you just complied? You just fucking *left*?'

There's silence for a moment. I lift the phone from my ear and consider throwing it to the kerb, watching it smash into its component parts. Only issue is, I'm essentially homeless right now and I need Prick Price to direct me to the Tube and find me a hotel. He might even need to front me a bit of cash. The business account is empty and the credit card is at its limit. Pierce will sort it, though. He's the man who makes things happen, even if he is more cunt than concierge.

'I left,' I say. 'They asked me to fuck off, so off I fucked.'

'Listen, Rob…' He's trying out his serious voice. 'This is still salvageable. I want you to turn around, go back to St Paul's and find yourself a nice friendly camera crew. Wear your album T-shirt, hand out badges, talk about social protest. This is free fucking publicity, mate, and you're *literally* walking away from it.'

I decide not to tell him about the prepubescent presenter who asked for an interview, but I also decide that I'll not go back to the camp without some preconditions. If I'm going to risk arrest for a quid or two then I want my pro quo.

'After that,' I say, '*if* I do that, will you get me a hotel?'

'It would need to be on your dime, Rob.'

'Transfer me some more, will you?'

'You can't afford more than the agreed *per diem*. The advance needs to last you.'

'It's not enough, is what I'm telling you, Pierce.'

What's the issue? The other chunk of the advance will come to me when the album's released next month, so that should make a dent in the credit card, and then we're into royalties and performance fees. Why would we penny-pinch now? Is it just because it's fashionable – is that it? Fucking austerity – the word was in danger of slipping out of the dictionary until all this financial shite started, and now it's repeated like a fucking catchphrase all across the country.

'Tell you what,' Pierce says, with a sigh shadowing his words, 'go back and talk to the press, then jump in a taxi and come and stay with me. I'll text you the address. God knows what my wife'll say, mind you.'

'*Wife*!' I always presumed Price to be a chronic masturbator. Either that or a prostitute-prowler. I certainly didn't expect him to be married. Not to a woman, anyway. A horse or a fucking standard-lamp, sure, but not a woman.

'Just go back,' he says, and hangs up.

The hi-vis-vests swarm like wasps and I buzz, because that's how you deal with the boredom. The whole cocking enterprise is bloody boring, so bloody boring, with the police keeping us away from the clean-up and the folk up on the steps of St Paul's standing there behind their banners that say 'This is just the beginning'. They're chanting or booing or cheering like a crowd at a football match, but with this resignation to it, as if they've already been relegated but are enjoying a final match in the big league. How would you deal with that? When Bobble-hat shows himself, on the fringes, it's not only myself who'd feel the sting of urgency. It's not only me who'd ask him if he has any left, if there's any I could make use of. It's not only me who'd lead him over to a doorway in the next street but one, out of the eyeline of the police but desperately close when you get to thinking about it, and hand him one of the advance copies of *Measures Taken* so that he can cut out two thin lines on the plastic. It's not only me.

'I'm a musician,' I say into the camera. With cocaine pulsing, I don't just tell my story, I fucking rewrite it. 'From the city of riveters and welders – one of the cities of... and, in many ways, I've been orphaned by society, y'know, cut adrift. So I ride the rails and I tell my tales and, wherever I find people, I listen to their stories – properly *listen* – then my songs reflect all of those gathered experiences and ideas. They act as a book of condolence for the world as it was, or as a blueprint for the world as it could be – ha ha.

'My debut album is out next month, and I've just been down this way over the past few nights to lend some credibility and celebrity – well, not celebrity, but you know – ha ha – because this is a hell of a movement that's started down here – and off in those other countries, with the Arab Spring and the Americans and – wait, was it OK for me to say "hell"? – right, OK, hell yes! – so that's why I'm here and then these guys show up, these ones, and – well, what are the press doing, is what I want to know – what are *you* doing, now, other than standing here recording it all, watching it all happen – '

It takes a long time before they get to pulling down the wooden barricade, shaped like Noah's Ark in the midst of a sea of onlookers, with steel drums and wooden pallets and stacks of shelves being dragged away, until the dozen or so protesters remaining stand stranded and surrounded. One by one they're pulled down and carried off to the police vans. There are whistles and shouts of 'shame on you'. Then there is a cheer as one of the protesters wrestles an orange-vested bailiff to the ground with him. I join in with the cheers, but stay towards the back of the crowd.

Pierce rings. 'How's it going?' he asks.

'They're removing the last of the protesters now,' I say.

'But how are you getting on? I can't see you on the live stream.'

'I spoke to one camera crew, but…' I pause. 'Listen, Pierce, where are all these folk going to go – after this, I mean?'

'Who? The Occupy lot?'

'Yeah.'

'Up to Finsbury Square, they're saying on the telly. There's some place in Islington called the School of Ideas, but that's been cleared tonight as well. Why?'

In the pause, I think of all the protesters trudging up to Finsbury Square, being met by Flick, who'll sit them down and question them, one by one, about their motives.

'Why, Rob?' Pierce repeats.

'No reason, really,' I say. 'Just wondering.'

'You going native on me, is that it?'

I shake my head, but stay silent.

'Anyway, give out a few badges and that and then get yourself in a taxi, OK?'

'OK,' I say. 'Pierce?'

'What?'

'What do you think of Occupy, as an idea?'

'Crock of shit.'

'That's what I thought,' I say, and hang up.

The police, in their riot gear, are eyeing the steps up to St Paul's. They'll be clearing those as well, someone says, and giving them a deep-clean. As they advance, the street-sweepers get to work behind them, brushing up the last of the debris from the dismantling of the camp. The police cordon around the square has relaxed now, with the attention focused on those still gathered up on the steps. As the media move forward, I take out the plastic bag of badges from the side-pocket of my rucksack. *Measures Taken*, they say in white against red, or *#protestwithwords*, in red against white. Quietly, without drawing attention to myself, I bend down and pour them out on to the ground. They will be trampled, cracked, scattered. Perhaps a journo will feel one beneath the tread of their boot and pick it up to examine it; maybe a photographer will notice one lying off on its own and think it an interesting subject; it might even be that a policeman will lift one and take it home so that he can search the internet for these odd phrases, to see if they signify a new protest group or even a militant uprising. In all likelihood, though, they will be swept up. Either from the small mound I left, or in ones and twos, they will be swept up.

Turning, I walk back towards Ludgate Hill in search of a taxi.

GLASGOW

He was always going to come to me. It was inevitable. Two days before the showcase gig, as I work on the bridge of the song about Maddie, Ewan shows up on my doorstep. I'm not surprised to see him, but I am shocked at how cut-up he seems to be about it all. His eyes are swollen and welling with unshed tears. In keeping with convention, he's brought a CD to listen to. He hands me a copy of Laura Marling's *Alas, I Cannot Swim* as if it's a note explaining his despair and heartache.

Sitting on the futon in my attic bedroom, he slowly and systematically destroys my beermats as he speaks. I became a tegestologist at the age of sixteen, a year or so ago, after my dad bought me what he thought was my first ever pint at a country pub out near Balfron. He suggested I keep the beermat as a memento, but he probably didn't imagine that I'd then hoard away another from the first time I was served in the pub down on Dumbarton Road, and another from when I tried my luck by carefully whispering 'serve-ace-a' at a bartender over in Almería. I must have caught the collecting bug from my mum, who has display cases filled with antique silver spoons. I've accumulated only a dozen or so beermats, though, not the eighty-nine-piece collection my mum's cultivated over the past twenty years. It takes Ewan no time at all to shred my keepsakes, one by one, by dragging his fingernail repeatedly across the surface until the white shows, flakes and falls.

I can't stop Ewan, can't protest, because I am to blame for his misery. Whether he knows it or not, he's punishing the right person. I'm just thankful that it's only my beermats he's flaying.

'Did she say why?' I ask.

He shrugs. 'Not really. She just said it wasn't working.'

'And was it?'

'Was it what?'

'Working.'

He drops the beermat Gemma brought back from her holiday in Boston. 'I thought so, Rab.' He shrugs again. 'Like, we get along really well and she's really easy to talk to, so…'

'Was it something else, then?' I ask, wanting to hint at bedroom deficiencies, but mindful that I'm meant to know no more than Ewan has told me.

'We were pretty happy, so far as I know,' Ewan says, scraping at the edges of a fresh mat. 'She's a really good listener, y'know, and I thought that… like, with all that shite with my mum, she was really good about it.'

I bow my head into a nod. It's not only shame I feel, but also something sharper, closer to jealousy. Ewan has never spoken to me, not properly, about the events three years ago that led to his mum leaving her husband and two sons and moving to the south coast of England with this barman-turned-poet from Falkirk. I asked Ewan whether he'd noticed a difference in his mum in the weeks before she left and he said that she'd been 'fidgety'. It made me think about my own parents: the way my mum craves attention from my dad but only ever gets half his concentra– is she likely to go looking for a barman? For a poet?

Ewan's never given me more than the bare facts of it, yet he's told Maddie within the first month of knowing her. There's something about that, the intimacy, that causes my cheeks to flare and then to burn. I grasp for his wrist and dig my fingers in until he drops the beermat he's holding to the red cushion of the futon.

'That's the beermat from my first proper gig,' I say, as both apology and accusation. 'Don't tear it up, OK?'

The gig was last year, along at the Bowling Club. My uncle's a member and was sorting the entertainment for the Christmas do. I played 'Fields of Gold' – know your audience – and received a half-pint of shandy and a piece of Battenberg as payment.

Ewan looks down at the scattered scraps on the cushion around him. 'Sorry, man,' he says. 'I didn't even realise I was doing it, not really.'

I pick the beermat up and place it out of reach, on the desk behind me. I make a sweeping gesture with my hand, intending to say that he should forget it, but he takes it literally and begins using a cupped hand to gather all the wisps and curls into one pile.

'I told her things I've never told anyone,' he says, as he does so. 'About the state it left my dad in, the state it left *me* in…'

I wait for specifics. I want to know if that's the reason he left school as soon as he was able, in spite of what the rest of us said; whether it was then that he first stole that piece of oily cannabis resin from his older brother so that we could smoke it through a pierced fizzy-drink can, inhaling the carcinogens of the burning aluminium along with the smoke. I want to know why he said no more to me about her, over the years, if it had hurt him so deeply. There was plenty of opportunity, after all. We spend more or less every weekend sleeping over at one another's houses. We come as a pair. Ewan shares in my mother's chiding about staying in playing computer games and, after a night up at the woods, I benefit from his dad's tradition of cooking a Saturday morning fry-up.

'Where's your bin?' he says, instead, looking up at me with an apologetic smile and nodding down at the neat mound of my former keepsakes.

'I'll do it,' I say, scooping up the pile. 'Is there someone else, d'you think?' I ask, treading carefully as I step over to the bin.

'Someone else?'

'With Maddie.'

'Honestly,' he says, biting at his lip, 'I never even thought about that.'

'She didn't say there was?'

'D'you think there might be?'

'What do I know?' I say, tipping my hand so that the cardboard fragments flutter down towards the empty bin. They're replaceable, I'm thinking. Even at the showcase gig, just two days away, there's bound to be a beermat that I can slide into my guitar case. Depending on how the evening goes, it might even trump all the others. 'Listen, it's always a possibility, is all I'm saying.'

The showcase is on Sauchiehall Street in an old converted cinema. Out front is one of those backlit signs that for years announced the arrival of the latest blockbuster, and, as I hurry along from the bus stop, I'm fully expecting to see my own name up there: RAB DILLON. Instead, the black letters spell out UN IGNED SHOWCASE, with a squint S resting against the base of the sign.

My disappointment at not seeing my name up in lights is tinged with relief, to be honest, because over the past few days there's been this tension across my shoulders that locks and grips at my muscles every time I think of the gig. I self-medicated with sloppily rolled joints and stolen sips from my dad's whisky collection, but the muscle-spasms continued to near-throttle me as I tried to wrestle the right chords from my guitar.

Ewan meets me at the door to the club. He wears a grey suit that is far too small for him: pinched in at the armpits, tight at the crotch, and showing his socks at the ankles. He looks like Bruce Banner when he's slightly peeved: stretching the stitches but with no torn fabric. Smoothing his blue checked tie, Ewan hands me a warm bottle of beer and leads me up to the first floor. When he turns, I frown and gesture up the stairs to the main room – a gutted-out cinema screen that serves as a massive stage and hangar-sized dance floor.

'No, mate.' He smiles. 'We're in this bar. They're running their normal night in there, I think.'

'Even better,' I say. 'An intimate gig.'

As with the sign outside, the smaller venue takes the pressure off and unpicks the knots of nerves, but I wouldn't want the evening to unravel any further or my shoulders might start to sag and slump.

'I'll introduce you to the artist manager,' Ewan says, pointing over towards the bar. 'Guy called Pierce Price, from London.'

'So he made it, then?'

'Of course. And your parents are over there.'

'You invited my *parents*?'

He shrugs. 'Of course.'

My mum and dad stand off to the back of the room. Mum is trying to appear inconspicuous by swaying gently to the music, even though everyone around her is still. As I look over, she catches my eye and gives me a broad wave and a broader smile. I return both with smaller, tighter versions, then she nudges Dad – who is staring at the grey ceiling tiles as if they're the clearest starry sky – and I have to repeat my greeting.

'What about Cammy?' I ask Ewan.

'The girls are here, but Cammy…' Ewan shakes his head.

'He's not coming?'

Ewan shrugs. 'Didn't even say why. Bit of a dickhead move, to be honest.'

My mind flicks through the times that Cammy could have seen me with Maddie over the past fortnight or so: from his treetop perch that night in the woods, or along Great Western Road the next weekend, and countless times since then walking Silo in the grounds of Gartnavel or on the streets up around Broomhill. We've not been particularly careful about not being seen.

Thoughts of being caught by candid Cammy are quickly chased away, though, by the approach of Pierce Price. He is short, but seems to spring upwards with every step. Dressed in jeans and a navy shirt with block-white collar, he is perpetually fidgeting – scratching at his ear, pulling at his cuffs, resetting his glasses, passing his hand over his thinning brown hair – but he stands still long enough to hold out a hand.

'Mr Price,' I say, shaking it. 'Lovely to meet you.'

'Pierce,' he says. 'Call me Pierce. Manager and, for one day only, judge extraordinaire.'

'Rab.'

'Well, Rob.' He smiles. 'Looking forward to tonight, then? Should be a good gig.'

'Should be good, aye.'

We keep up the stilted conversation for a minute or so, but I spend most of it nodding while Pierce whispers conspiratorially that what he's looking for – what he's *really* looking for – is something 'fresh' and 'contemporary', with a 'unique sound'. My throat feels like sandpaper and the warm beer doesn't moisten it, so my voice comes out as a rasp when I try to answer him.

'It's…' I cough thinly. 'It's contemporary music I play, yes.'

'Is it political?'

'In what way?'

'Like, does it speak to current affairs; does it give an *opinion*?'

I shrug, then nod.

'Because I saw your clips online, those covers, and I liked the passion behind them, Rob. Is that the kind of thing you're interested in?'

'What kind of thing?'

'Like, would you write a song about university tuition fee rises, maybe? Or about the protests around it all, at least?'

I'm spared *Question Time* by Teagan and Gemma, who come across with primary-coloured cocktails in plastic glasses.

Gemma, never known for being backward, enfolds Pierce into a hug that leaves his hand, held out for a handshake, awkwardly positioned. Teagan, for her part, steps in close and holds his hand for a moment longer than is necessary, then another moment and another.

'I may have played up his importance a touch,' Ewan says, leaning in towards me.

'In what way?'

'All I did was list bands,' he smiles. 'Just listed them and then asked the girls if they'd like to meet Pierce Price, the band manager. I didn't say the two were related in any way. It wasn't even a white lie, really.'

'Why go to the trouble?'

'My thinking is that it would do no harm if music-man had a beautiful girl flirting with him all night, and that if the girl happened to be your friend – well, all the better…'

'Gemma?'

'I was thinking Tea was more his cup of…' Ewan holds his hand up. 'Fuck. Terrible pun, sorry.'

I shake my head, smiling all the while. I can't fault his plan, though, because the attention of a girl like Teagan will be sure to please Pierce Price. She's tall and slender, is Teagan, with tumbledown brown hair and grey eyes. Beautiful, with a constant need to be told so. If she and Pierce spend an evening searching out the bare skin on each other – with her fingers swatting against his arm in mock annoyance at his teasing, and with him resting his arm on her shoulder as he leans over to reassure her that she's the prettiest girl there – then where's the harm?

'What the fuck is *she* doing here?' Teagan's manner shifts abruptly.

We all follow the direction of her glower, over to the bar. Maddie stands there, with a bottle of beer in her hand, trying to avoid the collective stare. Her attempted disguise is a checked shirt and a black beanie hat. If it were a '90s gay bar she'd blend in perfectly. Her eyes slide across to us and she tries a tentative wave. It's Gemma who responds in kind, and I manage to give a brief wave of my own before Teagan slaps at our wrists.

'What the fuck are you doing?' she says.

'She came to support Rab,' Gemma says. 'It's sweet of her, really.'

'And what about Ewan?'

'It's fine, Tea, honestly,' Ewan tries.

'The bare-faced cheek of it!'

'Honestly, Teagan…'

'She's *such* a bitch. Is she stalking you or taunting you, Ewan? Or is she just so full of herself, so up-her-own-fucking-hole, that she wants the drama?'

Pierce taps me on the arm and pulls me to the side. Angled away from the group, I manage to catch Maddie's eye and give her a quick wink. When she does the same, Teagan erupts. 'Did you see that?' she screeches. 'That wee witch is fucking winking at us – '

'I'll introduce you to the other acts in a minute,' Pierce says, drawing my attention away from the potential cat-fight behind us. 'But I wanted to run something past you first, if I could? Something that follows on from our chat about political songwriting a minute ago.'

'– we should fucking take her. Right here, right now.'

'Sure,' I say. 'What about it?'

'Well…' Pierce pushes his glasses up his nose again. 'I have a label, an imprint of a major, who're looking for something young and edgy. Not urban, though; they have plenty of urban. They want folky. Like the protest songs back in the '60s…'

'– what're you looking at, you fucking minger? Eh?'

'… something angry, something authentic…'

'– I'll scratch your eyes out and then we'll see if you can wink, bitch.'

'… broken Britain songs to capitalise, or not capitalise… to speak to disaffected youth.'

I smile, I nod and I skim through the three-song set-list in my mind to see if there's a political slant. The first song has one line, 'skip the line in the waiting room, won't ease the pain', that could be about the NHS. That's not what I was intending, fair enough, but it's better than the vague sentiment of artistic endeavour that I had in mind when I wrote it. The second song is the one I wrote about Maddie, so it's mostly soppy shit, but there's a lyric in there about the price of popcorn on a cinema date, so that's (sort of) about the economy. Then the third one talks about melting chocolate in tin-foil parcels on the heating pipes in the history classrooms at school, so that's education covered, although it does also repeat a chorus about 'getting laid' that would struggle to make it into most manifestos. The melodies, though, are authentic. They're mostly lifted from old folk songs – tried, tested, and out of copyright – so they'll sound the part. The lyrics can always be changed to suit.

By the time I take to the stage, I've reworked the three songs into a stump speech. Something Billy Bragg would be proud of. I grip the microphone in my trembling fist and mumble that the songs are about 'my experience of living under this government', then I look down at the stool they've set up by the DJ-booth to see if Pierce Price approves. He nods appreciatively. The rest of the crowd, only a couple of dozen strong, look up at me expectantly. They are waiting, but I struggle to get my fingers to settle on the strings of my guitar.

Ewan, Teagan and Gemma stand directly in front of me. Their grins produce a tightness across my chest that forces a thin breath into the microphone. It sounds out as static. Looking off to my left, over towards the bar, I search out Maddie. She raises her eyebrows and makes a 'hurry up' gesture by rolling her right hand in the air.

'I'm Rab, by the way,' I say, then launch into the first song.

The three songs pass quickly. I stare into the single spotlight, pointed off to my right, and focus on the smell, somehow both sweet and sour, that rises from the metal mesh of the microphone. I trip over two chords but stumble directly into the next, managing to cover the errors, and my voice cracks on one note but holds apart from that.

The applause at the end is strengthened by a wolf-whistle from Ewan and a scream from Gemma, but it's the thumbs-up from Pierce Price that gets me smiling. I don't look directly across to Maddie, but I can see her clapping. Nodding my thanks, I make my way to the side of the stage and gulp at the warm bottled beer they've set out for us while the other two contestants play their sets.

Although the girl after me constantly looks down at her guitar as she tries to find the chords, she has a voice that travels through me as a shiver. Rising to the high note at the end, she closes her eyes and forgets about the strumming, but no one seems to mind. After her is a band. Five-piece. The singer has this powerful throaty voice and the bassist does these runs and licks that cut through the dross of the lead guitar.

That's it, I think: I've got no chance of winning. I'm just being realistic. The girl, cute with straight, black fringe and dimpled cheeks, is capable of haunting a wet dream or two with that voice. And the band, with a bit of work and a new guitarist, would look the part on the main stages of all those summer festivals.

Packaging is important, right? Crisps are beige but the bags they come in are brightly coloured. I'm scrawny – all neck – with an Adam's apple that looks like a mouse being swallowed by a snake. I'll never be a crooner or boyband-bait, so the best I can be is folky. Peaked cap, trimmed beard, harmonica on the rack. That's not a good look.

I manage to drink three bottles of beer before the end; the release of tension means I'm more or less inhaling them. When I walk on stage for the announcement of the winner, I'm light-headed and in desperate need of a piss. Pierce Price stands in front of the three acts and tries his best to inject some tension into the silent room.

'And the winner of the 2011 Glasgow Unsigned Artist's Showcase is…'

There is no drum-roll, no rising-pitch soundtrack.

'… and don't forget that the winner gets a studio recording session and the possibility of being represented by my very own agency…'

The urgency in my mind is the need to urinate, not the need to win.

'… the very-talented… the *super*-talented…'

Piss, piss, piss.

'… Robert Dillon!'

There's surprise when he calls my name and it spreads as a numb disbelief rather than a feeling of pride or accomplishment. I step forward to shake his hand. My foot catches in a trailing lead and I have to pause and hop forwards to untangle myself.

It's then that I make a mistake, a significant one. As I shake hands with Pierce, I look out into the audience. I don't look straight out in front, though, at my friends, or to the back of the room and my parents. Instead, I look off to the left to Maddie, standing by the bar. She's the first person I share a smile with. And, just a second later, as I look down at Ewan, Teagan and Gemma, I realise my mistake. Gemma looks up at me with wide eyes, Teagan glares over at Maddie, and Ewan, with his suit jacket riding higher than his shirt-tail, has already turned away.

BRIGHTON

It is Luke who helps me open it up. An abandoned pub on the ground floor of a red-brick building on one of those streets off King's Road. Near the seafront. Our neighbours will be a high-end hotel and a florist. We find a way in through the weed-thicket of the back garden, then force a latch on the bathroom window.

'We found it like this, OK?' Luke says, after he's finished gouging with his screwdriver and prising with his chisel. He's left a brown-red rust mark against the flaking white paint.

'Of course,' I say.

'And remember to put your notices up after you've fitted the lock,' he says. 'Let everyone know that you're aware of your rights.'

'Section 6, legal warning,' I say, holding up the plastic bag Luke brought. In it are the laminated notice, the bolt-lock, a screwdriver, a torch, and a primus camping stove. 'Sorted.'

'As it stands you're perfectly legal here,' he says. 'The new law only applies to residential properties, so don't let them tell you that you're a criminal, OK? This is a *civil* matter. And you're homeless, seeking shelter in a disused building.'

'Yeah.'

I resent his attitude, this take-charge tone. He has no right to be repackaging my situation as a cover story and repeating it back to me. After all, it wasn't him I called, it was Flick. Unfolding the scrap of paper she'd smudged her phone number on to, that night at the party, and breathing through my mouth to avoid the foetid-funk of the phone box, it was Flick I called.

Maybe it was the nasal note to my voice that caused her to hesitate; maybe she thought it was someone pretending to be me, or she didn't quite catch what I said.

'It's Rab,' I repeated, just in case.

'I heard,' she said. Pause. 'What can I do for you?'

'It's about squatting. We were hoping you could help us get started, me and a…' I wince away from the word 'friend' '… an acquaintance.'

'Oh.' Her voice brightened. 'Of course. Let me see, who do I know down there?'

It's a rhetorical question, but it leads to silence. 'Just a bit of guidance, really,' I say. 'From yourself.'

'Yes, but we need to do some research to make sure the building isn't actually in use, or just about to be. We want to be careful about it, you know, do a proper recce.' Another pause. 'But there's Luke, of course, isn't there? He'd help.'

'Would *you* not – ?'

'He'd definitely help you out.'

From that point on I had little or no input. I was busking with Luke at the weekends – he was at uni during the week – and every Saturday he'd show up with a story about a former restaurant he was scouting, registered to an overseas tax haven, or an office block that had been abandoned because of rising damp, stripped of the copper wire from the walls but otherwise structurally sound. And with each update he'd slip in a compliment about Flick: 'She's so *engaged*… so *politically aware*… so *creative*… so *awake*.' We're all *awake*, you dozy prick! I wanted to scream. It's not the fact that she's fucking *awake* that makes her special. Instead, I smiled and asked the kind of question you'd ask an estate agent. 'Does it have outside space? A kitchen? Plumbed toilet? Running water? A roof?'

114

Eventually, three weeks in, the rehousing committee of Flick and Luke settled on this pub. It belongs to a Swiss financier who bought it as an investment back in the boom and is now waiting out the bust so that he can make his money back.

I'm less interested in the details than in the revelation that Luke travelled up to London to meet with Flick. To discuss the logistics of opening it up, over a drink or two. And we all know where that leads to with Flick. They're beyond phone calls and fawning now, and I'm the social-project pillock who brought them together.

In the overgrown garden, with thorns plucking at my jeans, I ask Luke why he had to travel up to London. He sighs: it's not the first time I've asked the question.

'We just wanted to get you in before winter started in earnest, Rab. It's October. It's cold.'

'Aye, but – '

'It's best to have you situated, as well, with the change to the squatting law and that.'

'I appreciate your help, Luke, really…' I say. 'I do.'

'I'd love to be joining you, to be honest,' he says, clapping me on the shoulder. 'Maybe I will, soon. But this term's just too important at uni, you know.'

'Aye, that makes sense,' I say. 'Besides, I'm not sure Sage would welcome you with open arms, anyway…'

We left Sage slumped at the mouth of the underpass between West Street and the beach, guarding the bags. We're going in through the toilet extension, out the back, and if there's squeezing/climbing/lifting to be done in opening it up, then he isn't the ideal candidate. Besides, he has a tendency to refer to Luke as 'the duplicitous dentist', and I don't want to test Luke's reaction to that particular Victorian-farce nickname.

'You go on in,' Luke says, 'and I'll go and fetch Sage.'

'Do you not want me to go?' I ask.

He hesitates, and looks up at the loose window-latch, tap-tapping in the breeze.

'Flick said there should always be one person inside. But, I don't think I should... because I'm not actually squatting... it's not...'

'Fair enough, you go back,' I say, smiling into the darkness and adding 'if you're too scared' in a whisper, once he has walked on out of earshot. Then I clamber up on to the windowsill and start to slither through, feet first, into the darkness inside.

The squat will be an improvement on the tent, no doubt about it. As I shine my torch around the lounge area, I catch sight of the ghostly shapes of plastic-wrapped tables. I flick the light switch on and off a few times, but it produces nothing other than a tutting noise in the darkness. When I turn the tap behind the bar, though, water gurgles then splutters out.

This will be my home. Or at least the closest thing since the attic bedroom of my parents' house. For over a year, I've been in transit – hotel, hostel, hobo – but now I have a home. In the hotel, Price was always at the door and the room was always re-set by the time I returned at night; on the streets the wariness scratched at sleep and the chill gnawed at dreams; and up at the pitch-and-putt the Rough Sleeper folk were always showing up, or the police would rustle at the canvas in an attempt to give an officious knock. But here, hopefully, people will finally just leave us alone. Leave us in peace.

Which reminds me about the lock. I make my way to the front door and turn the Yale. The door swings open without a creak. Taking the bolt-lock out of the plastic bag, I set to work with the screwdriver. The wood chews and splinters, but I get the screws to hold eventually. I run the bolt back and forth a few times, to make sure. Then, I consider how to fix the laminated notice to the outside. There are eight screws, in total, on the bolt-lock, but I'm not willing to sacrifice the security of even one of them to affix the sign. Instead, I use my fingernail to remove a small screw from the camping stove Luke gave us and use that. Then I shine the torch up on to the notice.

LEGAL WARNING

*Section 6 Criminal Law Act 1977
As amended by Criminal Justice and
Public Order Act 1994*

TAKE NOTICE

THAT we live in this property, it is our home and we intend to stay here.

THAT at all times there is at least one person in this property.

THAT any entry or attempt to enter into this property without our permission is a *criminal offence* as any one of us who is in physical possession is opposed to entry without our permission.

THAT if you attempt to enter by violence or by threatening violence *we will prosecute you*. You may receive a sentence of up to *six months' imprisonment* and/or a *fine* of up to £5,000.

THAT if you want to get us out you will have to issue a claim in the County Court or in the High Court, or produce to us a written statement or certificate in terms of S.12A Criminal Law Act, 1977 (as inserted by Criminal Justice and Public Order Act, 1994).

THAT it is an offence under S.12A (8) Criminal Law Act 1977 (as amended) to knowingly make a false statement to obtain a written statement for the purposes of S.12A. A person guilty of such an offence may receive a sentence of up to *six months' imprisonment* and/or a *fine* of up to £5,000.

I don't keep the front door open for long. As soon as the notice is up, I close it and draw the bolt across, then go back into the main lounge to explore. Some of the plaster has flaked from the walls, to lie like confetti across the floorboards, and there are enough discarded cable ties for an illegal detention centre, but it's not in a bad state overall. A smell like a stagnant pond and some black-streaked mould on the skirting boards is about the worst of it. No excrement smeared like graffiti across the walls, or needles lying clustered in the corners to sting at your ankles. In fact, other than dusty bootprints and a few stray leaves, there is nothing to indicate that anyone has been in here since the last of last calls.

It is unnervingly quiet, though. A silence that seems to be listening for the smallest noise from me. I tread slowly, picking out objects with my torch beam. There is a pile of cardboard in the far corner and a patch of wall pock-marked with tiny holes, save for a pale circle in the centre. I search for a dartboard behind the bar, but stop looking after my trainer crunches on the brittle bones of what must once have been a mouse.

By the time Sage arrives at the door, without Luke, I've unwrapped a pew-style bench with a cushioned base, and found an ice-bucket so that I can start heating water. We have no teabags, but sitting on a cushion and cradling a cup of something hot will be luxury enough.

'Is that to wash with?' Sage asks, nodding at the water on top of the hissing camping stove. 'Good idea.'

'It could be, I guess.' I frown. 'Although I'm not sure if we have a functional bathroom.' I came in that way, but I can't for the life of me remember. Taking the torch, I go down the hallway to check. There is a sink, but the hot water tap runs cold and there's brown staining, in veins, across the base. No bath – that would be too much to hope for – but two dry urinals and a cistern-toilet that doesn't flush.

'We can boil water and carry it through to fill the sink, so we can have a standing wash at least,' Sage says, from behind me. 'Now give me that torch, will you?'

I shine the beam across to where he stands, in the doorway to the bathroom. He has two of the tent poles in his hands and he clumsily clanks them together in an attempt to get them to fit. Squinting into the light, he grins. 'I thought I'd be able to do this in the dark, after all the practice we've had, but…'

'Sage,' I say. 'Do we really need the tent?'

He stops fiddling. The tent poles, one clutched in each hand, look like nunchucks.

'You agreed,' he says. 'We spoke about it and you agreed that we'd use the space, use the shelter, but pitch the tent so that we could move on.'

'But, as long as we keep the place tidy…'

'Rab – '

'There's cushions on that bench there, so…'

'No!' he bellows. It causes me to look nervously at the ceiling. Are there people in the flat upstairs? If there are, they'll either call the police or turn the telly up, depending on the type of neighbours they are.

'It just seems such a waste,' I w-hiss-per. 'When we could sleep on cushions.'

He shakes his head. 'We had a deal.'

'Will you keep your voice *down*?'

'Gladly,' he says. 'Will you stick to your promises?'

'*Yes.*' I pull him, by the arm, away from the bathroom. His voice seems to echo in there. 'It just seems a shame, is all I'm saying.'

'But you'll keep your word?'

I nod.

'Good. I'll get the tent up; you make a start on filling the sink.'

'Actually, I was going to have a cup of something hot first.'

'Do we have tea?'

'Well, no – '

'Do we have cups?'

I shrug. There was a broken hand-whisk, as well as the ice-bucket, underneath the bar, but I hadn't seen any crockery.

'Wash it is, then,' he says. 'Priority number one.'

We work in silence, with Sage erecting the tent by torchlight while I stumble down the dark hallway with a sloshing bucket of scalding water held out, at arm's length, in front of me.

'I was worried about you, you know,' Sage says, as the ice-bucket is set on the stove for the second time. They are the first words either of us has spoken for five minutes, maybe more. 'I really was, lad.'

'In what way?' I ask. He is in control of the torch, pointed down at his feet, so I'm not able to study his face, only the laces – one black, one brown – on his scuffed shoes.

'I really thought you might...' He pauses. 'Go down *that* road again. When we were camping along at the lagoon and you were going off with the duplicitous dentist. When you didn't turn up that time, I really thought...'

There is a catch to his voice; it causes his words to flicker and putter like the flame beneath the ice-bucket. I stare down at the water as the first bubbles start to bead then rise to the surface.

'I've not,' I say, softly. 'I won't.'

'I know you haven't,' he says. 'But I was worried you would.'

We both stand, staring at the water as it rolls into a boil. The missing screw has left the stove lopsided, so that it rattles against the wooden top of the bar. I expect the next words out of his mouth to be 'let me tell you a story'. There is a cautionary tale to be told, about how far I've come and yet how easy it would be to find myself right back at square one. Something about a bungee-cord or the collapse of the housing market in Ireland – you never know if you'll get wank or whimsy from Sage.

'That's the reason,' he says, instead. 'For the tent. It might not be much, Rab, but it'll still be there even if we get evicted from this place. It's the constant, the stability. OK?'

I nod.

'I think you need that, lad.' He reaches out to lift the bucket from the flame. 'Maybe we both do.'

Once we've filled the sink another inch or so, we top it off with cold water and Sage takes the first wash. I go searching. As I made my last trip with the ice-bucket, it occurred to me that a pub is likely to have two toilets. Sure enough, when I flicked the torch up on to the door, there was a little gentleman there. So, as Sage sploshes, I go in search of the little lady.

There are steps over to the left of the front door. I shine the torchlight down them, but they turn sharply to the left. There could be any number of things down there in the basement. A kitchen, perhaps, and a women's bathroom. Maybe even a storage room with some food and supplies. Then again, there could be rats and roaches. Dead bodies or decomposing animals. Fuck's sake, there might be a hatchet-man living down there for all we know. Or just a junkie willing to protect his turf with a stab-stab of his needle.

I sweep the torch beam in front of me as I descend, as if it were a lightsaber rather than just white light. At the bottom of the steps are two doors. The little lady is on the one to the right. The left hand one has a sign saying 'Private: No Entry'. I decide to ignore it. As I creak the door open, I rock back on my heels, preparing to dive away from whatever will come rushing out. Nothing stirs, though.

The room used to be storage. The beer pipes, hanging loose, come into here. There are two metal barrels over in the corner, but the rest of the room is empty. Across the floor, though, is a thick black mulch. The damp's got in, either from spilt beer or floodwater. It rises on the walls as a rash. The smell is strong enough to catch at the back of my throat.

I shut the door against it and turn to the Ladies. It's worse. Black mould up the walls and fungus – sodden brown sponges with white rims – strung together across the floor. I pull the collar of my jumper up over my mouth and take a pace inside the door. Just to check whether the toilets are intact. There are two cubicles. The toilet bowl in one is cracked and the brown rot seems to be seeping and spreading from its base, but the second one is only stained. I don't step across to check the flush. The Gents is definitely more usable.

After ten minutes, Sage comes padding through to the lounge, with his blanket wrapped around him as a towel, and I go through to the bathroom. The water, I'm sure, is brackish and brown. As if the veins on the base of the sink had burst. There are probably slicks of grease on the surface and floating islands of clumped hair. In the darkness, though, that doesn't matter. All I concentrate on – as I cup my hands and lower them in – is the heat of the water. It seems to seep into my skin.

We have no soap so I scrub myself as best I can with my bare hands. By the time I drain the sink, I feel a new man. Baptised. The flushed zeal of it fades, though, as I dry myself with the grimy red T-shirt I've worn for the past few days. I found it in a bin-bag of clothes left in a charity shop doorway, which is also where I found the checked boxers. They have only been in circulation for a day, so I pull them back on, throw the T-shirt on the floor, and go through to find my blanket.

Sage has managed to attach the torch to the light-fitting in the centre of the ceiling. It shines down, casting a circle of light in front of the tent: the fire of our indoor campsite. I smile, from the doorway, but then catch sight of Sage himself. He sits at the mouth of the tent, rocking backwards and forwards into the torchlight. And he is sobbing, softly. Cross-legged, with his blanket stretched from knee to knee. With his bare shoulders shaking and his head bowed to the carpet, he weeps.

I'm not sure if he's broken down from despair or relief. Relief at being clean, or closer to clean, and at having a ceiling above and four walls around. Knowing that the front door is shut and bolted and that the wind that whips in from the sea will do no more than rattle the windows.

Stepping forward, I avoid the pool of light and sit myself down beside Sage. He sniffs and drags a hand across his eyes to smear away the tears.

I reach out my hand and rest it on his calf. The hairs beneath my fingers are coarse. I know what I'm doing, as I bring my hand up against the grain, towards his knee. I want to be close, to give pleasure. Here in this squat, so far from

122

where we first met but remembering the circumstances of our first meeting, I want to show my gratitude. I want to draw his mind away from his troubles – from *our* troubles – and give him those moments of intense forgetting.

His breath shortens as my hand slides in underneath the blanket, and I know that he is squinting down at me. I avoid his gaze, though, and focus on the pool of light out in the centre of the carpet.

His cock twitches to the touch of my fingers.

'Rab, what is this?' he asks.

I curl them around the ridge of his foreskin.

'Seriously, Rab – '

Closing my eyes, I begin to slide my fingers up and down the shaft.

'No!' His hand is on my wrist, pulling me away.

'I thought you'd…' I say.

'What?'

'When we first met…'

'No.' He shakes his head. 'Don't.'

Then he turns and lumbers back into the tent, with this noise like a low growl coming from his throat. For a moment, I sit stunned and shaking. Then I look over at the bench and at my clothes bundled up, where I left them, against the cushions. That is where I'll be sleeping tonight, I know, while Sage sleeps alone in the tent. Because of my clumsy attempt to give pleasure, to be close.

LONDON

'Christ, it's awful.' Pierce's voice bleeds through from the kitchen. 'Listen to this: "Dylan speaks to the ninety-nine per cent with condescension worthy of the worst of the one per cent"… Fuck, and this: "Whether you have ten pounds in the bank or ten million, this album isn't worth the cover price." Bloody hell, he's given the thing half a fucking star. Zero-point-five stars. Fuck.'

I roll over, towards the window. More air hisses out of the slow leak in the blow-up mattress. I can feel the floorboards against my shoulder. I've been on the floor for the past three nights, since I was sick on their light grey sofa. Red wine, kebab sauce, Jägermeister – it left a stain on the cushions like a portal to hell.

'It's only one review,' Lydia, Pierce's wife, says. 'Maybe it won't matter.'

'*Fuck*!' Pierce replies.

I'm not sure how Lydia feels about me. She gives me mixed signals. In the evenings, before she goes off to her classes, she's all bundled up in scarves and tweed trouser suits the texture of scouring pads. In the mornings, though, she wanders around the house in this lace-trimmed, slinky blue robe that shows a spiked triangle of leg.

'There'll be more reviews,' she says. 'Better ones.'

'But this reviewer, Lyds, is meant to be *sympathetic*.'

'In what way?'

'Bower knows him, hand-picked him. He's all into the Occupy movement, spent time up at the Bank of Ideas, delivered talks on journalism to the protesters and – '

'You're overreacting, anyway.'

I can't decide whether Lydia's casual robe-wearing is slovenly or slutty. It's always when Pierce is out of the house, so I'm fairly convinced it's an invitation, but it usually takes me until tweed o'clock before I can shake off the lethargy of my hangover. Besides, Lydia isn't stunning. Not that she matches her nursing home name; she's just a bit plain beyond the blonde-hair, decent-body of it.

'It's not just this, though,' Pierce says. 'There was that magazine article last week that said the name change was the equivalent of an author calling himself Charlie Dickens or Ernie Hemingway...'

'Keep your voice down, he'll hear you – '

'... and there was that blogger who didn't even bother with a review, just scrawled "sacrilege" across the picture of the album sleeve.'

There's a trickle of laughter from Lydia. 'My favourite line from this so-called sympathetic reviewer is "this album should, indeed, spark protests".'

'It's not good, Lyds.'

I draw my tacky tongue across my lips, trying to give them moisture. Last night was spent at the local bar, buying drinks for those who'd spend a minute chatting. London is a lonely city for the most part, but you can always find a student or a tourist who'll sit over a beer. It's becoming harder to search them out, though, for some reason. And I shouldn't have to. I have an album coming out; I should have the gravitational pull of a small planet by now.

'Rob.' Pierce sticks his head around the door, his glasses catch the sunlight. 'We need to meet with marketing after lunch, OK? Half-one.'

I nod. 'Was that a review, Pierce?'

'Yes. Not good.'

'They're the establishment, though, aren't they? The Fourth Estate,' I say.

He presses his lips together, until his mouth is no more than a line.

'Will I meet you there, then?' I ask.

'Quarter-past. Don't be late.'

'See you then.' I drag a hand over my eyes. When I look again, Pierce has gone. The offending newspaper now lies on the floor, just inside the door. It is folded open to the reviews page. I leave it where it is. The front door slams, signalling Pierce's departure, and I prop myself up on my elbows and wait for Lydia to come through, as she does every morning. She will turn on the telly and sprawl herself out on the stained sofa. Her robe will hang slack, showing suggestive shadow. We'll watch until the end of *BBC Breakfast* and maybe catch the start of *Jeremy Kyle*, then she'll get her laptop out and make a start on her work, whatever it is she does, and I'll go through to raid the fridge for a cure. By the time I've had a shower, she'll be out of the robe and into jogging bottoms and hooded jumper, her halfway stage of clothing.

One of these mornings, though, she'll ignore the sofa and the telly and her books. Once the front door slams behind Pierce, she'll step into the front room and untie the silken robe. It will fall from her, more with each step, until she lifts her foot from the last shimmering of it. Then she will slip in underneath my blanket and, together, we'll take the last gasp of air from the mattress. One of these mornings.

We take a taxi from the label offices. Pierce is still stressing over this morning's advance review, checking his phone every two seconds, so it's left to me to deal with Innes – this marketing monkey who sits across from me and claps his hands like miniature cymbals.

'I'm super-excited about this,' he says. 'You'll love it. Guaranteed.'

I grunt.

'We'll have everyone talking about you… darling.'

He does this a lot, Innes, even in the short time I've known him: adds a flourish to the end of his sentence, a second too late, as if to convince us that he is actually gay. I don't quite believe it – in spite of the carefully contoured eyebrows, the ruler-straight side-parting and the way he stands with his hip cocked forward. He's trying too hard. Like some drama student's idea of a dandy.

'It's not trending, anyway,' Pierce says. 'And if you put your name into the search engine there are thirteen pages of the other Dylan before it comes up.'

'What's not trending?' Innes asks.

'Bad review,' I say.

'Reviews don't matter.' Innes waves the idea away. 'So long as you've got a hook for all the little fishies.'

'Like what?'

'You'll see. A lightning bolt – a flash – a uniqueness.'

The spark of inspiration Innes has come up with turns out to be the same one that's been singeing Scotsmen for years. We pull up outside a kiltmaker's just off Savile Row. I'm already shaking my head as we get out of the cab, and anger smoulders in my throat as we enter the shop to the dirge of bagpipe music. This will be the tartan tomb my career is buried in.

'No,' I say, turning to Innes and ignoring the perky shop assistant, who has stepped forward with a '*Fáilte*' and a smile that should come with a shot of insulin. 'No chance.'

'Not tartan… lovely,' Innes says. 'But a tweed or a leather one.'

'Not a *fucking* chance,' I repeat. 'I'm a singer, not a novelty act.'

'A moment,' Innes says to the assistant. She has taken several steps back already. Her blonde hair is in the same style as Innes's – shaved on one side and long on top – but she suits it better than him. Especially with the addition of thick-rimmed black glasses.

'No offence,' I say to her.

'I know it may seem derivative... darling,' Innes says. 'But we want to remind audiences that you're Scottish, and this would be a way to be fashionable with it. Fashionable and memorable.'

'It might play well in the American market,' Pierce says.

'Try again,' I say.

Innes stands where he is, blinking. He needs a moment to process the idea that his campaign – magazine articles speculating on whether I'm a 'true' Scotsman, internet chatter about what I keep in my sporran, photo shoots with my kilt being blown by an updraught – will never win an award for being '*brave*-and-*heart*felt' or whatever hackneyed hogshite he's fantasised about.

'What about...?' he begins, then falters.

'We have some wonderful flat caps,' the shop assistant says. 'That could be his thing, maybe. He could wear one every time he plays.'

'Like a bunnet,' Pierce says. 'That would be Scottish *and* folky.'

'A stylish cap could work, yes.' Innes nods.

'Or a tin hat, even,' I say. 'I could make it myself – out of kitchen foil.'

'Oh, no.' The assistant wrinkles her nose. 'I don't think so.'

I'm beginning to go off her, to be honest. I think she might be siding with Innes. They might even be old friends – met in the queue at the hairdresser's, maybe – or be working some scam whereby she gets the steam from every tartan-based turd of an idea that he comes up with.

The bunnet suggestion is not as bad, fair enough, but it would copy the corduroy cap from the cover of Bob Dylan's first album. I'd look like a cheap imitation.

'Don't be so *resistant*, Rob,' Pierce chides. 'Innes is the expert in this PR work, after all. You need to be open to a bit of polishing, image-wise.'

I shake my head. 'We'd need to blow layers of dust off these ideas before they could be polished.'

Innes straightens his cuffs. He takes a great deal of time and care over it. When he eventually looks up, he examines me from top to toe. I'm wearing a white T-shirt and beige chinos; nearly a blank canvas. His gaze settles on my bare wrists.

'How about some ornamentation for your arms?' he says.

'Like what? A bracelet?'

'Maybe, or a leather cuff. Give me a moment... lovely.'

He steps over to the assistant and whispers to her. She beams up at him as if the sun has just started shining out of his arse and then scuttles off to the back of the shop.

'Be *open*, Rob,' Pierce whispers. 'We need help with this side of things.'

The assistant comes back with a cardboard box filled with offcuts. Some of the fabrics are tartan, but most are fairly modest. It reminds me of the dressing-up box we used to have at home and how I used to argue with Ewan for the chance to wear the pirate costume. Innes wastes no time in plunging his hand in and rummaging through pieces with frayed edges or with shapes snipped from them. He comes up with two long strips. One is garish – mustard yellow and purple – the other is grey pinstripe.

'Right.' Innes juts his hip forward to make his pitch. 'Your music is accessible to everyone, correct? This concept gives something that can act like a symbolic membership to your club – your gang – without it being expensive or...'

He reaches out and ties the garish one around my right wrist.

'All different colours, no uniformity. Everyone who listens to your music can wear one, can tell their friends why they're wearing it, but without losing their individuality. It's like a badge, almost. A statement. But subtle... darling.'

'We could cut a strip from your tent,' Pierce says. 'The one from St Paul's.'

I don't tell him that the tent ended up in the bin-van on the night of the eviction. Instead, I move my wrist up and down to check that the fabric won't interfere with my strumming.

'It might work,' I say. 'Not too bad, certainly.'

'Rags on wrists,' Pierce says. 'Like a play on rags to riches.'

'You should have been in marketing,' Innes says, meaning it as a compliment.

This is certainly the least objectionable idea they've come up with – third time lucky – and I'm not keen to see what the bottom of the barrel looks like, so I raise my ragged wrist and give Innes a thumbs-up.

'Let me try the grey one, though,' I say.

By the release date, in late March, I'm on to my fourth rag. The first one – the grey – was discarded after some youngsters asked me where the rest of my suit was; the second – green and blue tartan – was removed at the request of a bouncer in Islington; and the third – the colour of sand – fell victim to a particularly brutal nosebleed. I would have worn the fourth today anyway, because it's been specially made – a black and white print of my album cover on a square handkerchief.

We travel, by car, around London. Innes is in tow, of course, but he's also brought a camera crew. At every stop we make, they clamber out with their bulky camera and boom. And heads turn. I've *arrived*. Rab Dylan, debut artist, busking outside the Royal Festival Hall, in Trafalgar Square, on one of the streets just off Piccadilly Circus. Because of the camera, I draw a crowd at locations where I'd normally struggle even to get spat at. At each, I play a couple of songs and we hand out postcards with a code to download a free taster from the website.

St Paul's Cathedral is our longest visit. I'm on the steps for over half an hour. I play the renamed 'Ivory Towers' again and again, because they're planning a low-budget video for the single with what they've shot today. They have enough footage of me tuning up the guitar for a Cannes entry – looking for different angles as I strike the tuning fork against the steps and then hold it between my teeth as it sings out. They seem more interested in that than in the song itself. I stand and strum, no more than mouthing the words, looking off along Ludgate Hill. The last time I was here, less than a month ago, the protesters were gathered down to my right, but no trace of them remains. They've all been hosed off the limestone – leaving it pristine for the tourists.

'Could we not… darling,' Innes says to Pierce, 'put up a banner or erect a tent or something – for *aesthetics*.'

'I don't think the police would, erm…' Pierce doesn't look up from checking the sales ranking of the album on his phone '… appreciate it.'

'Such a shame.'

'We could put some stills in the video, though, from the images we took last month. There are tents in those. Protesters too. It might even help to put those photos in beside this footage – show that Rob's the last man standing.'

'Oooh… I like that.'

Instead of playing to the dispossessed, the disenfranchised and the disheartened – as the blurb for my album puts it – I gather a clutch of Japanese tourists. They take photos because there's a larger camera focused on me, they accept the scraps of fabric Innes hands out because they're free, and they clap along because Pierce starts to. Then they all gather around me on the steps and hold up their garlanded wrists.

'Cheese!' one of them screeches into my ear.

Innes gives them all a badge and a postcard with details of how to download the taster. They examine the foreign words – the unknown symbols – with blank expressions. Most of them will put it in the bin; some of them might take it to the Starbucks at the side and try to exchange it for a complimentary coffee.

'Can we move on?' I ask. 'I'm not convinced this is useful.'

'Is there somewhere we can go... lovely,' Innes asks, 'where there are still tents and banners and all those accoutrements.'

There's Finsbury Square, where Flick is, with all its acute-remnants of protest, but the thought of turning up there and handing out rags causes me to tense up. I've avoided it – and her – over the past month. Something, close to shame, makes me turn to Innes and shake my head.

'No,' I say. 'This was it, all there was, and it's gone.'

On the way to our final destination – a converted chapel – we stop at a record store. The album has been under embargo until today, so I want to see it up on the shelves and maybe even sign a copy or two. First I look at the displays at the front of the shop, by the security gates, but have no luck there. Then at the 'New Releases'. There's no sign of it in 'Folk and Country', either, but I finally find two copies by flicking though the Ds in 'Rock and Pop'. I lift one and place it on the stand at the end of the row, in front of some no-hoper who came seventh or eighth in one of those talent shows on the telly. Dozens of copies of her face smile out at me from either side of the single copy of *Measures Taken*.

'You see it in the wild, then?' Pierce asks.

'Only two copies.'

'Strange feeling, isn't it? Feels like you should be able to pick it up and walk away – it's *yours* – but it's not, it's for sale in a shop, y'know?'

'Two copies, Pierce.'

'In that one store, buddy.'

I settle back down into the seat and we drive off. The camera, rolling to catch my reaction as I stepped out of the shop, is lowered. I put my hand in my pocket, feeling for pills. I'll just take one, to take the edge off the disappointment.

'They'll all be going to the wall soon anyway,' I say. 'Who buys CDs these days?'

The venue we're filming at is one of the ones I came to at Christmastime. I bought a ticket on the door for some local nu-folk band – I forget their name. There was no alcohol

132

allowed in the chapel, so I downed a couple of shots of whisky at the bar and then took my pew. All through their set – choral arrangements, double bass for rhythm – I was looking around and behind myself, at the people watching silent and still, and imagining what it would be like when I was up on that stage. My voice soaring, lifting listeners from their rows to dance in the aisles, raising their arms and closing their eyes, until they felt that music was born again.

It isn't like that, though. We arrive in broad daylight and set up in a hall that holds only echoes and stifled sneezes. Even with the addition of the sound and lighting engineers, there are only seven of us. Barely enough to stir the dust in the air.

I'm placed centre-stage – 'feet there, eyes forward' – and asked to play 'Ivory Towers' yet again. My fingers reach for the chords, as usual, I take a breath in all the right places, and each word is heard crisp and clear. But there's no energy to it. There doesn't need to be, because it will be the recorded version they will use. This is just for show, for appearance's sake.

Still, it would be gratifying to have the murmur of appreciation, the feeling of sets of eyes focused on me, breath held as they wait for the next line. The electricity in the room that comes, on my part, from nerves, and on their part from anticipation. And, most of all, the moment, right at the end, when the last chord fades out and applause patters then fills the room. Rather than a second of silence and a single shouted –

– 'Cut!'

GLASGOW

I pass up three opportunities to speak with Ewan before I screw my courage to the sticky subject.

The first is directly after the gig, as Gemma rallies around to congratulate us. That is cut short, though, by a replying text from Cammy to confirm that he has indeed seen me out with Maddie on a Silo-stroll. Zipping up my guitar case with the haste of a gunman on the run, I leave the club and make my way to the rendezvous point at the bus stop around the corner, where Maddie herself is waiting with a kiss and a double-decker getaway vehicle that groans up hills and smells of stale piss.

The second is excruciating. It has been arranged, a week in advance, that Ewan and I will spend our Sunday repainting the back wall of Cesare's café. It's a cash-in-hand job. Cesare wants the wall to be 'mocha'-coloured because he's seen the paint sampler and thinks it might put people in mind of coffee. At the very least, he reckons, it will be a conversation-starter. Not for us, though. We stand in silence, slapping sullenly at the wall with our paintbrushes. Even when Cesare cranks up the bullshit – *I had a trial for Glasgow Celtic, boys; I gave up a career as a stunt man to go travelling in Malaysia; I invented the gingerbread latte, that they all sell at Christmas, yes?* – we don't share so much as a secretive smile, as we normally would, or respond with anything other than a grunt.

The third is at the recording session I won at the showcase, so on the face of it it should be impossible for us not to talk. Ewan sends me a text to confirm the arrangements, though, and when I text him back, to ask if he'll be there, he doesn't answer. There's a sofa outside the live room, where Ewan could hang out, eating the softened crisps they've laid on and smoking a joint or two, but when he does turn up he only stays for long enough to listen through the first track with the sound engineer.

I should go through to speak with them. Especially because I've been having a running discussion with the engineer about the vocals on the chorus. He wants them 'thickened'; I want them raw. So, for the ten minutes Ewan is in the building, I should really get him to question what exactly is happening at the mixing desk. He's still my manager, after all. Instead, I stay in the airless live room and practise the guitar track for the second song.

It's on a Monday, a fortnight and four days after the showcase gig, that I decide I really need to find out whether the hatchet that I've taken to our friendship can be buried. It may be the prospect of double biology that convinces me, more than guilt. Whatever the motivation, I skip class and make my way down to the shoe shop on Byres Road where Ewan works.

The shop is not a trendy one. It sells sturdy shoes with cushioned insoles to pensioners. Ewan is good with the old dears; he doesn't cringe at the sight of a corn-pad or grow tired of explaining that they no longer accept cheques as payment. He's not here today, though. I make my way over to the manager, a middle-aged woman with a mole on her cheek who blinks in surprise at the sight of a youngster in her shop, and ask after him.

'Not in today,' she says. 'Called in sick. Said he's had the flu all weekend.'

'Oh, OK,' I say. 'Called in sick... so, maybe...' Her eyes narrow, and I realise that my arrival might call Ewan's illness into question for her. Conspiring to get him sacked from his job would probably not serve as an effective apology for stealing his girlfriend, so I quickly backtrack. '… it's just, I've not spoken to him in ages… I've been travelling, you see, to Malaysia, and I lost his number… so… but I knew he worked here, so I thought I'd try on the off-chance.'

'Oh. I could give him a ring for you, if you like.'

'No, no.' I smile, and backtrack right out of the shop. 'I'll try later in the week, maybe.'

I know where he'll be. As soon as she said that he'd called in sick, I knew where he was. The same place I, or any of our group of friends, would go.

The woods are different in daylight. You can see where the mud, underfoot, is congealed enough to tiptoe through without sinking, and the littered debris of our drinking makes the foliage look corporate-sponsored, with cans hooked on thorns, crisp packets caught on bushes and plastic bags flapping from tree branches. The train station, just visible through the trees, seems closer because of the echoing announcements and the regular trundle of trains.

Ewan sits on the uprooted tree-trunk. He holds a bottle of cooking sherry. It is half-empty, but he doesn't look drunk. Hollow-eyed and slump-shouldered, he picks at the bark and throws the shavings down to the ground.

'You think she's Yoko, don't you?' I ask, sitting down next to him.

'Get over yourself.'

'What?'

'You're no John fucking Lennon, mate.'

I smile, conceding the point. I'd like to laugh as well, but I'm not sure it would take the venom from his words. He stares at the ground, digs the toe of his trainer in underneath a root, and takes a swig from the sherry.

'Why are you drinking that?' I ask. It's a daft question – the sherry is obviously the only thing he could lay his hands on.

'Listen,' I try, 'we really should talk about this, Ewan.'

'Yeah?'

I nod. 'I know it hurt you, but I waited until the two of you had split up…'

No response.

'… and it doesn't have to change anything between us…'

Nothing.

'… although, Pierce wants to take over as my manager…'

He takes another drink.

'… so maybe you guys could talk and work something out?'

'Do you remember,' he says, 'we used to hang out together all day, around Naseby Park then up around Broomhill? We'd talk about all sorts, Rab. Not girls at that stage, but other shit.'

'And we'd stick football stickers to our shorts before we played,' I say. 'As though that would give us the skills of Giggs or Bergkamp or whoever.'

He nods, but doesn't smile. 'You said to me once, just before we started secondary school, that you'd like to be a pharmacist when you grew up, because you were amazed that moods could be altered, that pain could be taken away, just like that.' He snaps his fingers.

'Right,' I say, although I don't remember saying it. 'But maybe that can be done with music as well.'

'All with one little pill, you said.' Ewan holds up his finger and thumb and pinches the air. 'So I went rooting through my mum's medicine cabinet that night and found her anti-depressants and I thought…' He stops, takes a drink, shrugs. 'I thought you were a fucking soothsayer, y'know.'

'This was all before I started playing the guitar, though.'

'And I thought, maybe he's destined for great things, our Rab. Maybe he can find a cure for my mum – a permanent one – so she'll stop bursting into tears when my dad asks her how her day's been.'

'It was before I started playing the guitar, though, wasn't it?' I repeat.

'Aye.' He looks up at me. 'But I thought the reasoning behind it was great: that you wanted to save others from pain, even if it was only a headache. That was a noble thought for a boy of eleven or whatever age you were…'

If I ever wanted to be anything other than a singer, it has long since been forgotten. Even my exams, this summer, seem pointless. I already have three Highers, from last year, and I see no need for the two more I'm taking now. Pierce will manage me and I will produce album after album, year after year. Other folk can work in pharmacies, cafés, shoe shops – they get their wages and buy my music; the world keeps spinning.

The demo I recorded at the studio is being mastered by a producer Pierce knows, just to tweak the sound a little. Before he sends them out to labels, Pierce wants the tracks to be 'vibrant, *amigo*, with a pulse of anger'. Hopefully the producer has a button for that.

'What do you want me to talk to Pierce Price about?' Ewan asks.

'Well…' I bite at my lip. 'Pierce just wants to make sure that you pass on the management duties fully…'

'You mean he wants to buy me out?'

'Well, we – me and you – don't actually have a contract. So it's more a courtesy, really.'

Ewan shakes his head. 'I don't want your money.'

'I'm not offering you any.'

I want to reach out and take the sherry from him, both to save him from it and because a swallow would do wonders for easing the tension. He shows no sign of relinquishing his grip on the neck of the bottle, though. I stretch out to uproot a sapling instead, to give my hands something to do. Systematically, I strip it of its leaves.

'We can still be friends, Ewan,' I say, 'surely.'

'Rab, I'm not that upset about Maddie. If truth be told, like, she wasn't my – ' He stops, sighs, sips. 'But I still wish you'd come to me, y'know.'

'I would have – ' I say.

'You didn't,' he replies.

We both sit and stare at the ground beneath our feet, flecked with the bark shavings.

'I don't think,' he says, 'you would have made a good pharmacist after all. Because you don't need a pill to ease your pain. You have no concept of brooding on something, letting it eat at you. Letting it affect you, change you. You just forget, you just carry right on… I kind of envy you that.'

I look away, through the trees, towards the commuters gathered on the train platform. I have answers for Ewan – that I'm interested in progressing and succeeding, whereas he doesn't seem to have any drive, any desire whatsoever – but I think it would be unkind to take him on in his current state.

'Will you talk to Pierce if he gives you a call?' I ask.

He nods. 'Of course.'

'And what about Maddie?'

'She won't call,' he says, trying out a smile.

'I mean, are you OK about her and me?'

'It was never about Maddie, Rab.'

I nod, but don't press him further.

The woods in the daylight are different: the patchy grass is trampled smooth in places, there are branches snapped and bowed towards the ground, and the uprooted tree-trunk has been picked bald and bears the burns of countless cigarettes and the carvings of sets of initials. And, even with half a bottle of sherry in him, Ewan doesn't laugh or lash out. There is no anger to him, no temper. Instead, he sits with his hands on his knees and his back hunched. He swallows, sways, and stares at the mud. Then he hawks up some sherry-thick saliva and spits it slowly out so that it trails down, forming one continuous thread between his lips and the ground.

I spend more and more time with Maddie through the Easter holidays. Her mother and father split five years ago, with enough by way of alimony and acrimony that she can tell one she is staying with the other and never be caught out. Her dad shuttles between London and Glasgow for work, so we take over his flat when he is down south. I tell my parents that I am staying with Ewan, knowing that our own split means he won't call to contradict.

The only time we spend apart, really, is the last weekend in March, when Maddie takes a bus down to London to stay with her dad and take part in this anti-cuts, anti-austerity march. She argues that I should be going down too, that this is the equivalent of a massive one-day workshop for my songs. Hundreds of thousands of people all willing to talk to me about contemporary politics and how the government cuts affect them. I tell her that I'd rather get the music down first and worry about honing the lyrics later. That's only part of the reason for staying in Glasgow, though. Truth be told, I'm willing to miss out on the opportunity to ask the government why they're screwing the country if it avoids the prospect of Maddie's dad asking me the same question about his daughter.

Through April, Maddie stresses about revision for her exams. She has covered a wall in colour-coded timetables, charts, fact-sheets and quotations. You can find a detailed diagram of the urinary tract and the poetry of Edwin Morgan side by side, or a list of the devolved powers of the Scottish Parliament and a summary of the Stanislavski system. In the mornings, I sleep late and Maddie rises to add another layer of notes. After lunch, I pluck and fret on the guitar and she pores over past papers. It's only in the late afternoon, by half-three or four o'clock, that she's ready to be distracted. We go back to bed and try to make the walls shake, try to loosen the annotated wallpaper.

It's on a Wednesday, a few weeks after the recording session, that I get the final mix of the demo. I've just run out to the chippy and we're sharing a post-coital cod supper when my laptop chimes to tell me I have a new email. With vinegar-soaked fingers, I open it up. The producer has sent it to Pierce as well as myself, so I'm aware that I'm listening to my pitch for stardom as I play the first track. Maddie shuffles along the sofa towards me, after the opening chords, and folds her greasy fingers into mine. We sit in silence and listen.

Track one is good. The producer has kept the layered vocals on the chorus and added some reverb, so it fills out over the basic chord progression of the guitar. Track two suffers a little by comparison, because the vocals trail off before the harmonica section, but the lyrics sound crisp and clean and *confrontational*. Pierce will be pleased. It's track three, though, that stands out. The song about Maddie. The melody is strong, the vocals throaty, and the lyrics heartfelt.

My first thought is that I'll need to send it straight on to my Uncle Brendan, because you can really hear the hammer-on in the first intro – the pick-and-jab – and the intricate finger-picking on the second. There's also a lick on the third track that's as clean as I've ever heard it. Brendan would appreciate that. But then I start to worry about the lyrics. He's used to political, after all, and I'm not convinced that all the lyrics are *there* yet. It's only a demo; it's not Bragg-worthy yet.

As the last track fades out, Maddie pushes me back against the cushions and reaches a hand down to rub against my crotch. I am fully clothed; she is wearing only a T-shirt and shorts. With a smile, she slides off the sofa and on to her bare knees, lowering her head to give me a blowjob that, at first, has the faint sting and tingle of salt and vinegar.

'You must be proud,' she says afterwards.

'It was you that did all the work really,' I reply, with a grin.

'About the songs, you wanker.' She slaps at my arm. 'They sound great.'

'They do, don't they?' I smile. 'Let's just hope Pierce Price agrees.'

'He will.' Maddie cuddles in against my chest. 'Definitely.'

I reach out a hand for a chip, but they have gone cold. The congealed cod curls in underneath a clump of them. I scrunch

141

the wrapping up, leaving fingerprints against the brown paper, and set it down on the arm of the sofa.

'Will you move to London?' Maddie asks.

I peer down at her. 'What?'

'Now that you have a manager down there,' she says. 'Would you move to London?'

I shrug.

'I'd need a record contract first. But there's no reason why not, I guess.'

She sits up. 'Am I not a reason?'

'Well, I'd take you with me, wouldn't I?' I grin.

She turns away from me, towards the door. Bringing her legs up on to the sofa, she hugs her knees to her chest. Then, with her fingernail, she starts to scrape at the red polish on her toenails. Flecks and flakes of it settle on the sofa cushion.

'Why did that annoy you?' I ask.

The laptop chimes again – another email.

'Maddie? Why did that annoy you?'

I squint at the screen – it's from Pierce Price.

'Answer me.'

I don't lean forward to open the email. I can't, yet. I need to concentrate on Maddie.

'Maddie? All I said was that I'd take you with me. What's wrong with that?'

'You weren't being serious,' she says, into her knees.

'I was.'

'Fuck off, Rab.'

'I *was*.' I reach out a hand and rest it on her shoulder. 'Honestly.'

She half-turns, a frown creasing her forehead. 'What about our exams? And university?'

'They have universities in London, don't they?' I say.

She nods and turns fully. The frown has not disappeared completely, but it has smoothed out a little. Her eyes – those wonderful, wide brown eyes – flick back and forth across my face.

'We've not been seeing each other that long, though.' She bites at her lip. 'And you'll probably have girls tripping over their fake tits for you down in London...'

I lean across to kiss her. 'I only want you, Maddie.'

That convinces her. A smile breaks through. She nods down at the laptop on the table and asks a question with a lift of her eyebrows.

'Email from Pierce,' I reply.

'Are you *serious*? That was quick.'

'It's a brave new age of technology we live in,' I say. 'No more carrier pigeons or – '

'Is it good or bad that it was so quick?' she interrupts. 'Why haven't you opened it?'

'You were upset,' I say. Although, now that she's raised the possibility, I'm also nervous about what it might say. A rejection – polite or impolite, dismissive or encouraging. Nothing is signed yet. I don't want to open it in front of Maddie, don't want to dash her hopes as well as my own. I can't tell her not to look, though, or ask her to leave the room. 'Let me – ' I begin.

'Just tell me what it says.' She screws her eyes shut. 'I can't bear to look.'

I click, I scan it quickly. The words blur.

'It's just what he's looking for,' I say. 'He'd like me to come down to London to discuss it and to finalise the paperwork... he'll send it out to some record companies in the meantime... there's one called Agitate Records that are on the lookout for this sort of thing... and, listen to this, right at the end. *Buckle up*, it says, *buckle the fuck up, buddy*.'

Maddie opens one eye. She studies my grinning face, then opens the other. With a yelp, she jumps at me, rocking me backwards against the arm of the sofa. The remnants of our cod supper fall to the carpet. We both ignore it. Fuck it, we'll be eating caviar from now on.

BRIGHTON

'Let me tell you a story,' Sage says. He sits, perched, on the edge of a table, still wrapped in his blanket. He has been waiting for me to wake, but I have no idea how long he has been sitting there or what the time is. Streaks of grey light angle through the grimy windows to show the lines and sags of his face. He doesn't give me the opportunity to stumble over an apology, launching straight into his story before I've even had time to flush red at the memory of last night.

'My research, at university, was all about the writers buried in Bunhill Fields cemetery up in London: John Bunyan, Daniel Defoe, William Blake. They were all classed as Nonconformists, you see, either because they didn't follow the teachings of the Church of England or because they advocated religious liberty.'

He glances at me, to check that I'm listening.

I nod.

'The idea was to investigate this form of social activism – of dissent – and how it came across in their writings. So, I was seen as the go-to guy in the department for any discussion of literature that could be called *political*. I was only a doctoral student, but the undergraduates came to me if they were having trouble understanding Orwell or if they wanted a bit more Marxist theory. And there was one Masters student, maybe five or so years older than most, who came to see me for dissertation advice.'

Sage clears his throat, the sound crackles through the silent pub like static. His purplish tongue pokes out from his mouth and moistens his lips and the lower fringes of his beard. I don't hurry him, or make any sound beyond my shallow breathing. This is going to be a confession – perhaps even a coming out – and I don't want to so much as unsettle the air between us.

'Emma Scribbens,' he says, as if carefully pronouncing the name of a disease whose potency should be both feared and admired. 'Emma, that was her name. This bright young woman doing research on political theatre, on verbatim theatre specifically – have you heard of it?'

I shake my head, but I'm not sure whether Sage notices, or is interested. He stares intently at the far wall.

'Verbatim theatre is interesting, worthy of study. You take interviews and found material – newspaper articles and television pieces, maybe – and you structure it all into a play. It's like a documentary, but the staging and the *presentation* of events is all-important. It's a really interesting concept, as I say, and Emma… Emma was fascinating.'

Sage closes his eyes and goes silent. For several long moments he holds his breath, before letting it out as a sigh. When he speaks again, his words are weighty, spoken slowly and softly as though dredged from his memory.

'She had this long red hair. Proper fiery red, so that it caught the gleam of sunlight. And her eyes were pale grey, but they had a glint as well when she spoke of the theatre. So, looking at her, there was something… something… *elemental* about her.

'We spoke for hours about the power of the theatre, and about all the plays that were being put on at the time – that summer – about the financial crisis and the London riots – how it was the theatre that was able to give an *immediate* response. And there, in my office, with the dead debris of my research around us – books and articles and drafts of useless chapters – it felt as if we were discussing something *vital*, something that could change the world, or at least a corner of it.

'Suddenly my own work – Blake, mostly – seemed archaic, hopelessly out-of-date and out-of-touch. Here we were in central London, with the Occupy protesters setting up camp just round the corner from the dissenters' graveyard, and I'm looking at those who're dead and buried rather than those actually *participating*. Students were talking to me about tuition fees rising and I was answering by quoting poems from *Songs of Innocence and of Experience*. It all seemed like studying the atom rather than the splitting of it...'

He pauses, shakes his head, draws in a breath.

'Maybe that analogy doesn't work, but it seemed laughable to look at these long-dead writers when there was history happening outside the office window. And Emma, she was my connection to all that. She was so *engaged* with it, Rab. Not because she was a ringleader or because she'd chain herself to railings or lie down across the street in the way of traffic, but because she knew the arguments and *understood*. She'd been on the anti-cuts marches, had campaigned for that financial transaction tax on the banks – the one they called the "Robin Hood" tax – had supported the strikes and the student protests.

'Every teacher has crushes, you know, just as every student has crushes. And I was infatuated with Emma, entirely. All through that term, as she worked towards completing her dissertation, I devoted myself to our discussions, to finding her obscure sources in the British Library and helping her transcribe the interviews she'd conducted at the Occupy camp. Then, when she handed it in, I felt this hollow anti-climax, this numbness at realising that I didn't want her to hand it in, that I wanted her to keep working, keep researching, keep visiting, and...'

Sage sags forward, his elbows against his knees and his head propped up by his hands. I draw my feet up towards my chest, to leave some of the bench empty. Without looking at me, he levers himself down on to the cushions and leans back until his head rests against the wood. He stares, unseeing, at the ceiling.

'That evening,' he says, 'she showed up at the office, offering to buy me a drink by way of thanks. Of course – *of course* – I said yes, and we got the Tube to a pub near her house and shared a bottle of wine. Only it wasn't the same as the chats we'd shared in the office, because there was no *urgency* to our words. And, when I walked her home afterwards, I had this dread, this horrible anticipation, about what would happen next.

'So, we reached her door and she grasped for my hand. And she thanked me for all my help, you know, and her grip on my hand got tighter and... and then her left hand started plucking at my shirt until I bowed my head down towards hers. And, all the while, her eyes are on mine. These grey eyes that are electric with imagination and intelligence...'

He pauses. I am fully upright, fully awake, waiting for him to finish.

'And I told her "no". Just that one word,' he says.

'But why?' I ask, breaking my silence.

'Because...' His eyes are on me now, an intense gaze. It is the first time he's done more than glance at me in all the time he has been speaking. 'Because it would have been selfish of me. She was too beautiful and brilliant, too young, and too ready to believe that I knew more than I did, that I held more answers than I did. She was trying to recapture the intimacy of those months in the only way she knew.'

'How much younger was she?'

'Than me?' Sage shrugs. 'Maybe ten years, no more than that.'

'And did you explain it to her?'

He shakes his head. 'Not really, no.'

'You just refused her?'

'For her sake,' he says, still staring directly at me, 'as well as for my own. I didn't want to tarnish what we had shared,

147

didn't want the meeting of minds to be no more than foreplay or for our friendship to be based on less than it was, so that there would always be the question – *always* – of whether it was all just building, or built, towards that point... We're all too eager to mistake intimacy, any intimacy, for sexual feeling.'

Sage's eyes hold an electricity of their own. It takes me a moment to work up the courage to meet his gaze, to hold it. There is pain there, and also this desperate need – as if the question he is about to ask is the most difficult, most vital question of his life.

'Do you understand, Rab?' he asks.

'Yes,' I say. 'I think I do.'

Several hours pass before we speak again. In the meantime, I've dozed on the bench and Sage has ventured out with the last of our money to get provisions. As the grey early-morning light turns golden, he stands at the bar and rattle-boils water on the stove.

'Tea?' he asks, holding up a tin can.

'What's that?'

'I raided next door's recycling. This one was beans; the other was soup.'

'Tea would be nice, thanks.'

He nods and sets about pouring. His movements are hunched and hurried, with the wild wisps of his newly clean beard and the trailing cuffs of his once-white shirt giving him the look of a mad scientist at work. The concoction he hands me, though, is definitely tea – hot, milky and sweetened by sugar.

'Now,' he says, 'how about some breakfast?'

It's my stomach that answers, with a rising groan that sounds like a question.

'Porridge,' Sage replies. 'The food of your forefathers, Rab. It's cheap, it's nutritious and, with a bit of milk and sugar added, it's just about bearable.'

'OK.' I smile as a memory comes back to me from childhood. I'm unsure how to bring it up; it's only rarely that I volunteer information about the past. 'Let me…' I start. 'My granny… she lived up in St Margaret's Hope, on the Orkney Islands… and she used to have a drawer, in a wooden chest of drawers, that was lined with greaseproof paper and then filled with porridge oats. Cooked, covered with treacle. When we visited, she would open the drawer and cut me a slice. And once the drawer was empty she'd just refill it and leave it to set.'

'Like flapjack,' Sage says.

'And my mum always tells the story that, after one of our trips north to see her, I came back and pulled the clothes out of all the closets, wardrobes and drawers in my parents' room because I was looking for – '

' – the flapjack,' Sage finishes the sentence.

'Exactly.' I nod. 'So this brings back some memories for me.'

Sage looks at me over the ice-bucket, through the steam, and smiles. He is using the broken hand-whisk from beneath the bar to stir the oats. From time to time he adds a splash of milk from the carton beside him.

'Sage?' I say, softly.

'Yes?'

'Is she the reason you left the university?'

'Who?'

'Emma Scribbles.'

'Scribbens,' he corrects me. He sets down the whisk and lets out a sigh. The steam disperses and I see his face clearly as he shakes his head. His eyebrows hang low, shadowing his eyes. 'It wasn't her, no. I just ran out of funding, pure and simple. At the end of my three years, I ran out of money.'

'Did you not have a contract, though?'

'I had a three-year contract,' he says. 'But it was based on me finishing my research within the three years and… well, I didn't, and they didn't offer me anything or help me out in any way… so I had no way, really, to continue.'

'So what about all the work you'd done over the three years?'

He shakes his head. 'I had drafts and bits and pieces completed, but... well, basically, they found out that I was sleeping in the office, that I was washing in the staff toilet, that I was sneaking sandwiches from the catering trolleys left in the hallways, and...'

'Could you not finish now, then?' I ask. 'Do you still have the research? Could you not find a computer in the library and do some work on it?'

'Stir this,' Sage holds out the whisk.

I rise, in boxers and blanket, and shuffle over to the bar. The porridge looks done; it is thick, and it rises and falls as if breathing. Every couple of seconds the surface breaks into a glugging bubble. Quietly, as Sage roots through his rucksack, I lift the pan from the heat and turn the gas off.

'This,' Sage says, 'is the culmination of three years of research. This is all of it.'

He hands me a CD. It has no case and the surface of it is scratched and worn. A single word – *THESIS* – is inked across the front of it in red. At best, it is damaged; at worst, unrecoverable. I decide not to tell him that.

'Would you like to work on it again?' I ask, instead.

He considers. 'I'd like to rework it, Rab. I'd like to take all of the research I did on Blake, and all of the research that I did for Emma, and join the dots between them. I'd like to use the past to shed light on the present, maybe.'

'Well, why don't you?'

'To tell the truth, what I'd most like to do is to read again. For pleasure.'

'I thought you loved teaching as well?'

'I do.' He smiles, gently. 'But nothing I have to say is worth what the students are being asked to pay for it. My wages, as a teaching assistant, were only a grand more than a year's tuition. For one student. And I was teaching fifteen or twenty of them per tutorial, seven or eight tutorials a week.

Universities are businesses, pure and simple, and those who're successful within them are businessmen and businesswomen. Let me tell you a story – '

'Why not do what you suggested, then?' I interrupt.

'What was that?'

'Open this place up for some lectures – free ones.'

Sage nods. 'It would be nice to have some conversation. Just people sitting around and chatting about things. That's all I need, Rab, to keep me going.'

'We could invite Luke, maybe,' I say. 'And Flick.'

Sage takes my tea tin from me and pours the dregs down the drain. Then, using the broken whisk, he scoops some porridge into the tin. There is no spoon, so I tip it towards my mouth and use my fingers.

The porridge is hot and sweet. I have to force myself not to gulp and slurp at it. To slow down and savour the fact that we have time to spend over meals now.

'Well, now that we've spent the night,' I say, 'don't you reckon we should give the place a name? A pub deserves that.'

'Absolutely,' Sage beams. He has porridge clumped, like a skin condition, in his moustache. 'What was it called before?'

'Don't know. They've taken the sign down.'

'What were you thinking, then?'

'Sage and Onion, maybe.'

'You being the onion?'

'Aye.' I smile. 'Because I smell like a field.'

'And you bring tears to many an eye.'

'That'll be the smell, too.'

He chuckles, then raises his porridge tin again. His fingers dislodge most of the moustache-meal as well.

'In my student days,' he says, 'my undergraduate days, that is, I would have named it something horribly, horrifically Marxist. Something properly left-wing, you know? The Trotsky, or On the Side of the Engels, or something…'

'Aren't you still a Marxist?' I ask.

He shrugs. 'Is anyone? It's too complicated, maybe, with the way the world's changed, to call yourself a Marxist and not find yourself handed all the baggage of Stalinist Russia and Maoist China. But the central idea... it still resonates: "from each according to his ability, to each..."'

'What else could you have called it?'

'"... according to his need",' he says softly, then, 'What's that, Rab?'

'What other names could you have called your Marxist pub?'

'I don't know,' he considers. 'The Hammer and Sickle, maybe, something like that. Keep it nice and simple.'

'Maybe we could call it The Sick Little Hammer, then?' I suggest. 'Since you're not a Marxist any more.'

'That's good, that,' he says. 'A fitting pub for modern-day Britain, maybe.'

'To The Sick Little Hammer,' I raise my tin.

'And her swift recovery,' Sage hits my tin with his own, producing a dull *clank* that doesn't ring or echo.

LONDON

I sit in the outer office and shred a leaf between my fingers. The plant it came from is beside my chair. It might be plastic, might not. That's why I'm tearing it apart: to investigate. That's also why I poured the last of my latte into the pot beneath: to see if the plant would wither and die from the caffeine.

Over the past hour or so I've smoked two joints, one on the walk to the Tube, the other by the bins at the side of the building that houses the label. They dulled the nerves about what Bower would say. What can he do, after all? What can any of us do? It's only another bad review – bad reviews – so all we need is a good review or two and some decent sales. Simple.

'Ready, Rob?' Pierce has arrived. He steps in the coffee dribbling out from the base of the plant pot and his eyebrow lifts to his creased forehead. 'Why is the carpet all wet?'

'Do you think the plant is real, Pierce?'

'I don't know – does it matter?'

I shrug and let the scraps of leaf fall to the ground.

'Now,' Pierce says, 'let me do the talking, OK?'

I try to suppress a smile, because it sounds like a line from a film. Not a good one. This is serious, though, I know – so I manage a nod and I rise to follow him to the wooden door. He knocks, and we wait until Bower's deep voice calls out, 'Enter.'

'Thanks for coming in,' Bower says, stretching his bulk across the table to grip at Pierce's hand, then my own. 'Not a crisis meeting, understand, just strategy.'

I've never been in his office before. It is oak-panelled like a headmaster's study, but with photographs and framed cover art on the walls in place of bookshelves. It's not these that draw my attention, though, or the view out over north London; it's the potted plants on either side of the desk, with dark green leaves that have that same sheen as the plant in the hallway outside.

'Pierce,' Bower begins, after we've taken a seat, 'I imagine you've seen the download figures I sent through?'

'Yes.' Pierce nods eagerly. His glasses slip down his nose. 'Not good, I know.'

'Not great, no.'

'That's only digital sales, though, so...'

Bower holds up a hand, to stop Pierce. 'I've also had an email from that *Guardian* journalist who did that profile down at St Paul's,' he says. 'With the proof copy of the article attached.'

'Any good?'

'Let me read you a snippet...'

Bower reaches across to click at his mouse and clack at his keyboard. Monkey with a typewriter, I think, but I say nothing. He finds what he is looking for and clears his throat.

'"This is a young musician full of failed promise and empty rhetoric... he is arrogant enough to presume to speak for everyone present, whether they want him to or not."'

'Yes.' Pierce tries out a grin. 'There seems to be a bit of resistance, y'know? A bit of protest about the idea of a protest album, because it's not...' he lifts his hands to bunny-rabbit quotation marks '..."*safe*".'

'It was never supposed to be safe,' Bower replies. 'We've done this type of topical record with urban music and made it work. It doesn't need to be safe, but it needs to be half-decent.

It needs to appeal to a specific demographic, a particular market.'

'I'm confident,' Pierce says, with a wavering tone that undermines his words, 'that we will appeal to that market, definitely, if we are patient and rely on word-of-mouth and social media, maybe.'

'Maybe,' Bower says. 'But there'll be a bit of damage limitation in the short term.'

'Meaning what?'

'I'll call the journalist and try to get her not to run this piece, or at least not all of it, and our publicist will try to lift one or two positive quotes from the rest of it.'

He pauses and looks directly at me.

'But it's looking like saving the sweetcorn from a steaming shit, at this stage.'

Pierce shifts in his seat. This time he accompanies his grin with a nervous giggle, but Bower meets both with an impassive stare. There's talk, then, of the co-headline tour being 'under review' and the release of a second single being delayed until they see how 'Ivory Towers' does with radio play and downloads over the next month or so. The single needs to do well to support the album, and the album needs to support the single. They want me to bend over backwards while standing up straight, basically.

'We'll be limiting our exposure to it,' Bower says. 'That's the bottom line.'

'What does that mean?'

'We'll scale back the ad campaign,' Bower says. 'And – '

'Just until this blows over, though, right?' Pierce asks.

Bower nods. 'Sure.'

'And what can we do to help it blow over?' Pierce leans forward.

'Find something positive to highlight and get on social media to build up a following.' Bower shrugs. 'And, I don't know, play some gigs, I guess. That's always a good plan for a singer-songwriter.'

I think back to those weeks over Christmas when I went from venue to venue, cap in hand, asking for gigs. I could do that again, of course, but there's something vaguely indecent about doing it when you're an established artist. Isn't there? Like the Queen having to ask for a visitor's pass to Buckingham Palace.

'Is there a – well, any sort of a…' Pierce hesitates '… budget for that?'

'From this end?'

Pierce nods, but also holds up his hand as if to apologise for the question.

'The pot is empty from this end. I suggest you use the advance.'

The room falls to silence. I sit back and watch Pierce squirming in his seat, as if he's trying an escapology act – trying to raise an objection without any direct confrontation.

'I've got a question,' I say.

'Yes, Rab?' Bower turns to me.

I want to ask about the plants, obviously, but there's also another question which has emerged from the fug and falsehood of the last ten minutes. It is such a basic question, so fundamental, that I have to think carefully about how to word it.

'Well,' I say, 'have you listened to it?'

'The album?'

I nod.

'Bits and pieces of it, yes,' he says.

'But not all the way through?'

Bower pauses. 'I don't need to.'

When the silence returns, I softly chuckle through it. It is a dry laugh, from the throat. It marks my victory over Bower, over the music executive who didn't even bother listening to his latest release. All those journalists, the reviewers and the bloggers, are probably exactly the same – they looked at the cover and they read the press release and then they *decided*. It is a hollow victory, but it's a victory nonetheless, because it means that I can lift a stiff middle finger to the industry and wait, just wait, for the general public to make up their own minds. The success I have will be grass-roots and organic; it will be busker-to-billboard rather than manufactured pop.

It's only been a month since the album was released, anyway. There's plenty of time to win people around, to find folk who'll actually *listen* to the lyrics. I just need to take the music to the people, right? Travel the country by rail the way Woody Guthrie did in dustbowl America. If only the trains weren't so fucking expensive.

'Second question, then,' I say. 'What's the deal with these pot plants?'

'It's my house; I can wear what I want!'

'But it's misleading, you must admit.'

'Misleading?'

'Well, it's all shiny and silky.'

'So I *misled* you with fabric, then?'

'No – well – '

She draws in a breath. 'It's a dressing gown.'

'Yes, but – '

'And let's get this straight: even if it was a leather corset and stockings, even if I had chains hanging from my nipples, I'd still have every right to wear it in the *privacy* of my own house.'

This is not going well. Lydia is breathing heavily, granted, but it's not from desire. I blame the sleeping tablets I popped last night, washed down with a solitary glass of wine. I'm rested, I'm alert. There were no twitchy fingers as I placed my hand on her thigh and slid it upwards, no doubt in my smile as her eyes met mine. All was going to plan until I noticed that her jaw was open wide enough to dislocate and that the panties I was inching my fingers up towards were not high-end lingerie but plain white cotton. She slapped at my hand, then at my cheek. The sting from the second slap was what caused me to accuse her of leading me on.

'Maybe I picked up the wrong signal, then,' I say.

'Damn right you did, you…' she searches for the right insult '… scrotum of a boy.'

'No harm done, though, right?'

'You're just a horny teenager, aren't you?'

'I didn't mean – '

'I teach every evening, and I sit and translate shitty romance novels all day, just to scrape enough money together.' She draws her robe tightly across her chest. It causes the hem of it to ride further up, but I don't think it's the moment to be pointing that out. 'So if I want to sit for an hour or so in the mornings, over my coffee, in my *pyjamas*, then that seems perfectly acceptable to me – '

'Absolutely, I – '

'I have that right, surely. And I have the right not to be sexually assaulted by whichever fucking street performer my husband's decided to bring home this month.'

'Come on, that's a bit strong.'

Her eyes flash and her cheeks flush. This needs defusing, I realise; this needs careful handling or I'll end up kicked to the kerb. The mattress in Pierce's front room may be more floorboard than air, but there's a roof over my head and free food and drink in that scavenging hour between Lydia going off to her classes and Pierce coming home. I can't lose that.

'So you're a translator, then?' I ask, in a conciliatory tone. 'I didn't realise.'

'And it never crossed your mind to ask, Rab?' she replies. 'No?'

I stay silent.

'You didn't ask because you don't give a fuck,' she says. 'You thought I was just a mannequin, sealed in silk for your after-cornflakes shag, didn't you?'

'No – '

'You lie there every morning disturbing my early-morning routine, clearing your throat every few seconds and making my front room smell like a back-room brewery, and I tolerate it because my husband's got so much invested in your shitty little career, but all the while – '

'It was only a question,' I mutter.

'Yes, I translate. Italian into English. And I teach. Italian. My mother was from Bologna.'

I nod. I wish I could reply in Italian, just some short phrase to ease the tension, but I did French at school. Short of watching the Italian football on a Sunday afternoon when I was a boy, I've got nothing. Maldini, I think, Baggio, Batistuta – fuck, he's Argentine – Del Piero.

Instead of reciting the names of footballers, I try another apology.

'I'm sorry,' I say. 'Really, Lydia, I just…'

She has folded her arms and crossed her legs. She sits angled away from me, squinting sideways at the muted tabloid talk show on the telly.

'… I've only ever had one proper girlfriend, and she broke my heart. That sounds like a crap cliché, I know, but she did. And, after her, I've only slept with one other girl and she, well, doesn't think much of me at all.'

'Was this up in Glasgow?'

'The girlfriend was. The other girl was down here.'

She nods; she looks across at me. She's not melted, but there's a crack in the ice. I keep talking, both because it feels good to speak openly and because I need to convince Lydia not to tell Pierce about this faux-fumble-pas.

'The Glaswegian girlfriend,' I say, 'was supposed to come down here with me. We would have had a set-up like you and Pierce. Us against the world. She was planning on working in a café or something, just while I got established in the music industry, and then I'd support her though her university studies.'

'And what happened?' Lydia looks at the telly, then back at me.

'She…' I falter. 'She bailed. There were reasons for it, on her part, but she bailed.'

159

'Mitigating circumstances,' Lydia says, softly.

I look across at her. 'So, I know I'm not the best with gir– with women – but it's because I'd worked out this version of my life, this settled version, where I only ever needed one girl to like me, where the rest of the world could do as it pleased. And it didn't work out.'

She nods, unfolds her arms. For a moment I think she's going to reach out to touch my arm, but she holds back. 'It's tough, I know, but you're only a young boy, really. Patience is all you need, you'll see.'

'Maybe you're right,' I say. 'But I sometimes make bad decisions, is all…'

I stare across at the sunlight angling in at the window, so that I don't have to meet her eye. I don't want to tot up the misjudgements or the times I've strained at the leash until it snaps, because the scorecard – this morning, in this light – might cause the embarrassment of the situation to slip towards shame.

'What you and Pierce have…' I begin. 'It's important, isn't it, to have someone to draw you out of your worries, drag you out of your own thoughts, towards, er, reality – '

'Some perspective.' She nods.

'Pierce is always positive.'

'Yes.'

'I envy him that.' I pause. 'And I think a lot of that's down to you.'

'I'm more than a scrap of silk, certainly.'

'Agreed.'

We share a smile, but it's still a little forced on her part. Taking a breath, I decide to test the limits of our new-found understanding.

'Lydia,' I say. 'Can I ask you a favour?'

She raises an eyebrow.

'Please don't tell Pierce about this.' I pause. 'I'll get my act together and leave you two in peace soon, once sales pick up, but it's really difficult for me right now.'

'You're lucky I'm not telling the police, Rab, never mind Pierce.'

She looks back across at the talk-show on the telly. A paternity DNA test is being slid from an envelope... the phrase *Is he the father?* scrolls along the bottom of the screen. The presenter says something and the potential dad jumps from his seat and starts dancing in celebration. Without the sound, it's impossible to tell whether he's happy because he's gained a child or because he's lost one.

'You're on notice,' Lydia says, softly. 'Best behaviour from now on, OK?'

GLASGOW

My father dated my mother for twelve years before he finally got around to asking for her hand. By that time, she'd developed a habit of clicking her tongue against the roof of her mouth – a tic of her biological clock – as if to remind him that time was running out on her dream of having a big family. She was thirty-seven when she had me and, according to my Uncle Brendan, forty-one when she accepted that I would be an only child. The tutting stuck, though, as a continual prompt for a question that came a decade or so too late.

Marriage probably just slipped my dad's mind. Since his early twenties he's been a collector of anatomical oddities, both professionally and privately, so it's more than likely that it was just distraction as he set up the display of surgical instruments, or absent-mindedness as he labelled the bell-jars of aborted fallow deer. If Mum had just asked him, I would be eight or nine years older and surrounded by siblings. Instead, she clung to the traditions of her Presbyterian upbringing even in the absence of any religious conviction: the man must ask.

Uncle Brendan told me all this two years ago at the whisky-soaked wedding of my cousin Gerard, his own son, and I tell it all to Maddie on the walk from her dad's flat to dinner with my parents. It will explain the drift to Dad's sentences, and the noises from Mum that bring him back on topic. It will lessen her shock at the detailed anatomical sketches on the walls of the dining room and prepare her for Mum's ability to studiously avoid phrasing any attempt at conversation as a question.

We begin with prosciutto-wrapped melon pieces and a short, polite tut-tut from Mum. It only lasts a second and could slip, unnoticed, between sentences. At the sound of it, Dad stops folding and unfolding the corner of his napkin and looks across at Maddie.

'So, Madeline,' he says, 'you've just finished your exams as well, I take it? As well as Robert, that is.'

She nods, smiles. It never occurred to me that her name must be Madeline, that Maddie is a shortening. Maybe it never dawned on her that my name was Robert either. I bloody well hope not, anyway. Dad is the only one who uses my full name.

'Maddie is a year behind me,' I say. 'But she did five subjects this year.'

'I would imagine,' Mum says, 'that Maddie is applying to university and that she could tell us all about the wonderful things she's going to learn and the wonderful career she's going to have.'

We all look at Maddie. She wears an olive-green summer dress, with a black shawl over her shoulders. The gold necklace that I gave her for her seventeenth birthday, a fortnight ago, hangs around her neck. The treble-clef pendant rests in the shallow at the base of her neck.

'I'm hoping to go to university, yes,' Maddie says, answering the unasked question rather than the asked one. 'I've applied to a couple up here and a couple down in London. To do theatre studies.'

'There must be a difference between that and drama, otherwise they wouldn't bother calling them different things,' Mum says. 'There must be a difference.'

'Theatre studies is more academic maybe, focused on the history and the theory of it all,' Maddie says. 'Whereas drama is more practical. The two are close, though, you're right.'

163

Dad is concentrating on furrowing his melon rind with the edge of his spoon. He is thinking, no doubt, of the book on anatomists he is currently researching. Either that, or visitor numbers for the past year. The tongue-tut from Mum is louder this time. The spoon is laid to the side.

'Are you musical, Madeline?' he asks.

It is the wrong question. A short, sharp tut cuts over the top of it.

'London will be a good city for theatre, anyway,' Mum says. 'Much better than Glasgow, I'd imagine. For both of you. Theatre and music.'

Maddie nods. 'It's a bit more expensive in terms of tuition fees and cost of living, and I'll need to do well in my exams because I only have a conditional offer – '

'The newspaper says,' Mum interrupts, 'that the tuition fees are going up.'

'That's right. For England, at least. But that's for students beginning next year, so I'm getting in just before it rises, hopefully. Unless I need to stay and do a sixth year at school to get enough qualifications.'

Mum stands, abruptly, and begins to stack the plates. The clash and clatter of crockery covers the noise she makes while she tidies. It is like an attempt at Morse code – *short, short, long*. An irregular rhythm.

'Your spoons are very beautiful, Mrs Dillon,' Maddie says, nodding up at the display case of silver on the wall. 'Gorgeous.'

'Thank you.' Mum sets down the plates and moves over to the wall. 'They're mostly silver-plated, but there are some interesting ones up here.'

She plucks five from the rack that holds them and spreads them out on the table in front of Maddie as though setting the place for a quintet of desserts.

'The first one that got me interested was this simple Victorian teaspoon, which was mixed in with a batch of vicious-looking surgical instruments that Douglas, Rab's father, picked up at some auction or other.' She smiles across at her husband, but he doesn't seem to be listening. 'It was the only object I could recognise among all the blades and gougers and – '

'She was taking the edge off my dad's collection,' I try, but nobody laughs.

'And this one,' my mum continues, 'is double-struck, you see, with the design on the front and the back.'

'Ah, it's lovely,' Maddie reaches a hand towards it but stops short of touching.

'Then we have salt spoons. And this,' Mum lifts one, 'is a moustache spoon, with a guard on one side to protect the moustaches of Victorian gentlemen as they sup their soup. Isn't that ingenious?'

As if suddenly aware that she might be boring Maddie, she gathers the spoons into the palm of her hand and slots them into position in their display case. Then she goes back to the task of clearing away the starter, her tongue clicking away at the roof of her mouth.

I turn to Maddie, to check that she's surviving, and slip a hand beneath the table to grasp at her knee and give it a squeeze. The noise from my mum gets louder. Maddie flinches and tries to brush my hand away, but I keep it where it is and nod across towards Dad. The tut-tut is a prompt for him.

'And your contract's all sorted, is it, Robert?' he asks, looking up on cue.

As she walks to the kitchen, Mum lets it be known that she disapproves of the question. This tut is designed to carry. She's busy getting the lamb cutlets out of the oven, though, so I take the opportunity to answer Dad. It'll give Maddie a break, at least.

'Signed and sealed,' I say. 'The first album will be released early next year.'

'It's an exciting time.' Maddie grins.

The recording contract is for the first album, with an option for a second. It took a bit of back-and-forth to agree the production budget and whatnot, because Pierce was assuming that the major label, the parent company, would be footing the bill but then the imprint, Agitate, kept on pleading poverty. What do I care about details like that, though? Let my manager handle that and sort out things like the publishing rights. If there are creases, he's the one to iron them out.

'As soon as we move down I can start in the studio,' I say. 'Try to get the whole thing recorded in the next few months, before the turn of the year, and then...'

'Take on the world,' Maddie finishes my sentence.

Dad stares at the gravy boat that Mum sets on the table, as if wondering what it could possibly be for. It was probably a wedding present, but he's not noticed it properly these past nineteen years.

'Pierce says that the advance will be enough to put us up in a hotel for the first while, with a small weekly allowance, but then we should start looking for somewhere more permanent. Not to buy, necessarily, until the royalties and that really begin coming in, but just somewhere more settled.'

There's a meeting scheduled with an accountant. The idea is to set up a business account for the advance and then work out an allowance – a *per diem* – from that. Like pocket money. I asked Pierce what was stopping me from taking a hammer to the piggy bank and spending the lot of it and he just shrugged. Nothing, he said. Other than the fact that, once Pierce has taken his cut and all the bills, food, and accommodation are factored in, there'll barely be enough for a piggy bank, never mind a hammer.

'It sounds like a lot of expense, I would say,' Mum says, bringing the potatoes through. 'It must be, to keep two people fed and watered in London.'

'I'll get some sort of job,' Maddie says. 'As well as my student loan – '

'Just in the meantime,' I cut in. 'Until the album hits the shops.'

As she hands Maddie the carrots, Mum's tongue tuts again.

'Will you have enough money, the two of you?' Dad asks.

I stay silent, because we've just answered that. There is no noise from Mum, though, so it must be the correct question. I spoon out some mint jelly and look at Maddie. 'The record company puts up all the start-up costs. For production and marketing and whatever else,' I say. 'Until the sales come through.'

'Those must be two of the least secure professions imaginable,' Mum says. 'A musician and an actress. Truly, there are probably statistics to prove it if you knew which expert to ask.'

'Maddie doesn't necessarily want to act,' I reply. 'Maybe just direct or work in the theatre in some other way. As long as she's involved, y'know, then it'll be worthwhile. And, in case you've forgotten, I've already got a contract. It's *secured*.'

I wave my hand in the air, swinging an invisible contract from side to side. Dad, catching sight of it from across the table, blinks and looks down at his plate.

'This is lamb, then, is it?' he asks.

We lie on the bed in my attic room and stare at the shard of moon visible through the skylight. My jean-clad leg is folded over Maddie's bare legs, but I make no moves beyond that.

'I see what you mean about your mum's clucking noises,' she says. 'She's very beautiful for her age, though. You didn't tell me that. Especially when she was animated – taking about her spoons.'

I frown, consider. My mum is in her mid-fifties, at the stage where her brown hair is beginning to thin and thread itself with grey. I've never thought of her as anything other than my mother, never had occasion to switch to thinking of her as Hannah Dillon.

'You think so?' I say. 'It's not something I've ever – '

'She's got your green eyes,' Maddie says. 'Or you've got hers, maybe.'

Music plays softly from my laptop. It was Patti Smith, but now it's shuffled on to some soppy shite that Maddie must've downloaded. If she hadn't just turned to nestle against me, her head on my shoulder, I'd get up to change it.

'Can I ask you, Rab…' she begins.

'Yes.'

'Are you worried about moving to England?'

I try to crane my neck around to kiss her on the forehead, but can only brush across her temple. Strands of her blonde hair catch and trail against my lips. They smell of macadamia shampoo but taste of nothing. 'No,' I say. 'We'll be fine.'

'Not because of us, though.' She bites at her nails. The sound and shudder of it, next to my ear, is like the crack and rumble of thunder. 'Because you're a Scottish singer, right? But if you go down there then you lose that a little bit. If you write about Glasgow, you'll be accused of no longer living here, and if you write about London then you'll be called an outsider.'

I shrug. It stops her nail-biting.

'And,' she says, 'Pierce wants you to sing about politics, doesn't he? But is that *Scottish* politics, or *English* politics, or *UK* politics, or what?'

'What's the difference?'

'Are you serious?'

Her legs disentangle themselves from mine and her head lifts from my shoulder. She sits up and crosses her legs beneath her on the mattress. I take the opportunity to flip on to my front and dangle off the side of the bed so that I can scroll through the music.

'They're all Conservatives down there, Rab. Maybe not in London, not fully, but in the countryside all around it. Surrey and Sussex and Suffolk and…' She pauses. 'Whereas up here we're lefty-leaning. You know how many Tory MPs there are in Scotland?'

I shake my head, settle for Belle and Sebastian and push myself back up on to the bed. I'm curled in against Maddie now, with my head in her lap. She strokes at my hair.

'One,' she says. 'There's only one, right down in the Borders.'

'Are you a closet Nationalist, then?' I ask.

'It depends.' She stops stroking. 'If it's about identity or patriotism, about whether I *feel* Scottish or British, then I don't care. Not at all. But if it's about a value system, if it's about whether I'd rather have a welfare state and a public-funded NHS and tuition provision for students, and if an independent Scotland can provide that, then I'll proudly call myself Scottish, yes.'

'You mean aye.'

'What?'

'You said yes; you meant aye.'

Maddie was too young to vote in the Scottish Parliament elections at the start of the month, but she took part in all the social media twittering about it and she seems to have convinced herself – along with the majority – into supporting the Scottish Nationalist Party. Her opinions tend to be a hundred and forty characters long.

Her face flickers into a frown. I smile and reach a hand up to cradle her cheek, but she leans away from it.

'There are plenty of folk down south who aren't in any way right-wing,' I say. 'Plenty of them even protest about the government cuts, like that march you went to, so – '

'But there's a mandate.' Maddie is still frowning.

I don't know what the word means, not fully, so I settle for nodding.

'They can cut those things because enough of the country supports or can be convinced to support them,' Maddie continues. 'Whereas a Scottish government doesn't have public support for any of it, even if they wanted to. And independence would give us a chance to build, maybe, to dream – '

'There needs to be money for all those things, though.'

'Absolutely. But it seems like the independence debate is all about national fucking pride, rather than just a discussion about how we could go about affording all those things. Building a Scottish state that truly represents the values of the Scottish people. On the Scandinavian model, maybe.'

'How do we pay for it?' I repeat.

'North Sea oil,' she says.

'Would we not just be in the pocket of the oil companies, then?'

'That would be the challenge, granted: keeping their influence out of the politics, even though we need their money. Especially because green energy's so important to the economy as well.'

'And what about all those people, down south, who don't want the Tories?'

'Newcastle can join us, if it likes. Wales too.'

'Not Manchester, though?'

Some of the anger seems to have seeped out of her. She twists my hair through her fingers and gently – from her throat – hums along to 'The State I Am In'.

'What's all this got to do with *us* moving to London, though?' I ask.

'Because…' she tugs at my fringe '… I don't want you to lose your *decency*, Rab. Like, if you start making money hand-over-fist, I don't want you to develop a sense of entitlement or – '

'*Don't forget your roots*, is that it?'

'Not your roots.' She smiles. 'You're as middle-class as they come, mate.'

'What, then?'

'Don't forget that it's people, not profit, that matters.'

I grin, circling my arms around her waist and wrestling her down towards me. We kiss, and I can taste the sourness of the stewed plums we had for dessert. My breath catches as we pull apart. 'I love you, you know,' I say.

'Is that because I keep you right?'

I shake my head. It takes me a second to place the reason, though. It's that she'll sit through dinner with my parents, swallowing all their eccentricities and Mum's stinking stewed plums without complaining, but then come upstairs and get to the point of tearing hair out – mine, of course – about politics and Scottish independence. But it's also that she turned up to support me at the showcase gig even though she knew that my friends – that Ewan – would be there, and that she didn't just clap and cheer, but she told me to hurry up when I started fucking about on stage. It's that she's honest to the point of being brazen, but with enough softness about her to carry it off.

'It's because you're beautiful, to the point where I still have to do a double-take when I wake up with you beside me,' I say. Which is true as well, but not what prompted me to tell her I loved her, here and now.

'My dad once told me,' Maddie says, 'that the reason he married my mum was because being with her was as easy as being alone. I was about twelve when he told me that. And for a while I thought it was a really sad thought, but then I started to think that what he was saying was that they were entirely comfortable with one another, that they could completely be themselves…'

I stay quiet. She looks beyond me, over my shoulder, with her eyes unfocused. I hold her hand in mine, but it is limp and doesn't respond when I tighten my grip.

'Two years later, he left us,' she continues. 'And I thought back to what he'd said. If it's as easy being with her as being alone, then why be alone? And did the fact that he left mean that he didn't like her, or didn't like himself…' her voice drops to a whisper '…or didn't like me?'

'No,' I say. 'No, it doesn't mean that.'

'No.' She shakes her head. 'It means that marriage was convenient, at the time. There was no struggle to it, no obstacles to overcome, no difficulties in getting to fully know one another. There was no challenge about it, maybe.'

'Right,' I say, leaning closer to her so that her eyes focus on my face.

'I love you too, Rab,' she says. 'But only if we keep each other right, OK? Only if we challenge each other.'

'Deal,' I say, sealing it with a stolen kiss. 'There's nothing like conditional love.'

BRIGHTON

We advertise on the streets. From a pound shop, we buy a pack of multicoloured chalks and use them to scrawl on the pavements up around North Laine. *Gandhi & Occupy*, we write, *free lecture*. Then our address and the start time underneath. On the first couple I add: *Donations gratefully accepted*. Sage catches sight of it, though, and comes across to spit at the words and scuff them with the toe of his shoe.

I tell Luke about the lecture and he says he'll spread the word at the university. When I offer him a piece of chalk, he lets out this choked cough of laughter and holds out his smartphone. I ask if he can invite Flick as well and he nods, but there is the slightest hesitation and the ghost of a wince. He puts the phone back in his pocket.

We tidy away the tent in the lounge area and push the tables into the corner. Sage says that he doesn't need notes or anything, that he'd rather it was a freewheeling discussion. He's had this fascination with Mahatma Gandhi ever since he found out that he was influenced by some Englishman called John Ruskin. Several times, over the past couple of days, Sage has tried to tell me more than this, but I've managed to convince him that it's better to save it for the event itself.

Ten minutes before the start, it looks as if the only attendees will be myself and Freddy, the Danish teenager who lives along at the pitch-and-putt in Hove. Faced with such a sparse turnout, Sage grumbles something about wanting to wash, and locks himself in the bathroom. In the week or so we've been in the squat, he has had two or three sink-baths a day, producing sounds worthy of a storm at sea and leaving the lino-floor flooded. It's like he's engaging in a cleansing ritual, to rid himself of the stigma of the streets.

By the time Sage emerges, with his long hair dripping on to the towel draped over the shoulders of his shirt, Luke has arrived with reinforcements. He has brought two of his friends, but no Flick. It is five lads who sit in the corner – three of us on the bench and two on chairs to either side – to listen to Sage. He stands barefoot in the centre of the floor, dressed in brown corduroy trousers and navy shirt, with a white towel for a tie.

'We'll start with the central idea, OK, the defining idea of Gandhi,' he says. 'The practice of *satyagraha*… that's sat-ya-gra-ha… which loosely translates as an insistence on truth or a quote-unquote "truth force".'

'Calm it down,' I say, under my breath.

He paces back and forth. It doesn't seem to bother him whether he's facing the audience or not. He steps towards the bar, then parries away to the side as though making for the door, before advancing again, from an angle, and spinning to face us. The whole performance is like a fencing match against an invisible opponent.

'Gandhi used this word – a compound of the Sanskrit words for "truth" and "holding firmly to" – to signify his concept of non-violent resistance, in which there would be no response to physical or verbal assault.'

Sage pauses. He has stopped mid-lunge, with his right leg extended towards the bench and his arm out to the side. He reaches up and whips the towel from around his neck, throwing it behind himself, towards the bar. It lands a foot or so short.

'Calm the fuck down,' I mutter again. 'Take a fucking breath.'

'And what's really interesting for the Occupy movement,' he launches in again, 'is that Gandhi also set up communities in South Africa that operated as collectives. He bought one hundred acres of land at Phoenix Settlement and used it to house his newspaper *The Indian Opinion*... but he also allotted the land in three-acre, erm, plots... and it was at this point that he took a vow of celibacy, even in relations with his wife. How's that for commitment to the cause, eh?'

There is a sharp shout of laughter from Sage, which causes Freddy, at the other end of the bench, to flinch. Beside me, one of Luke's mates fidgets. He has a braid of long blond hair which he by turns chews and tucks behind his ear. Reaching into the pocket of his jacket, he brings out a half-bottle of whisky, which he twists open.

'The most famous example of Gandhi's non-violent protest is the Salt March, when he marched to the coast to produce salt because... well, I should give you some context... the British Raj taxed salt in India as a way of collecting revenue from the native population... and Gandhi realised that – '

'Here.' The braided boy holds the bottle of whisky out towards me. He speaks at a normal volume, interrupting. I look apprehensively at Sage. His navy shirt now has shoulder-patches of moisture and a scattered pattern of drops down the front. He glares across at the bench.

'Thanks,' I say, in a whisper, and take the bottle. I've been trying to avoid alcohol recently, but this is a special occasion.

'*So,*' Sage says loudly. 'What is the lesson for Occupy? Well, the Salt March had both a practical and a symbolic significance. It wasn't an empty protest, because it cut off a revenue stream for the Raj as well as showing disobedience, but it's difficult to categorise it as an aggressive action...'

I pass the whisky back and it is handed on. Sage rocks forward and back on his leading leg, like when you used to pause a video and the still picture would skip.

'... so the lesson is that people wanting to protest against rail fare rises would be best trespassing on the lines; that those annoyed about inadequate social housing should squat in unoccupied buildings, as we're doing here...'

Sage nods at me. I smile and return the nod, but I also remember back to the day when I first suggested squatting and he compared it to breaking-and-entering. If I'd called it satay-grey-ha living he'd have been all for it from the start.

'... and the Occupy London movement should have been at the London Stock Exchange, as was the original intention, or posting up details of bankers' bonuses on ATMs for the customers to see... The interventions they make should, in a non-violent way, disrupt or call attention to the actions of the banking system...'

The braided boy next to me is pointing both of his index fingers at Sage and moving them up and down, as if playing at being a cowboy. *Bang-bang*. For a moment there is no reaction from Sage. Then he seems to stumble back a step... hit by an invisible bullet.

'What are you doing?' he asks.

'It's a hand signal,' Braids says. 'We use them in meetings to show when we want to speak – it makes discussion easier.'

'Right.' Sage puts his hands into his pockets, holstering his guns.

'I'd like to give a direct response to your point,' Braids continues. 'Which is that those have all been done, to some extent. Can we not do something more *positive*?'

'I'll take questions at the end,' Sage says. 'But the – '

'Even Occupy London,' the braided boy interrupts again. He is sitting on the edge of the cushion, with his hands passing restlessly over one another. 'Occupy London set up the Tent City University, and the Bank of Ideas and School of Ideas were all about exchange of knowledge, so it wasn't just about disruption and protest.'

'There's a brilliant initiative in a town near here,' Luke says, from the chair to my left. 'Just up the road. They've set up their own local currency which is exchangeable for normal currency, but you can use the local one in all the shops there... like the butcher's or the bakery...'

'That's the kind of thing,' his mate replies. 'Practical.'

'Because Gandhi...' Luke holds out an arm towards Sage '... was trying to promote community and co-operation and to *build* something new, it sounds like, rather than just pull down the old structures. Is that right, Sage?'

Sage doesn't reply. He has become ominously still and silent. He stands, turned towards the wooden chair, with his sodden shoulders rising and falling. For a moment I wonder if he might be sobbing, but his eyes are widened and angry when he eventually turns back to us.

'This is the problem. *This*,' he hisses. 'You try to talk about the important lessons of the past, about one of the most important civil rights activists the world has ever known, and fucking *students* interrupt to talk about some stupid provincial scheme – '

'Calm down, mate,' Luke says to Sage. 'We're interested, is all.'

'If the government...' Sage speaks through his teeth '... is intent on packaging off bits of our NHS to sell to private companies and decides to declare disabled folk fit for work when they're not, then a local fucking currency isn't going to help, is it?'

'But...' Braids speaks up, again '... a series of community movements might make a difference, is all I'm saying. So, if the government starts to sell off bits of the health service, communities could set up a not-for-profit to take over or – '

'The Big fucking Society, eh?' Sage sneers.

'No, something more active than that, which proposes an alternative – '

It is at this point that Sage decides to take action himself. He reaches down to the floor and lifts the wet towel. Then, stepping over to the bench, he drapes it over Braids, covering his entire head. There is no reaction. Either Braids is too stunned to respond, or he has decided to follow Gandhi's example. Whatever the reason, he sits for five seconds or so with this damp hood over his face before he removes it.

'As I say…' Sage stares at him '… keep your questions for the end.'

Afterwards, we go to a pub on the next street along. A fully functioning pub, with the beer and spirits our Sick Little Hammer lacks. Sage stays behind to seethe, and to snap and snarl if we have any unwanted visitors. There's no need for both of us to play guard dog, though, so I follow Luke and Braids. In exchange for a pint of bitter, I sit quietly while they take the piss. Swaying on their stools, they compare Sage to a character in a computer game, walking into a brick wall and then persistently marching on the spot but going nowhere. Over the first shot of tequila, Braids interrupts each and every attempt at conversation with, 'I'll take questions at the end,' and then erupts into laughter. Over the second, Luke gives a detailed account of the diverse ecosystem he believes to be dependent on Sage. In the hair, he says, there must be lice, but also something larger to feed off them – perhaps a small bird. Maybe they nest in the beard and fly up to feed. Then, in the cavity of the ear, there would be enough dense fauna for an insect or two, maybe a tiny lizard. In his armpits there are miniature swinging monkeys by day, and a population of bats by night, and there are snakes slithering and cockroaches scurrying through his innards. It's the bellybutton – for some reason – that leaves Luke breathless with laughter, that has him slapping his hand on the table, his eyes streaming tears.

'Just imagine…' he snorts. 'Just imagine… a set of eyes, in the fluff-filled darkness there, peering out and darting from side to side.'

'Doesn't even matter what animal,' Braids says, smiling.

'Fucking dragon, maybe,' Luke says.

'Bunny rabbit.'

I'm grateful that they stop at the bellybutton, that they're not going any lower. I've heard enough of it, though, so I rise from my seat. It's not just a protest but a necessity. The room is beginning to tip, the table sliding away from my resting elbows. We have been in the pub for only twenty minutes and we've already had two pints and two shots, in addition to the whisky back at the squat. I've been cutting down on the alcohol and the pills over the past few weeks, so the tequila is having a real effect. The chemical smell of it singes my nostrils, and the taste of it cuts through the thick trub of the bitter.

'We might have taken that a bit far,' Braids whispers, thinking that I'm out of earshot as I stagger-stumble towards the back of the pub.

'Where are you going, mate?' Luke calls.

'The toilet.' I turn back to them.

'Good.' He gets up. 'Don't go running off anywhere. I've got a bit of a present for you. It's up in the car, in the multi-storey – '

'You can't drive, Lukey, not after tequila,' Braids says.

'I'm not going to *drive*, am I? All I need to do is open the boot. I'll just be a minute.'

When I get back from the toilet, Braids is sitting alone, nursing the last inch of his beer. He smiles across the table at me, but the smile is wary now. 'You know we were only poking fun at your friend, yeah?' he says. 'No harm meant.'

'I know…' I hesitate. 'But he is a mate.'

'No harm meant,' he repeats.

I nod.

'And there's a serious point…'

I stare at the empty glasses on the table, wondering if his serious point will be that I haven't bought a round, that I haven't even offered. The next running joke will be the various species of moth that live in a Scotsman's wallet.

'He talks about non-violent resistance,' Braids continues, 'but not about where to direct it. Because the government privatises everything from crèches to parking and then there's this choice, right, about whether you protest to the government, for selling it on, or the company, for not delivering the service.'

'Unless they do deliver the service, that is.'

'Well, yes, obviously.'

'The government are still in control, though.'

'Are they?'

'They can cancel the contracts, change the system.'

He shakes his head, so that his braid whips out from behind his ear and becomes a pendulum in front of his face. 'It's the big corporations who're in charge,' he says. 'And not the coffee chains or the electronics manufacturers or the burger joints, but the private security firms and the defence contractors. All of them with these vague, non-specific company names, like something a Bond villain would think up.'

The barmaid comes over to clear our empty glasses and I tighten my grip on the edge of the table, worrying that she will ask if we want more drinks. She tidies without a word, though, and then walks off.

'*That's* the problem, if you ask me,' Braids says. 'That people are annoyed and have this feeling that the system's unfair, but they don't know who to blame or where to direct their anger, because it's not like the British Raj in India, a central power-base. Instead, every company, every public body, has its own Raj system – hierarchy is everywhere, Rab. And then all the different mini-empires fight each other in the market.'

'What's the solution to that, though?' I ask. 'Is there a solution to that?'

He shrugs. 'Break down each and every hierarchy, one by one.'

'But, that's – '

'Not really possible. Or it's difficult, at least. So, instead, we take on inequality and injustice wherever we find it. Don't look for the big picture, just a series of tiny, pure brushstrokes. Like pointillism.'

'Or a mosaic, with tiles?' I ask.

'Sure,' he says. 'Tiny fragments of pure colour.'

'Right.'

'People think of anarchism as anti-state,' Braids continues. 'But it's actually anti-hierarchy. Free association, consensus politics. Often just at a local level.'

'Are you an anarchist, then?'

'Yeah, although with a small "a", you know?'

'What's the difference?'

'I'm a pointillist anarchist, maybe.' He pauses, then smiles. 'Pointillist, not pointless, mind.'

'Is that a thing?'

'Not until this moment, mate, no. But this might be the start of something, eh?'

He's lost me, but it doesn't matter because Luke has returned. There's no need to ask what he's brought me; it's obvious from the size and shape. He holds the guitar out to me, by the neck, and gives me a wink.

'Thought you might want to borrow this,' he says. 'To get going on your song-writing again.'

'Luke...' I say. 'Thank you.'

He waves it away. 'You're a musician, mate, you should have an instrument.'

The fabric case is a little dusty. I wipe at it with my hand. The zip snags, but I manage to force it open. And there it is: the same guitar Luke lets me borrow for gigs.

'Thank you,' I repeat, my voice catching.

'You going to give us a song?' Braids asks.

I shake my head. 'As Luke says, I want to get writing again.'

We sit for another five minutes, but all the talk is of football, film and telly – searching for something to agree on, something in common. Braids reminds me of Maddie – the way he can burn with argument one minute, then hold not even a flicker or smoulder of it the next. His talk of anarchy has slipped into comparing mobile phone upgrades with Luke. I tune out when they start with the 'remember that time' stories.

Outside, Luke and Braids go off in the direction of West Street and I make my way down to the stones of the beach. It is early evening, but there is enough winter sun left to take the bite out of the breeze. Hooking the strap of the guitar case over my shoulder, I crunch my way down towards the shore.

A year ago, with a different guitar on my back, all I wanted was to have an album out. It would be there, in the shops, with my face across the front and, with that, I would be a singer. It's not as simple as that, though. The music has to be something you're proud of, something you'd defend. It's like folk who say they want to fall in love and get married. It's not as simple as that, either. The person you fall in love with matters – the person you settle down with. It can be shit-awful as well as happy-ever-after. It's not just the existence of it, it's what it actually is, how it actually works. The music matters, not just the packaging.

Maybe I was caught between two ideas with the album – the political and the personal. And, while one of them was meant to be all conviction, the other was all doubt.

Stepping out of my trainers, I peel off my socks and tuck them inside the pockets of my jeans. Then I dip a foot into the waters of the English Channel. The cold cuts keenly at my ankle. I hold my foot there, though, then bring the other one forward to rest beside it. After a moment, the slitting pain of the incoming waves fades to numbness.

I was offered a short-cut, I realise that now, and I didn't understand the steps that others had taken to get to the same stage. The pain, the hard work. And there's a practical purpose to all that struggle, all the shit you have to put up with along the way. It gives you a thick skin, sure, and it leaves you able to deal with the criticisms and the reviews and the uncertainty. And it means that you can look at the album up on the shelf and know that it's not just your picture on the sleeve – that it's also your songs on the CD. But, more than that, those experiences give you something to say. When you sit down to write your songs, you have something to fucking say.

LONDON

My tour bus is a battered Volvo estate that Pierce borrows from his uncle. The red paintwork has worn to white, in places, and the scratches have been daubed over in a different shade. It rattles and shudders its way out of London. We're making for Guildford to play a Tuesday night gig in a bar there. It was the only booking they could find – or so Pierce says – because any decent London venue is scheduled months in advance.

The booking agent had originally scheduled a nationwide, co-headline tour with another artist on the Agitate imprint for May. This rapper called Brink from Tottenham Hale. He's been getting some traction since the release of his album, *Hale and Hearty*, and the idea was to tour the two topical singers together. At the last minute, though, Bower decided not to mix genres. Instead, a support slot was lined up with one of those West London nu-folk bands that are big at the moment. That seemed to fall through even before the tickets went on sale.

As a result, I'm in the car heading to Surrey. Pierce offered to drive in preference to getting the train, because he's got this anxiety thing with the rail network. His dad used to work for British Rail, back before it was privatised. His job, day-to-day, was rail maintenance and repair, but he was often first on the scene when there was a jumper. And, over dinner, he'd tell his family about the damage done: the businessman who left one side of his face a hundred feet up the line; the young mother who passed her baby up on to the platform at the last moment; the teenager who misjudged her leap and ended up with two broken legs and a fractured spine. His favourite story, Pierce says, the one he tells at parties, is of a colleague walking down the tracks at Clapham Junction, whistling, with a suicide's disembodied leg slung over his shoulder. Desensitised to it himself, Pierce's dad had traumatised his son with stories that caused the younger Price to see every train as a speeding bullet.

I don't complain about being driven door-to-door. Sitting in the passenger seat, I listen to the radio on the off-chance that Radio 1 decides to ignore its playlist and give airplay to 'Ivory Towers', the first single from *Measures Taken*... but also so that I don't have to make conversation with Pierce.

I don't know if Lydia has told him about our dressing-gown dalliance, but Pierce hasn't been his usual chatty self recently. Ever since our meeting with Bower last month. He works just as hard – harder even – but there's this crazed, frantic look when he hangs up the phone with the promoter for the weekend festival or the producer at the local radio station. Even when 'Ivory Towers' gets played on an 'introducing' show, he sits with his head in his hands and rubs at his hair as if trying to spread his bald patch. I've got two more gigs lined up over the next week – both of them outside London – but, instead of smiling about that, he just stabs away at his calculator and frowns.

The album still hasn't sold many copies, true, but in these days of downloads a flatline can spike at any moment. Not because of gimmicks like rags on the wrist – long since abandoned – but with social media or word-of-mouth. Or gigging, even. It only takes a spark to kindle a fire.

On the back seat of the Volvo, my guitar rests against a short stack of CDs and a folded pile of T-shirts. The fee the bar is paying should cover petrol costs, but any profit will come from merchandising. Later in the week, for the longer trips to

Brighton and Southampton, we'll do well to break even. The margins are *razor*-thin, Pierce says, slicing his hand through the air.

He has high hopes for Guildford, though. There's a large student population and the campus newspaper ran a piece about *Measures Taken* last week to try to drum up interest. The bar itself is up a narrow alleyway, off the high street. It is starkly lit, so there is no disguising the fact that only three folk wait for me to set up. There are two girls who look barely eighteen and a young bloke with a black and white patterned scarf swirled around his neck. As I use my tuning fork to tune my guitar, a fourth comes in, but he turns and leaves when he sees that there is live music on. I look over to Pierce, sitting behind his table of merchandise, but he avoids my eye. Without a word of introduction, I launch into my first song.

I play the album from first track to last, without variation. If it weren't for the feedback on track two and the pause I take after track six to give a little speech about 'Ivory Towers' being available now, then the effect would be the same as putting in the CD and pressing play. Because I know that Pierce is driving straight back to London afterwards, I do my drinking during the set rather than after, so I use the brief gaps between the songs to gulp at the triple whisky and Coke that the barman has set on a stool to the side. It is warm and flat.

After I finish – no encore – I stand at the side of the stage to meet my adoring public. One of the two girls steps forward. Neither of them is stunning, but it is typical of the night I'm having that it's the one with the lazy eye who approaches. She smiles, crookedly, and holds out a copy of the album and a black permanent marker.

'I wrote the article,' she says.

'Sorry?'

'In the campus newspaper. I wrote an article about your album.'

'Oh,' I say. 'Thanks.'

She is still holding out the CD. I take it from her and flip it open. Scrawling my signature across the inside sleeve, I look beyond her to her friend. She is at the merchandise table, trailing a fingertip over the CD cases. She has bobbed brown hair and a sleeve tattoo. I consider whether she's worth the effort, but decide there isn't enough drinking-time to make her an attractive proposition.

'What did you think of it?' I ask her friend, the one who wrote the article.

'The album?' She pauses. 'It was good, yeah. Catchy melodies. Although some of your ideas about higher education are flawed, if you ask me.'

Yeah, well, who did ask you? I want to say. Instead, I nod. 'In what way?'

'Your lyrics seem to blame the universities for the tuition fee rise, but it's the government that cut the teaching budget for higher education.' She shakes her head. 'It's a common mistake, but the new fees don't really raise the universities' income, it's just that the money's now drawn mostly from undergraduates rather than the taxpayer.'

'Right.' I hand her back the signed album. 'Well, thanks for coming.'

She walks back to her friend and the two of them leave. The guy in his black and white scarf sits in the same spot in the far corner, still nursing the same pint, in a way that makes me wonder if he was part of the audience or just a lone drinker. With nothing else to do, I wander over to where Pierce sits. For a moment, he doesn't look up. When he does, he has this dazed look.

'Three people,' he says. 'And a barman.'

'We sold an album, though, right? At least one.'

He frowns, shakes his head.

'To the girl who wrote the article. The one I was just – '

'No,' he says. 'I sent her a review copy.'

I let out a snort of laughter. Pierce continues to stare up at me, but he doesn't see the funny side. A sixty-mile round trip to play to three people and sign a free copy of *Measures Taken*. If you take the postage and packaging of the review copy into account, we're probably running at a loss.

'Let's go for a pint,' Pierce says. 'We need to have a chat.'

My smile fades. Nerves flutter through my body, in the way they should before a gig, not after. There had been no tension tonight, though, because the audience was barely enough to fill the Volvo, never mind the bar. It is the thought that Pierce will bring up the subject of Lydia, that the purpose of the pint is to issue a wife-warning, that causes my stomach to clench.

Without taking care about chipping CD cases or creasing T-shirts, we bundle all the merchandise into a holdall. Then we leave the bar and go back down the alleyway to another one, with faux-Tudor wooden beams across the outside. We settle ourselves in the corner with two pints of dark ale. I hold my guitar, in its case, between my knees. There are animated fish on the table, projected from above. They swim around our glasses and I trace patterns on the table, as if to disturb the water.

Pierce puts his elbow down on a lily-pad and rests his cheek against the heel of his hand. There's mild interest, on my part, to see how he brings up the subject of his wife. *Listen, old bean*, he'll say. Or, *I'm not convinced that's sporting, buddy.* Fuck, he'll probably give me his blessing just to avoid the confrontation.

He doesn't, though. There is no mention of Lydia. The conversation is not marital, it's material. With blunt matter-of-factness he tells me that the advance has gone and that we're operating on credit. These three gigs – Guildford, Brighton, Southampton – need to turn a profit, because we're running on empty. The label is waiting for the further sales figures but – who're we kidding, buddy? – they're not going to be good. The publicity won't pick up, the advertising budget's been spent, social media is silent, and the single didn't chart anywhere near the Top 40.

His elbow slides and his head sinks to the projected pool. I can't move across to comfort him; I can only sit and watch. While I sit picking awkwardly at the strings of my guitar through the fabric of the case, Pierce gently weeps.

Two days later, I play Brighton. It is much better. The venue, a small pub underneath the promenade on the seafront, is nearly full. Less than a hundred people, more than fifty. They listen attentively, applauding after every song, and we even manage to sell four albums and a T-shirt. I'm not the headline act, granted, but I'm sure as many folk turned up for me as for the local three-piece who recently featured on the cover of the *NME*.

As the headliners play, Pierce and I sit by the merchandise table and drink our profit in celebration. Over a steady succession of rum and Cokes, we plot our future assault on the charts. It's true that we needed the draw of the other band on the bill for this particular gig, but word will spread and soon I'll be the one giving a leg-up to other acts. Other managers will be phoning Pierce to beg a favour. Success, when it comes, will be the hard-won result of this series of small shows we've driven to in the consumptive Volvo estate.

'I have faith in you, Rob,' Pierce says, pointing to the *Measures Taken* T-shirt he's wearing. 'It's just that we were maybe naïve in expecting everyone to pick it up so quickly.'

'New ideas always take time to catch,' I say.

'New ideas *do* always take time,' he echoes, nodding.

'But the album is good, and they'll all come to realise that.'

Pierce sags his head into a nod again, taking a sip through his straw at the same time. We've decided to sleep in the tour bus tonight, partly so that he can have a drink or two and partly to save petrol money. We'll drive to Southampton in the morning, for the next gig.

'I can't go back to Glasgow, Pierce.' I say this softly.

Pierce looks up at me. 'What?'

'I can't go back to Glasgow,' I repeat. 'It would be too much of a step backwards, too much of an admission. You know what it's like: you saunter off with a massive *fuck you* and, if you come back, then people will... folk will...'

Maybe it's the rum loosening my thoughts, or the joint I smoked after the show, but suddenly I feel like telling Pierce everything. All about Maddie. And Ewan. About those final weeks, between the record company offering me the contract and leaving Glasgow for good.

'Why would you go back to Glasgow?' Pierce frowns. 'You've just recorded your first album, you've just released a single. For fuck's sake, buddy, you're a proper musician now. Why would you go back?'

'But I can't stay with you and Lydia for ever...'

'No.'

'And I can't afford to move out, either.'

'No.'

I stop there. I don't want to keep listing the negatives. Maybe the joint was a bad idea, after the emotional drain of playing a set. Maybe a snort of coke would serve me better, smooth the doubts. 'Do you have anything stronger?' I ask, nodding at the drink.

'No.'

'But you used to carry some,' I protest. 'You used to – '

He shakes his head, but puts his hand into his pocket. When he unfolds his fingers, he's not holding a baggy of white powder but a small brown bottle with a black lid. It is half-filled with liquid.

'Poppers,' he says. 'Best I've got.'

'Fuck me, this budget-cutting is brutal,' I say, but I take the bottle and unscrew the cap. The chemical smell of the poppers rises to my nose even before I bring my hand up. Lifting the bottle to my nostril, I take a sniff. Then another. There's a warmth, a flush, a pulsing in my head.

'You could go back, though, if you needed to,' Pierce says, 'right?'

'What?'

'To Glasgow.'

I hand him back the poppers. 'No.'

'Why not?'

'There's a girl…' I breathe out slowly.

'But if you *needed* to?'

I shake my head, but I can't put the reason into words. Not the exact words needed. It's the reason that Lydia can't tell him about my fumbling attempt, that the album can't fail, that the gigs can't dry up, that the record company can't drop me. Because then Maddie will have been right. All along, she will have been right.

'Well, anyway,' Pierce smiles, 'it's not going to be an issue, is it? Because I've fucking decided that you're going to be a success, buddy. From the start, I decided that. And you know what they say…' He pauses, expecting me to say it along with him like a catchphrase. 'The Price is always right.'

'… is always right,' I echo, a moment too late.

I go absent-without-leave after the Southampton set. Out of the back door with Celine, a girl from the casino foyer I was playing in. She stood at the bar, with restless eyes scanning the room. Twisting the straw in her glass like a periscope, she saw me and smiled. Well, not smiled. But her mouth twitched and her eyebrows lifted ever so slightly towards her straight black fringe. It was enough for me. After I finished playing, I bought her a cosmopolitan and she handed me a yellow prescription bottle. I swallowed two of the pills down with a double vodka-lemonade.

Pierce can go fuck himself. He can sleep in the front seat of his Volvo estate for all I care, like he did last night. I'm not curling up in the back seat, though. I'm out on the town. After the gig I've just endured, I'm out in the clubs of Southampton with Celine and her mystery pills.

The casino is not a proper venue – it's roulette wheels and blackjack tables and a corner where I sit and play for the amusement of the fuckwits who've just lost their week's wages. They shout out requests for 'Brown Eyed Girl' and Michael fucking Bublé as if it was a cruise. When I keep playing my own material they start to pelt me with chips – the potato kind, not ones I could take to the cashier. The ketchup makes them stick, so they spread it on thick and aim for the face. I cut the set short and make for Celine and her tight black mini-dress. Like everyone else, I walk straight past Pierce's merchandise table.

Celine leads me up to Bedford Place and we queue for this club on the corner. The bouncer points at my guitar case and asks me what's inside. I reply that it's not what he's thinking, there's no shotgun. Then I wait a beat and say there's just two swords and a musket inside. In Glasgow that would get me a laugh or a crack in the jaw, depending on the mood of the doorman, but down here the dickhead just looks at me levelly and narrows his eyes, as if deciding whether to take me seriously. I swing it around and pluck at a string through the fabric – to prove that it's just a machine to kill fascists – and he waves us on through.

The pills make Celine the ideal companion. She doesn't try to shout in my ear to make herself heard over the music, or engage in that ridiculous sign-language where you have to point at yourself and mime taking a piss – in great detail – to let it be known that you're going to the toilet. Instead, she stands by the speakers and reaches into her handbag for a steady succession of pills from prescription bottles. A modern-day Mary Poppins, she is, only without the spoonful of sugar. I take each and every one she hands over, not knowing whether they're uppers or downers, or whether they're her own prescriptions or the result of a shotgun-in-a-guitar-case raid on a local pharmacy. To tell the truth, I don't care. Celine could vacantly feed me an overdose and I wouldn't protest. I'm too preoccupied.

What the fuck was the booking agent thinking with the casino? What was Pierce thinking? At least with the Guildford gig it was just a case of no one turning up. The venue was fine. And Brighton was a solid choice, even if I was only the support. But having to play to a packed room where everyone is turned away from you, towards their own particular vices, was humiliating. Even before the chips were thrown.

Celine kisses me. There is no preamble. She steps towards me, lifts on to her tiptoes and kisses me. Her tongue tastes of peppermint, which makes me wonder if she's been feeding me placebos all evening, but then she cups my crotch with her hand and I start to think it's chemical castration she's working towards. There's not a stirring, not even a flicker of interest down there, as she presses her body close. She steps away and her eyebrows lift towards her fringe again. Maybe she's a rogue pharmaceutical scientist, testing her concoctions on unsuspecting members of the public with a reckless disregard for regulations. Or maybe the pills are making me paranoid.

That's the last I remember, properly, of Southampton. There are snatches of other memories, like the fading details of a dream: walking over the largest concrete bridge I've ever seen; being led down a lane by the belt-buckle by Celine; sitting on the steps of a kebab house and playing my guitar for chips. It's only when I've managed to wander my way back towards the city centre in the early hours, and my thoughts start to string together again, that I realise the irony of that. And of the fact that I've developed a headache. Celine is nowhere to be seen, though. So I find a twenty-four-hour garage to buy myself some painkillers, on the credit card, and ask for directions back to the casino.

The Volvo is still in the car park. Slumped in the front, his jacket up over his head, is Pierce. It might still be because of the anger from the evening before, the pills from Celine or even the two painkillers I took on the walk down, but, whatever it is, I decide that Pierce deserves a bit of a fright. So I go searching for the biggest stone I can find. Then, arcing my arm back, I throw it towards the car, aiming for the bonnet. Mid-flight, it occurs to me that it could smash the windscreen, that it might even hit Pierce. I needn't have worried, though. It falls short, skitters across the concrete and stops against the far wall.

As I search for a second – slightly smaller – stone, there is a blast of noise from behind me. It takes me a moment to turn, to unfreeze from my crouching position. When I do, though, I see Pierce sitting upright in the driver's seat of the Volvo, reaching out to press at the horn again. He does not look as if he slept well.

GLASGOW

I won't start recording until later in the summer. The month or so between, Pierce says, will give me time to write a 'songbook'. He wants me to research the austerity policy of the government, the events of the Arab Spring, the European bailouts. Like revision – maths, geography, more fucking maths. At the end of our last phone call he did say that the songs didn't all need to be topical, that Dylan quite often went *introspective*. Even that required some schoolwork, though, because I had to look the word up in the dictionary.

Maddie doesn't help – or, rather, she helps too much. She worked herself into such a lather over her exams that, even though she's finished, the suds are still clinging to her. I sit in my attic reading about NHS funding and she looks at my laptop over my shoulder. Or I'll go down to the kitchen to make us a sandwich and when I get back she'll have bookmarked all these pages on banking regulation for me to read. She emails me links to newspaper articles and video clips in the wee hours of the morning. It's like having my own personal spammer except, sad to say, with fewer and fewer invitations to fuck.

At the start of July, we have our first proper argument. It's because I click on a link about the scrapping of the Education Maintenance Allowance in England. I don't even take notes. All I get down is *EMA?* before Maddie, never more than a single stride away, pounces.

'You're not going to write lyrics about that, are you?'

'Why not?' It seems like a crowd-pleaser, one to rouse the rabble – the government taking away the weekly allowance of youngsters who are seeking out some education. Like a parent spending all their money on mai tais and then deciding to deal with the hangover by cutting their children's pocket money.

'Because,' Maddie speaks slowly, 'it was only in England. You can still get it up here or in – hell, I'll be applying for it if I need to stay on another year.'

'But only in Scotland,' I say.

'I think they kept it in Wales too.'

'No – what I mean is, you'd only apply if you were staying in Scotland.'

'Yes.'

There's a gap. A pause. It infuriates me because Maddie fills it by looking at me with that expression – laughter suspended in disbelief – that seems appropriate only for moments of ridiculous stupidity. If I'd slid my sandwich into a postbox, say, or tried to string my guitar with shoe-laces.

'If you don't believe me,' she says, 'then look it up properly.'

This is another peeve I've taken to petting. Every time I discuss something with Mads – every time I take a stance – she goes straight on to the search engine to disprove me. With facts and figures. It's impossible, in her eyes, to have an opinion without the support of some statistic. Which isn't good for songwriting, since bugger-all words rhyme with 'percentage'.

Back when we were twelve or thirteen, Ewan and I climbed the wall at the back of the Bowling Club and made ourselves a temporary shack in among the bushes there. We used wood and sheet metal we pinched from the allotments behind. Then we sat there in our clubhouse looking out over the green, flicked mud pellets at one another, and chatted until our eyes were crossed and our T-shirts dotted. We didn't talk about politics, but about girls. At that stage, what we knew wouldn't have filled more than a byline in a lad's mag. Still, we talked it through, between the two of us, in that draughty shelter that didn't have a bar of signal for our phones never mind an internet connection. That's the way to learn, isn't it? Discuss it all, see what you can figure out and go looking for specific details about the stuff you don't know. Because if you just type 'sex' into a search engine then you're going to learn some pretty skewed stuff.

'Fucking talk to me about it,' I hiss at Maddie. 'Don't just find me a clip from a *Panorama* programme or a quote from Jon bloody Snow – '

'Are you serious? I'm trying to talk to you about it.'

'You're trying to *lecture* me about it.'

'You're the one who deals in soundbites, Rab.'

'Yeah?'

I want to point out her reliance on social media, that she needs a virtual thumbs-up before she'll actually make a statement, but we've not had sex in three days – *three days* – and I don't want to wound her so deeply that it can't be kissed (or licked) better.

'Maybe if you would actually debate,' she says, 'actually look into these things and have it out, you'd find this lyric-writing a bit easier – '

'All I need is peace and quiet!' I shout back.

'I can leave, Rab; you just say the word!'

I backtrack; I rethink. I've no wish to extend our record into a fourth day, especially if it leaves open the possibility of five days, or six, or the full *week*. Laying a hand on her arm, trying an apologetic smile, I compromise.

'Will you give me an hour, maybe,' I ask, 'to try and get some lyrics down? And then we can spend some proper time together.'

'Can we go to the cinema or the bar or something?'

'Maybe, yes.'

She frowns, but then nods. 'I'll wait for you downstairs.'

'Perfect,' I say, reaching for my guitar.

It becomes our routine – Maddie watching telly in the living room while I pick away at my guitar in the attic – but the distance doesn't seem to help my songwriting. The paper in front of me remains pristine white. I smoke a joint to coax the words out, but still my pen hovers an inch or so above the page. When I eventually write a word – any word – I immediately scratch it out. Then the page is ruined, spoilt, so it goes in the bin and I start again from blank.

For weeks it goes on like this. I get through reams of paper without using more than a squid's squirt of ink. There are minor successes, of course, that get placed on the floor to the side. Two lines about tax – 'You say avoidance is part of the equation/But offshores and loopholes are just plain evasion' – that might find their way into a verse somewhere, and a melody that seems to suit my lyrics about non-violent protest: 'Where you choose to sit, mate, is a political act/If it's in a bank lobby or repossessed flat'. The problem with that one, though, is the word 'mate' in the first line. It should be more specific, giving more of that sense of common purpose. 'Comrade', maybe, if I could say it without slipping into Soviet stereotype, or 'brother' if I could get it to fit the phrasing.

My wider issue, I think, is that the lyrics are too obvious. They don't give a slant on the facts at all; there's no *angle*. They may as well be the lists and charts that Maddie favours. Whereas those other folk singers – Dylan especially – can talk in metaphor and through... I think the word is *illusion*. I should be hinting at these things without naming them, right? There should be another layer of meaning.

I could always go downstairs and run some ideas past Maddie, but that's become an even less appealing option. It's not just her any more. My mum's gone part-time at work, so she's back in the afternoons now to fuss around, make endless cups of tea, and tut-tut her way through Maddie's daytime programming. I wouldn't be going down to ask one or the other for help; I'd be going to stand in front of a panel, a committee. I can hear them nattering down there – enough wasted words to fill all the sheets of paper I've thrown away – and the last thing I want is for their tut-and-snigger to shift from the stupidity of the quiz show contestant on telly to my writing.

It's on the issue of cuts to the health service that I finally manage to go abstract. With the help of a joint rolled from my last few skins. The smoke from it is still uncoiling around me as I scrawl: 'Put a fence around health spending to help protect the sheep/Let the foxes burrow underneath'. I need to change the guitar riff from three-four time to common time to suit, but it begins to come together with the chorus of: 'There's money in diseases/Cash in your coughs and sneezes'.

In the normal course of things I'd celebrate with another cheeky joint, but I've run out of papers to roll with. I set about constructing a makeshift bong instead. It's like an episode of *Blue Peter*, only without the sticky-back plastic. I use a fizzy drinks bottle, nearly empty; my pen, minus the ink insert; scissors, from my desk drawer; and a scrap of kitchen foil, from a tiptoe-trip downstairs.

'You must be about done now,' Maddie says, climbing the ladder to the attic. It's been half an hour – more, maybe – since the bong. 'Are you?'

My face melts into a smile. 'Done, done, *done*,' I say, getting lower with each one so that it sounds like an effect from a horror film.

'Anything you want to play for me?'

Since the NHS song, I've been messing around with some love songs. I'm not convinced that they work quite as well, though. I persisss-persisted (funny-sounding word) with this lyric about a heart being broken 'like the shell of an egg', but I struggled to take it further because I've never really experienced that, y'know? Maybe I should ask Ewan. Call in the expert, eh?

'I'll play you them later,' I say. 'Is it nearly dinnertime?'

'Another while yet.'

She looks at me with narrowed eyes. I respond by narrowing my own and meeting her stare.

'Should we maybe go for a walk or something?' she asks.

'Up to you, babycakes.'

'I think we should.'

We go round to the park and sit on the swings, side by side. Maddie rocks slowly back and forth, with both feet on the ground, but I stay still and twist the chains in my hands.

'When was the last time you spoke to your mother about her work?' Maddie asks after a spell, breaking the silence. After a silence, breaking the spell.

I look up, surprised. 'In what way?'

'Like, whether she's happy.' Maddie shrugs. 'Or even what it is she does.'

My mum has worked at the solicitor's office for a dozen years or so. When I was in primary school, she worked part-time so that she could pick me up in the afternoons, then she moved to full-time as I grew older. Other than her brief try at university, she's been nine-to-five ever since. The recent switch back to part-time is from financial necessity, on the company's part, rather than personal flexibility on hers.

'She does admin work,' I say. 'Receptionist or personal assistant, maybe.'

'Those are three different jobs, Rab.'

'She's a multi-tasker.' I grin.

Maddie shakes her head. 'She's an administrator and book-keeper.'

'That's two jobs.'

Maddie stares down at the rubber surface beneath the swings. It's coloured bright green. Not the natural green of grass, but the shade of a children's crayon. She tries to dig the toe of her trainer into it.

'I was talking to her about it this afternoon,' she says. 'How they moved to Glasgow for your dad's job, the same one he's in now, and she never really pursued anything else because she wanted to be there for him. For you as well.'

'Right,' I say. 'Nothing wrong with that, surely?'

'But I was asking her – there must have been something beyond that, y'know? Things that she wanted to do, to achieve, for herself.'

'My Uncle Brendan always said she wanted a bigger family.'

'Beyond that, even.'

Maddie seems to be driving at something, but she's determined to take the scenic route. True, my mum rarely shows enthusiasm for her job – she's certainly not cocooned in it like my dad is – but she's never actively complained about it either.

'Just that she must have other interests,' Maddie says. 'Like her spoon collection. I was showing her how to use those online auction sites to look for new pieces, Rab, and she got all excited and suddenly – '

'She *can* do that, though. That is another interest.'

'But could she not take it a step further? Really engage with it, y'know, by taking a silversmithing course, maybe, or working at an auction house?'

'There's a big difference between a hobby and a career, Mads.'

'Is there, though?' Maddie goes silent. She sways back and forth on her swing. 'Why could she not pursue the thing she loves to do and take it further?'

'Maddie, you're…'

I've lost the word I was looking for. She's shifting her own ambitions on to my mum. Not even my mum, really – some imagined version of her when she was younger. And Maddie doesn't know the first thing about it; she wasn't there that evening that my mum burst into tears because of the pressure of returning to university. True, that was for accounting or something, rather than for spoons, but the principle is the same.

'Listen...' I change tack. 'Not everyone who collects spoons wants to move to Sheffield and become a master silversmith, right? Just like not everyone who can strum three chords together necessarily wants to become a singer-songwriter. Shit, there's a world of difference between – '

'But she should have had the opportunity to try,' Maddie says.

'She did, didn't she? Have the opportunity, I mean.'

'No.' Maddie shakes her head emphatically enough to rock the swing. 'Because she was always thinking of you guys. Supporting your dad in his career, bringing in an extra bit of cash for the family, and then – '

'Maddie, honestly, I don't think she has any interest in it.'

'We could get her some leaflets on courses.'

This is the central focus of Maddie's chat. We've arrived, finally. She wants to act as a careers advisor, admissions tutor, for my mum. Fuck knows why. Maybe she's thinking that everyone will pursue their separate studies and then, in a few years, we'll form some sort of family troupe. Son on guitar, mother on spoons: a sell-out stadium tour.

'Glasgow Uni,' she continues. 'Or one of the colleges.'

'Really, Maddie – '

'If you and your dad supported her. Emotionally, more than anything.'

'You can't go to uni to study fucking *spoons*!' I half-shout it, irritation causing me to clench my eyes shut. I wait a beat, then open one eye. Maddie is staring at me, chewing at her bottom lip and shaking her head.

After that, she decides to go to her mum's house. I'm fairly certain that she would be welcome for dinner at mine and she could probably stay over if she didn't mind taking the spare room. That way we could spend the evening together. She says she'd rather sleep in her own bed, though. Later in the week, she says, her dad is flying down south and we can be together properly. Overnight. By that stage, I'll be like a sailor on shore-leave.

I walk her back, but on the return journey I get this burn of impatience in my chest. I want to *do* something, *go* somewhere. A pint would douse it, I'm sure, but without the possibility of calling Ewan or Cammy – more accurately, without the possibility of them answering – I can only trail my feet homewards to dinner with my parents.

This time last year, during the summer months after our exams, we were out each and every day celebrating. I forgot what sober felt like. There were afternoons in the woods, of course, but also day trips to Edinburgh, Stirling, and Troon, out on the coast. It was at festival-time that Ewan got so drunk on cheap vodka and so stoned on skunk that he kept freaking out and running away from the rest of us because he didn't recognise any of the streets. And I had to keep chasing after him, to sit him down on the kerb and explain it to him: there was no point in looking for the direction home because he was in the wrong city – Edinburgh, not Glasgow.

When I get home, my parents are already halfway through their shepherd's pie. Mine is in the oven, forming a crust. I shovel forkfuls of it into my mouth, even though it tastes mostly of salt.

I don't forget about the conversation with Maddie – no, ma'am – but I still can't help thinking it's her own issue. Besides, the opportunity to talk to my mum about anything Deep and Meaningful never quite comes up, because she's so busy canvassing my dad about a late summer or early autumn holiday up to the Orkney Islands. She drops more hints than a shy salesman, but the closest she gets to a commitment is an acknowledgement from my dad that September isn't the busiest month at the museum.

After a slice of lemon tart, I leave my dad to decode my mum's tut-tutting over coffee and retreat to my attic to work on my songs. I'll smoke another bong, I reckon, and then take another stab at this austerity budget.

BRIGHTON

Neither of us owns an alarm clock, but there was never a chance of us sleeping late. It is still dark outside when Sage comes through from his morning wash, drip-drying his newly cut hair on to the tiles of the floor. I need to click on the torch to brush the lint from his second-hand suit and straighten his Mozart tie. Then I set up the stove to make his porridge.

'What d'you think they'll ask you?' I say.

'The usual.' He shrugs.

'Like what?'

'Have you never had a job interview, Rab?'

I go quiet, busying myself with measuring out a half-tinful of oats. The only time I've ever been interviewed was by Cesare, back when I was sixteen. He asked if I liked coffee, because if I did then he couldn't employ me as a barista. In case I stole. I stuttered and swore a hatred for the stuff, not realising until my second or third shift that it was his attempt at humour. Somehow I don't think Sage's interview will be like that. Maybe it will be closer to my meetings with Bower: full of jargon and casting-couch promises.

'They'll ask about my teaching at university,' Sage says. 'And about what qualifies me to talk to those with what you might call *vulnerabilities* to alcohol and drugs. Or those with mental health issues.'

'And what does qualify you?'

'Experience,' he says, simply.

The job is with a community centre up near Hollingdean, working with folk to try to increase their employability. Teaching CV-writing skills, interview techniques, time-management and the like. Basic stuff, far removed from Gandhi or the poetry of William Blake. That might be no bad thing, though. He won't be telling people how to think, just how to get from nine to five.

I asked Sage, the other day, how the position was funded, and he replied that it was a mixture of gambling and begging – the Lottery and private donations – but Luke reckons that he's just being cynical and that there might be a bit of city council funding as well. Especially down here, with the Green Party being such a strong presence.

The duplicitous dentist has really come through for us. Not only is he coming over to squat-sit this morning, to guard against unwanted visitors, but he's also helped out with money towards the suit and haircut needed to get Sage from looking as if he's been living underneath a hedge to just looking as if he's been dragged through one backwards. Dishevelled is acceptable – look at the Mayor of London – but stained and shaggy is not.

In any case, Luke has his own fundraising to do, because he's hoping to volunteer over in Tanzania for a year after he's qualified, so it was good of him to donate his share of the money from the two gigs we played last week to what we dubbed the 'suit and shave' fund. He's got plenty of time to make it back, he says, and he's always got the option of taking out a loan. Sage's need is more urgent.

The second gig, at a pub out Rottingdean way, wasn't about the money, though. Not on my part, at least. It was all about the moment, right at the end of the set, when Luke stepped to the back of the stage and left me seated on my stool at the front. Alone. With my eyes closed, I trickled my fingers over the strings and let my voice falter and break over the opening lyrics. All the while, I knew that each note I picked out and every word I sang would build, until the sound filled the small bar. Then every conversation, every pint glass, every turning head and texting thumb would be stilled.

It's called 'Bethnal Green'. A new song, written on my borrowed guitar, about those days after I was thrown out of Pierce's house. And not to sound arrogant, but it's *good*. No one else has told me this, there have been no compliments; I just *know*. As I belted out the chorus, the words rose from deep inside and the guitar melody scaled my spine as a shiver. Out in the audience, I knew that toes were tapping and that if I opened my eyes I would see the eyes of others closed, with a smile spreading.

I know it's good. Which made it all the more annoying when I fucked up. Right towards the end, as I came out of the last chorus. My fingers hovered over the strings. I reached for the F chord, the same one I've played a thousand times, and it slipped. Not for long – I quickly recovered – but the spell was broken.

Afterwards, I took a tenner from the fee and bought myself a whisky. It went down, without a grimace, in a single swallow. As Luke came over, I stalked away to the toilets at the back of the room. They were empty, but I caught sight of myself in the tarnished mirror above the sink. With a yell, I slung the loose change in my hand at my reflection. The coins *pinged* and *cracked* across the room like shrapnel. Instinctively, I ducked and raised an arm to cover my face, and it was in that crouched position that I remembered that the money was not mine to throw away. It was for Sage. Dropping to my hands and knees, I crawled across the floor to pluck up the six pound coins and three twenty pences. I left the ten pence coin where it lay, in an ever-spreading puddle beneath the far-end urinal.

We walk briskly, and I worry about the rattle-wheeze of Sage's breathing, and about the sour-sweet smell of his body odour transferring itself to his suit. It's mild out, even though we're at the start of November. At St Peter's Church I make a point of stopping and taking off my zip-up hoodie. I wait for Sage to remove his jacket, but he is pacing small circles on the pavement and muttering to himself.

'Would you not like to keep your jacket nice?' I ask.

'What?' He turns towards me.

'It's warm enough for just your shirt and – '

'I'm fine,' he says. 'Fine. It's this way.'

We turn on to the bottom of Ditchling Road, past the ornate balconies, leafy trees and bistro pubs. There's graffiti on the walls, but it's trendy – art rather than hatred.

As the road begins to pitch upwards into a slope, leaving the city centre behind, I find I can't stop thinking about the suit jacket. It is difficult to keep anything decent when you're squatting or sleeping rough. Everything you own – seems like everything you touch – takes on the seeping smell of either your skin or your surroundings. It only takes days, less than a week definitely, before you get to the stage of not having anything fit for the likes of a job interview. Then it takes money to buy new clothes. Money you don't have unless you save and sacrifice. Or steal.

'What if you don't get the job, Sage?'

He frowns, but says nothing.

'I'm not saying you won't. But if you don't get it then you'll want to apply for other jobs, won't you? And it would be good to have the jacket clean for that, no? So that it doesn't need a dry-clean.'

He reaches up and wrenches the jacket from one shoulder, then the other. I want to tell him to be careful of the shape and the stitching, but I stay silent and wait for him to hand it off to me. I don't point out that I was just in time, that the armpits are damp with perspiration and that the white fabric of his shirt is beginning to develop that telltale yellow tint at the collar. Instead, I fold the suit jacket over my arm and follow, a step or two behind, as Sage strides on.

The walk is long. We pass streets lined with disused shops and abandoned houses, with wooden boards across windows and tattered 'To Let' signs in overgrown lawns. As we continue climbing, I wonder whether Sage has carried on past Hollingdean and is making for the South Downs. That was his original plan, after all, before the squat: run for the hills.

As we begin to return to terraced streets, though, we take a turn to the right and make our way down into a dip in the road. Sage's pace begins to slacken. He doesn't stop, exactly, but he sways and begins to feel his way, hand over hand, with the help of a garden wall.

I grasp him by the elbow. 'What's the matter?' I ask.

'Why bother, Rab?' He turns to me. His beard is neatly trimmed and his fringe no longer trails across his forehead, but there's despair in his eyes. 'Why fucking bother?'

'They invited you for the interview,' I say, shaking his elbow. 'They think you're suitable for the job, Sage. For fuck's sake, you *are* suitable. You love teaching.'

'I'm only on their list to fill some quota, tick some box…' He trails off and looks at a clutch of shops further down the road. 'Sure, we gave the homeless guy an interview, we even gave him a fucking bourbon biscuit, but he smelt of the *gutter* so we gave it to the young graduate who smells of the new car his daddy bought him.'

'Come on,' I say. 'It won't be like that.'

'You're right: they won't give it to the graduate either. It'll go to the interviewer's daughter or the board member's son.'

'You'll get it, Sage.'

He doesn't look convinced.

'Is it one of those buildings there, then?' I ask.

He nods and points. 'The brown one, with the blinds in the windows.'

'It doesn't look so scary, mate.'

The shop front has no sign. Brown-painted wood cladding surrounds a display window with off-white blinds, shut. To one side is a newsagent, to the other, a fish and chip shop.

There is no movement around them, but a couple of smokers stand outside a betting shop a couple of doors closer to us.

'I should have had a drink,' he says. 'To take the edge off.'

I shake my head. 'Fuck that.'

'They'll take one look at me, though, and…'

This is the main problem with rough sleeping. More than the crotch-rot, the cold and the constant threat of violence – *this*. You get to the stage where you can't imagine anyone looking at you and seeing anything of value. Too used to glances sliding away, eyes flicker-skipping past. It's the self-doubt that clings to you worse than any dirt. And fuck me, it's difficult to clean off once it starts seeping into your skin.

'Let me tell you this,' I say. 'In the centre of London, in pubs and restaurants, there's a steady stream of young graduates. Fucking leaders of the future, these folk. And, when they meet, they reminisce about that one lecturer who spoke about contemporary politics and took the time to bloody *talk* to them about the world outside the walls of the university. And at the end of the table this woman with red hair blushes, because she had a massive crush on that lecturer. Then someone raises a glass, and they all toast to – '

'What's your point, Rab?'

'That you've never valued yourself by quotas or tick-boxes. Or *money*, for that matter. You value yourself by the difference you can make, the impact you can have.'

'And you think that *they'll* do the same?' he snorts.

'Why not?'

Sage stands, slumped, with one hand still on the garden wall. His Mozart tie is askew, showing the missing button halfway down his shirt-front. Shaking out the suit jacket, I hold it out for him. Putting it on, one arm at a time, forces him to stand upright.

'The job is to help people, right?' I say. 'It's to give them the confidence and the skills for them to survive on their own. It's basically about making them feel human again, instead of dog-shit on the sole of a shoe, yes?'

He nods.

'Well, you've done all that for me, mate. All that and more.' I try to meet his eye, but find that I can't. 'These past few months, Sage. Without you I'd be nowhere. In fact…' I falter. 'In fact, remember where I was. When you first met me. Remember where I was. If you can take these folk half as far – '

'We're both still homeless, Rab; we're no further along – '

'*Fuck* that.' There's venom to my words. 'I've grown up a huge fucking amount in these past few months. And yes, I might not have as much money – as much credit, maybe – but, mate, I *understand* more. Am I better equipped to face the world? Damn right. Is that because of you? Fuck, yes.'

'I don't know what to say, Rab.' He speaks softly.

'Say that you're ready.'

He looks up. 'What?'

'Say that you're ready for the interview. Less of this self-pity shite.'

'It's a two-way street, Rab,' he says. 'We all need somebody to talk to and – '

'Just say you're ready,' I interrupt.

'Yes.' He smiles. 'I'm ready.'

'Fuck, yes,' I say. 'Damn right.'

We walk on to the brown building. To the side of the window is a simple metal plaque: 'The Commons'. I reach forward to push open the door. Inside, there is a wooden reception desk with partitions around it to hide the rest of the room. Behind the desk is a middle-aged woman with blonde hair that, scraped back into a ponytail, shows its brown roots at the front. She has damp eyes and a smile that she struggles to keep in place.

'Hi, there,' she says. 'You here for the benefits advice session?'

I shake my head and wave Sage forward. He shuffles up to the desk, with his hands clasped in front of himself. In a whisper, he gives his name to the receptionist and then half-turns, as if preparing to leave.

'Ah. So you're the new employability tutor, are you? Excellent, excellent,' she says, and I pick up a hint of the familiar Glaswegian accent. She looks at her watch. 'You're a touch early, but I think they might be ready for you. I'll take you through. Your friend can take a seat here in reception if he wants to wait?'

She turns to me with a raised eyebrow. I nod and take two steps backwards, until a chair nudges at the back of my knees. Sitting, I flick through the leaflets on the table beside me. They're all about temporary housing in hostels and B&Bs, about getting on the waiting list for social housing. They use the phrases like 'priority need' and 'first-stage' or 'second-stage accommodation' that I recognise from my visit to the day centre in London. I search for the words they used to describe me that day: 'intentionally homeless'. As if it was all part of a plan, all leading up to that proud moment. When I grow up, I want to be –

'Would you like a cup of tea or anything while you wait, honey?'

The receptionist has come back through. She stands, behind her desk, smiling at me. And I find it difficult to answer. When I open my mouth, it feels tacky and the words won't form themselves. Even after I clear my throat, loudly, the best I can do is shake my head and offer up an apologetic smile. She gives a single nod in response, and sits down to busy herself on the computer. The opening for conversation is passing; the social situation is slipping into silence.

'Are you from Glasgow?' I ask. It comes out loud. Abrupt.

'I am indeed,' she says. 'Or close by, at least. Cambuslang. Why, where are you from?'

'The West End, just… Broomhill.'

'Lovely.' She smiles. 'So what brings you down this way?'

It used to be, in pubs and at parties, that I fished for this question. It's been a while, though, since anyone has seen me as anything other than homeless. Even with my guitar, I'd not be described as a singer, but as a busker. Or, worse, a beggar.

'I was a singer,' I try. 'And guitarist.'

'Is that right? Well, Brighton's good for the music scene – or so my nieces tell me. What kind of thing do you play?'

'Folky stuff. Acoustic mainly.'

She nods and then looks back at her computer screen. She shakes her head at something, then reaches for a pen and a piece of paper. All the while, though, the index finger of her left hand points at me, over in my chair, as if to remind her that our conversation is not over.

I hold my breath through the seconds of silence. Maybe she's thinking of forming a band and needs a guitarist. Or she might be thinking of setting me up with one of her nieces. Neither is likely, granted, but you never know.

'So,' she says, finally, 'you must need somewhere to practise? Are you sleeping rough at the moment, or…?'

'Squatting,' I reply, taken aback by the directness of the question.

'Yes, must be difficult to get peace. Definitely. But we have rooms upstairs here that are free most days.' She points to the ceiling. 'If you want somewhere quiet to practise.'

'Thank you.'

'All these government directives and incentive-linked benefits are about getting people into offices or labs or…' She waves a hand vaguely in the air. 'But it makes precious little provision for artists or musicians or writers.'

She goes silent. I'm nodding, but she doesn't look up.

'Those professions with little or no stability but plenty of value, you know?' she continues. 'Because we've got a culture to be proud of here, and in most countries they'd be celebrating it.'

'Absolutely,' I say, in a whisper she probably doesn't hear.

'And it's not that artists or musicians want money, in my experience,' she says. 'They don't want a handout, you know? All they're looking for is time and space.'

I'm back to the dry throat, the words that won't come. I've forgotten what it's like to engage in a conversation without the lubrication of pills or alcohol. Just an everyday exchange. Next up on the list is the joke I've just thought up. It's fully formed, ready to go. Fuck it, it's even funny. But my mouth gapes open, gulping in the air, and the seconds tick past.

'We're like physicists that way,' I breathe. It's quieter than the inhale before it or the exhale afterwards, but the words are still there.

She looks up, surprised, and smiles. 'What was that?'

'I said, musicians are like physicists that way: only looking for time and space.'

'Very clever.' She chuckles. 'Very good indeed.'

I sit back in my chair, pleased with myself.

'Aye,' the receptionist says. 'It would be nice to have some music about the place – good for the soul. And if your friend is up this way anyway, most days, then it would make sense to tag along and pay us a visit, you know?'

'I'd like that, yes,' I say. 'Thanks.'

'Just say that Sandra said it was OK. That's me.'

'Nice to meet you. I'm Rab.'

She nods, takes a note.

'So…' I hesitate. 'Is he likely to get the job, then?'

'Your friend?'

I nod. Can an unemployed man teach employability? Can a homeless man teach stability? He's either the most or the least qualified candidate imaginable. I just can't decide which.

'He's got a teaching qualification,' Sandra says. 'He's worked with university leavers on employability, *and* he's got an understanding of the limitations and issues these people are dealing with. So, honestly – ' she looks across at me ' – we'd be lucky to have him.'

'All he needs is an opportunity, definitely,' I say.

From somewhere behind the partition, Sage and his interviewer start to talk. It drifts through to us as a bass note, from Sage, with the occasional melody of a question from the woman interviewing him. In the hard plastic seat I close my eyes and listen, remembering those nights down at the shore when his stories would distract me from wakefulness. Like when he told me the origin of the word 'sabotage' – how French workers would throw their wooden clogs, or *sabots*, into the gears of the looms to protect their jobs from the new machines. Or the time he tried, with his tongue twisted by alcohol, to explain that the word 'assassin' came from hashish-influenced murderers at the time of the Crusades: *ha-sha... ha-sha-shin... hash-ah-shin*. And I smile, even though I know that the memory shouldn't be a happy one.

LONDON

I give the interview outside Bethnal Green Tube station. To the guy from the *Standard*. As we talk, the Olympics commuters stream down the stairs, making for the Central Line to Stratford. They are red and white with excitement, against the blue of the early evening sky. The warm mouth of the Underground swallows them, then belches out a trickle of returning afternoon spectators. I have to shout to make myself heard above all the coming and going.

'It's the difficult second album, isn't it?' I say. 'That's the one they warn you about. It's a tricky one, most definitely. Need to follow up the first, of course, but also build. *Develop.*'

I've taken a seat. On the paving slabs. It's not the tonic wine; I'm used to that. I think it must be the co-codamol. Over-the-counter pills, but strong enough to slump me down to the ground with my back against the phone box. My interviewer remains standing.

'The first one wasn't brilliantly received, no. But that might be timing as much as anything, d'you not think? With the Olympics this summer, and the royal wedding last spring. People don't want social critique. They don't want political activism, do they? Look around.'

Everything seems to have been taken over by the Olympics recently. It's everywhere. Not that I've seen much of the action myself. Not since I left Pierce's house. We split at the start of

214

this week, the Monday after the opening ceremony. 'Artistic differences'. No matter, though, there are plenty of singers out there without managers. Going it alone is in vogue – triumph against the odds, the Olympic fucking spirit.

'It's important for the songs to retain that political message, certainly, but I'm also looking for more by way of *hooks* in this second album. It's useful if they're catchy as well, you know. Not manufactured pop – no, sir – but with enough, erm, ingredients of… elements of… to…'

I told Pierce that I slept with Lydia. I told him out of boredom, maybe; out of frustration. After Bower confirmed that the option for the second album wouldn't be taken up. No gigs since Southampton; no money since the advance dried up. Only a couple of nights in Kentish Town where I had to pass the hat around after playing to get payment in loose change, and a so-called 'blog tour' that consisted of me updating some other musicians' websites free of charge. That was the sum total of Pierce's 'management' in those weeks. So I told him that I fucked his wife.

'I'm between labels at the moment,' I tell the *Standard* man. 'Although the songs are there, ready to go. It's complicated, you understand? I was signed to an indie-style label, but they were owned by a major, and they didn't like, maybe… with the social message… didn't like the *truth*.'

Of course, I didn't get near Lydia. There was nothing there, other than that morning I made a pass. Pierce deserved some pain, though, after what he put me through. Chiding me – day after day, night after night – to get on with writing some new songs. Even though I'd just recorded an *album*. Hadn't even toured it properly, or had it reviewed other than those amateurish attempts around the time of release. But we needed an EP's worth, Pierce said, to take to Bower. The option was coming, the option was looming, the option would strike without us knowing. An epic fucking armageddon.

In the end, we only got to play Bower one of the three new songs. At that meeting near the end of July. Just one. Then his massive finger stabbed at the CD player. He hit stop, he hit pause, he hit fucking fast-forward. The music stopped. Then, with careful detachment, he told us that the money men, the suited saps upstairs, had decided against the second album. *Measures Taken* would be the only release on Agitate Records.

'It's a fickle business, sure. But there are plenty of labels, plenty of second chances, don't you think? It's not a closed shop, surely? You don't only get one shot. Brother, all you need is a bit of *buzz*, a bit of fucking… well, momentum. And that can be got. That can be got. Right here, right now, with these fine folk making their way to the Olympic Park, I could busk and make a… earn a… isn't it?'

It was in the taxi on the way back to the flat that I told Pierce about his wayward wife. I was sober, as well. I'd taken something with codeine in it, sure, and those benzos the doctor gave me for anxiety were on constant rotation, but I hadn't had a drink since the night before. I'd kept a clear head for the meeting, just to please Prick-Price.

He didn't say anything. Not in the taxi. He just stared straight ahead, so that I began to wonder if he'd even heard me. There wasn't a word spoken on the stairs, either. Even as he started to lift my clothes from the floor, as he squashed them into that rucksack I'd taken – all those months ago – to the last days of Occupy London. Nothing from Price. And nothing from Lydia, sitting startled on the sofa.

Within minutes, I was on the street. Rucksack on my back, guitar in hand.

But I never found out if he confronted Lydia, if they had a marriage meltdown over it or not. Nothing was said in front of me, anyway. Except for those two words – 'we're done' – directed at me rather than at her. Maybe Pierce did say the same to her, but she wasn't kicked out. I waited for her. I expected her to come out sobbing, in that slinky slip of hers, and walk, on bare feet, along the rain-slicked pavement towards me. It didn't happen, though. It rarely fucking does, apart from in books and plays and films and fucking *songs*.

'The main thing with the second album,' I tell the *Standard*-bearer, 'is to make sure that it taps into something bigger, you know? Like, there's still a lot of anger around, on the streets and that, in spite of the Olympics… papering over the crack-whores, is all this is… because of the inequality of… because Britain is still a rich country, isn't it? In spite of this recessi-deficit shit, there's no reason for anyone to… if they're hungry or…'

He steps further away from me, in his red bib. He holds out copies of the *Standard* to the folk coming up from the Underground. They avoid me too. They step past me, around me, and bury their heads into the paper to read about the running-jumping-cycling heroics they've just come from. All is well; all is golden.

'Sure I get nervous before playing live,' I tell them. 'But the fans have paid their money, they deserve my best. And I feed off their energy, you know?'

Parents place hands on their children's shoulders, to steer them away from me. But the kids look back, unafraid to meet my eye.

'The music thing is all I have,' I say. 'What would I be doing otherwise? Probably still working in coffee shops, eh? The daily grind, if you like.'

I think I hear laughter: faint, underground. I acknowledge it with a slight nod.

'Of course I'll play you out, glad to. How about a first play from my second album? An exclusive, just for this show. Since we're friends.'

It takes another three days to run out of money completely. There was enough in the dregs of my credit card to fund a stay at a B&B up Camden way, paid in advance, but once that's used up I don't have so much as a copper coin. It's not as if I spend the time productively, either. In the daytime I wander the streets, and in the evenings I call Pierce and Bower. Using the hardened calluses on my plucking fingers, I dial again and again. They pick up a couple of times, but all I can give them is bottle-bile, a booze-bollocking, before they hang up. After that, I'm forced to reason with answering machines.

'It seems like…' I swig. 'One album isn't a lot to try with, you know?'

'What about a development contract?' I sway. 'Is that not a thing? Does that not exist?'

'A fucking year is all I get, is it?' I spit. 'What's that? What the *fuck*'s that?'

They must be talking to each other about my queries, liaising about my comeback. That's why they've not got back to me as yet. They're letting me stew in the florid heat of the B&B to give themselves some leverage for the contract negotiations. The second album is the difficult one, after all; they want to make sure that I'm *tough*. That I'm hardy-fucking-ha.

The landlady is very nice about my credit card being refused. She wears a patient smile and goes off to try my debit card. She's even pleasant enough when that doesn't work, but she turns fucking frosty when I ask if I can have another night on tick. She's insistent on payment in advance, this lady. It doesn't seem to matter that I've been staying here all week. There's no fucking loyalty system. Once she's established that I'm penniless, she can't get rid of me quickly enough. She even tries to cheat me out of my final breakfast, in spite of the fact that I've bloody *paid* for that. I have to count them off on my fingers to show her.

After my oily sausage and egg – the sour bitch overcooked the yolk as punishment – I go out on to the streets of Camden Town with my rucksack and guitar. Later, I'll go to find the day centre that the landlady pointed me towards. For now, though, it's worth finding a decent busking spot and making the most of the warm weather and the goodwill-generosity-guilt of the summer shoppers.

I'm mindful of the reviews as I play. Instead of 'Ivory Towers', which that one magazine described as 'infantile',

I play a Kinks cover. Rather than continue past the intro to 'Baby and the Bathwater', slated as 'cringingly clichéd' on the Indie Idol website, I pause and then play a bit of the Boss. Even the musical outro to *Measures Taken*, which that newspaper reviewer described as 'the one track blissfully free of screeching and saccharine lyrics', only gets a brief airing to check that my guitar is in tune.

By the time I leave for the day centre I've earned a grand total of six pounds and seventy-two pence. Probably more than I've earned from royalties so far. It's enough for an unbranded pack of co-codamol and one of those plastic bottles of table wine. I'm thinking that I'll sort myself out with some medicine and then this shelter-place can sort me out with a hot meal and some accommodation. Job done.

Not a bloody bit of it, though. I have the good sense to hide the half-empty bottle in my rucksack and tuck the pills away in my pocket, but the sweat-bucket at the desk still gives me a lecture about the centre being 'dry'. *Is that right, fella? How about you fucking mop your brow, then? Why don't you take some BO spray to what those armpits of yours are giving out?*

I think he might be related to the B&B landlady, to tell the truth. He's of the same build, and his shirt is made of the same material as her curtains. More than that: both of them twitch their blank expressions into a frown every time I try to answer their questions. That's a genetic thing, right? That's a family trait. They must be mother and son, I'm thinking, with old mum passing on her residents to her child so he can fleece them further. That's how it works, isn't it? If you've got work in the family, then you pass it on. If you don't, you're fucked. Necro-something, you call it. Maybe that's why he keeps on asking about my parents, about my 'monetary situation'.

I lay it all out for him. The royalties will start coming in, of course they will, but in the meantime I have a cash-flow problem. Pierce's floor is off-limits, and I know no one else in London.

'You have alcohol problems?' he asks. No loosening questions, no ice-breakers.

'I like a drink,' I reply.

'What about drugs?'

'For anxiety, yes.'

'Heroin?' He raises an eyebrow.

'No,' I say. 'Prescription only.'

What is it with the English? They think everyone from north of the border is from that book – you know the one. Fuck that. I've no interest in making a Braille novel of my arm. Never had. I'll smoke and I'll snort, but I'd never stick myself with a needle.

'And do you have any family you could stay with?'

'Only up in Glasgow.'

'Is there anything *preventing* you from going back to them?'

'My career.'

There is no flinch-frown now. To be fair, he doesn't exactly laugh either. It's more of a splutter-cough. But it's enough for me to want to uppercut one of his chins. Maybe that and a knee to the goolies, then back up to the B&B to see to his precious mother.

I stay seated, though, and manage to restrain myself. It's up to him whether he passes me back to his family business or on to a hostel or whatever, but I want my bed for the night.

'We can only give advice, Mr Dillon,' he says. 'But your family might be the best option. Because you're not priority need. In fact, it could be argued that you're intentionally homeless…'

'Fuck does that mean?'

'You have a place to stay in Glasgow, correct?'

'So what? Are you telling me to walk home, is that it?'

Am I like shite going back to Glasgow. With my tail shoved up my arse, never mind between my legs. Turning up with a cheery wave for my parents and my friends after giving it all that on the way out. And Maddie? After what I said to Maddie,

I need to be going back with platinum records, platinum credit cards and a platinum-blonde girlfriend. I need to show her she was *wrong*, don't I? Am I like shite going back.

'We can send you to some of the direct-access hostels,' he says. 'But they fill up. Fast.'

'You look like you fill up fast too, mate.'

'What?'

'Nothing, nothing.'

'Take these leaflets.'

He gives me some promotional literature for hostels – probably run by his aunts and uncles – and a cheeky one about alcohol dependency. Then he stands up. He waits for me to do the same. It takes a minute, though. Because where the fuck am I meant to go? There are all these streets in London, all these houses and public buildings – my *A–Z* is full of them – but not one of them would welcome a failed and friendless folk singer.

And it's at that moment that I get homesick. Not for the shallow-eaved safety of my attic bedroom or the bare-skin warmth of Maddie's bed, but for the woods up at the back of Hyndland train station. Our old drinking spot. Where the trees stand silent and still, the bushes rustle only with the breeze, and the shouts and siren-sounds are faint and far away.

Instead, I end up on the pavement outside the centre. I turn one way, then the other. I reach into my pockets, hoping to find an unnoticed note or a coin caught in the fabric. Nothing. So I begin walking down the street to my left. As I go, I scan the shop doorways, the entrances to lanes and loading bays, the underpass and the archways, the concrete foyers outside the office blocks and Underground stations. I'm looking for a good busking location, certainly, where I can hopefully make enough in spare change to fund a night indoors. But I know that whichever spot I choose will probably be more than that. It will probably be where I end up spending the night.

GLASGOW

I have five tabs open on my browser when the phone rings. One is a solo brunette with red lingerie and searching fingers; the next is blonde lesbians sharing oil and dildos; then an Asian blowjob scene; a little latex number that caught my eye; and, finally, a racial-harmony threesome – one black, one white, one latin. I look down at the clock in the corner of the laptop screen: 3.17am.

'Hi,' I answer my mobile. 'I was expecting you to be asleep by now.'

'Are you at home?' Maddie asks.

'Yeah, I got in about twenty minutes ago.'

I was out with Gemma. Pub then club. To celebrate my eighteenth, three days early. On my actual birthday I'll be going out for dinner and drinks with Maddie and my parents. I'm thinking that none of my friends would accept an invite – they've all sided with Ewan – except for Gemma who would bend over backwards – dislocate her spine, even – to preserve our friendship. The night out was a compromise, to save her the embarrassment of being the only one of the group at the dinner. Gemma spoke earnestly of the past all evening, as if flicking through a photo album of our times together – school, parties, gigs, holidays. The woods. The time the police came, torches sweeping the trees, and Teagan, running away, tripped and fell in the mud, then turned to the policemen and said, 'For fuck's sake, will you look at the *state* of me now.' Or the night

Ewan sliced his hand on broken glass and, instead of going to the hospital, just washed it with whisky and then continued to help Cammy build a fire. We were full of stories.

Neither of us mentioned Maddie, though. She was carefully clipped out.

'Are you busy?' Maddie asks, on the phone. 'I'd like to talk to you about something.'

'No.' I look at the laptop. The threesome, muted, is continuing without me. 'Go ahead.'

'There are a couple of problems with the move south, Rab. For me, I mean. Like, the exams I'd be taking would be A-levels rather than Highers so it would be a whole different education system to – '

'We've talked about this, though.'

Maddie didn't do as well as expected in her exams. Drama was her only A. She would need to stay on for a sixth year at school to get the grades she needed for university. Nothing wrong with that, of course, but she seems resistant to the idea of doing that down in London. Even though that was the plan. *Our* plan.

'But as well as that,' she says, 'there's also the tuition fees issue, isn't there? Because if I go next year then it'll be more expensive than this year, but in Scotland it's free, whichever year I go. That's a big difference, Rab.'

'So now you've decided to stay up here for uni as well?'

'I've not decided, no.'

'We can make the financials work, Mads. It's only money.'

'It's debt.'

'What's the difference?'

'Well, if I want to go on and get involved in theatre…' She hesitates. 'I'm not choosing this career for the massive wages, put it that way. It'll all be internships and temporary contracts. And if I'm saddled with debt right from the off…'

We've had this same argument, over and over, for the past fortnight. Since the exam results came out. If I could give her my own results, from last year and this, I would. As it is, though, I don't see the problem with her getting a job during the day and studying for her exams at a college in the evenings. Then, next year, she can go off to uni and I'll support her. She probably won't even need the loans. If she does, it'll only be short-term.

'I'll look after you,' I say. 'We'll be fine.'

'But,' she speaks softly, 'I *like* the idea of free tuition fees, Rab. Not just because it suits me. I also think it's right, you know. Our generation's going to be contributing for the next forty-odd years, so the tab for our education is picked up. That's *right*.'

'Sure,' I say, closing down the threesome and clicking on the Asian blowjob scene.

'It's the equivalent of your advance, really. The government puts out the initial outlay because they're expecting to recoup that money from the graduates in taxes over their lifetime. Like the label. And one or two individuals might not earn the money back, but it supports the development of – '

'Uh huh.' Japanese porn is often pixelated, but it's still worth a watch. 'You just said, though, that you'll not be earning massive wages, so you probably won't contribute enough to cover your free tuition anyway, will you?'

'I just said…' There's a sigh from Maddie and a smile from the porn-actress. 'That's assuming that the only *contribution* that can be made is monetary. What about a fucking *cultural* contribution?'

'You can make money and culture at the same time, surely.'

'Make culture?'

'You know what I mean – '

'Anyway, we're getting sidetracked.' She sighs again.

I move on to the solo brunette. She's a definite looker. I decided on her because she reminds me a bit of Gemma. Not that I've got a thing for Gemma, but I did spend the whole evening with her, and she was so attentive. Always laying a hand on my arm, or leaning in for a cuddle after one of her 'but you're such good *friends*' or 'you've known each other *such* a long time' entreaties about Ewan. The brunette is a passable way of letting the night reach its natural conclusion while staying faithful to Maddie.

That might be drunken logic, I admit, but I drank a fair few whisky and Cokes at the club tonight. Then a shot or two of sambuca before closing. To get me through the last of Gemma's chats. The tearful one.

'And there's another option, isn't there?' Maddie says.

'What's that?'

'Well, you don't actually *need* to move to London, do you? Like, you'll need to be there for the recording, I guess, and for certain events, maybe…' She pauses. 'Look, I don't know how it works, but do you really need to be in the same city as your label?'

'You mean I could stay in Glasgow?'

'And travel up and down.'

Pierce suggested the same thing. After signing the publishing contract, in the offices of the parent company: the major label. We'd had meetings the whole day with the lawyer and the accountant – Pierce's men – then the product manager, the A&R man, and the publicist, from the label. This music lark's not as simple as walking into a studio, with a guitar, and recording a track or two. There are folk to tell you how to walk in, to argue that the guitar should really be a five-piece band, to take the tracks and remix them so that all that remains of the original is the opening chord and five seconds of the chorus. I'd met so many people that day that, by the end of it, I was reaching forward to shake hands with the filing cabinet and imagining a fitted pinstripe suit on the coat-rack.

When it was just me and him again, Pierce took me to the side. It's easy for your feet to lift from the floor, he said, just an inch or two. With so much going on, so many voices in your ear. It might be best to stay where you have friends and family around you. Glasgow, he was saying, would be a good base for me, with regular visits to London whenever they were needed.

There are two ways of looking at that, though. Pricey was saying that the folk I grew up with would keep my feet on the ground, but I was thinking that they would drag me down.

'We need to be in London, Maddie,' I say. 'It's the only way.'

'But the advance will only keep you for – what, six months?'

'Seven or eight.'

'Really?'

'Of course, through to the release. That's the idea.'

The accountant gave me a spreadsheet that details spending for six months. It's based on one month in a hotel, then five in a rented room. I can make that stretch, though. Because all he put in the 'income' column is the advance from the label, nothing extra. And I can pick up some money from gigs. Hell, I can even busk if things get tight.

'Seven or eight,' I repeat. 'Through to release.'

The solo girl is boring me. She's not varying her routine any. I close her down in favour of the lesbians. They'll challenge each other, push each other on to ever greater feats. Besides, they're *oiled*.

'Rab,' Maddie says, 'I can't.'

'Can't what?'

'Move away. It's too soon for me. I'm a year younger than you, don't forget…'

'What difference does that make?'

'You're just turning eighteen. You can drink – legally – in bars and… I just think I need another year up here. To get everything settled and then go on to uni next year.'

There's some furious movement on-screen, but the girl's gasps and groans to camera are only silent mouthings. It looks as if she's screaming, swearing, at me. As if to blame me for what the other girl is doing to her with the dildo.

I watch numbly.

'I need to move to London,' I repeat. 'It's the only option.'

'It can't be.'

'It is.'

She goes quiet. The blondes change position.

'How much do you even know about Agitate anyway?' Maddie asks.

'Fuck's sake, not this again.'

This has been another constant conversation over the past fortnight. Because Maddie found some story on the internet, about this young rapper named Brink who was signed by Agitate last year. After releasing an EP, the label planned to drop him because of poor sales. Then, at the start of this month, his track 'Riotously' enjoyed a spike in downloads after the riots down in London. He wanted to move on to a different label, but Agitate held him to the terms of his original contract and plan to release his debut album next year.

Maddie brings up Brink as a warning, but I see him as a success. His track is about racial tensions in Tottenham Hale – it's *contemporary* – and Agitate took a risk on it. Sure, he was cut adrift after the EP, but the label soon recognised their mistake. There are two sides to every story, aren't there? From the label's point of view, they're just recouping their initial investment by holding him to his contract. Fair enough, I say.

'You've heard some of their artists,' I say. 'I played you that electro-pop outfit Hemmed In, didn't I? And that singer, Sasha Coburn, still comes on the radio from time to time.'

'She's nowhere to be seen now, Rab.'

'Not everyone can make it big.'

'But, that's the point – ' She breaks off, so abruptly that I have to check my mobile to see if the call is still connected. It is, so I look back to the laptop and wait. One of the blondes is saying something into the camera. I try to lip-read but can't make it out.

227

'All I'm saying is,' Maddie continues, 'you can't expect everything to just magically take off, you know? It'll be hard. Really fucking hard. And even then it'll be a dice-roll as to whether it all actually goes anywhere or not.'

'Exactly,' I say. 'So I need to be on hand for when it all happens. To take advantage.'

'I can't take that risk, Rab, is what I'm saying.'

I draw breath. 'You really do love your drama, don't you?'

'What does that mean?'

It means she's even better at manufacturing emotions from nothing than the blondies. That her reactions are just as overblown and fucking fake. It means that everything was sorted – all our fuck-a-ducks were in a row – up until this phone call. At 3.17am. When Maddie, lying awake in her bed, started groping around in the dark for some shit and a fucking fan.

'There's no issue, is all I'm saying, Maddie. It's only because it's late, maybe, or because you're a wee bit nervous about the move – '

'You're not hearing me, Rab,' she says, and I can hear her breath catch. 'I'm not going.'

'You'll be able to study at – '

'I'm staying.'

The video on the laptop stutters then buffers. There is skin on screen, but it's difficult to make out which blonde it belongs to or where, on their body, it is. I click: pause, play, pause, play. Nothing happens.

'Rab?' Maddie says. 'Do you understand what that would mean? It would mean we would break up.'

I stop clicking. 'Why?'

'Unless you stayed in Glasgow, of course.'

'Why the fuck would it mean we'd break up?'

'Long-distance wouldn't work, Rab.'

'Let me get this shit straight.' The words seethe out. 'You'd be OK with me travelling up and down – *daily*, for all we know – for my music, but there's not a fucking chance of you getting the train down on a weekend, no?'

'I just… it's just that long-distance never seems to work. And if you're concentrating on your music down there and I'm concentrating on my exams up here – '

'So it's all about concentration, then, is it?'

'No. What I mean is, you'll be settling into it and – '

'Are you shagging someone else, is that it?'

There's silence on the other end of the line, then static as Maddie lets her breath out. The lesbians on my lap start up again, but I stab a finger to get rid of them.

'Fuck you, Rab,' Maddie says.

'That's it, isn't it? This is all just a way of worming your way out. There's no fucking crisis about moving down there; it's only you trying to find some grander excuse – some other *motivation* – that's not just you getting horny for some other guy – '

'What other guy? Where is this coming from?'

'There's always another fucking guy.'

'How could you even think that?'

'It's what you did to Ewan, isn't it?'

She goes quiet. I listen to her breathing. When she speaks, it is barely above a whisper.

'We're done here,' she says, then hangs up.

It takes a minute, staring at first phone then laptop, before I'm able to process what just happened. Maybe I shouldn't have had that joint as I was browsing for video clips. I definitely should have closed the laptop and just focused on the call. This is what comes of multi-tasking. Now, as well as the headache-hangover in the morning, I'll have this ball-ache breakup to sort out. This misunderstanding. Because that's all it is, surely. We've *decided* to move down south, we've talked it through. It's the next step, in both our careers. I mean, for fuck's sake, she wants to work in theatre. London's the place to do that, isn't it? She must see that. Why stay in Glasgow's West End when you've got a chance to move to *the* West End, eh?

The lesbians have gone, so I move on to the latex. The black shiny suit covers her whole body, with only two slits in it. One for breathing and one for... I get it playing and reach down into my boxer-shorts. It's only fiddling and fumbling, though; there's nothing stirring. Nothing.

Tomorrow I'll go round to see Maddie, face to face. We can talk it through properly. Maybe browse online for some flats in London. Then, over the weekend, I could use some of my advance to take her down on the train – fuck the spreadsheet, I'll just withdraw the money and sort it later – stay in a hotel, see a play or a gig. In fact, it might even be possible to schedule a set or two of my own to make the trip pay for itself. Short notice, yes, but I could call Pierce to see if there's anything available. Show Maddie that it's the place I *need* to be for my music.

It's maybe the gimp mask that's killing my lust. If I could see her properly, then I'd be more interested. She's showing no signs of taking it off, though. I turn the volume up instead. So I can hear the sighs and the squeaking. Then I make a last, concerted effort to salvage what I can from the evening.

BRIGHTON

Sage settles quickly into his job. Every morning he's up and out before the winter sun has taken the knife-chill from the air. I rise an hour or so later, when the frost along the base of the window panes is beginning to soften. Steeping a teabag in my tin-cup until the liquid is dark and bitter, I curl my fingers around the warmth to thaw them for the morning's practice.

He tells me about 'The Commons' in the evenings. It's not your usual community centre; not just a charity or an advice centre. The place is organised as a community benefits society, where everybody has a say. Everyone living within a certain distance of the building is invited to be a member – rough sleepers can join too – and then they all vote on how to spend the budget.

As a result, Sage isn't only teaching employability, he's also been asked to do some literature classes. He's starting with *Brighton Rock*, for the local connection. Using books borrowed from the library. And he's proposing that they all group together – the members – and write a verbatim play about the community. Not just about cuts to the benefits system or the government vilification of the unemployed, but about the strength and humour and kindness between them as well. They'll vote on whether to go ahead with that project in the next few days.

We've spoken about submitting a proposal for me too. Sage reckons I should offer guitar lessons or even songwriting classes, but I'd rather keep that separate. Instead, I'm working on something else to present to them, scribbling in the margins of the Christian pamphlets given out at the food bank we go to. A simple idea, but something I would enjoy.

For now, though, I stay in the squat during the day. To protect it from the heavies the landlord has employed. In the early days, within a week of arriving, we had the police round. They were easy. Sage gave them a lecture through the letterbox – about the morality of buildings sitting empty when folk are sleeping rough on the cold streets – and they were satisfied.

The heavies, however, are not content with the sign on the door or a shouted invitation to have us evicted through the civil court, using repossession orders and court-appointed bailiffs. They are not patient men.

At first I knew them only as noises. As voices whispering, then snarling. As thumps on the door, rattling the locks. But, one afternoon, I see a hand and then a peering set of eyes. They are up on the flat roof of the toilet extension, pulling the felt away and then ripping at the wood with the claw of a hammer. When the hand appears, I wonder what weapon I could use to strike out at it. To leave it bent and broken, with the wrist snapped and the back of the hand lying flat against the ceiling. It's a panicked thought, though, and one that is quickly followed by the realisation that they'd have me up on assault charges. So, when the eyes look down through the hole, I try reasoning with the man behind them.

'This was an empty building,' I say, gasping and grasping at the words. 'We know that the owner has no immediate plans to redevelop it, that it's just for his portfolio, and – '

'You need to get the fuck out.' The eyes narrow. '*Now*.'

'If he wants to discuss his plans for the building with us, we'd – '

'No. You need to do one. Today.'

I try a different tack. 'You're damaging his roof. This building is structurally sound, but if you tear open the roof then you'll leave it exposed to – '

'Right, mate. I'm coming in, then.'

'There are about a dozen of us in here!'

I shout this as a warning. I've barely held it together up to this point – hearing the footsteps overhead, the blows of the hammer, and then seeing the disembodied, dangling hand – but the thought of them coming in, dropping down from the ceiling, really sets me off. Taking my tin-cup, I clatter it against the sinks, against the cisterns. I stamp my feet. Then I start a conversation with myself – one moment shrill, the next deep. The words are nonsense, are just noise.

'We'll fucking smoke you out, then, won't we,' the heavy calls.

They keep working to widen the hole, but now I'm not sure if it's to gain entry or to set a fire. How do you tell if someone means something like that literally or not? If you can't see the eyes, the face, but only the grabbing hand.

I run through to the main room and lift the ice-bucket from the primus stove. With it, I drum at the wooden bar and use my spare hand to strum at the open strings of my guitar. It's not enough, though. So I start wailing – a thin, primal note that rises above the racket.

'Ain't nobody going to take my home from me, no,' I sing, then, in a bass note.

'Ain't gonna take my home,' in falsetto.

'Ain't nobody gonna leave me on the street.' Bass.

'Don't you leave me on the street.' Falsetto.

'I've fallen far enough, I'm on the fucking floor.'

'Don't kick me no fucking more.'

I lose my rhythm, but I work hard to find it again and repeat my chanting. Drumming, strumming and screaming, I keep up the noise as best I can. Concentrating, losing track of the passing of time and the words coming out of my mouth. When, eventually, I trail off, there are no sounds from the toilets at the back.

Swinging the bucket in front of myself, I advance to the Gents. There is a cold wind swirling in through the hole in the roof, which is twice as big as it was, but there are no hands or eyes above. They have been scared off. Probably more by the thought of one lad with mental health issues than by the promise of a dozen reinforcements, but a victory's a victory.

'Ha!' I shout upwards. 'Thanks for the skylight, dickheads!'

Then I retreat back to the main room and begin to barricade the door to the toilet. I use chairs and tables, trying to prop them up underneath the handle. They won't hold, though, so I prise the panelling from the bar. Rusty nails come away with the wood. It takes me about ten minutes of frantic work to hammer it across the door jamb, using the butt of our screwdriver. All the while, I'm listening out for their footsteps on the roof or the thud of them landing on the tiled floor on the other side of the door.

Once I've finished, I sit cross-legged in the centre of the floor and clasp my hands together in my lap. To try to stop the shaking.

Sage comes back from work about an hour later. I ignore his first knocks, even though they're in the agreed pattern – three rapid, three slow, then three rapid again. I sit where I am and stare at the door. It's only when he repeats the knock and calls out – 'Rab!' – that I rise to unbolt the lock.

'What's the matter?' he asks.

'We'll have to use the Ladies from now on,' I say.

'Did they try to get in?'

'Through the roof.' I nod. 'Should we phone the police, maybe?'

'And what?' He smiles tightly. 'Invite them in for a cup of tea while they take our details?'

He has bought dinner on his way back. There is bread and pâté, bananas, and grapes. One tin of beer, for me, and one of cider, for him. When he sees the state I'm in, though, he lets me have both. We ignore the fact that I'm trying to cut down, trying to loosen the grip of that particular vice.

234

We sit in the darkness and talk. About the need to move out. Not back to the streets, but somewhere stable. It's getting close to Christmas – just a month away – and that means even colder weather. We don't want to find ourselves sleeping rough again, or moving from one emergency accommodation to another: churches, hostels, B&Bs. It's nearly New Year, and we make a resolution to find something more permanent as soon as we can. Now that Sage is earning a trickle of a wage.

'There's a room in one of the members' houses,' Sage says. 'Nice lady. Used to be a crossword compiler for a national broadsheet until her eyesight started to fail.'

'Has she offered it to you?'

'Almost. She told me that it would be useful to have the help and the company…'

'Why didn't you tell me?'

He shrugs.

'Just one room?'

He clears his throat. 'That's the thing.'

I look over into the gloom, but I can't see anything other than the bulk of him.

'I can't leave you.' He says it that plainly. 'We're a pair, you and I. But maybe if we could find you somewhere as well, and if we could get your proposal off and running up at the – '

'I could ask Luke if he knows of anywhere,' I say, thinking of the student flat up in Elm Grove.

'Do that,' Sage says. 'And in the meantime – '

'We tough it out here?'

'Absolutely,' he says. 'In our Sick Little Hammer.'

'Getting sicker by the day.'

'Today, yes,' Sage chuckles. 'But it's not so bad. Just a bit like myself – rotten body, rusted head.'

I go to an internet café a couple of days later, to type up my proposal. In the normal course of things I might have gone to the day centre to use one of the computers there, but I

235

don't want to leave the squat unattended. So I wait until the evening, when Sage is back from work, and then take the scraps of paper I've been scrawling on to a place up by the train station.

The sullen owner takes my money and brings me coffee, though I asked for tea. Unwilling to go up to the counter to complain – knowing I would be addressing his leather-jacketed friends as well as him – I sip at the coffee. It is cloyingly sweet.

It's been a long time since I typed. Back in Glasgow I would have been clacking away at online chats with two or three people at once, but now I can only stab at the keys, one at a time. I feel the eyes of those up at the counter on me and wonder if they see me as being like one of those elderly dears who claps and yelps excitedly every time they successfully get a word up on the screen.

I soon get back into the rhythm of it, though, and the document – with a bit of formatting – spews out of the printer as one sheet. For a moment, my mind drifts to the single-page promo sheet for *Measures Taken*. Quotes from other artists on the label and then a glowing gush from the publicity folk – 'Ready to take on the mantle of his namesake, Dylan is the troubadour for troubled times, the balladeer against the banks, the oracle for Occupy, the prophet of protest.'

My attention is snapped back by the clicking fingers of the café owner.

'Twenty pence a copy,' he says.

I hand over the coin and get the sheet of paper, slightly creased and dented at the edges, in return. Smoothing it out, I read it through. It's short and to-the-point. Smiling, I look back at the computer screen. I still have twenty-five minutes of my hour remaining.

It's been months since I checked my email. There have been times, at day centres or even at parties with Luke and his mates, when I could have, but it's been something I've avoided since… since when…? The day before I left Pierce's house, maybe. July. Fuck, I've been off-grid for the best part of five months. I take a breath, then open them up.

Seven pre-approved credit card offers.

Five emails about online gambling.

Four from dating websites.

Two from Bower.

One from Pierce.

One from Ewan.

Nothing from Maddie.

A grand total of twenty emails across five months. Four a month. Not a good showing from the Voice of a Generation, eh? I open up my junk folder, just for the spike in popularity that the six emails in there will bring. There's nothing of interest, though; nothing from Maddie. So I go back to the Inbox and click on Ewan's. It is formed of blunt bullets, three of them:

- *Call your mother. She's worried and she doesn't understand.*
- *I've listened to the album, a lot. It's not perfect, but there's something there.*
- *Get in touch, Dildo. For fuck's sake, get in touch.*

It's the use of the nickname that causes my chest to clench and my eyes to prickle with tears. More than the mention of my mum or the (faint) praise for the album. There's no reference made to the name-change or all the Maddie-mess between us, just a straightforward request to hit 'reply'. I do, but then sit staring at the blinking cursor.

Ten minutes pass. I close down the empty email and open the first one from Bower. It's chatty, asking if I made it back to Glasgow and telling me he'll keep in contact with sales figures for *Measures Taken* and anything else that might come up. His second is briefer, just asking for a forwarding address for their files and to pass on to the Performing Rights Society. As for Pierce, his email is full of the usual guff – how he thinks it

237

could have worked, but we maybe rushed it all a bit. He asks if I knew that Bob Dylan's first album sold poorly. That, for a time, Dylan was known as 'Hammond's Folly' at Columbia Records because they all thought that the talent scout, John H. Hammond, had made this huge mistake in signing him up. I didn't know that. I'm not interested.

There is no mention of Lydia. Thinking of her stirs memories of silk and shame, but I hold back from sending a confession to Pierce. I type her name into the search engine instead. And there, among the image results, is a photo from last month – early October. It's a press photo from a book launch. Lydia stands in a grey trouser suit, by the book-stack, and Pierce stands beside her, with his hand resting on her shoulder. They both smile at the camera.

I open a reply to Ewan again. The email remains blank. I wonder what would come up if Ewan, or my mum, were to put my name into the search engine. They'd get dribs and drabs of information from before the launch, then a spate of reviews from the release, and a final drip-drip of write-ups from the gigs in May. And then? Nothing, most probably. Not a single result – no photographs or listings on venue websites.

I pause to consider, then hit 'send' on the empty email. That way Ewan will know I'm alive. He can tell my mum. It's enough. Just barely, but it's enough.

Rising from my seat, I lift the proposal and leave, ignoring the calls of the owner, who's anxious that I don't miss out on the last moments of my connection. Or the remaining granules of my sugar-coffee.

They sit in a circle on the floor, for the most part, although two of the elderly members and a pregnant woman sit on chairs to the side. There is a gap in the group for me, so I sit cross-legged between Sage and a young girl with frayed blonde hair piled on top of her head and an even more frayed infant heaped on her lap. This was not how I was envisaging the pitch. I was expecting to have to stand in front of them all, with a whiteboard perhaps, and deliver my ideas that way. Like a performance. Instead, I hand the single-sheet proposal to the girl next to me and it is slowly passed around the circle.

'Essentially,' I begin, 'it would just be a few tables along the back wall, behind the reception desk. In the empty space there. And all that would be needed, for start-up costs, would be enough for a coffee machine and those few bits of furniture.'

There are sixteen people present, including Sage and Sandra, who don't have a vote. That's fourteen folk to convince. Nerves seize at my vocal cords, lengthening the silence. I swallow and start again with a stutter.

'B-but... the primary purpose is to offer a meeting place. Because I've noticed that – erm – people come and go and wait about, but it would be good if they had somewhere to chat.' I gesture towards Sage. 'Before and after class, even. So that they're not just turning up for class then leaving again straight after. So that it's a community hub, rather than a...'

I'm wearing a shirt, but I'm glad that I turned down Sage's offer of a loan of his Mozart tie, because everyone else is dressed casually. They're all spread and splayed over the carpet, relaxed, while I sit straight and watch their faces for a flicker – smile or frown – as they read through the sheet.

'So it would be like a café,' I continue. 'But with not-for-profit at its core. I'd be paid minimum wage, then any profit would go back to the centre to spend on other projects.'

'Once the coffee machine is paid off,' the girl next to me says.

'Of course.'

'I bake,' an older woman, seated on the edge, says. 'Could we maybe sell cakes or buns as well? If I donated them.'

'We'd need to pay you for ingredients,' someone else chimes in.

'I don't need a wage, though.'

'So the only wage would be yours, then?'

It takes me a moment to realise that this question is directed at me. 'Yes,' I say.

'Could we not reclaim furniture rather than buying it,' another voice. 'From skips or something?'

'I'd be happy to fix it up a bit.' Someone else.

'And it makes no sense…' this is Sandra '…for all this to be stuck behind the reception desk. Better to move me to the back wall, so that the first welcome is the – what would you call it – foyer, maybe?'

'That might attract outside customers,' someone says. 'Other than members.'

'It's important, that, if it's going to make money.'

I'm finding it hard to follow the conversation. My eyes dart around the circle as if I'm trying to follow a fast tennis rally and the angles, the players, the lines on the court, all keep changing. I'm pretty certain it's going well, but the proposal is no longer confined to the single sheet.

'You'd have to be answerable to this general meeting.'

Again this is directed at me. I nod.

'And it would have to be part-time, at first,' the pregnant woman says. 'Until we see if it works out and – '

'That's a point – you said it would be minimum wage?'

I nod again.

'Let's make it a living wage, surely?'

'How about seven-fifty an hour?' someone else suggests.

'Any concerns with that?'

Silence. I look around the circle. All the folk on the floor – whether they're leaning back on their elbows or perched forward on their knees – are listening intently. Most people have spoken, but even those who haven't are paying attention. One man, directly opposite, takes notes.

Sage explained to me, last night, how the meeting works. The facilitator – Sandra, today – will eventually ask whether there are any 'stand-asides' or 'blocks', and then they'll decide on the proposal. Hands held up in the air, fingers waving, for agreement. I don't point out to Sage that he's explaining jazz-hands to me with a straight face when only a short while ago he put a towel over Braids for using hand signals.

'There's a sink in the back for washing cups,' they start up again.

'And someone will need to check with the council, to see if we need to register for licences or whether it can all be tied in with – '

'I'll do that,' Sandra says.

'Excellent, then…'

There is a pause while everyone draws breath. The proposal has worked its way back round to my hands. The white space around the typed words has been filled with scribbled notes. 'Baking,' it says, and 'How about a living wage?' Then, in tiny, cramped handwriting: 'just tea/coffee facilities – no need for staff'. An objection, down in the corner.

I look up. One of the older members on the fringes stands. He holds his cloth cap in his hands. When he speaks, there is a rattle like a loose ball-bearing in his throat.

'Seems to me…' He coughs. 'Seems to me we could just have a kettle and all make our own. I've no need for anything fancy, and the money could maybe be better spent – '

'If I may…' I say, rising to my knees. I don't want to stand because the rest of the group is sitting, but I also feel that Cloth-cap has a bit of an advantage in standing over me. 'The idea is to more than pay my way. As in, we should be able to turn a small profit, hopefully, for re-investment, and perhaps even hire more staff eventually. It's not a hand-out I'm looking for.'

'We could have a trial period, maybe,' the pregnant woman says.

'Three months?' comes the suggestion.

'Let's vote already.'

'OK, any stand-asides or blocks?' Sandra asks.

She raises her own hand, palm flat, to show that she's abstaining, and Sage does the same. They both show how they would have voted, though, by smiling warmly up at me from the floor.

Cloth-cap sits looking out of the window, his hands on his lap. I'm waiting for him to raise his hand and then clench his fist. That would be a block and the proposal wouldn't go through. He doesn't make any move, though.

'OK,' Sandra says. 'Two stand-asides. And the rest of you?'

I watch as hands go up. There are twenty-six of them. Fingers start to wave in the air. The only person not agreeing is Cloth-cap, who has stood to show his hands held downwards. That's OK, though: there's still a consensus. Proposal passed.

'I'll check with the council,' Sandra says. 'And Rab, if you could source a coffee machine that suits, then…'

'OK, any other business?' someone asks.

The rest of the meeting passes in a blur. They split into working groups: one to discuss using social media to raise awareness of the Commons; one about problems folk are having with the benefits and housing offices in town; one to start advance planning for a community Christmas dinner. I go with Sage to a group with two others, which is all about organising a theatre trip to see the panto. It's fairly big of Sage to get involved, considering they shot down his verbatim play idea. It was a tight vote: eight to six. Some months ago – weeks even – Sage might have seethed at that, broken the circle and stormed out. Now, though, he calmly swallows his disappointment and suggests calling the box office to see if we can get a group discount for *Peter Pan* along in Hastings.

I tune out. Not because I'm not interested, but because I'm already imagining the shiny coffee machine I will buy. And the hiss and swell of steam it will send out over the chattering members – no longer cross-legged in a circle on the floor, but seated in threes and fours at tables in the main foyer of the building. My nostrils are already filled with the familiar smells of bitter coffee and warm milk, and I can see the rug I'll hang on the far wall, to create the backdrop for the small stage. Where I can play a few songs at the end of my shift.

LONDON

It's the feet that go first. Because you're in your shoes all day long, trudging around the streets or sitting sweating. In the August heat. Wear the same pair of socks for two days in a row and you're sunk. From that moment on, you trail the stench of a rotting corpse around with you.

After three nights in doorways, the Street Rescue folk find me and refer me on to this hostel near Colliers Wood Underground. Nice enough, to tell the truth, with a narrow bed in a narrow room. But the smell of *feet* in the building! Every evening it creeps through the corridors like a toxic cloud, seeping in underneath the doors and settling on the sleeping men, piled up on the mattresses, and their belongings, piled up underneath the beds.

In the mornings, the staff get the bleach out and there's a brief spell of clinical-clean before we all leave for the day, but I know that when we return the nostril-singe smell of the chemicals will be overpowered once again by our collective trench-foot.

On my second night in there, I dream of the First World War. A vivid, reeling nightmare in which I stand alone among the mud and barbed wire and listen to the piercing screech of a whistle. In my hands is a gas mask, but I can't find the opening for my face, can't unfasten it quickly enough as the mustard gas wisps and weaves its way across No Man's Land. I don't know if it's the chemical warfare in the corridors that brought that on, or the afternoon I spent wandering through the Imperial War Museum, but I wake with a panicked conviction that the cold sweat on my face is poisonous.

It's becoming the dominant emotion now – fear. Out on the streets it's the thought of someone swiping the guitar case from the ground in front of me, taking away my day's earnings and the prospect of a drink along with it. I begin keeping one putrid trainer on the case as insurance. That seems to affect my takings, though, so I take to kneeling instead. With my feet behind me and the fabric case like a prayer mat in front. There's still the possibility of someone robbing me, of course, but they'd have to physically move me first.

At night, in the hostel, the worry is the men around me. Screamers and squinters, they are. The screamers come into the communal lounge and shout and babble as if they're having a seizure, while the squinters log on to the computers and start watching porn, right out in the open, but without looking at the screen. Instead, they keep glancing sidelong at me.

For the most part, I stay in the room I share with a screamer. I sneak in half-bottles of whisky, even though the hostel forbids it, and drink quietly beneath the fluorescent lights. With a skinful, I secure all my belongings in my rucksack and then tie the straps to the leg of the bed, so that it can't be taken during the night. Even my trainers – the same ones that inspire German gas attacks in the small hours – are bound by the laces to the bed. It reminds me of something Ewan and I used to do in primary school. Every day for a year or so we'd put our schoolbags over our chairs and our shoulders, then our jackets on top, so that if there was a fire alarm we could stand quickly and try to take everything we owned – no more than crayons, a packed lunch, and a plastic chair that actually belonged to the school – with us.

The only thing I don't tie down for the night is my guitar. From the second night I spent in doorways, I've been putting it into a locker in a place in Tooting. It costs four quid a pop, which is normally what I set aside for food, but it doesn't eat into my drinking budget and it means my wage-earner is secure for the next day.

All of this will make for a great story one day. This is the *authenticity* Pierce was looking for, right? Grit under my nails, a husk to my voice, a tremor to my hand as I reach for the chord. This is the *experience*. I'll talk about it on chat shows and at award ceremonies – 'that was when my music got its *edge*' – all with a patient, fixed smile that masks the shrieks I hear in the empty corridors of my mansion and the stares of the haunting hobos I see in the crowd at my sell-out gigs.

Strangely enough, it's not the fear of the screamers and the squinters that leads to me leaving the hostel in the end. It's not even the eau de feet.

A few days into my stay, one of the staff members takes me to the side and talks to me about payment. At first, it's all along lines I can understand: they would like a contribution of seven pounds a week from me. That's OK, that's do-able. One pound a day, set aside from busking. Then he starts talking about how they'll need to sort it with the housing benefit and see to it that my Jobseeker's Allowance starts coming through as well –

I react. The bloody, shitty-faced cheek of it. The pissing, fucking nerve of this *boy*. On some voluntary-intern-work-experience to feed the fucking destitute, the down-and-outs, because he read Orwell once, he bought the *Big Issue* with his first pocket money, he gives to the Christmas appeals. Because he goes to church, or browses the *Guardian* website, or watched an art-house film where the homeless guy had a heart of gold. He's on a self-improvement kick disguised as a society-improvement mission, this middle-class Melvin, and so he thinks he can look down his nose – talk through his nose – at me.

'I'm not fucking *unemployed*,' I explode. 'I'm not fucking – '
'Language,' he chides.

'I'm a singer, for arse's sake.' It's the best censoring I can manage. 'I'm out singing every day. I have an album out, *mate*, I have newspaper reviews and radio play and – '

'All I'm saying is that the benefits office could – '

'I'll have gigs in a week or so, once the Olympics are over. Because it's all a distraction, isn't it – the… people don't go out much. But I'm not unemployed, you stupid wee…'

I trail off, remembering that I'm not meant to swear but also because I see the anticipation of hurt on his face – the widened eyes, the dropped smile. Even with a half-bottle of whisky in me, I don't want to offend this lad who must be no more than a year or two older than me. Still young.

'Would you have called Woody Guthrie unemployed?' I reason with him.

'I don't know who that is,' he says.

'Well, there's your problem, then, grasshopper. He was an American singer – the figurehead of the folk movement.'

'What does he have to do with your benefits, though?'

'I'm not unemployed,' I repeat, through my teeth. 'I'm a *singer*.'

To prove the point, the next morning I decide to pay Bower a visit to collect my royalties directly. It's been over a fortnight since I left Pierce's house. Enough time for sales to have picked up, surely, or for Bower to have listened to the new tracks and reconsidered his decision about the second album.

So I make my way to the office in St John's Wood. Not the vast, shiny offices of the parent company, but the converted townhouse that holds the Agitate imprint. Only four or five staff and my old friends the potted plants.

The secretary is a blonde woman in her thirties with a piercing, just above her top lip, that she prods and probes with her tongue. Her nose curls up, either sneering or sniffing, as I begin speaking. Trying not to falter, not to let it affect me, I tell her my name and that I'm here to see Bower.

'You're Bob Dylan?' she repeats.

'Rab.'

'Yeah.' She drawls it out. 'And I'm Erica Clapton.'

'Do you not remember me?' I ask.

'I've heard of you, certainly.'

'Ah, you have? Good.'

'But you're with Columbia Records, love. I think their office is over in Kensington somewhere.' She's enjoying herself, plastering the sarcasm on as thickly as her eyeliner. 'They'll be delighted to see you.'

'I'm not *fucking* joking. I'm an artist on *this* label.'

She sits up straighter. 'No need to take that tone, *sir*.'

'How long have you worked here?'

'Since June.'

That explains it. That clears up the misunderstanding. She's a new member of staff, drafted in since *Measures Taken* hit the shelves. She wasn't around in the months before, for all the frantic preparations. Maybe she was around for the option meeting, at the end of July, but that was a manic time. It's fair enough if she's forgotten. She's probably only ever seen the album listed in the sales figures, maybe heard the songs playing, and she hasn't connected me with it because I look – this morning, with all my belongings in the rucksack and a guitar slung over the other shoulder, with fringes of plastic bags visible at the tops of my trainers, where I stuffed them to protect my last clean pair of socks – I look… dishevelled.

'Do you have any promotional material there?' I ask. 'Catalogues, or – '

She shakes her head.

'CDs, then?'

My thinking is that if I can just get her to look at the cover art for *Measures Taken* then she'll realise who I am. It even crosses my mind that it might be worthwhile running out to – where, Maida Vale, maybe? – and finding a record store that stocks a copy. I've only got £2.33, though. It's possible that it's been discounted, by now, but hopefully not by that much.

'Listen,' she says, 'we've got nothing to give you, nothing that you can – '

'Search me!' I shout, suddenly realising the simple solution.

'What?'

'On the internet. Put in "Rab Dylan" and "Agitate Records" and you'll get *pages* of results.'

She still looks unconvinced. There's no need for me to reach across and type it in for her, though, because the door to Bower's office opens and he emerges with a stately-looking black woman. She has shaved her head to a neat skullcap and she no longer wears her trademark vinyl trousers, but I recognise her immediately as Sasha Coburn, the singer who had two hit singles in the early Noughties.

'Rab?' Bower says.

'Hi there,' I say, brightly.

'What are you doing here?'

'I wanted a quick catch-up,' I say. 'A follow-up.'

'Right.'

There's a look exchanged between Bower and the secretary. Then a shrug from her. It's Sasha Coburn who takes the awkwardness from the situation. With a single stride, she comes across to me and holds out a hand.

'Sasha,' she says, smiling.

'Rab. I'm a big fan.'

That smooths everything over nicely and I'm ushered into Bower's office to wait while he sees Sasha out. I take the opportunity to tuck the plastic bags on my feet firmly into my trousers.

'She's still a big earner on the songwriting-publishing side of things,' Bower says, as he comes back in. 'Not on the recording side so much, not any more, but we keep her sweet for the big bosses...'

I nod. 'Thank you for seeing me, Mr – '

'An album every couple of years,' Bower cuts me off. 'At a loss. With the songs they can't get other artists interested in. She does a *lot* of writing.' He sits down and stares, for a moment, at the wooden desk. 'Prolific songwriter and a real hard worker.'

'I remember seeing her on telly,' I say.

'She was our first real success.' Bower shuffles some papers. 'Although, funny thing, we actually had a similar problem with her in the early days. Similar to you, that is.'

'Is that right?'

'With the name thing, I mean.' He pauses, as if considering whether to go on. 'She spelt her surname Cock-burn, you see. Like, C-O-C-K. And we thought that might be a bit too, well, pornographic for the mass market. A beautiful black woman, wearing leather, with…' He pauses, then finally meets my eye. 'We make these decisions all the time. Sometimes they work out, sometimes they don't.'

'Absolutely, Mr Bower. I understand that.'

'So, what can I do for you then, Rab?'

'Well…' It's my turn to avoid eye-contact. 'I need some money.'

'What for?' Bower leans back in his chair. There's a sigh, but I'm not sure if it comes from him or the cushion underneath him.

'Just to keep me going. Accommodation, maybe some new clothes so that I can start chasing gigs in pubs and clubs. I'm planning on working the scene a bit harder – '

'No,' he interrupts. 'I guess I don't mean what *for*, so much as what *from*. I mean, what would I be giving you money *from*? Your album's not earned out its advance, far from it, and there's fuck-all coming in…'

'What about my royalties?'

'Son…' Bower leans forward. 'Your advance, the production costs, a packing charge – all that – is recoupable from your royalties.'

'What does that *mean*, though?'

'It means you have an empty well to fill, mate, before you get a bucket of water for yourself… sorry.'

That knocks the breath from my lungs. It's a setback. Because I felt sure there'd be a small amount – even just a few hundred – accumulating since my last visit. I mean, what have they been doing since then? Where are all those shiny CDs? Are they all just sitting in a warehouse somewhere?

'I thought we'd spoken about this,' Bower says. 'Me, you and Pierce.'

'I'm no longer with Pierce Price,' I say.

'OK. So you don't have a manager at the moment, then?'

'I've decided to self-manage.'

In the silence that follows, I cross and re-cross my ankles underneath the chair. I immediately regret it, though, when I see that Bower has registered the rustling of the plastic bags.

'Listen,' he says, 'these things can turn around. Of course they can. But I'm not going to lie or sugar-coat it. The album hasn't done well and we're not going to throw good money after – '

'I'm ready to work harder, do more promotion,' I interrupt.

'It's not that.'

'And now that I've not got a wannabe game-show host for a manager – '

'It isn't that, either.'

'What *is* it, then?'

Bower reaches across to his computer and starts key-tapping. He takes some notes on a pad of paper, then reaches into his trouser pocket. He brings out his wallet.

'The train fare up to Glasgow is a hundred and twenty-five quid,' he says. 'Here's a hundred and forty. So you can get yourself some grub as well. Take it and *go home*.'

I smile, and shake my head. 'My career's down here.'

'Listen, Rab…' He leans across the desk. 'Not for now it isn't.'

'But – '

'This isn't money from the label. Or money you've earned. This is a personal loan – gift, even – from me so that you can

251

get yourself home. So you can get your shit together and...'
He trails off. 'You need to regroup, Rab.'

'You think I should form a band?' I ask. 'Get a group together?'

'No, Rab. *Re*group.'

'Maybe if we re-recorded some tracks with an orchestra?'

'I'll see you out...'

'Or got a rapper on board as a featured artist? Brink, maybe?'

'And keep in contact...'

'Maybe Sasha could write me a song?'

'Let us know when you get home...'

'Or I could get a bit of exposure on one of those TV talent shows?'

'Take care.'

I walk. Aimlessly. Up Abbey Road – yes, *the* Abbey Road – and over the train tracks, before turning towards Queen's Park and then crossing back over the tracks. I find myself in a maze of small streets intercut with the arterial lines of the Underground and Overground. There's a depot somewhere nearby. I stand on a railway bridge and watch the trains trundling below.

I think back to Pierce telling me about his father, how he would clean up the scattered limbs and torsos of folk from the lines as if they were no more than store-window mannequins – and I wonder what damage a slow-moving suburban train would do. Just a short fall and an impact. Maybe some scarring or a lost limb, maybe worse.

I've always had this fascination with trains as they pull into the platform. The suck and rush of air and the moment, just a split-second, where you could sway forward, out in front, but instead you shuffle back. What would happen if you stepped out? Or dropped down? Not in front of an express train or one picking up speed, but just an ordinary one, travelling fast enough so that you feel the collision like a collapsing, crumpling punch – massive, all-over and somehow welcome. Like the hit of a rugby player, that leaves you bruised but not broken. Is that possible? Does that happen? Or do all jumpers, all steppers, droppers, and divers end up being scooped off the tracks by Pierce's dad?

What if you did survive? By some miracle. If you got up off the ground with all your essential organs still in place. What then? Does that make the papers, maybe? Do they tell your story in the press: the failed first album, the couple of weeks of homelessness, the triumphant return to playing gigs with only one arm – no, wait – only one leg, maybe. And a *Phantom of the Opera* mask to cover the missing portion of your face. Does that affect sales? Out of all those hundreds of hard-luck, triumph-in-adversity, against-the-odds tales, does that one make it through?

There are bushes and spindly trees on either side of the bridge, behind the advertising billboards and the flattened fence. They lead steeply down to the tracks. Waiting until there's no traffic on the road, no pedestrians on the pavement, I push myself up on to the top of the wall and then jump, sideways, on to the embankment. My feet slip, but I reach out for a fistful of roots and weeds to steady myself. Then I crouch in the undergrowth and watch the carriages rattle past beneath me, no more than a few feet away.

Although there is blazing sunshine overhead, it is murky down here. The shadow of the bridge and the overhang of the branches means that I can't make out the two shapes properly at first. Instead, I hear them. Snapping twigs, rustling leaves, grunting.

I peer through the trees, thinking of the night – up at the woods in Glasgow – when I saw Maddie with Ewan. The two shadows, two shapes, are doing something similar. Fucking or fighting. They grapple at each other's clothes, their feet kicking and their toes digging as they try to find some grip on the loose earth. To stop themselves rolling down, still in their embrace, on to the tracks.

This goes on for five minutes or so, about ten feet to my left. Then, abruptly, one of the two scrambles to his feet, rearranges himself, and starts to shuffle and slide his way over towards the bridge. Towards me. I shrink back, into the bushes. If he sees me, though, then he doesn't acknowledge it. Instead, he reaches for the top of the wall and, with difficulty, levers himself up and over.

I wait, breathing shallowly, for the second one to follow suit. Carefully, I inch backwards, further up the slope. He is larger than the first – fatter – with the same hobo's uniform of thick beard, tattered khaki jacket and stained trousers. He sits still for a moment, with his head cradled against his knees, and I wonder if he's weeping. But then he rises and stumbles his way over towards the bridge. When he catches sight of me, his step falters and he has to reach out for a branch to steady himself. I wait, with my breath stuck in my tightened throat, to see what he will do.

At first, it seems as if he will carry on past me. But then he hesitates. Stops. Turns.

'You're not thinking of jumping, are you?' he asks.

'Me?' I say, as if there are others around. Behind other bushes, beneath other bridges. 'It wouldn't really be a jump, would it? Not from here. More of a slide.'

'Still,' he says, slowly, 'if you are thinking about it… don't.'

Fuck me, I think. How's that for advice, eh? All that fancy psychiatry and psychotherapy shite they do and all they actually need is a single word – *don't*. That's it, all that's needed. Back from the brink, off the ledge. Keeping the noose from the overhead beam and the toaster from the bathwater.

'I'll be fine,' I say. 'Thanks anyway.'

'Can I tell you a story?' he asks. He's reaching down to fiddle with his fly. To re-zip it after his quote-unquote 'wrestling match'.

'Sure.' I watch him warily. 'Why not?'

254

'Back in the nineteenth century...' he crouches a couple of feet away – a safe distance '... there was always smog over London. Thick clouds, nicknamed pea-soupers, from all the household fires – of course – but also from the industrial work of the city. It was the physical manifestation of all the *activity* of the capital, you know?'

I don't know if I'm supposed to answer. So I settle for nodding.

'And people were anxious not to live with this constantly,' he continues. 'Breathing it in, and letting it settle on their skin, on their food. So they took trips to the seaside for fresh air and a break. Just to the south coast. Brighton, Eastbourne, wherever.'

'Makes sense,' I say. 'What's your point?'

'Well, the smog's gone now. For the most part, at least. Because the industry's been replaced by *commerce*. There's just as much movement and activity, just as much noise and stress, but it doesn't create clouds of coal soot or...' He stops, clears his throat. 'It's an invisible smog, rather than a visible one, but it's just as thick, just as toxic.'

'It's a frantic city, no doubt about it,' I say.

'Exactly.' He looks across at me. 'And when was the last time you went to the seaside for some fresh air?'

'Well...' I consider. 'I played a gig down in Brighton, a good one, a few months ago. But I didn't really spend time on the beach or – '

A train goes past below us. The clatter of it breaks my sentence. A thought – a brief thought – flits through my mind: that, without the interruption of this smoggy storyteller, the brakes of that train might now be squealing. And I'd not be having this thought, or taking this breath. Or this one, or this.

'I don't mean literally,' my companion says, once the train has passed. 'When was the last time you escaped all the pressure and expectation – all the smog – of London, is what I mean.'

255

My hand goes to my pocket. To feel the edges of the banknotes that Bower gave me. They were earmarked for a different trip, of course, but one that I never intended taking. Maybe they can take me in a different direction. Give me a chance to – what was the word Bower used? – *regroup*.

'I know you think,' the man says, 'that *this* might be a way of escaping it. But it's not really, because it all adds to the smog – the fug – of it all. Think of the driver, for instance. How do you – how could you – recover from something like that? From – '

'I'm Rab,' I say, stretching out my hand.

'Pleased to meet you,' he says, taking it. 'The name's Sage.'

'Sage?'

'Like the herb.'

GLASGOW

The birthday dinner is a smokescreen. With much tutting and straightening of ties, my mum bundles us into a taxi and directs the driver to Kessington Hall, on the road out to Milngavie. Not the Italian restaurant on Byres Road.

By the time the heavy doors are swung open and the lights are flicked on, the shouted 'Surprise!' is a little redundant. Sure, I stare as if I've been caught unaware by a flashbulb and I shake my head in amazement, but by that stage it's about assessing who's bothered to turn up for my joint eighteenth/ leaving-do.

There's a table of relatives, including Uncle Brendan and his lot of children and grandchildren; then a group of dad's work colleagues, all carefully inspecting the labels on their beer bottles as if expecting to unearth previously undiscovered ingredients; and a clutch of my mum's gathered gossipers, mostly neighbours and old dears she's adopted on her daily rounds of the supermarket aisles. All these partygoers are to be expected – they're duty-bound, by the blank squares on their calendars, to accept any invitation – but I'm surprised to see the table of my mates over by the raised platform of the stage. Gemma is not a shock, nor Teagan at a push, but the sight of Ewan and Cammy causes me to take a step back towards the door. It takes a moment to realise that I can't be intruding, can't be an unwelcome guest, at my own surprise party.

All in all there are probably a couple of dozen folk. They don't really seem to be mingling, but their paths are at least crossing en route to the bottle bar over by the back wall. As my dad comes back from his own trip, and places a beer in my hand, I scan the room for Maddie. She doesn't fit neatly into any of the tabled groups, but I'm hoping that I might have missed her standing over in a shadowy corner or hiding by the coat racks. 'No Maddie, Dad?' I ask.

'Sorry?'

'Could Maddie not make it?'

'You'd have to ask your mother.'

I could make my way over to where Mum is talking to the bloke who comes fortnightly to clean our windows, but I shrug instead. After all, Maddie already cried off from the cover story – saying she thought it was better, in the circumstances, if she didn't come out for the meal – so it's foolish to think she'd be crouched in a cardboard cake or seated in front of a bulb-framed mirror preparing for a sultry rendition of 'Happy Birthday'.

We formalised the break-up two days ago, on the afternoon after the 3.17am phone call. *She* formalised the break-up. In Kelvingrove Park, with a picnic suitable for my hangover – two bags of crisps and a can of Irn-Bru. Nothing wrong with keeping in touch, she said, but better for the two of us to do what we want to do, where we want to do it, instead of building up resentment – and debt – by trying to stay together through it. She's as practical as an asset-stripper, is Maddie, underneath it all.

It's not that I wanted tears or a full-scale breakdown, but a snivel would have been gratifying. It was the clear eyes and calm tone that hurt me most, I think. She began by saying 'I love you, but…', then listed the reasons we should split up. I should have pointed out that if you love someone you don't make lists. Not of their faults and limitations, at least. A shopping list is fine – practical. A wedding list – somewhere down the line, maybe. Not a break-up list, though.

People talk about their heart breaking, but that's wrong. It's more like a collapsing of all the arteries and valves, so that it feels as if it's no longer pulsing in the centre of your chest but is twitching in the corner instead. And your lungs deflate along with it, your stomach slips and all of a sudden there's this void in the centre of your body where, it feels like, all of your hopes and plans – expectations, even – used to be stored.

Still, I thought there'd be enough sentiment there for her to turn up for the party. So that, when my mum climbs up on to the stage and invites me to play a few songs, I wouldn't have to look down at the mistimed toe-tapping of my dad's co-workers or the sullen faces of Ewan and Cammy. Instead, I could have played her one final love song. To make her change her mind.

'We're very proud of Robert,' Mum says, smiling down at me. 'For following his dreams and making a success of himself...' She pauses. If she clicks her tongue as punctuation, I'm too far away to hear it. 'But we know that London is an expensive city – we all know that – so we were hoping that you'd all contribute something to help him out, if we "pass-the-hat" while he plays us a few of his songs. Brendan, I think, wouldn't mind lending a hand.'

Uncle Brendan rises from his seat and, with a flourish, pulls a flat cap from his pocket. Showing a ten-pound note to the room, he stuffs the money into the hat as if he's performing some reverse magic-trick. Then he sets off around the tables with the hat held out in front of him.

'Just before I invite Rab to play, though,' Mum continues, 'his father and I would like to give him a small gift of our own. Rab, if you'd come up here, please.'

While I make my way up to the stage, my mum reaches down for her handbag. From it she pulls a long, thin case. Shit, I think, she's only gone and got me a bloody spoon. Maybe a fiddle thread one, with a stem that looks like a fret. As if my own spoon, in its own fucking carry-case, will keep me from poverty in London – 'Please, sir, can I have some more? I brought my own spoon.'

'Thanks, Mum,' I say, with an edge of sarcasm, as I take it from her. I snap the case open and feel my frown lifting. The case doesn't contain a spoon at all, but a metal tuning-fork in a velvet inset. I lift it to show the room and then reach down to strike it against the edge of the stage. A single note – a pitch-perfect A – rings through the room.

'Thank you, Mum,' I say again. My voice holds a quaver. I play a chord through it, on Uncle Brendan's guitar. The one I learnt on. 'Any requests?' I ask.

'"Streets of London",' one of the old dears says.

'Dougie MacLean,' someone calls. 'The one from that advert.'

'No,' Cammy shouts, with an edge to his voice. 'Play your own stuff.'

'I'll have to charge you, then,' I joke. But I move the capo down the fret and then pick out the intro to the song I was working on yesterday. It's untitled. About folk settling for the safe option rather than taking a risk. The chorus rhymes 'armchair resistance' with 'insistence' and 'persistence' and, half, with 'commitments'. There are rough edges, certainly, because I'm not sure what the main focus of it is yet. Scottish independence, maybe. Or the austerity cuts. It might even be a more general anti-capitalist anthem. I can fill it out later. Once I get down to London.

After three songs I clamber off the stage, waving away the calls for more. Three is enough of a set. I want to save my voice. Besides, the hat filled with notes and loose change has already done a full circuit of the room and a second pass would be mortifying. I'm not a bloody busker, you know; I've got a recording contract.

Uncle Brendan plugs his laptop into some portable speakers and we get a mixture of wedding music and old ballads – Phil Ochs, Pete Seeger, John Martyn, some early Billy Bragg – from the treasured collection that he finally transferred from vinyl to digital after his youngest grandkid left his Joan Baez record to melt on top of the radiator.

People keep on getting up to dance, midway through a track, and then having to sit down again when the next protest song comes on. After a few rounds of this game of musical chairs, my mum fusses Brendan into making a politically neutral playlist and folk begin to settle into that self-conscious dancing you get when there's too much by way of light and not enough by way of drink or drugs.

Gemma and Teagan are straight up on to the dance floor and Cammy, as he tends to do, has gone off wandering, so I take two bottles of beer and go to sit next to Ewan. He keeps his eyes on the girls, but accepts the beer with a nod.

'We split up,' I say.

'You and Maddie?'

'Yeah.'

'I heard.'

I frown and pick at the label on the bottle with my fingernail. How has he heard already? We only broke up, properly, the day before yesterday. So unless my mum or dad had a word with him, then…

'I leave for London a week on Monday,' I say.

'Where are you staying?'

'A hotel, for the first while at least.'

He whistles softly. 'Big time, eh?'

I don't know how to answer that, so I stay silent. Out on the dance floor, Teagan turns as if to make her way back to the table. Gemma, looking across at us, catches her by the arm and pulls her away in the other direction.

'I've done a wee bit of research,' Ewan says.

'Yeah? On what?'

'Call it my last act as your manager…' He looks at the back of his hand, as if to check crib-notes. There's nothing there, though, except for a bit of dry skin. 'It's rare for a debut album to earn out its advance. In fact, only, like, two per cent of albums released sell more than five thousand copies. And if you're only making, what, ten to fifteen per cent? Plus you'll need to pay back production costs and session musicians and – '

'I've read my contract, Ewan. More to the point, I've been through it with a lawyer, you know?'

'Yeah. All I'm saying is, you need to be realistic with it. Like, even if you have a best-selling album, it's unlikely that you'll make more than, say, a schoolteacher in the first year.'

'Nothing wrong with a schoolteacher's wage.'

'Well…'

There's another gap in our conversation. The girls are back to dancing. They keep glancing over to us, though. Even from a distance, they can probably see the tight grip I've got on my beer bottle, can probably hear my teeth grinding.

Why does everyone keep telling me I'm going to fail? Congratulations, kid, you'll never make it. Great opportunity, lad, you're sure to blow it. Never mind the bastards, Rab, you'll grind yourself down.

'It seems like you'll make the most money from live gigs,' Ewan says. 'And from selling merchandise like T-shirts and that. But you need to make sure the label don't get their hands on a percentage of that – '

'No offence, but I've been through all this.'

'Sure.' He takes a swig of beer. 'It's just easy to get stung. They've got these things called 360-degree contracts, where they take a slice of *everything*. And this is London we're talking about. Up here, at least, you've got some knowledge of the scene, but – '

'Have you been talking to Maddie, is that it?'

'What?'

'Is that where this whole pissing-on-my-parade bit is coming from? You and the ex recon-fucking-ciling over a shared desire to see me fail?'

'I don't want to see you fail, Rab.'

'No?'

'No.'

My phone sounds as I stare him out. It's the opening to 'Maggie May' by Rod Stewart. I used to sing the first line to Maddie, substituting her name, in the mornings after I stayed over. I've not had the chance to change it yet. Fumbling the phone free from my pocket, I open her text message.

'Right on cue,' I mutter. 'Probably just finishing your sentence, eh?'

'What's with the paranoia, Rab? Remember, it was me she left to go out with you. So this jilted lover act doesn't really fly, does it?'

'It's just a bit of a coincidence...'

I trail off, because I'm concentrating on the message. It's an apology for not turning up. Half-arsed. At the end she asks me to come round to her mum's house tomorrow so she can give me my birthday present. Probably another lecture. An echo of this one from Ewan.

The message causes me to tense, to tighten further. She should have come tonight. She should be here and she should have had the confidence in me – in *us* – to move down to London. She's allowed second thoughts, of course she is, but they should have faded by now. She should be bursting through the door of the hall, bags packed, laden with regret – not sending text messages.

'Nothing,' I say to Ewan, eventually. 'Never mind.'

'Ewan, be careful with that olive branch, mate,' Cammy's back, to interrupt. 'He'll only end up shafting you with it.'

'Fuck off, Cammy. What do you know?' I say.

He snorts. Ewan holds out a hand to quieten him.

'Singers are sold this dream and then it's hard work and the rewards aren't really...' Ewan begins. 'Like, most folk would love to play a gig in a stadium. But playing a six-week tour in small venues like this, with most of the money going back to the label to pay recording costs or... there's a high suicide rate; lots of instances of breakdowns or rehab because of the pressure.'

'I won't do a Kurt Cobain on you, don't worry,' I say.

'Which part?' Cammy asks. 'The shotgun or the sell-out?'

'Cammy,' Ewan says. 'Seriously, ease off.'

'I'm not going to fucking fail, OK?' I say. 'Next time you see me, lads, I'll be on a stage ten times as big as that one – ' I point to the platform ' – playing to a crowd a hundred times bigger than this – ' I wave an arm at the room ' – and my bank balance, *my* fucking earnings, won't only be a thousand times bigger. They'll be tens of thousands, hundreds of thousands – '

I stop there. I should go on; I should round on Ewan. I have the right of reply. You've questioned me, ballbag, now here's yours. Why didn't you find me a recording contract, eh? Too busy selling shoelaces? And why didn't you fight to represent me? Was our friendship brittle enough to be broken by Maddie, is that it? For fuck's sake. If it was, why didn't you fight for her, at least? You've bent over to be buggered every time, mate, yet you have the cunting *nerve* to lecture me about getting screwed. Well, here's yours – you think I've sold my soul, but all you'll ever sell is fucking insoles, maggot, because you don't have the stones, the fucking strength of character, to take a leap of faith.

'I hope you're right, Rab,' Ewan says.

'You can fucking count on it.'

I've never been beyond the front door of her mum's house. All through our relationship, when we were looking for a place to 'watch a film' or 'practise guitar' or 'revise', we would always end up either at her dad's flat or in my attic bedroom – where we could place inverted commas around our activities without being disturbed.

Maddie's mum is, similarly, a mystery to me. I've only ever caught sight of her in a picture posted online, from some family occasion. She's hiding her face from the camera. I know her only as bleached blonde hair, cut in a bob, and an outfit that's all cardigan and cleavage.

'Right on time,' Maddie says, as she opens the door.

'How are you?' I ask.

'Fine, fine. Come on in.'

The blue shirt I settled on is buttoned right to the top, so that it scratches at my Adam's apple. I hook a finger in to pull at the collar. In the hallway, I pause, wondering if I should kiss Maddie – on the cheek, maybe – or lean in for a hug. I'm halfway to offering a handshake, but then decide against it and cover by smoothing my palms against the legs of my jeans.

I've only had one joint, just a thin trail of resin, so the clamminess is only nerves. The tightness to my throat is just because I know that this is my final chance to convince her.

'Come into the living room,' Maddie says. 'Would you like a mug of tea or something?'

I shake my head and follow her into a room to the right.

'My mum has gone out to the shops. To give us a chance to talk.'

'OK,' I say, trying to keep the relief from my voice. 'It's a nice place, this.'

The living room is typical of Glasgow's West End, with a high corniced ceiling and bright bay windows. Among all the antique lamps, framed prints and carefully ordered bookshelves, though, are cluttered heaps of play-mats, stuffed animals, changing bags and the like. There's a cot in the corner. My first – frantic – thought is that Maddie has had a baby and that fatherhood is going to be my birthday surprise. Then I do the maths. I choke back a laugh, a chortle.

'I'm going to get myself a beer, I think,' Maddie says. 'You sure you wouldn't like something?'

'Well, if there's a beer going…'

'Back in a second.'

I ease myself down on to the sofa. The cushions, plumped up, seem to want to bounce me back to my feet. It takes two or three sittings before there's a comfortable indent. Once I'm settled, I look around the room again. There really is a *lot* of baby stuff. The thought flickers again, then catches: maybe she had the baby before she met me – before she met Ewan even – and she's never found the right moment to tell. She didn't want to scare me off. So she left it with its grandma and carried on as normal. And, of course, she didn't want to move to London without the wee blighter. Is that so far-fetched? Is it?

'Thanks for coming over.' Maddie comes back in and hands me a bottle. 'I wanted to do this in person.'

'Yeah?'

She nods. 'I feel like we didn't leave it on the best of terms the other day, so I wanted to make friends again, you know?'

I gulp at the beer, swallowing down the idea of Maddie being a teenage mother. There's nothing going on here except a clear-the-air meeting. I'm just being paranoid, looking for a reason why she's been a bit off with me these past weeks, why she backed out of moving away. Shit, I'm just looking for a way of softening the brutal break-up.

'I don't want you to think that I'm a bitch,' she says, seating herself on the sofa opposite. 'It's not that I don't care or that I don't think you'll do well for yourself. It's just that the timing's not right for me.'

'Maybe the timing will be right in the future,' I say, softly.

'Maybe.' She smiles. 'I'm still really young, you know. The year between us might not seem like a lot, Rab, but there's a big difference between seventeen and eighteen, in terms of – '

'It's not really to do with age, though, is it?' I interrupt.

I can't rid myself of the idea of this *baby*. From the corner of my eye I see the toys scattered across the carpet by the window. Maddie's mum is too old to have a young child, surely? And Maddie doesn't have any brothers or sisters who might be new parents. There's more stuff, though, than for a passing visit from a niece or a family friend. This is a baby-in-residence, a critter who's marking their territory.

'Well…' Maddie looks at me with narrowed eyes. 'There's also the university thing, and there's the debt question attached to that. I don't want to make the wrong decision there, really, because it feels like that's what could set me up, one way or other, for the rest of my life.'

I don't want to show myself up – act the arse – and question her about all the baby debris in the room, but maybe there's a way of being subtle about it. Ask without asking. Just see if she flushes at the mention of the child – if she avoids the topic.

'It's a nice house,' I say, breezily. 'Nice room.'

'Thanks,' she says, and takes a gulp of her beer.

'I've never been in here before.'

She nods, but her brow is furrowed into a frown. She catches her bottom lip in her teeth and chews at it while she watches me. Not a sign of a guilty conscience – not necessarily – but she doesn't look comfortable.

'Is there a reason for that, maybe?' I ask.

'A reason for what?'

'For my… for you not inviting me in.'

'Well, you've never even met my mum, have you?'

I shake my head, thinking about the line I could use – *She's not the only member of this family I haven't met though, isn't that true?* – if only I were more confident about my Sherlocking skills.

'Is there something going on with you?' she asks.

'How d'you mean?'

'You're acting odd.'

I shake my head again. 'Is there something going on with you?'

We're reaching the reveal. The point at which Maddie makes her confession, thinking it's a plot-twist worthy of the worst of those soaps my mum watches, and I respond by offering to support her and the baby. After some soul-searching, obviously. And only if I'm certain that Ewan isn't the father.

'Seriously, Rab,' she says, 'what is it?'

'What's what?'

'Are you stoned, is that it?'

267

'No.'

'Drunk, then?'

'No,' I say, then let my gaze drift across the cot, the changing mat, the picture books piled on the coffee table. I search for the right phrase, the right line, but I'm mindful of giving myself an out in case I'm wrong. 'You must have realised that I'd notice, Maddie.'

'Notice what?'

'All the *baby* stuff.'

'Yeah.' She shrugs. 'So?'

There's a moment, in which I raise my eyebrows to invite her to come clean, and then see her eyes widening. In horror.

I've made a mistake.

'My mum's a child-minder, you dick,' she says.

It's an understandable mistake, surely.

'She's a child-minder. For other people's children.'

I didn't actually *say* anything, did I? I never actually *asked* outright.

'I mean, for fuck's sake. How could you think…?' She slams her beer bottle down on the table. 'We don't live in Victorian times, do we? Do you not think, if I had a baby, I'd bloody *tell* you about it?'

I try to laugh. It comes out half strangled. 'I didn't… think that – ' I begin.

'We've been seeing each other for, what, six or seven months, Rab.'

'Yeah.'

'And you think I hid my baby away from the world for all that time, is that it? How fucking heartless d'you think I am?'

'I wasn't saying that,' I say, more forcefully. 'Any of that. I was just saying there was a lot of baby stuff, that's all.'

She's sitting perfectly still, but there's a flush rising up her neck and her fists are buried into the cushions of the sofa. A mistimed memory: her rigidity in the moments before orgasm, tensing before the release.

'It's not...' I take a breath, then launch into my defence. 'You could have left the baby with your mum, maybe, while you were with me.'

'Yeah, cause you'd have come first in that scenario, Rab, wouldn't you?'

'I didn't actually think that, though. I was just wondering... about all the stuff.'

She goes quiet again. There's an accusation in the silence – she's judging me because she thinks I've judged her. Even though I didn't actually *say*. It was just a theory, based on the available evidence. She's the one that's twisted it, blown it out of all fucking proportion.

'How the *fuck* could you think that, Rab?' she asks, quietly.

'Well, you can't blame me, can you?' I spit back.

'What's that supposed to mean?'

'You invite me round for a birthday surprise and...'

'What – *surprise, I'm a teenage mum*?'

'Yeah, you're right,' I say, dropping my voice to match her sarcasm. 'That wouldn't be a surprise at all. I've always known you were a wee slapper anyway. Why wouldn't you have some diseased bastard-child falling out of you?'

She stands. 'Fuck you.'

'Fuck everyone, isn't that your motto?'

'One minute the perfect girlfriend, the next a useless whore, is that it?'

'Come on. We both know you only think with your cunt.'

She turns and walks out of the room. The sudden silence drains the blood from my face. I can feel it as a chill. As a realisation that I've gone too far. The bottle of beer sits sweating on the coffee table. I lift it and swallow a couple of mouthfuls.

Of course, it seems irretrievable. I've found myself up shit creek and I've decided to scuttle the fucking boat. And sure, you could argue that if I hadn't had that wee joint before I got here – if I'd kept a clear head – then I might not have lost my paddle in the first place. But here's my counter-argument – wait for it – all the things that happen in the world, good and bad, must happen to someone. Somewhere in the world, odds are a teenage mother hid her child from her boyfriend – why not here?

'This is your birthday present,' Maddie says, coming back in. Her eyes are black with smeared mascara, her cheeks wet with tears. 'I saved for it. So that you'll think of me – of us – when you're playing all those gigs down there. When you're famous.'

She half hands, half throws the guitar. The wood sounds out hollowly as it strikes my chest. It's an acoustic, with red-hued wood and a white trim. Steel strings. Without thinking, without pausing for an apology or a word of thanks, I strum out a G-major. It's a little out of tune, but the tone is deep and mellow.

'You're welcome,' Maddie says.

'Maddie…' I look up. 'I'm sorry, I – '

'You can see yourself out.'

'Seriously – '

'Seriously just fuck off.'

She turns and leaves the room again. I hear her footsteps on the stairs.

I'm left holding the guitar. Across my lap, with the neck cradled against my shoulder.

BRIGHTON

There's only room for five tables in the foyer. As well as the reception desk against the back wall and a high bench with the coffee machine, baked goods, and fresh fruit over to the side. One of the members has made up some cushions, though, so there are extra seats along the windowsill. Above the radiator.

The biscuits and cakes are contributed by Enid, the woman who volunteered during the proposal meeting. She comes in twice a day, wearing a dusting of flour rather than her usual talcum powder, and restocks. Laying a hand on my arm, she talks animatedly of Victoria sponges and rocky road slices as if we were a young couple planning our future together.

Around each of the tables are three chairs. Sandra found them online, going free to a good home. They're old church chairs – with hymn book holders in the back – that only needed a once-over with sandpaper to clean them up. We've taken to putting second-hand paperbacks in the holders, so that folk can browse while they're drinking their coffee. It's Sidney – with his cloth cap – who sources all the books and takes half of the pencil-scrawled price to supplement his pension.

The excess books are beginning to stack up along the walls, piled high as extra insulation against the December cold. At the last meeting, we talked about using some of the money from the café to buy built-in bookshelves. I think we're currently on the lookout for a carpenter – someone local – to come in and measure them up.

I sit on a stool to the side of the bench, ready to drip the espresso or steam the milk. Occasionally I read or lift my guitar from where it stands, propped up against the wall. For the most part, though, I just listen. To the layered noise of conversation. The hushed hiss of scandal, the strained sob of desperation, the cheery chatter of two schoolfriends meeting somewhere other than the job centre. The clap and roll of laughter.

In the mid-afternoon, at the end of his classes, comes Sage's bass-note. It doesn't drone on, uninterrupted, as it used to though. It rises at the end as he asks a question or rumbles off into a chuckle. He does the rounds of his learners, then drags a chair over to where I sit. Making up two cappuccinos, with a sprinkling of cinnamon on the top, I take a break and add my voice to the others in the room.

This is our daily catch-up, now that we live apart. He tells me about the classes upstairs and I tell him about the gossip downstairs or what I've been reading. We move easily from one topic to the next, covering as much ground in half an hour as we used to in an entire day beneath the arches on the seafront. Now that every second sentence isn't about the chill that pierces until it scrapes at your bones, the hunger that you try to drown with the dregs of your tonic wine, or the despair that creeps over you with the insistence of an incoming tide.

We're talking, more and more, about Occupy. Even though the camp has gone and my interest in it – my musical motivation – should have faded. It wasn't where my interest in politics was stirred, where I felt the full hardships of camping on concrete, or where I finally found out what it meant to be *engaged* with the world around me. But it was a seed. At least, it was a seed for other folk. And, even if it only means that they talk to their neighbours more often, or that they campaign against the closure of a local library, it's had an impact. It was a space where people were listened to. Those months outside St Paul's Cathedral were worth it if only for that. Although, on my part, all the positives that could have come with that experience – the companionship, the debates, the sense of self-worth – only trickled through later, once I found the smaller, safer forum of the Commons. And once I was willing to listen to those around me.

Sage has moved in with the crossword compiler. Cruciverbalism, he calls it – the setting of crosswords – though it sounds more like a vegetable-based diet to me. Every night, they sit together and he reads to her from her old cryptic clues. It only takes a moment, he says, before she smiles at her youthful cleverness. Sage has to wait a minute or two more and then ask if he's got the right answer.

I've moved out of the squat as well, but I've not yet found myself a permanent room. There's a friend of Luke's who has a space, and the plan is to have a drink with him after the gig tomorrow and see if we get along well enough. For now, though, I'm sleeping on Sandra's floral sofa. She lives just around the corner from the centre with a ginger cat, named Molotov, who's as warm as the cocktail he's named after. Every night he curls up on top of my duvet and we sleep through until one of us stretches ourselves awake.

There's a routine to it all now. Centred around the ten-till-three shift in the café. But it's not all-consuming. There are no stress dreams about whether the Kenyan blend coffee is really fair-trade, or late-night anxieties about whether Enid's bakewell tarts should be a pound or a pound-fifty. There's no grip of panic when a customer complains that the milk tastes sour or comments that the chain bistro in town makes patterns on the top of their lattes.

If I ever feel the arrival of *that* voice – the one that tells me that I *should*, I *must*, it's *time* – then all I need to do is look up at the chalkboard on the left-hand wall. Above the bolted-together packing crates we use as a stage. 'Live music', it says. 'Every Thursday and Friday, from 3pm'. There is no mention of my name, no reviews or recommendations in different

273

coloured chalks. Just the simple promise of that regular gig, in front of a crowd of no more than a dozen. Every Thursday and Friday.

Luke and I play together, of course. We've been working on our covers, with myself on rhythm guitar and vocals, and Luke on lead guitar and backing vocals. More excitingly, though, we also had a couple of days last week when Flick came down from London and we worked on setting her lyrics to music. As I strummed and experimented, adding my voice to the chorus, I felt the thrill and swell of her words pulsing through the music. Words that *mean* something. She'll repeat a word, like an incantation, until you've forgotten the meaning of it and you're just listening to the sound. Then she'll tell you what it is, what it does, and why it's important to her. And you'll never again hear that word, or see it written even, without the whisper of her voice in your ear.

There was a brief disagreement, over coffees afterwards, about what to do with the songs we'd come up with. Luke was all for recording them and sending them out to some scouts and managers. Not in the hope of landing a recording contract – he knew that was a sore topic – but more with an eye towards a publishing deal. Because that's where the money is. Someone else singing your songs.

Flick sided with me, though. Two against one. If the songs are picked up organically, through someone seeing us performing or whatever, then fine. If they agree with the ideas, the sentiments, of the lyrics. But we're not in the business of putting words in people's mouths.

She'll be down tomorrow as well. Flick, that is. To join us for our Thursday afternoon set. We're planning on playing our two gigs here and then busking up around the Theatre Royal on Saturday. For the Christmas shoppers.

After work, I make a shopping trip of my own. To the pawn shop where I hawked the guitar Maddie gave me. It's a blue-painted store up in Kemptown, with electrical goods in the window and jewellery locked away in glass cases that double as a counter. With the cash clutched in my hand – my wages plus a loan from Sage – I could have bought a telly that some single mother had to sell to fill the kitchen cupboards, or a console that had to be pried out of a child's hands so that the rent could be paid. No sign of my guitar, though, among the instruments hanging on the wall behind the counter.

I smooth the slip out on the counter and explain that, although it's beyond the loan period, I'd be willing to pay full price for the guitar if they still have it. The paper's been in the inner pocket of my coat for months. The ink has faded and the edges have frayed.

The young lad behind the counter goes off to check. And, in that moment, I realise that I'm not really that bothered. There's no attachment to the guitar. It signifies only a flop of a relationship and a break-up with an album. It's not like the tuning fork, in its velvet-lined carry-case, which my parents gave to me and which is nestled away in the inside pocket of my jacket – or even the harmonica lying in there beside it – both of which have kept me going these past few months. It doesn't mean as much to me as the guitar lent to me by Luke, which is safely stowed behind Sandra's reception desk. There's this vague feeling of guilt, this nagging expectation, that the red-hued acoustic from Maddie should be precious. If it's been sold, I should be putting an advert in *The Argus*. I should be so anxious to find it that I plaster posters on lamp-posts and go door-to-door with a photo of the guitar and me, taken in happier times.

I put my hand into the pocket of my jeans, to smooth my thumb over the pebble I keep in there. Sage gave it to me on my nineteenth birthday, the week after we arrived in Brighton. He had nothing else to give. After an hour, maybe more, at the tide-line selecting the stone, he spent another half-hour polishing it with the corner of his blanket. It is blue-green with a ripple of white. Like a wave breaking on the shore.

When the lad comes back, shrugs and explains that the guitar must have been sold, I find myself smiling. I shake my head, I say that it doesn't matter – never mind – and I take the slip from the counter. Maybe I'll keep that as a memento instead.

On the way back to the centre, I hum a melody I've been working on. A vocal hook. At first it's under my breath, into my scarf, and quiet enough that the folk passing me can't hear. As I climb the hill, though, the volume increases.

If – when – I go back to Glasgow, I'll not be able to take Maddie's guitar with me, but I will carry songs that I can proudly play, whether it's on the fallen log in the woods behind the train station or on stage at the Barrowlands. I'm resolved on that. And it's not because I'll force the lyrics from search-engine snippets or solder together melodies from the songs Uncle Brendan taught me when I was younger. It's because there's a seam of experience, a harmony of gathered voices, that's ready to be mined.

It's been an hour since my shift ended, since we stopped serving coffees, but there are still a few stragglers sitting around the tables in the foyer. The heat from inside has misted the bottom of the window pane. As I enter, Sandra looks up from her desk and smiles. I unwind my scarf and unbutton my coat, hanging them on the rack by the door, then stand for a moment waiting for the tingling sensation on my cheeks to fade. For the warmth to seep through.

There's a blank wall beside me. Beige. Maybe we could think about asking if anyone fancies painting it. Not mocha-coloured or anything. A mural or a series of scenes, perhaps, done by those members who're artistically minded. I'll bring it up at the next meeting.

I go over to Sandra and lift Luke's guitar. Then I make my way over to the cushions on the windowsill and curl myself into the corner. From the inside pocket of my jacket I take out the tuning fork and strike it against my kneecap, then set it on the sill beside me and tune the fifth string to it and the other strings relative to that. The people gathered around the tables pay me no attention. From upstairs, I can hear the faint sound of Sage's voice. He's been helping a couple of folk with college applications, after hours. The deadline is coming up.

Trickling my left hand over the fret, I begin to pick with my right. Playing the lick that will, eventually, become an intro or a solo. It echoes the vocal melody that's stuck in my head. I let it ease out into a chord progression, a counter-melody, that can be softly strummed. It takes me a moment to work out the rhythm. Then, with my eyes closed, I hum the hook over the top. Knowing that the words will come.

Acknowledgements

Thank you to my superb editorial team of Holly Ainley and Vicky Blunden and to all at Myriad Editions – Candida Lacey, Corinne Pearlman, Adrian Weston and Emma Dowson. Thanks also to copy-editor Linda McQueen (for crossing my eyes and dotting my tees) and to proofreader Dawn Sackett.

I gratefully acknowledge financial support from Arts Council England and research support from Pete the Temp, Sam Brodbeck and Martine McDonagh. Thanks to David Ashford for the London Zoo penguin story. Several books were vital to my research, including *A Race of Singers* by Bryan Carman, *Coming Up From the Streets* by Tessa Swithinbank, *The Democracy Project* by David Graeber, and *Music: the Business* by Ann Harrison.

I am fortunate to have wonderful first readers. Thanks to Gavin Goodwin, for sharing his experiences and providing such knowledgeable feedback and conversation. To Brendan Henderson for unqualified support and the early cultivation of a tea habit that I still can't shake. And to Nina de la Mer for writerly chat and critique over ginger beer that was only sometimes alcoholic.

My love and gratitude to my family – my wife Orla, parents Ann and Charles, sister Katy, and newest addition Emmett. Thanks also to Dougal, Andrew, Fraser, Ainsley and Finlay for teenage days in the studio and allowing me to sneak a lyric into the book.

Finally, this book owes a great deal to the lifelong friends I made in the woods behind Hyndland train station, Glasgow.

If you have enjoyed *The Busker*, you might like Liam Murray Bell's critically acclaimed debut novel *So It Is*.

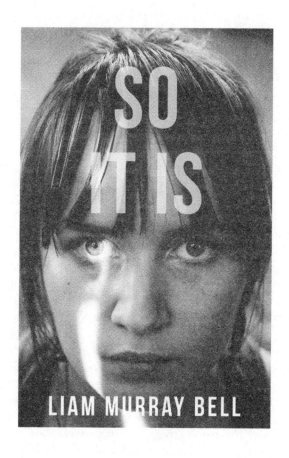

For an exclusive extract, read on…

1

I wait for Whitey in the Regal Bar, sipping at a tonic water.
Typical Loyalist hole, the Regal is, with portraits of the
Queen and Norman Whiteside side by side on the walls.
Usual crowd in too: stubbled heads, rolled necks, beer guts,
tattoos. It takes two hours for Whitey to arrive, with his
friends, and take the corner table. They're all nudges and
winks, seeing the ride at the bar with the short skirt. He's not
sure whether to take it serious or treat it all as a great geg.

'Can I buy you your next one?' he asks, as he approaches
the bar.

'Would you be having one with me?' turning to him then
so as my knees brush against him. He nods and we go to a
table. Around the corner, out of sight. I play with his hair
and pluck his shirt away from the nape of his neck. He has a
tattoo there: a single screw. Inked so as you can see the detail
of the thread. I ask him about it, even though I know rightly.
His dad was a prison guard, died three years ago, in '93. I
ask him about his job, even though I know that too. He's an
RUC recruit, fresh out of school. I've done my homework.
He can tell me nothing that I haven't already found out. I've
scouted out the whole area. A man walking about around
here with a sports bag over his shoulder would be pulled to
the side. Not me, though. A woman's inconspicuous. Even
months after, when someone lands up in hospital, they never
suspect the ginger-haired girl who sells jewellery door to
door. Why would they? For five months I've been calling at

Whitey's house, selling his mother earrings and necklaces. His photo sits on her mantel beside a cracked Charles and Diana wedding plate. I listen to her proud stories of her son. Over tea. Terrible thing, a mother's love.

'Get that pint down you and we'll get you a real drink, eh?' I says to him. Then I swallow the rest of my own. Leaning over I press my lips against his. Count the seconds – one, two, three. He'll be my third. Only two I've done before this one. Two in just under two years. Plenty of time between. Healing time.

Whitey's perfect. Eager enough that he'll not think twice before, green enough that he'll think twice about telling anyone after. As I stand up, I lift my handbag and the empty miniature tonic bottle.

'Wait there a minute,' I say, and make my way to the ladies'.

Aoife's mammy started to have problems with her mouth in the weeks after Eamonn Kelly was shot by the Brits. It started as a tingle, she told the doctor, like a cold sore forming at the corner of her lip, then it began to scour at her gums as though she was teething. It was when it started to burn, though, like taking a gulp of scalding tea and swilling it around… when it began to feel like the inside of her mouth and throat were nothing more than a raw and bleeding flesh wound… it was only then that Cathy Brennan phoned for the doctor.

In those weeks, as the pain intensified, she'd call Aoife or Damien over to her with a wee wave of the hand and reach into her apron pocket for a five-pence piece. Tucking it into Aoife's school pinafore or into the torn remnants of Damien's shirt pocket, she'd send one or the other scampering down the street to McGrath's on the corner to buy an ice-pop. All different colours, they were. Aoife liked the purple ones best, while Damien liked the green. Neither of them would ever even think to buy the orange ones. They would race home and give it to their mammy, who would clamp it unopened between her thin lips. Lengthways, like the flutes played during the Twelfth parades. She would keep it there, between closed lips and beneath closed eyes, until all the white frost had melted and the inside of it had turned to brightly coloured juice. Then, opening her eyes and letting out a wee sigh, Aoife's mammy would lift it away from her mouth, snip the end of the plastic with the kitchen scissors and hand it to whichever of her children had run the message. Give it to them so as they could squeeze at the sugary slush with their fingers and suck on the end of it like a babby.

'How come Mammy needs ice?' Aoife asked her daddy.

'Her mouth burns her, love.'

'Why?'

'It's psychoso…' Shay Brennan lifted his daughter onto his knee, clearing his throat as he did so. 'It's all in her mind.'

'So her mind's burning her, then?' Aoife paused, waiting for her daddy's nod. 'Why?'

'It's what happens, wee girl,' he whispered, 'when you go touting to the peelers.'

'Is that right?' Aoife asked.

'Not a word of a lie. It's what happens when you feel guilty about turning on your friends and neighbours.'

Eamonn Kelly had been a neighbour of the Brennans for as long as Aoife, with all of her eleven years and ten months on this earth, could remember, but as far as she knew he'd never been a friend to either her mammy or her daddy. In fact, she'd have sworn by all that was good and holy that she'd heard her daddy talking of Eamonn as 'nothing more than Provo scum' at Mass one Sunday when he was having the craic with Gerry from down the way.

Still, it had fair shook her mammy when the Army raided the house, two doors down, where Eamonn was living. Aoife had seen it as well, even though Cathy had pulled her daughter's head in against her chest and kept it there with a firm hand. By twisting her neck a wee bit, Aoife had managed to squint out and see the whole thing. She'd seen the soldiers shouldering in the door without so much as a knock, even though Sister Beatrice at school said it was rude not to. She'd seen Eamonn squeezing out of the upstairs window then, as the soldiers crashed and shouted inside, and jumping from the sill – feet-first like Hong Kong Phooey – onto the lawn below. She'd seen him landing, with his right leg part-buckled beneath him, and then springing up and hobbling out the garden gate. She'd seen the Saracen then, from further down the street, speeding down towards Eamonn and she'd heard the shout of 'Get your hands up, you bastard!' She'd seen him limp on for a pace with his gacky half-run, and then heard the shot. Then she'd felt her mammy flinch as Eamonn crumpled to the ground.

'Did you like Eamonn, then, Daddy?' Aoife asked.

'Ach – ' he bounced his knee beneath her, so that she felt as though she were on a juddering bus ' – it's not that I liked him, love, but he was a member of this community, is all.'

Aoife paused at that, her arm up around his shoulder and her hand nestled in at his neck. She didn't look him in the eye, as unsure of her footing now as Eamonn had been when he'd left those two footprints – one deep and straight, the other shallow and slanted – in the tiny square lawn, two doors down.

'Joanne from school said...' she started. 'I tell a lie – Joanne's brother said to her, and she says to me, that Eamonn was making bombs in that house.'

Her daddy shrugged. Aoife felt it up the length of her arm.

'If he was making bombs, though,' she continued, her thoughts stumbling on ahead of her, 'is it not right for Mammy to be telling on him?'

Another shrug and a settling of the bouncing knee. 'There were other people she could've talked to, Aoife,' her daddy said, 'if she had worries.'

'What if the bombs had blown up, but?'

'Eamonn was being careful, love.'

'What if – '

'I'll tell you this.' Her daddy lifted her down. 'These houses we've got, all in a row, they're near enough bomb-proof, so they are. Remember what your mammy told you, when you were wee, about them windows – triple-glazed. As long as you're under this roof, you'll be protected rightly, OK?'

Aoife nodded.

'Besides, a wee girl like you shouldn't be concerning herself with bombs or any of that there.' He smiled. 'You and your mammy both, you're too fond of the gossip.'

Aoife's mammy hadn't even said that much. It wasn't like she'd come out and gone, 'That Kelly lad on the other side of Sinead is making bombs for the IRA.' If she'd said that, then there'd have been cause for all the ructions that had taken place since. Instead, all she'd said was that there was a powerful smell coming out of Eamonn's house sometimes and that the windows, from time to time, did steam up like the wee window in the kitchen did when the dishes were getting washed after dinner. That was all she said, Aoife's mammy, and every word of it the truth. Out on the doorstep, as the woman from the social came out from seeing young Sinead O'Brien and her two fatherless children. Aoife had been there, with her shoulder against the door-jamb, watching Damien as he plucked the black and orange striped caterpillars from the bush near the gate and set them down on the windowsill. He collected a brave amount of them, all slithering slowly across the sill and clambering over one another as though they'd a notion to make it to the other side before Damien's grubby fingers could scoop them up again.

Still, nine days later Eamonn Kelly was spread out across the concrete with his arms splayed out to the sides, as though he was trying to make a snow-angel and hadn't realised that it was springtime.

'She works for the Brits,' Aoife's daddy had said to her mammy. 'She's a Prod and she works for the Brits and she's from East Belfast. Come on to fuck, Cathy, you know that if you tell them the time of day they're liable to take the watch from your wrist.'

Aoife wasn't meant to hear this. She'd been sent upstairs to mind Damien after all the commotion had died down. She'd crept back down the stairs, though, because Damien's room faced the road. As she sat on his bed and read to him from his Roald Dahl book – about George stirring in a quart of brown gloss paint to change the medicine to the right colour – her eye kept being drawn to the bloodstain, out in the middle of the pavement outside. Further down the road, beside the peelers' meat wagon, was another patch of liquid. It was as slick as the blood, but darker and with a swirl of colour at its centre.

'That's it over and done with, though,' her daddy continued. 'Enough with the waterworks. You're not to be blamed for what that scumbag was up to, Cathy, so don't be beating yourself up over it.'

He'd looked up then, Aoife's daddy, and seen her standing in the doorway, staring beyond him at her mammy, who lurched to her feet and felt her way across to the sink, using the worktop as a handrail. Then she set the tap running and twisted her neck in beneath it, making a bucket of her mouth. As the water passed her lips, Aoife could have sworn she heard a sizzle, like the first rasher of bacon hitting a hot frying pan.

Whitey is stocious by the time we leave the Regal. Absolutely full. That's how I need them, though, so I've no complaints. I lead him down Conway Street. Past the UVF mural with two sub-machine-gun-wielding paramilitaries guarding plundered poetry written in black and gold:

Sneak home and pray you'll never know
The hell where youth and laughter go.

He follows me on down Fifth Street, not noticing that we've turned right and right again, not noticing that the flags on the tops of the lampposts are changing. Out onto the Falls Road. We've skirted right around the peaceline. Whitey seems happy enough, though. Like a dog following a scent, his eyes on me, his hands grabbing for me and, for the most part, missing. Leading him on, past the garden of remembrance. More words in black and gold, but no poetry to them. Lists of the Republican dead.

Whitey stops under the first mural of the Hunger Strikers and mumbles to himself. As though he's trying to memorise the quote painted on it. Unlikely he'll remember much of anything from the walk home. He'll remember the rest of the night, mind. Pain sobers you up quickly. I steer him to the right before the second mural, the one of Bobby Sands MP. Down Sevastopol Street, then Odessa. Doubling back on myself. It was Baldy who set me up with the place. A safe house. Number forty-eight. The house beside has woodchip across the windows, fly-posters plastered on the woodchip and weeds sprouting from the posters. I check the other side, Number fifty. All the lights are out. I don't want there to be kids in next door when Whitey sets to squealing. That sort of thing can leave a kid shook for life.

'Whitey, love –' I step in close, searching his acne-scarred face ' – are you going to be of any use to me?' I reach a hand down to check. Something stirs. I smile. 'Good lad.'

Aoife and Damien were about equal with the ice-pop runs, purple versus green, when the steady supply of five-pence pieces stopped. Aoife made it home first that day, near clattering into her mammy as she slid around the lino-corner into the kitchen. Her mammy was on her knees in front of the fridge. The butter and milk and all were spread out across the floor, giving her enough space to get her head right in. Aoife caught on to what was happening. Rushing forward, she clawed at her mammy's cardigan until her head came out of the fridge.

'What are you at, Aoife?' her mammy asked, a frown on her as though she'd caught Aoife at the biscuits before dinner.

'You're looking for a goose!' Aoife shouted.

'A goose?' The frown deepened. 'What're you on about?'

'It was how Big Gerry's sister committed sue-side.'

'Suicide.' The frown disappeared. 'She'd her head in the oven, love.'

'And she died, Mammy.'

'That she did, Aoife.' She was smiling now. 'But a fridge wouldn't do that to you, now.'

'Well, why did you have your head in there, then?'

'Because I'm burning up.'

'You wanting me to run for an ice-pop, then?'

'No, love.' Her mammy shook her head. 'I'll call for the doctor, maybe.'

Aoife's daddy had told her about Caoimhe McGreevy – Big Gerry's sister – one Saturday afternoon when he had the smell of drink on him. She'd had to wrinkle her nose against the whiskey breath. Caoimhe's husband had been put in Long Kesh prison for planting a bomb down near Newry somewhere, then Caoimhe got herself blocked on the gin and put her head in the oven so as she didn't have to live the life of a prisoner's wife.

'Why'd she put her head in the oven, though, Daddy?' Aoife had asked.

'Why?' Her daddy had thought for a moment, then chuckled. 'She needed to see if her goose was cooked.'

'Really?'

'Really.'

'And was it?'

'It was, and she passed on up to Heaven, love.'

'Can a goose do that to you, but?'

'If it's cooked, love, then it can. Only if it's cooked.'

The doctor came during the day when Aoife and Damien were out at school and gave Cathy Brennan a wee white tub of pills that had her name neatly typed across the side. Their daddy warned them not to be touching them, said they were only for mammies and that if Aoife or Damien ate one then they'd find themselves frozen stiff and still, unable to move even their arms and legs.

'Is that why Mammy takes them?' Aoife asked. 'Because she likes ice?'

'What d'you mean, Aoife?'

'Like, she says her mouth burns her, so are these pills to cool her down?'

'Aye, that's exactly it, so it is. Exactly.'

The pills certainly seemed to work for their mammy, anyway. In the late afternoon, Aoife and Damien would come home from school and run into the kitchen to find her by the sink, with her back to them and her hands plunged up to the wrist in the soapy water. For hours she'd stand, staring out of the wee steamed-up window, moving only to top up the basin from the hot tap every now and then. Aoife reached up to dip her finger in the water once, after it had just been drained and refilled, and it was scaldingly hot. Her mammy's hands stayed in there, though, getting all folded and wrinkly like her granny's skin. It seemed to Aoife that her mammy had real problems getting herself to the right temperature: before the pills she'd been roasted and was always trying to cool herself down, and after the pills she was baltic and was constantly trying to warm herself up.

The benefit of having their mammy spending the majority of her time at the sink was that Aoife and Damien found they had free rein. They'd sprint from room to room of the terraced house, playing at chases or hide-and-seek. Damien took to carrying the bow-and-quiver set that he'd been given for his seventh birthday wherever he went and firing the plastic arrows at anything that moved, whether that be the neighbourhood cats in the garden outside or Aoife as she made her way from her bedroom to the bathroom. After her mammy had been taking the pills for a few days, Aoife realised that she could reach up and take the biscuits from the cupboard beside the stove without being noticed. Their daddy was working on a garden out near Hillsborough and wasn't back at night until darkness had taken control of the streets outside. By the time he trudged in, Aoife and Damien were both tired out and would be sprawled out on the sofa in the living room, watching the telly and nibbling on biscuits. Their mammy would be in the kitchen, her hands deep in the warm water, until her husband put his dirt-stained hands on her hips and walked her, dripping, across to the dining table for dinner. She'd feed herself, and smile vacantly, but there was no conversation from her, and Aoife's daddy had to steer her away from the kitchen and up the stairs to the bathroom after they'd eaten to make sure that she filled the bath, rather than the sink, for her nightly wash.

The days slid by and the dishes piled up by the side of her mammy's misused dishwater. The mountain of clothes began to spill over the top of the laundry basket like a saucepan boiling over, and the floor around the telly became littered with biscuit wrappers and mugs of half-finished tea with floating islands of congealing milk in the centre of the brown liquid. Damien came in from school with a mucky blazer and it fell to Aoife to scrub at it with the nailbrush. The newspaper boy came knocking and she had to root through her mammy's pockets for enough change to pay him with. Her daddy dandered in with the smell of whiskey on him and asked her to wet the tea leaves and put the chip pan on for their dinner. It took all this, and more, for Aoife to grow scunnered of the new way of things.

On the second weekend, after putting on the wash, running out to McGrath's for the messages, taking the dirty dishes up the stairs to the bathroom sink and scrubbing at the tomato ketchup stain her daddy had left on the sofa after he came in blocked, Aoife stood in the doorway of the kitchen and picked up Damien's bow-and-quiver from where it lay on the worktop. Stretching out the string, she imagined aiming one of the plastic arrows at her mammy's back. She imagined pulling it back as far as it would go and then calling out in a loud voice, with an unfamiliar accent, 'Get your hands up, you bastard!' She could see her mammy's head twisting, then, to look over her shoulder as Eamonn had; could hear the *twang* from the taut string as it was released, a second noise coming just moments after the shout of warning; could see the arms lifting up, raising themselves as Eamonn's had, suds flying up and around, splattering the lino like blood against concrete.

Instead, she soundlessly set the bow down on the side and leant against the door-jamb to stare at her mammy's back. The shoulders of Cathy Brennan, either because the water had gone cold or because she had caught the arrow of her daughter's hatred, shuddered and then were still.

The place is a dive. They always are. Streaks of damp down the walls, single mattress by the radiator in the upstairs bedroom. Bare. With a bottle of whiskey beside it. Like I asked for. I lead Whitey over to the mattress, ease him down, tie his wrists to the radiator, and then clamber on top of him. Lifting the whiskey, I keep him drinking whilst I straddle him. The smell of the alcohol rises like antiseptic.

'You think I'm a ride, don't you?' I breathe, into his ear.

'Aw, Cass,' he mumbles, from between thickened lips. 'Aw, Cassie.'

'You ever killed a man, Whitey?' I ask. 'Or hurt him so as he'll never recover?'

He looks confused by that, shakes his head. I reach in underneath my skirt and tug my underwear to one side. I can feel the thing inside, shifting as I shift, moving as I move. Waiting, it is, impatiently. As I pull his fly down, he murmurs something about having a packet of rubbers in the pocket of his jeans. He tries to point with his bound hands.

'I've plenty of protection,' I say. Then I ease my body up, seeking the angle. There's a whistle and a wheeze coming from him now, he's fair fit to burst. Like a kettle near boiling point. With a blissful smile spread across his face. He's drunk as a lord, getting his hole. All is right in the world of Whitey. For now. Just a final movement of my hips, a final positioning, and then I'm ready. I grit my teeth and wait for his thrust. Always wait for the man, just for those few seconds of deadly anticipation.

A sudden, high-pitched screech of pain. He's squirming and twisting beneath me. I'm not for letting him go, though, not yet. Clamping my thighs, keeping him in. My own teeth set together with the agony of it. I close my eyes, grind down, and listen as the screams grow louder and sharper. I listen as the hurt and sorrow of it all penetrates through his whiskey-addled confusion. I'm for waiting until his cries crack, until the tears stream, until he's ready to plead.

MORE FROM MYRIAD EDITIONS

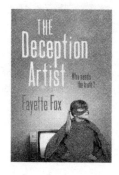

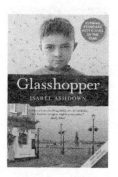

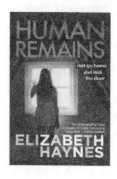

MORE FROM MYRIAD EDITIONS

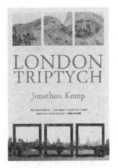

MORE FROM MYRIAD EDITIONS

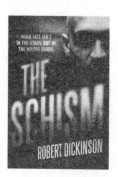

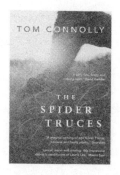

www.myriadeditions.com